George Harris, B. W. Richardson

The Autobiography of George Harris

George Harris, B. W. Richardson

The Autobiography of George Harris

ISBN/EAN: 9783337075149

Printed in Europe, USA, Canada, Australia, Japan

Cover: Foto ©Raphael Reischuk / pixelio.de

More available books at **www.hansebooks.com**

THE
AUTOBIOGRAPHY

OF

GEORGE HARRIS,

LL.D., F.S.A.,

OF THE MIDDLE TEMPLE, BARRISTER-AT-LAW,

Author of "Civilisation Considered as a Science," "The Theory of the Arts,
"The Nature and Constitution of Man," etc., etc.

WITH A PREFACE BY

DR. B. W. RICHARDSON.

" Homo sum; humani nihil a me alienum puto."
TERENCE.

Printed for private circulation by

HAZELL, WATSON, & VINEY, Ld.,
52, LONG ACRE, LONDON, W.C.

1888.

PREFACE.

THE learned author of these memoirs, feeling the failure of his own powers, has asked me to add a few words of preface. I undertake the duty with pleasure and pain: pleasure in that I am about to help an old friend whose studies have, in many ways, run parallel with my own; pain in that he is himself unable to give the finishing touch to a work which he is desirous of leaving behind him as a token of remembrance to those who have known him best, and who have read his many essays with interest and satisfaction.

The book is a diary. In its original form it was never intended for the public eye; and twenty years ago it would have been out of place. Now when most of the individuals referred to are enrolled with the great majority, and when nearly all the incidents recorded are old enough to be considered historical, there is nothing in the publication except what is purely biographical and in many senses curiously quaint as contemporary history. It is right to name this fact in order to explain some passages in the volume—in the personal parts especially—which might be considered egotistical, and which would be so considered, and rightly too, if they had been written at the present date and by way of recollection. Chronicled at their own dates, as thoughts and aspirations and impulses of the author, fresh on his mind, it would have destroyed not only the originality, but also the honesty, of the work to have changed its form or modified its matter.

The reader, therefore, who takes up this volume must kindly consent to read it with the clear understanding that, if he is out of the immediate circle of the author, he must meet with passages, on many occasions, which are possibly quite uninteresting to him. They connect the narrative, and that is all. Limited in interest as this part of the story may be, it still is not without its value, since the very simplicity of the narrative is the best proof of its sincerity. Moreover, it is not out of the range of belief that the personal matter itself may be of personal interest to some who, at first sight, would seem to be least taken with it. This world in which we live is, after all, very small ; and it is astonishing how the mention of one name often brings up, unexpectedly, a train of memories and recollections which are either pleasant or instructive, or both.

Apart from these considerations, the reader of the present work will be, incidentally, brought into communion with men of eminence who have made a distinguished figure in the history of the century. The conversations of its author with such men as Dr. Arnold, Bishop Lee the first bishop of Man-

chester—Lord Hardwicke, the Chevalier Bunsen, and
Mr. Macready; his description of the style and
manner of the different preachers whom he went
to hear—notably of the popular Montgomery and of
Sydney Smith; his visit to Prince Albert at Windsor;
his visit to Lord Brougham in retirement at
Cannes; his short, quaint introductions into the
inner life of the bar in the middle of the nineteenth
century; his correspondence with Darwin, with
Quatrefages, Bethell, and many others who were
interested in the same or kindred subjects to those
on which he was occupied; and his curious, sometimes humorous, incidents of foreign travel—these,
each and all, lend a value to the narrative which will
be appreciated warmly by all students of the future,
and by many of the present, who know and feel
how precious a thing it is to get the light of the
past from a reliable source.

As in Pepys' Diary, so in this, the singular candour
of the author is conspicuous on every page. In
reading the proofs I have often been so struck with
the similarity that I have caught myself under the
temporary belief that the work of the older author
was in my hand. This is from no spirit of imitation
on the part of my friend—who of all men is
least an imitator—but from natural tendency to
speak of himself, as of others, without reservation.
I have observed the same, precisely, in conversation with him. He has, in fact, in the fullest
degree I have seen in any man I have ever met,
the combination of self-abnegation with the intensest

ambition; a spirit of ready submission conjoined with a resolute will and resolution to hold his own. Proofs of this abound in these pages, as, for example, in his letter to Lord Brougham on the occasion of his losing the appointment of the Professorship of History—a position he so much desired—in the University College, London. Further proofs of the same spirit are shown in the records of all the worries and disappointments which he describes. A still more remarkable instance of the like kind was indicated, in another form, when he was finally putting together his most important work on "Man." In this task he sent proofs of chapters treating on subjects to which he had devoted the closest attention to other scholars, asking them to read what he had written and to tell him, without the slightest hesitation, their candid views on the points submitted. In every instance where an answer was sent he inserted the whole reply, whether it favoured his views or not. If the opinion given were diametrically opposed to his own, he still published it without demur, anxious only that every view which he considered competent should be presented, and that the truth, the whole truth, and nothing but the truth, as far as it could be obtained, should be the one thing, first and foremost.

The remarks he makes on his reviewers and critics are always equally fair and considerate, a fine proof of good-nature and of a sound understanding.

A long friendship with Mr. Harris and a personal knowledge of him have prepared me for all that appears in this volume. It is not often I have known a man who on the one hand has been so industrious and on the other has, so cleverly, concealed his industry. He tells us himself that some of his friends thought him idle, the idlest man they knew; but those who have understood him correctly are surprised at the abundance of mental work which in the midst of a busy professional and public career he has been able to accomplish.

To this industry he has added a perfect fund of good-humour, lighted up, at times, with touches of wit and with keen appreciation of wit in others which his ordinary grave manner would not bespeak. These qualities, quiet and deep, explain his striking power of hitting off in words and sketches the pictures of men and things that are met with in a number of places in the coming pages. His history of the Sheffield catastrophe, at pp. 317—320, is a good example in point.

As a last personal observation, bearing on the genius of the author and sustained in his present book, is a distinctive faculty of inventive skill, both in mechanics and imaginative constructions. I have been impressed with the idea, the more I have seen of Mr. Harris, that if, from the first of his career, he had followed out exclusively one particular line of labour, mechanical or literary, in which invention and description formed the heart and soul of the labour, he would have achieved some great and remarkable result at very much less cost of labour and trouble than he has expended on any one of the varied pursuits which have occupied his time and talents. In a word, without being himself naturally versatile, he has, I believe, by sheer industry forced himself into a versatility which has temporarily concealed him from the world.

It will be seen that even on the subject of law, in which he is specially learned, he is essentially synthetical and inventive in his method, a fact which the astute mind of the late Lord Westbury very naturally detected.

It will be found in one of the pages of this volume that an old friend of its author observed to him, in a jocular vein, that he (Harris) was a bold man to venture to bring out a treatise like that on the subject of " Civilisation as a Science," since it was one that could only gain immediate acceptance by coming from a man who had already obtained a great name. There is many a true word spoken in jest; and, probably, no truer word was ever spoken in jest than this, for if the book referred to had emanated from a man widely known, it would, in all probability, have become by the present time quite a renowned and classical treatise. The same may be said of the other works thrown off from his prolific and industrious, though, it may be admitted not always equally strong, mind. He has laboured under the disadvantage of not commanding immediate popularity, a fate which more than one philosopher has had to bear before, and which he can well afford to share. He will reap the reward he most desires if a future generation of scholars shall take up his works and shall gather from them some of the useful thoughts of a man who, in advance of his time, has spoken both well and wisely, but who in his own day has not been sufficiently heard above the voices of others who have neither spoken so wisely nor so well.

BENJAMIN WARD RICHARDSON.

TABLE OF CONTENTS.

—◆—

CHAPTER VII.

CHAPTER VIII.

CHAPTER IX.

CHAPTER X.

CHAPTER XI.

CHAPTER XII.

CHAPTER XIII.

CHAPTER XIV.

CHAPTER XV.

CHAPTER XXIV.

CHAPTER XXV.

CHAPTER I.

I HAVE been several times asked by intelligent friends, of kindred spirit, both to preserve an account of, and afford information respecting, various transactions of life in which I have been engaged, some successful and of importance, to a certain extent, to society at large, others (as in the case of most of those who undertake much) unsuccessful, and not reaching sufficient maturity to affect any persons beyond myself. As regards my individual career, although it has no pretensions to be regarded as a distinguished one, it has been somewhat singularly varied, and so far, to a certain extent, interesting. I have, however, neither the desire to gratify an idle curiosity, nor am I so vain as to consider that anything in my career is calculated to interest or to gratify the general public; yet, with all this, I believe that what I have here recorded will be both interesting and in a degree useful to persons who may be placed in circumstances similar to those which have befallen me.

To begin at the very beginning of the story, I may state that at three o'clock on the afternoon of Saturday, the 6th of May, 1809, at my father's house, which is in the centre of the then little but now large town of

Rugby,* I, George Harris, made my first appearance
upon the stage of life. So frail, however, was I in my early
days, that it was thought advisable at once to baptise
me privately, which was done by the Rev. John Sleath,
then one of the undermasters of Rugby School, curate
of Rugby, and afterwards High Master of St. Paul's
School, London. Later on—viz., on the 22nd of June—
I was baptised at church, by the Rev. George Innes,
who was also formerly an assistant master at Rugby
School, but at that time Head Master of the college at
Warwick, and whose second daughter, Elizabeth, I had
the happiness and the good fortune to espouse.

One curious fact connected with my early history I
may here narrate, which was that soon after my birth
I was given up for lost on account of my debility, and
so far considered by my friends to have passed the
verge of hope, that on the bell being heard to toll for
the death of a child about that time, it was generally
concluded to be the announcement of the termination
of my terrestrial career.

1810. I continued for some time very delicate, and
my tender and affectionate parents had much anxiety
about me, as appears by the following extract from a
letter written by my father, who was then staying in
London, to my mother in February, 1810, when I was
about nine months old, and their only child: "I do
hope that little George is going on well, and I pray
that he may be spared to us; but we must remember
that He Who gave him to us has a right to take him
from us whenever He sees fit, and I hope that we are
prepared to say, 'Blessed be the name of the Lord,'

* A handsome family red-brick residence of the period of
Queen Anne, purchased by my great-grandfather (together
with the rights of common in the open fields of Rugby, which
were subsequently enclosed and divided) about the year 1730.

whatever He may direct. I do not expect that our little darling will be quite well until the teeth which have been so troublesome to him have made their appearance." True piety and affection are here evinced. Both are genuine, and they are beautifully blended together.

As I have remarked in my "Treatise on Man," as regards faculties and disposition we are the children of nature, yet as regards the exercise and development and application of these we are no less the children of circumstances, so I shall endeavour (what to me will be a most interesting and, I believe, useful undertaking) to trace the growth and development of my different powers and the effect on my mind and character of different circumstances through life, commencing with those which are the earliest I can recollect. I am of opinion that one of the most truly valuable gifts which could be presented to the world would be a sketch, such as I here design, of the origin, rise, development, and progress, so far as they could preserve a recollection of it, of their mental powers and individual character, exhibiting the first feelings of growing strength and gradual formation and perfection of them, with the influences and modifications produced by different circumstances upon them,* by those who have differed from the common lot, either by their acquirements, their efforts, their penetration, or their intellectual capacity. A few such productions would afford the most valuable material for the mental philosopher to work upon, and would supply the noblest landmarks to guide in their career those who look for benefit from their

---

* I urged upon Lord Brougham, who did me the honour of consulting me on the subject, to carry this out in his autobiography, but unfortunately, before he commenced the above work, he had attained the age of eighty-four, with an enfeebled memory and diminished intellectual power.

exertions. The great hindrance to our observance of
the mind and character of others is that so much is
either industriously concealed from us, or is purposely
dissembled, so that the real constitution of the individual is never properly comprehended, or is altogether
mistaken. In self-examination, however, if we possess
sufficient candour and sufficient honesty for the task,
we may obtain the fairest and most complete view of
human nature. Nay, the very difficulties which stand in
the way of this pursuit—the very fears, and prejudices,
and disguises which here obtrude themselves to obstruct
our progress—by creeping out from their lurking-places
and exhibiting to us their nature and operation, may
contribute to assist our investigation, and enable us to
obtain the most complete view of the subject before us.

A letter which was written by my father from Rugby
to my mother, who was then staying with my father's
brother, John Harris, who was very ill at Magdalen
College, Cambridge, about this time, contains the following allusion to me : " Little George is rather at a
loss to account for your absence. He asked me once
if you were alive."

1814.   In 1814, when about five years old, I went into
Wales, to a village on the sea-coast near Rhyl, called
Prestatyn, in charge of some friends. I then first saw
the sea. I can recollect, with the most perfect distinct-
ness, the endeavours which I made before setting out
to form in my mind ideas of what the sea would turn out
to be, and of the waves of which I had heard people talk.
I well remember, too, the first glimpse that I had of it, on
descending the hill into Prestatyn, and the distant vessels,
with their white sails, dotting its blue surface, but I can
hardly recollect any of the circumstances of the journey.
Expectation eclipsed memory. We remained at Prestatyn
about two months.

Later in 1814, I was taken to London that an oculist might examine my poor little eyes. We travelled by a slow and heavy stage-coach, drawn by four horses, and called the "Balloon." It started from Lutterworth, passing through Rugby. We had to leave before day-light, and did not reach our destination until after dark. Travelling in those days was somewhat perilous from the number of mounted armed highwaymen who infested the roads, especially near London, and of whose doings I used to hear appalling stories. I recollect one of my uncles mentioning that in posting (from Devonshire, I believe) he carried a loaded pistol in his hand a great part of the journey. Doubtless I owe much to London as regards my mental vision. The observation which I made on reaching it was that "there was a fair every day"! I went to see the Tower, Exeter 'Change, with its wild beasts, and St. Paul's. The only record of this visit that I can find is a letter from my father, who accompanied me, to my mother at Rugby, in which he says, alluding to my travelling to London, "The little fellow was in high spirits throughout his journey."

Not long after this, I was again taken to London by my mother. In the autumn of the year 1814, I went with my aunt Emma (my father's youngest sister) to Sidmouth, where we were in lodgings for about a year. Mr. and Mrs. John Marriott* and my cousins

---

* The Rev. John Marriott, the rector of Church Lawford, Warwickshire, but who, being recommended to reside in Devonshire on account of the weak state of the health of his wife, my father's sister, for some time held the curacy of Broadclist, near Exeter. He was a man of considerable intellectual capacity, the friend of Sir Walter Scott, who dedi-cated to him one of the cantos of "Marmion," and also of Dr. Robert Southey. He was himself the author of several poetic

John and Charles Marriott* were also there part of
the time.

My aunt used often to say I made her laugh very
much by my remarks, and she predicted that I should
" turn out a genius," and some day do something in the
world.   She told her friends that I made such clever,
amusing observations, which she was in the habit of
relating, and mentioned to people in her letters about
what she termed my witty sayings and curious remarks.

My principal amusement at this time was endeavouring to construct ships with corks and pins, and other
mechanical contrivances.   I also tried to make a clock
and a balloon.   While here I had my profile taken, and
have it still in my possession.

When at Sidmouth I went to a day-school kept by a
Dr. Clarke.   I returned to Rugby in the course of this
year, and I recollect how much delighted I was to be
at home again.

1815.   In the spring of 1815 I went to Hastings.
After I had been some time at Rugby, my mother
asked me one day whether I would like to return to
Sidmouth, or to go to Hastings instead.   I preferred
the latter, and was accordingly taken there in charge
of my nurse.   I recollect quite well the news of the
battle of Waterloo arriving while we were there, and
the nurse telling me that our relation Colonel Miller, of

pieces, and much of the Border minstrelsy is said to have been
written by Mr. Marriott.   His poem comparing matrimony
to a Devonshire lane is full of exquisite humour.   Special
reference is made to him in Lockhart's " Life of Scott " (vol.
ii., pp. 151, 153).

* Charles Marriott also, to whom I was extremely partial, and
with whom I maintained a close intimacy after we grew up,
attained a distinguished position, was a Fellow of Oriel College,
Oxford, and the author of several writings which commanded
much attention.   He died when about thirty.

Radway, who led on the Enniskillen Dragoons, had been
severely wounded there.

1816.   I was subsequently placed at a school at
Hastings for little boys and girls kept by Mrs. Schaugh-
man, the widow of a German, with her sister, Miss
Harvey, who was related to those of this name of
gunpowder celebrity.   These ladies appeared to have
imbibed something of the quality of the article for
which their relatives were so renowned, and a little
spark served to inflame them to the utmost.   Some of
their pupils were treated with great severity.

1817.   My principal amusement here was drawing
and reading Æsop's fables, of which I was very fond,
especially when they treated of animals.

My mother, writing to my aunt Fanny Harris in the
spring of 1817, mentions of me, "I think we must
certainly have little George home for a little time, as
we must see him before the winter, dear little fellow !
I feel very anxious about him now, for he is getting to
an age when something must be done about his learning
a little more than he can do without some kind of
master, but I hope something may turn up in time.   I
feel quite happy about him now that I know he is
happy, but I should dread his going to a school
exceedingly."   I accordingly returned to Rugby for
a time, but in the summer of 1817 I again went to
Hastings, and was placed under the maternal tuition
of Miss W——, a somewhat ancient and still more
irritable spinster, who had a house looking on the sea,
which she called Priory House.   Another little boy, a
nephew of hers, was also with her, named Samuel F——,
son of Dr. F——, who, I believe, resided in Jamaica.
This good lady always treated me with kindness,
saving not a few occasional ebullitions of ill-temper,
of which, however, I believe I was not in very great

dread. She took in boarders at her house, and I used to accompany them on their excursions to see the neighbouring picturesque objects, the Govers, the Dripping Well, the Old Roar, and Hastings Castle, and we occasionally took, or attempted to take, sketches from nature. We also walked a great deal by the sea, in which I was constantly bathed, and in the products of which—its fish, birds, weeds, and shells—I took a deep interest. Indeed, I used to have my pockets so filled with stones and shells picked up by the sea-shore, that good Miss W—— told me that I carried a ton weight about with me wherever I went, and that this was a serious impediment to my walking properly, in addition to lameness from which I then suffered.

Miss W—— kept sundry pets besides her pupils already mentioned, including a brace of cats and a bullfinch, about which I used to joke and make my friends laugh long after I quitted her roof.

Under this lady's tuition I believe I really made some progress in information, especially in French and English history. The rudiments of Latin she also aspired to teach, but her pronunciation of it brought much ridicule upon me after I came to Rugby, especially my calling *huic hewich*, and *vos vaus*, errors which my father and my brother Tom of course corrected before I went to Rugby School. With the Greek language my learned instructress did not presume to claim an intimacy, though perhaps as well qualified in most respects to be a teacher as some of its more promising doctors.

1819. Miss W—— did not appear to entertain very high expectations as to what her pupil would do in after-life, for, when she was out of humour, which was perhaps indeed her ordinary mood, she used to exclaim

that it was very fortunate I was the eldest son of the
family, as she was sure I should never obtain a liveli-
hood for myself, but always be in need of their support
—a prophecy which up to an advanced period in my
career seemed to possess every probability of being
fulfilled. In a letter which she wrote to my mother in
the spring of 1819, she said, "Your little boy is quite
well, and, I hope, improving in all respects ; . . . but
he is so volatile and full of glee, that what I say to him
does not make much impression on his mind. I trust,
however, that in time I shall succeed better. . . . A
lady near here took the little boys to see some wild
beasts that were exhibited, and they were much delighted. . . . The boys' tongues have been running on
so about lions, tigers, and elephants, that I scarcely
know if my letter will be intelligible."

CHAPTER II.

EARLY BOYHOOD.

1820—1823.

1820. AFTER I had been with Miss W—— for
about two years, I returned to Rugby,
in the summer of 1820. My father taught me Latin
for a few weeks, correcting the errors which my
instructress had inculcated, after which he entered me
at the school of which Dr. Wooll was then the Head
Master. I was about eleven years old, and was placed
in the first form. Partly owing to delicate health while
I was very young, I was extremely backward as a
youth in everything as regards learning of each kind,
and much behind others of my age. This was a serious
discouragement to me, and led me to consider myself

for a long time deficient in mental capacity and considerably below par in this respect; this idea deprived me of all stimulus to exertion. On first going to school, however, I did very well indeed; and Mr. Bird, who was then the master of the first form, told me I was the best boy in that form. But I speedily became the worst, and got terribly idle. I was indeed never expert at learning grammar, and at no period have I ever been able to apply myself to a subject in which I took no interest. Where the topic has been one in which I have felt a desire to excel, I believe that I have not been inferior to others in my powers of application and assiduity. Except when I first went to school, at which period I felt some stimulus, I never exerted myself to advance in classical study, as I did not perceive any real advantages to be gained by it, and I could generally get through my work without any severe punishment, and with but little trouble.

1821. My idleness continuing to increase as I grew older, in the autumn of this year I was taken away from Rugby School and placed under the tuition of the Rev. William Sutton, who had private pupils at Bilton, about two miles from Rugby, and who had formerly been an undermaster at Rugby School. Here I made real progress in Latin and Greek, and began to be animated by a sort of literary ambition and desire to be an author. I actually commenced the composition of a book, an abridgment of a geographical work, with which, however, I did not proceed very far. Probably Mr. Sutton's talking to me about Addison, whose country seat was in this village, diverted my attention, for I recollect he used to tell me that Addison felt more pleasure in composing one of his *Spectators*, which are supposed to have been written at Bilton, than I could ever do in any games of play. While with Mr.

Sutton I began to take interest in my studies. I read the " Nut-tree " in Ovid with much pleasure ; and being appealed to by Mr. Sutton to explain Pope's meaning of the passage, " Fame has a thousand tongues," upon one of the pupils not understanding it, I gave the meaning correctly.

1822. While here I also read a good deal in a miscellaneous way, Paley's works, especially his " Theology," Sturm's " Reflections," the " Arabian Nights Entertainments," " Tales of the Genii," " Sandford and Merton," Mrs. Hannah More's " sacred dramas," and other works. Mr. Sutton's conversation, which was very improving and superior, was most useful to me, and led me to think for myself; and many of his remarks I have ever since retained. He was a man of some ingenuity and mechanical skill, and constructed an organ for himself while I was with him. In imitation, I tried to make small organ-pipes of alder wood ; and the first turn of an intellectual kind which appears to have developed itself in me was the attempt to construct ships and clocks and organs, and to invent little machines of various kinds.

In the year 1822 I returned to Rugby School, and was put into the lower third form. At first I did pretty well, and soon got into the upper third, then under Mr. A——. However, in a short time I became as idle as before, and seldom, if ever, looked at a lesson before going into school. I was pretty often flogged, though, as Mr. A—— told my father, I generally did just well enough to escape the rod. Mr. M——, who was my tutor, used also to complain of my irregularity in going to him, and once, when I happened to attend at the right hour, exclaimed before all the boys that it ought to be particularly noted down that on such a day and at such an hour George Harris actually came to his tutor at the proper time ! I was very expert at doing Latin verses, and used to make these for other boys, some of whom remarked that I was a clever fellow if I would but work. At this time I perceived fully the beauty of parts of the classics, especially Ovid and Virgil, and some of the quotations in the Eton Latin Grammar, which the masters of the school never attempted to point out.

I was much bullied at Rugby School. I believe, however, as I have often been told by others, that I was not at all fitted on many accounts for a public school ; and I have in later times felt surprised at my father sending me to one. To this treatment of bullying Roundell Palmer, eventually Lord Chancellor and Earl of Selborne, was also subject, as was the case with the great tragedian Macready. This custom at that time extensively prevailed ; but has, I believe, long been abolished, to effect which Dr. Arnold, who had when a boy suffered severely from the system, exerted himself strenuously.

CHAPTER III.

A MIDSHIPMAN IN THE NAVY.

1823.

MY grandfather, Admiral Chambers, lived in Rugby. Of him an admirable description and character are given in Moultrie's "Poems." He used to talk to me a great deal about the incidents of his naval career. Having myself been much by the sea, I was naturally led to think of a sailor's life; and I had, moreover, a great desire to see foreign countries, a

desire which has through life influenced me. The dislike of going into my father's office, which was my
only alternative, had also its weight here. It was ultimately determined that my wishes should be acceded
to, and matters were settled for my becoming a sailor,
a profession for which I was in several respects peculiarly well, and in certain other respects peculiarly ill,
adapted. Through my grandfather's influence, my
name was entered in the navy, and eventually on a
flag-ship. At first I was entered as a midshipman
in the *Sybil*, and afterwards I was transferred to the
Isis; but my name was put down for the *Spartiate*,
which was the flag-ship under Admiral Sir George
Eyre, a friend of Mr. Birch, one of the masters of
Rugby School. The captain of the ship, Captain
Gordon Thomas Falcon, was known to my grandfather,
Admiral Chambers.

In June, 1823, I accordingly left Rugby for the navy.
I was accompanied on my journey to Portsmouth by
my father and mother, my uncle, the Rev. W.
Chambers, and his then intended wife, Miss F——,
whom he married shortly after. We hired a barouche
for the occasion, and went first to Oxford, then to
Ashbury, the living to which my uncle was just presented ; afterwards we journeyed to Stonehenge, and
on to Winchester.

While going over the college at Winchester, I was
much struck by a Latin inscription, the exact words of
which I do not recollect, but the purport of which was
that all the wise and clever boys would aspire to a
mitre or the ermine, through the profession of the
Church or the law ; while for the fools were left the
army and the navy. I must say I felt rather keenly
this satire on my adopted profession, and did not cease
to think of it. After passing through the New Forest,

we reached Portsmouth, and were hospitably entertained there by Colonel Williams and the Rev. Mr.
and Mrs. Dusautoy, of Portsea. We went over the
Queen Charlotte, which was then the gun-ship in Portsmouth harbour, and paid the *Spartiate* a visit, where
we lunched on salt beef. As the ship was not ready
for sailing, we afterwards took a trip to the Isle of
Wight, where we spent some days. All this time I
was duly equipped as a midshipman, and liked the
thoughts of joining my profession very much, though
many of my friends had at different times tried to
shake my resolution. A Captain Chambers in particular
used often to rally me about it, and tell me I was not
fit for the service. I took a sort of *revenge* of him,
however, by persuading his only son to enter the navy
as well, much against his father's wish ; and he became
a very rising officer in that service, though he is now
dead.

The time at length arrived for my going to the ship.
My relatives, except my father, returned to Rugby,
and he accompanied me to the *Spartiate*, where I was
very kindly received by Mr. Sheffield Cox, the chaplain,
and some of the midshipmen. Among these I recollect
the names of Hamilton and Montgomery. Mr. Harness,
the purser, and one of the lieutenants of marines, were
also known to some of my friends. My father took
leave of me after depositing me in the midshipmen's
cabin ; and I well recollect watching him from the
quarter-deck as he rowed away towards the land, and
thinking I should probably never see his face again,
and how I tried to conjure up all sorts of reflections to
console me. Some of the midshipmen said they understood I came there to escape from quill-driving, but
they seemed to think it a very dismal life, with but
little hope of promotion.

At first I liked my new situation very well. We had a comfortable cabin to dine in, and salt meat every day for dinner, with hard biscuit and an allowance of rum-and-water, which latter, as I could not drink it, I gave to one of the sailors. Our sleeping berths were down in the cockpit of the vessel, and were very close, daylight never entering there. Several convicts were there, who were chained down, but who would be made to serve as sailors when the ship was at sea.

I slept in a hammock, and had the usual trick played me of letting it down one night after I had got into it. We had to rise at four o'clock every morning and to superintend the washing of the decks, without shoes or stockings, which I found very trying after coming out of the close atmosphere of the cockpit. In the day-time, I climbed the masts a good deal, and reached the topmast, but only by going through the "lubbers' hole." From some cause or other, the sailing of the *Spartiate* was delayed day after day ; and we remained stationary at Spithead, only swinging round with the tide, for about a fortnight.

This waiting I found excessively irksome and mono-tonous ; and the bustle of the ship, the smell of paint, and the badness of the water, which was then in its worst condition, from its having just been put into rusty iron casks and not having had time to purify itself, brought on a fit of illness and melancholy. I used often to get into a corner by myself, and felt very low, and on one occasion overheard the sailors say one to another that that young gentleman was quite unfit for the service. I also caught a violent cold, which brought on a fit of croup, attended with an extraordinary rattling in my throat, which was much noticed and laughed at by some of the midshipmen. Captain Falcon came on board the *Spartiate* one day, and was very kind and civil to me, as was also Admiral Sir George Eyre; and I believe that if we had sailed at first, all would have been well, and that I should have been in the navy still. A letter which I wrote to my friends at this time I have lately found, in which I said, "I did not like my naval life quite as much as I had expected to do, but I think that I shall like being in the ship pretty well."

I obtained leave one day to go on shore at Portsmouth, which I accordingly did, and called on the Dusautoys at Portsea.

My croup was then very bad, and Mrs. Dusautoy said I was extremely ill, and must not go back to the *Spartiate* that day. She immediately sent for a physician, Dr. Lara, who said I was certainly not strong enough for the sea, and could not think of it. She very kindly insisted on my staying at her house, where I was at once put to bed, and attended by Dr. Lara, who for some days thought me in considerable danger. Mrs. Dusautoy wrote off to Rugby, and in a day or two my father arrived.

He wrote word to my mother that "Dr. Scott, the navy surgeon, said he did not think that George would have lived six months at sea if he had had much salt diet. Dr. Scott also told me that he informed Captain Falcon soon after George went on board that he thought there was too great an appearance of delicacy about him for a seafaring life." In another letter to my mother, my father says, "I find that the midshipmen have to walk about early in the morning without shoes or stockings, and at four o'clock, and that the surgeon and officers are decidedly of opinion that he will not be able to undergo what the sailors term 'the seasoning.'" A letter written by my father a few days after the preceding one states, "Captain Falcon told me that he really did not know what they should have done with George if he had

sailed with this complaint upon him, as the accommoda-
tions on board are not calculated for so tender a subject ;
and had the complaint returned or left any unpleasant
symptoms, he would have been left at Madeira. . . .
I am glad to find from Admiral Chambers' letter to
George that he views matters as I do about his leaving
the ship. Indeed, there is but one opinion about him
here by those who have seen him. . . . The physician is quite amused with his answers to his inquiries. . . . George has never shown any dislike
to the service, and would, I believe, join the ship, when
he is well enough, with pleasure. . . . I never saw
anything like Mr. and Mrs. Dusautoy's kindness to
him. Mrs. D. has been with him night and day. . . .
She says that George was so considerate about her
taking him in, and asked her if she was aware of the
expense he should put her to. He said to her that he
was sorry we had been at so great an expense about
him, but seemed to console himself that he had had a
week's keep on board. He amuses Mrs. Dusautoy by
his oddities."

It was shortly decided that I must leave the navy, as
all the medical men who were consulted about me,
including the surgeon of the *Spartiate*, agreed that I had
not strength for the service, and my discharge from it
was accordingly obtained. The letters which were
written at this time about me are among my papers, as
also one which my grandfather, Admiral Chambers,
wrote to me, which is as follows : —

" MY DEAR GEORGE,—I am much pleased by your
letter, and am very glad to find you are getting better ;
and though you are obliged to give up being a
flag officer, I hope you will succeed in that way of life
your good father may think best to put you to. You
now, my dear boy, are old enough to see how anxious

your father has been to promote your happiness ; and
I hope and doubt not but you will follow your father's
good advice, whatever it may be.   Tell your father
that your letter to me was much better, at least plainer,
than *his*, so that I should think you will be able to out-
write him in the office.   I am sure you are very
fortunate in having such kind friends as Mr. and Mrs.
Dusautoy."

In the course of about a fortnight I recovered so far,
that I was able to go out of doors.   On the whole, I
was, I believe, not altogether sorry to escape the
navy ; but I had a great horror of being sent back
again to Rugby School.   Before I left Portsmouth, I
recollect very well walking on the ramparts and taking
a last view of the *Spartiate*, which was still lying
majestically at Spithead ; and I could not help shedding
a tear as I turned away from the scene of hopes and
expectations which were now all faded and gone.

I have several times since regretted that I left the
navy, as it is in many respects a profession which
would have suited me well, and in which I should have
greatly delighted.   I have often thought that if I could
go back to it as a captain, or even as a lieutenant, I
would gladly do so.

CHAPTER IV.

A SCHOOLBOY AGAIN.

1823—1825.

1823.   AS soon as I was well enough, I returned with
my father to Rugby, but was for some time
attended by Mr. B——, our medical man.   People of course
laughed very much at this abrupt termination of my nau-

tical career, especially as I still wore my naval uniform. After sundry deliberations about me, it was determined that I should be placed with a tutor in order to make amends for the neglect of my education, and that after a time I should go into my father's office. A master who kept a small private school at Totnes, in Devonshire, under the Pestalozzi system, and who was much patronised by my uncle Mr. John Marriott, then living at Broadclist, in Devonshire, was fixed upon as my master. Mr. Marriott told him that if he could make anything of me, he would have performed a miracle! On my way to Totnes, I stayed at Broadclist, where my aunt Fanny, my father's only surviving sister, was also living. The famous Dr. Southey was at this time on a visit to my uncle; and I recollect a conversation between him and Mr. Marriott about the Greeks and the Turks, respecting whom the public interest was at this time much raised. Southey maintained that the Turks were a much finer and nobler race of men than the Greeks. He also asked if a W—— C—— was "a serious man."

I arrived at Totnes by the Exeter coach one evening in September about seven o'clock. There were about thirty-seven boys then at the school. There were two under-masters: the Rev. John W——, a Cambridge man, and a Mr. C——, a German. My principal I never much liked or thoroughly confided in. In his principles he was an extreme Evangelical, and full of ostentation, always abusing other people and praising himself, more inclined to Dissent than the Church of England, and fond of putting himself forward at Bible and other avowedly religious meetings as a platform orator. He seldom, if ever, went to church, but generally to a Dissenting chapel, and had a great horror of anything approaching to High Church doctrines.

Some of the incidents connected with this school

cannot fail to remind one of Dickens' description in
"Nicholas Nickleby" of Dotheboys Hall, more especially
the intense amusement created among the boys on the
occasion of visitors coming to see the school, when the
mistress was heard to call out to the housemaid to run
at once and put clean sheets (which were immensely
needed) on the boys' beds, as visitors were coming to
go over the school. Unluckily the towels, which from
want of change had become very offensive, were not at
the same time replenished. To the above little narrative
we also add the periodical administration to the boys of
large doses of Epsom salts before breakfast, and the
subsequent fasting.

Whenever I now see an advertisement of a " school for
backward or unmanageable boys," I always think of
what I went through at this time, and what slender
hopes the most sanguine of my friends had of my ever
doing anything or ever rising to a level with the rest of
my compeers.

I disliked being at Totnes very much, as we were
kept under great restraint, and never allowed to go off
the premises unattended ; but now and then we had a
holiday and went long walking excursions into the neighbourhood : to Dartmoor, Holne Chase, Paignton, and
Torquay. I made considerable progress here in Latin
and Greek, and also in general knowledge. A letter
which was addressed to my father by the principal at
the end of my first half-year's stay here is at once
characteristic of the man, and describes, not untruly, my
intellectual condition at this period, but the same sentiments are expressed in a letter from my aunt which
follows. " George is not here yet. We expected him
last week, but as the winter holidays are not a regular
thing, Mr. —— is making his coming depend upon
his behaviour. We feared the other day that Mr.

E—— did not wish to keep him, for he wrote to
Mr. Marriott requesting him to meet him in Exeter
on Monday to talk about George, and saying, 'Your
nephew is very well, and very happy when at play,
but——' There he ended. Mr. Marriott did go to
meet him, and they had a long conference about
George. He says he has never had any boy whom
he found it so difficult to understand and meet in all
his little extraordinary ways and faults ; that at first he
found him disposed to get away and break all rules as
to bounds, etc., but he soon checked that, and now the
great difficulty is the making him exercise his mind
and fix his attention ; that in this respect he finds
him a great deal of trouble, and it is so very difficult
to make him do anything which requires thought,
etc., that he takes more of his time than the other
boys. He therefore gave Mr. Marriott to understand
that he should be sorry to give so much time to
him if he thought he could not carry it through,
and really have him under his care long enough to
make the good fruits of his system appear. He says if
you yield to George's wishes, he very well knows that
he will not return to him after the summer holidays. I
think George has said as much to him probably as that
he may do as he likes, and that you will not wish him
to remain if he does not like it.

" It can certainly be no object to Mr. E—— to keep
him, for he daily refuses boys for whom he has not
room, and he is a man of too much principle to desire
anything but the good of his pupils. We did not know
what your intentions were about George, but we think
the very fact of his disliking the school is the positive
obligation he is under to do something, and therefore it
is evident it is the proper place for him. We know so
well that he has every comfort and the greatest kind-

ness and attention from Mrs. E——, and that he could not be better off in that respect. I hope he will be with us in a few days. I have not forwarded his parcel, because we so fully expected to see him. I will write to you again when he comes. Mr. Marriott had a letter from him the other day very properly written, and expressing his great wish to come here.

" Mr. E—— says George does his Latin and Greek with great facility compared with the calculations, etc., which require close thought and reasoning. He does not despair of his greatly improving in time."

1824. I accordingly went to Broadclist for a short Christmas holiday, where my cousins John, Charles, Marianne, and George Marriott were then staying ; and this visit I exceedingly enjoyed, and have often thought of the Christmas games we had on that occasion, and the rides I took on a rough Dartmoor pony, which Sir Thomas Acland had given to John Marriott. Mr. Marriott told me while I was at Broadclist that Mr. E—— said I was much better at classics than at mathematics. Euclid's elements I never could bear, although very fond of metaphysical and other reasoning studies. But pure mathematics seems to lead to nothing. It is like cultivating ground which brings no fruit, or rather it is a sort of intellectual treadmill, on which, although you are constantly stepping, you are never advancing. At least, so it appeared to me then, and I have never got over my repugnance to it.

After my return to Totnes, I remained there until the midsummer of 1824, when I went to Rugby for the holidays, which were of some length, as Mr. E——'s establishment was to reopen at Teignmouth, where he had taken a large house, with some nice grounds attached to it. During these holidays a melancholy accident occurred, which threw a damp over the whole school. Michael Eaton, a schoolfellow, a very fine young man of about eighteen, was bathing in the river Dart, near Totnes, in company with some of the boys who stayed the holidays, when he was suddenly seized with the cramp, and drowned in their presence ; as the river was both deep and rapid, and as they were all quite young, they were unable to render him any assistance. A singular coincidence occurred connected with this catastrophe, which at that time received an ominous interpretation. About a fortnight before this event, just as I was leaving Totnes, one day during our one o'clock dinner, an owl was observed to fly four times round the house. This was remarked to be a prediction of a death in the family.

1825. Teignmouth I certainly found preferable to Totnes. The house was large and more commodious, and it was a great treat to be by the sea, besides which I was now high up in the school, associated with the head boys, and was under much less restraint. I also entered with great spirit into the different games which were played, of which the principal one was racing round the grounds with hoops. I used to read a good deal of natural history and craniology, as it was then termed, while here, though afterwards denominated by the more classical appellation *phrenology*. This latter study occupied a good deal of my thoughts ; and one speculation arising out of it, as to the nature and reality of happiness, formed the origin of my work " A Philosophical Treatise on the Nature and Constitution of Man." I also paid some attention to mechanical contrivances, which I occasionally projected ; and I made considerable progress in drawing.

CHAPTER V.

1825—1833.

1825. ON the 1st June, 1825, which was the commencement of the holidays, I left Teignmouth and came to Rugby. I was at this time very desirous of going into my father's office, and urgently entreated that I might be taken in there. This was not from any love for the profession, but from an ardent wish to escape from school and to live at Rugby, a place to which I was at that time most affectionately attached. I used to say I should live there all my life, which made some of the boys laugh ; but Mr. Croade, I recollect, expressed his opinion that I should do so, and that I was one who would go very quietly through the world, without making any stir in it.

Soon after my arrival at Rugby, my father set me to copy some writing in the house, and made me read Addison's *Spectators* in order to form my style, which, as my letters evince, did not at this period bear any close affinity to the Addisonian. In the course of a few weeks, I was taken into the office as a clerk, with the view of being articled. Among my colleagues there at this time were Matthew Bloxam, who is highly distinguished for his books and researches respecting architecture and antiquarian studies, besides being a Fellow of the Society of Antiquaries ; John Eyton, who had also a turn for antiquarian pursuits, who was connected with some old families in Shropshire, his brother being the historian of the county, and who, at the time of his death, was engaged to be married to Miss Disraeli, sister of the distinguished statesman ;

John Walcott, a Worcestershire man, who afterwards married Bloxam's sister; and Felix Knyvett, who subsequently became secretary to the Archbishop of Canterbury.

Bloxam and Eyton were the only two of the clerks with whom I maintained any close intimacy. To the former I believe I owe much as regards his influence over me, especially at this time, in directing my mind to intellectual pursuits and studies, especially those connected with the arts, which he well understood, and in which he had been instructed by his uncle, Sir Thomas Lawrence, at that time President of the Royal Academy, and some of whose choicest sketches the Bloxams possessed. Eyton especially, as also the other clerks, used to express their opinion pretty freely that I was not at all fitted for this sort of life, and that I should never do any good in the office.

1826. I possessed at this time but very little general information or love for literature, though I had a great turn for certain pursuits. Indeed, I have at different periods, especially about this time, been imbued with a threefold ambition, into which all my desire of glory might be resolved. This consisted in desiring to be either (1) a great painter, especially of epic subjects; (2) to be a great orator; (3) to be a great author. All that I have ever cared about of getting on at the bar or obtaining position, or wealth, or reputation, was only subservient to these, and to enable me to obtain them. But I must not anticipate. The first desire, I think, for some years at least merged into the third and graphonamata designs. The second, if ever accomplished, will be through lectures. I never had any ambition to be a great statesman, still less to be a great lawyer. Mechanics for some time occupied my attention; and I designed several really ingenious machines, among which were a flying machine, a locomotive engine, and a water organ, being a finger organ, the pipes of which were constructed out of glass bottles of different sizes, partly filled with water, by which the notes were to be varied. These two formed the germ of my scientific suggestions relative to those subjects. In conjunction with this pursuit, I studied " Joyce's Scientific Dialogues," and some other works of this nature, which I fully entered into. I also prepared some skeletons of animals, and stuffed some birds. Phrenology and natural history at this time engaged much of my attention ; and I read, among other works, Shakespeare, Milton, and Swift. In this sort of way I went on for about the first four years after I came to Rugby.

1827. I never gave my mind much to the subject of my profession, though I was obliged to attend regularly to the routine work of the office, and learnt in time to prepare abstracts and draw deeds as others had done before me. Of my intellectual capacity at this time, I believe the general opinion was a very humble one. One lady, who visited at my father's house, spoke of me as " that poor sort of half-witted fellow George ; " one gentleman said he " could not at all make me out : some things I said were very good, others so very foolish." Another, at a later period, pronounced me to be " a rolling stone that would never accomplish anything."

In the course of the year 1827 Dr. Wooll, who had always treated me with great kindness, and at whose house I occasionally dined, resigned the head mastership of Rugby School, and was succeeded by Mr. (afterwards Dr.) Arnold, with whom we also became intimate. During my leisure, I continued to practise drawing, and became very successful in copying heads and miniatures, and also in taking likenesses of several of my friends ; and I commenced painting in oils. In time I designed historical compositions, among them one of Satan's expulsion from heaven, one of Hamlet, Macbeth and Lady Macbeth, Cicero, St. Paul, and the raising of Lazarus, each of which I still have. I never had any love for my profession; and my father continually rating me about this, and telling me whenever any mistake occurred that my head ran upon painting, and that I was following two professions at once, served so far to extinguish the little spark of attachment towards it, that I seriously deliberated within myself about taking up the profession of an artist and abandoning the law. I never divulged my project to any one, but hoped when I went to London to have an opportunity of mentioning my wish to Sir Thomas Lawrence and obtaining his aid.

1828. In a short time, however, I was convinced of the wildness and impracticability of this scheme; and the sudden death of Sir Thomas Lawrence before I went to London extinguished my main hopes here. I continued nevertheless for some time to follow painting assiduously, and fitted up a studio for myself in the garden. I also modelled in clay and etched a few things on copper, pretty successfully. From the practice of the art, I was led on to study it in its highest branches; and I thought that I would sooner be a great historical painter than attain eminence in any other profession. In time I was induced to reduce to writing my notions on the subject of art and the highest principles of it, which I accordingly did in a series of rude essays, some of which are still extant, and which formed the germ of my work on "The Theory of the Arts," published in 1869. In the early part of the year 1831, after long deliberation, and after finding it impossible to follow up painting so as to attain real eminence and fame in it as a profession, I determined to give it up altogether, and to write upon it instead, and devote myself to general literature. I resolved also to continue collecting engravings and works of art and books on the subject, which I have since done; but with the exception of one or two pen-and-ink sketches and one or two copper-plate etchings, until I went to Manchester, when I had full leisure afforded me, I steadfastly kept to my resolution to abandon painting as a pursuit. I must confess, however, that as regards the expansion of my mind and the extension of my ideas and mental vision, I owe to art a debt of gratitude which it would be flagrant in me not to acknowledge.

1829. During the period of my articles, I routed out from a recess in the roof of the old part of my father's house, which was used as a lumber room, a number of old waste papers and letters of the last century, which had been lying there for years, among them letters and papers relating to the Donellan murder case, a letter from Sir Theodosius Boughton, several from his mother, as also a numerous correspondence about the Oxford Canal and Enclosure Acts. This was my earliest effort in the inquiry into ancient manuscripts collections, and was followed several years after by my researches at Wimpole, and completed in my origination of a Manuscript Commission.

In November, 1829, my grandfather Admiral Chambers died, in his eighty-first year. I was sincerely attached to him, and his epitaph most truly describes him as "a man beloved and esteemed by all who knew him." This character is beautifully and faithfully sketched in Moultrie's poem.

In 1829 I paid a visit to Kynnersley, in Shropshire, to my aunt Fanny, who had married Mr. Burn, the rector of that parish. My aunt, in writing to my mother soon after my visit to Kynnersley, said, "We

were very much pleased with George and Tom during
their visit to us. I was surprised at George's reading
so much as he did." While here I principally occupied
myself in making sketches in water colours of portraits.
The reading I was engaged in was that of Pope's
" Homer's Iliad," a large portion of which I studied while
here with great delight.

1830. The next year, which was in 1830, we made a
family tour through North Wales, going first to Bangor,
where we heard the news of the French revolution, the
abdication of Charles X., and the accession of Louis
Philippe. We subsequently ascended Snowdon, and
saw the magnificent prospect from thence during a
glorious sunset, but were romantically lost on the
mountain during our descent, and wandered about until
daylight, when we got to Beddgelhart, where we stayed
some time. I afterwards attempted a poem in blank
verse on the " Hermit of Snowdon," but being dissatisfied
with it, I eventually destroyed it.

1831. In 1831 my father was professionally employed
in a contested election for Northamptonshire, which
found me plenty of occupation. At this time I first
became acquainted with the Rev. James Prince Lee
(afterwards Bishop of Manchester), who had then just
been appointed one of the assistant masters at Rugby.
His first introduction to me was his meeting me in the
street at Rugby near the Bank, and asking me the state
of the poll, and wishing me success to the Tory side, at
which I expressed surprise, as I thought he had been a
Whig.

During part of the period of my clerkship my old
friend and tutoress, Miss W——, resided as a governess
in our family. Her frailty of temper had unfortunately
increased with her years ; and her visit was, I fear,
mutually unsatisfactory. We never saw her again, and

she died a few years afterwards, having written a novel
(we heard), which was to embrace her own biography,
and of which I ought to put in a claim to be a hero, but
the title of it we never discovered.

1832. In addition to the study of art and general
literature and the composition of essays in that department, I took up politics at this time, as also the question
of education. My principles were of the Tory school;
and in the course of March, 1832, my first effusion
in print appeared in a letter, inserted in the *Northampton
Herald*, to the electors of Northamptonshire, signed
" An Englishman."

On the 22nd February, 1832, my articles of clerkship
expired; and in April of this year I went to London. I
commenced keeping a diary during my residence in
London in 1832 and 1833, the following extracts from
which afford a correct notion of my pursuits and views
at this time :—

" *April 16th.*—Went to London to be admitted as an
attorney. Lodgings were engaged for me at No. 4,
Featherstone Buildings, on the second floor. Eyton
lodged at the house opposite. I should have gone up
to London before this, but the cholera was raging, so
that my father was afraid to allow me to do so.

" *17th.*—To-day I went about with Knyvett to see
London, not having been there since I was quite a
child. The morning very foggy, through which the
sun looked more like a new, bright penny than a
celestial body. Soon after I came to London I went
to the Court of Chancery to see the wonder of the day,
Lord Brougham, which was a general practice with
visitors to London at this period; and I well recollect,
and have still a very vivid impression of, the first glance
which I had of this very remarkable man, of whom I
had heard so much, and whose fame and exploits every

newspaper and every tongue was then occupied in discussing.

" He was then about fifty. His expression was hard and wolfish, with grey eyes of great fierceness. He leant back in his chair as though much exhausted by fatigue, and indeed his worn features and haggard looks afforded every appearance of this. His voice sounded very harsh, with a strong north-country accent.

"At this period I had a great ambition to be acquainted with three men whom I looked upon with fervent admiration, though each were very different in their way. These were Lord Brougham, William Cobbett, and John Martin, the artist. The first I have since known well, and visited and corresponded with pretty frequently. The second I heard speak on the most memorable occasion on which he addressed the House of Commons. The third I never saw, but I wrote a concise biography of him in the *Critic* soon after his death.

" *22nd.*—Easter Sunday. Dined at Dr. Sleath's, at St. Paul's School, who was exceedingly kind, and gave me a general invitation to his house, of which I availed myself freely, and was always most hospitably received.

" *26th.*—To-day I sent an essay, in the form of a letter, signed 'A Connoisseur,' on art generally, to the magazine called *The Library of the Fine Arts*, which was my first literary production.

" *27th.*—Dined at Mr. George Marriott's, in Queen Square. Marriott was then a police magistrate, and afterwards chairman of the Middlesex Sessions.

" *May 1st*, Tuesday.—My article appeared in *The Library of the Fine Arts* which was published this day. How my heart beat to see it, my first-born, in print !

" *3rd.*—Sent another article to *Library of the Fine Arts*, being an essay on 'The Composition of an Epic

Painting.' Both this and the former one I had roughly composed at Rugby.

"*June* 1*st.*—My article appeared in *The Library of the Fine Arts.* A notice to correspondents that a communication left for me at the publisher's. Felt far too nervous to call about it. Sent a messenger for it, but no answer brought by him. A parcel, however, left for me in the evening, containing the two last numbers of the magazine and a letter from the editor, thanking me for my contributions, and begging my acceptance of the numbers containing them. How delighted I felt! I could hardly speak on opening the parcel, which I found on my return home in the evening with Eyton, and handed to him. He said the articles were very creditable to me, and showed much research. I now began to consider myself a regular literary aspirant. Resolved to 'escape' from Rugby, go to the bar, try and obtain an income by writing, and to gain political distinction. I would have done anything then to procure an income of £100 a year, which would enable me to remain in London. The editor of *The Library of the Fine Arts* was Mr. J. Kennedy, afterwards M.P. for Tiverton, and subsequently a colonial judge. He was a Hull man.

"*4th.*—Went for the first time to the House of Commons. This was a period of extraordinary political excitement, when the Reform Bill was in the crisis of its agony, and all London was in a state of foam. I entered with great spirit into the discussions of the time, and frequently went down to the Houses of Parliament, and was there on the occasion of the second reading of the Reform Bill in the House of Lords, when the mob assembled in a very tumultuous manner, insulted many of the peers, hooted the Bishop of Exeter, and made a rush at Dr. Gray, the Bishop of

Bristol, who walked by near where I stood. They
would have murdered him had he not been rescued
by a body of the police. I also attended several
political meetings, and became a member of a Debating Society which met at the London University
College.

"*7th.*—Sent another article to Arnold's *Library of
the Fine Arts*.

"*30th.*—*Library of the Fine Arts* published to-day.
My article appeared.

"*August 9th.*—Returned to Rugby. The vacation
of this year I spent at Rugby. Read discursively,
and composed in the same style."

From considering art as proper to be employed in
the representation of human nature, I was led on more
fully to the study of the latter, to which I had been
also induced by other pursuits, and composed several
essays bordering on, and connected with, this subject.
Composed also an oration supposed to have been
spoken in the House of Commons in favour of a motion
the object of which was to abolish negro slavery, and
which concluded by exhorting " honourable members "
to vote for the motion, as, " by doing so, be assured,
you will have gained a more glorious victory, you will
have achieved an exploit that will entitle you through
remotest ages to more lasting honour and gratitude,
than all the victories of war and bloodshed that have
distinguished the most renowned of heroes. Theirs
was a conquest over skill and valour ; yours will be a
more magnanimous one over tyranny and injustice."

After the vacation I returned to London, when I
resumed my journal.

"*October* 15*th.*—Returned to my lodgings in
Featherstone Buildings this day by the Rugby coach
the ' Accommodation,' which left Rugby at a quarter

before seven in the morning, and arrived at the Three
Cups, Aldersgate Street, a little before six in the evening.
I commenced my studies, as a pupil of Mr. James, in
his chambers, 11, Gray's Inn Square. Mr. James was
a conveyancing barrister, and eventually became one of
the benchers of Gray's Inn. He was the eldest son of
the Rev. Dr. James, formerly Head Master of Rugby
School.

"31st.—To-day I hired the November number of
Arnold's *Library of the Fine Arts*. Among the
notices to correspondents it was announced that an
article which I had sent to it, 'On Imagination and
Invention in Epic Painting,' was not inserted on the
ground that the subject was not treated with sufficient
clearness, and that the writer either went too far, or
did not go far enough."

This article, however, appeared about a year
afterwards in a number of *Arnold's Magazine*, a
continuation of *The Library of the Fine Arts*, when
one of the critiques on this number remarked,
'Among the remaining articles is one very cleverly
written, and deserving great attention : 'On Imagination
and Invention in Epic Painting.' A notice of it in an
Irish paper asserted that ' whoever is the writer of the
article, he is capacitated to take a very high rank
in English literature.' The substance of this article
was incorporated in the chapter on the same subject in
my 'Theory of the Arts.'

"7th.—In the *Gentleman's Magazine* of this month
appeared an article by me on 'The New National
Gallery.'

"25th.—I sent some verses of mine on the loss of the
Rothsay Castle and an elegy for insertion in the
Mirror and the Casket, but could not ascertain whether
they were ever inserted or even acknowledged, my

only effort up to this time at getting any poetical effusion into print.

"*December* 18*th.*—Had a breakfast-party. We afterwards went round to see the preparations for the different metropolitan elections which were now commencing, this being the first election after the Reform Act. In Covent Garden I one day witnessed a regular exhibition of a Westminster mob in the good old style, and was near being annihilated by getting too deep into it. The mob was so dense, that baskets and cabbage-stalks, being thrown upon it, floated on the heads of the mass until the people dispersed.

" 19th.—I returned to Rugby for the Christmas holidays. Each day I attended regularly at Mr. James' chambers, from ten to four. Plenty of work, and read 'Coke on Littleton' and other law treatises. Found them at Rugby very busy with the election for the northern division of Warwickshire, for which there was a strong contest between Mr. Dugdale, the Conservative candidate, whom all my friends supported, and Mr. Dempster Heming, a Radical. The latter called a meeting of his supporters at Rugby, when he delivered a violent speech, especially against the Church. I attended the meeting, and afterwards sent out an address to the electors, under the signature of 'A Spectator,' in favour of Sir Eardley Wilmot and Mr. Dugdale, the two candidates of moderate views, in the form of interrogatories, instituting a comparison between the different candidates in the various capacities deemed most important. It took well and told with several, and my friends applauded it."

1833. About this time I composed several short essays on the subject of the education of the people and of that branch of politics which is connected with civilisation, which especially interested me. I also wrote several notes on topics connected with human nature, among them some on "The Improvement of the Mind," on "The Fallacy of Human Judgment," on "Men of Ability," on "Happiness," "The Immortality of the Soul," on "Innate Ideas," and one contending that there is in man "no innate principle of benevolence." This was quite early in the year 1833 ; and soon after my return to London, on or about the 16th February (as nearly as I can make out), I composed the plan of my great work "The Treatise on Man," and the title of which was as follows : " Essay on the Mind and on Human Nature in General."

After the Christmas holidays I returned to London, when my journal recommences.

"*January 2nd.*—Returned to London to-day.

" 14*th.*—Borrowed to-day the *Quarterly Journal of Education*, to which I had sent an article, but no acknowledgment of it. Sent the substance of it afterwards to the *Northampton Mercury*, under signature of ' G. H. R.,' where it was inserted.

" 21*st.*—A letter of mine in the *True Sun*, signed ' Honestas,' attacking the Government for prosecuting Hetherington when they had allowed so many revolutionists of their own party to go unmolested.

" *February 26th.*—At London University Debating Society. Although very nervous, I often used to speak at this Society, though but shortly, but in time I improved.

" *March 14th.*—I was at this period desirous of obtaining a situation in London as a managing clerk, so that I might remain there, and hoped in time to be able to get called to the bar, which I now resolved to do sooner or later. But I had also thoughts of going into the Church, and once determined to do so, though I never mentioned this to any one. Edward Cardale used to

say it would suit me better than the law, and to ask me
if I did not wish I had done so.   He said he regretted
not having become a clergyman.   He did afterwards take
orders.

"*April 4th.*—Dined at E. Cardale's.   Went to the
House of Commons in the evening.   An article of mine,
'On the National Gallery,' in Arnold's *Library of the
Fine Arts* of this month.

"*20th—22nd.*—Went to Mr. Halcomb's, at Highgate,
and stayed there during Sunday.   He was at this time
M.P. for Dover, and used to frank my letters for me,
and frequently took me to the House of Commons, so
that I was there constantly, which made me long to be
a member of it, and added fuel to the flames of ambition
which were now raging hot within me.

"*May 6th.*—My birthday.   Bought at this period
'Locke on the Understanding,' which I studied deeply,
much admired, and have always considered since as my
favourite work, also 'Locke on the Conduct of the
Understanding' and Bacon's 'Essays,' which I read
as well.   Montesquieu's 'Spirit of Laws' I also purchased
and studied, and was much pleased with it, and 'Locke on
Government.'   I purchased too several engravings after
the old masters."

I continued to attend Mr. James' chambers very
regularly, and devoted myself entirely to professional
matters during the hours of work, and made good
progress here.   Sometimes I thought of practising as a
conveyancer in Gray's Inn, but my general determination was to go to the bar as a common law practitioner,
espousing politics as well.

"16th.—Went to the House of Commons, having an
order from Mr. Halcomb.   The question of the evening
was Cobbett's motion to dismiss Sir Robert Peel from the
Privy Council.   The House much crowded.   Cobbett

commenced by reading a series of resolutions quaintly
worded and of great length, which he afterwards
handed to the Speaker, who read them to the House in
his dignified manner, forming a great contrast to
Cobbett's.   Cobbett spoke at some length, but hesitated
a good deal, and repeated himself constantly.   Peel's
reply, especially the conclusion of it, was very fine.   He
spoke under considerable excitement, and with great animation and fluency ; and his delivery as an orator was
really perfect.   He was enthusiastically cheered from all
parts of the House.   Cobbett's manner and appearance
were much against him, homely and undignified.   He
is tall and well made, dressed like a country farmer,
with yellow waistcoat, brown trousers, and very broad-
brimmed hat.   His hair is quite white.   His face
is round, and not strikingly intellectual.   He rather
stoops.   His voice is hoarse.

"*June 2nd.*—An article of mine on ' The Railroads '
in *Arnold's Magazine.*"

At this time I started a sort of domestic newspaper
in manuscript, which was to contain all the news of the
family, and to which the different members were to
contribute letters, bits of news, humorous and satirical,
personal hits, etc.   It was called *The Rugbæan*, and
came out monthly while it lasted, which was for a few
months, and was written out by different members of
the family by turns, and sent to John at Liverpool, to
Tom at Oxford, and to Rugby.

"*July 1st.*—Went to Rugby.

" *12th.*—Returned to London.

" *14th.*—Sent an article to *Arnold's Magazine of the
Fine Arts*, ' On the Repeal of the Stamp Duty on News-
papers,' which was duly inserted in the number for
August."

Here my journal of this period of my life ends.   I,

however, continued in London, and in Mr. James'
chambers, until September.

"*August 26th.*—I attended a debate in the House of
Lords, having had an order sent me through Sir Gray
Skipwith. I heard Lord Melbourne, Lord Grey, and the
Archbishop of Dublin speak."

One Sunday in September I dined and spent the
evening at Kensington, and did not reach home until
very late. I had not been long in bed, and had
scarcely got to sleep, when I was startled by an unusual
noise, and at once perceived an extraordinary glare of
light in my room. I immediately got up, and found
that the house in Hand Court immediately at the back
of the one I lived in was on fire ; and it soon became
enveloped in flames, which threatened also that where
I resided. I at once called up my landlord and his
daughter, who were very much alarmed at first, supposing our house was on fire, and eagerly inquired if the
stairs were burnt.   The house which was on fire
was only separated from ours by a small yard, into
which my bedroom looked ; and the heat speedily
broke the windows in my room.

The police and firemen were soon thundering at our
door, and six pipes from the engines were conveyed
through the passage in our house. The spectacle was
an awful one. The flames raged tremendously ; and
the noise of the tiles rattling down, and of the floors
falling, and the roof giving way, was very terrific ; and
it was unknown whether any people were in the house
or not, though all, I believe, escaped. Six houses were
destroyed, and ours was a good deal injured, and the
outhouses burnt down. About eight the fire was
extinguished.

This catastrophe made it very uncomfortable
for me to remain any longer in my lodgings ; and

though I had settled to stay with Mr. James until the end of the long vacation, and attended to all his papers in his absence, and drew all the drafts, etc., sending them on to him for approval, I mentioned to him how I was situated, and therefore left London and came to Rugby in September. I well remember the real fond, unaffected regret with which I left London, and turning round with genuine tears in my eyes to take a last look at it as I passed through Islington on the top of the Rugby coach.

On my return to Rugby I did not go into my father's office, or attend to any business for him, as I expected I should have done, but I was left entirely to myself until January. During this period I therefore pursued my favourite studies and read through " Locke on the Understanding" and other works. I also wrote some more articles in *Arnold's Magazine :* an essay in the October number, 1833, " On the Charges Made for Admittance into our Cathedrals," and one " On National Receptacles for Works of Art," which one of the critiques pronounced to be " excellent," and which the publisher in a letter informed me was much praised. The essay before alluded to "On Imagination and Invention," etc., and one " On the Study of the Fine Arts," both appeared in the number for February, 1834. But my most important occupation was the composition of what I may call the first edition of my " Treatise on Man," which occupied me principally during October, November, and December of this year. I now put my ideas into writing, and actually carried out my intention of composing a treatise on the topic I had so long contemplated. It was comprised in ninety pages of note-paper size, but very closely written. It cost me much thought, rude, and vague, and loosely written as it was ; I embodied in it the various essays on the several topics treated on which I had previously written. This edition was only composed to work upon, and to serve as a sort of scaffolding to build up to.[*]

—

CHAPTER VI.

BECOME A PARTNER IN MY FATHER'S FIRM.

1834—1838.

1834. AS I was sitting in my bedroom (which I used as a sitting-room also) late one evening by the fire, at the commencement of January, 1834, my father came to me, and, having shut the door, said, "Oh, George, we have been thinking of your joining us," and then told me that he had arranged with his partner, Mr. Wise, that I should be admitted into the firm, which, indeed, Mr. Wise himself was, I believe, the first to propose. I thanked my father for the offer, to which I, of course, assented ; but I remember very well thinking at the time how few young men to whom such a

* The following was the title of the work and the heading of the several chapters :—

ON THE GENERAL NATURE OF MAN.

CHAPTER I. GENERAL CONSIDERATIONS RESPECTING MAN.
,,   II. THE APPETITES.
,,   III. THE PASSIONS.
,,   IV. THE DESIRES.
,,   V. THE AFFECTIONS.
,,   VI. THE FEELINGS IN GENERAL.
,,   VII. THE CONSCIENCE.
,,   VIII. THE IDEAS.
,,   IX. REASON.
,,   X. GENIUS.
,,   XI. TASTE.
,,   XII. EDUCATION.

proposal had been made would have been so little elated
by it.   Of late I had been more and more desirous of,
and determined on, going to the bar, and I thought
that my surest chance of effecting this was to escape
from Rugby ; but I knew it was useless to propose
such a thing to my father, as he would not listen to it
for a moment.   He had of late made two or three in-
effectual attempts to obtain situations for me as a
managing clerk.   One of the letters for this purpose
I peeped into, and was surprised to find him describing
me as "a young man of good abilities and very steady."
My income was (nominally) about £400 a year, and I
continued to live with my father and mother as long as
the partnership lasted.

After joining my father's firm, I attended to business
regularly and punctually, though without taking any
real interest in my profession, and still hoping and
determining eventually to be a member of the higher
branch of it.   During my leisure hours, I continued
the composition of essays on various topics, particularly
those connected with the "Treatise on Man," "The
Arts," and "Education."   I also wrote out some orations
and perorations for imaginary speeches at the bar, and
in the House of Commons.   A great portion of the
essays was subsequently extracted for, or worked up
into, the "Treatise on Man," "Theory of the Arts,"
and "Civilisation as a Science."   I also resumed my
poetical attempts at this period, and composed a poem
on Poussin's picture of Moses striking the rock, and
one on "The Deluge," and some other pieces, and
designed a sort of oratorical tragedy or debate in verse,
entitled "*Raphael:* an Allegorical Tragedy," being a
debate in the shades below between Raphael, Michael
Angelo, and others, on the capacities and powers of
their art.   I occasionally, too, sent some letters and

political efforts to the *Northampton Herald* and other
newspapers on the passing topics of the day.

In August of this year I paid John (my brother) a
visit at Liverpool, and afterwards went to Ireland, and
made a short tour there, of which I wrote an account in
a journal. Dublin and the " Giant's Causeway " were
the principal objects of interest which I saw.

1835. I often had discussions with Dr. Arnold on
constitutional and philosophical subjects. By his per-
suasion it was that I was first induced to deliver a lecture.
On one occasion after dinner at his house, I had a good
deal of discussion with Dr. Arnold on the state of
Ireland, and expressed my opinion that the best plan
would be to dissolve the union, which he said was the
opinion of Southey and Wordsworth, whom he considered the two deepest thinkers of the day. Dr.
Arnold remarked that the only country Ireland could
unite with was America, that the dissolution of the
union would probably lead to a war between England
and Ireland, and that " in the end we should drive the
Celts into the sea."

On the 7th January, 1835, I delivered a lecture on
" Jurisprudence " before the Rugby Literary and
Scientific Institution, in which I inquired into the
first principles of laws of different minds, traced the
origin of government, and described the various kinds
of it, concluding with a eulogy on the British Constitution as " one that had ever been the admiration of
foreign rivals and statesmen, and which contained a
system of laws that had been the means of rendering
this country so truly great, so glorious, and so free."
Of this Society the secretary was Mr. J. Hooley
Lockyer, a chemist in Rugby, and father of that very
distinguished astronomer and philosopher, who was
born in Rugby, Mr. Norman Lockyer.

At this time Parliament was again dissolved, and we had another contested election for North Warwickshire, into which I entered warmly, and prepared several of the squibs, especially one about Pope Gregory absolving the voters from their promises, alluding to a handbill of Mr. W——, the agent for Mr. Gregory, the Radical candidate, telling the people they were absolved from their promises to vote for Mr. Dugdale, and which elicited much praise. Soon after the election was over, I composed a small political pamphlet, entitled " What have the Whigs done ? " containing a review of the various measures effected by the Ministry, and condemning them strongly. This I sent up to Mr. Valpy, to whom I was introduced by Mr. Charles Seager, then residing in Rugby as a tutor, who revised the proof sheets for me. It was printed by Mr. Valpy, and published by Relfe and Fletcher, of Cornhill. The price was sixpence, and it sold well, about four hundred being disposed of by the publishers, and a good many at Rugby and in the neighbourhood. It was well reviewed in some of the country papers ; and Mr. Homer, of Rugby, in a letter thanking me for it, termed it " a very able and well-written pamphlet." So much for my first work.

In July I paid a visit to Paris, of which a full account is contained in my journal on that occasion. My old master Mr. E—— and I exchanged letters in the autumn of this year. I wrote to him and sent him one of my pamphlets, and had a long reply, giving an account of his family and of some of my old colleagues.

On the 3rd of November I delivered a lecture before the Rugby Literary and Scientific Institution on " Painting and the Fine Arts," which was illustrated by several engravings. The substance of it is incorporated in " The Theory of the Arts." Some of my audience expressed themselves as much pleased with it ; and even my father, my mother told me, read it with great interest.

Of late I had been occupied in the composition of a constitutional pamphlet, inquiring into the first principles and respective advantages of different forms of government, and the preference of a mixed form like our own to any other. I also pointed out certain measures as inevitably leading to republicanism, and certain others as counteracting that tendency. This work I entitled "Prospects of, and Progress towards, a Republic." I sent it up to Mr. Valpy, who printed and published it. It occupied about eighty pages in an octavo form.

1836. In 1836 I recommenced keeping a diary, some extracts from which I here insert :—

" 14*th*.—Spent the evening at Rev. J. P. Lee's. Mr. Stevenson (a leading publisher of Cambridge) there, who gave me much useful information respecting the publication, etc., of books, and told me that newspaper reviews, etc., were not any real test of a book's merit. As I have already recorded, I became acquainted with the Rev. J. P. Lee in 1831, soon after he came to Rugby.*

---

* We became very intimate, chiefly, I fancy, through my fondness for metaphysical subjects, which we used to discuss a good deal together, in evenings especially, Locke, Dugald Stewart, and T. Brown, who he said he thought was the greatest of them all (chiefly, I suppose, because he devotes so much attention to educational topics), though I can't agree at all with him.

We also discussed art a good deal, and oratory. When, much later on, I was at the bar, and used to visit him at Birmingham, we frequently talked upon forensic topics, and he illustrated to me very well one evening the theory of cross-examination. In a letter which he gave me when I was a candidate for the professorship of history at University College, London, in 1860, he mentioned that my reading had been considerably above the tone of that of ordinary men.

"*2nd.*—A notice of my pamphlet in the *Leicester Conservative Standard Magazine*, in which they say I treat the subject ' in a masterly manner,' and term mine ' a most valuable and instructive pamphlet.'

"*3rd.*—Letter from Valpy, containing extract from a review of my pamphlet in the *Metropolitan*, and in which they term it ' a sound argumentative pamphlet, which ought to be read by every one who affects to love his country.

"*24th.*—On the 30th of last month Eyton wrote me a very long letter, principally advising me about my book, of which I afterwards sent him a copy, with a letter, and was daily expecting a reply, when this morning I received the following note from the Rev. P. W. Powlett, one of the masters of Rugby School, and a great friend of Eyton :—

" ' *Rugby, Wednesday.*

" ' DEAR HARRIS,—I am sure you will be shocked to hear that our poor friend Eyton died on Friday last of small-pox, after a short illness. My brother gave me this sad account by letter this morn-ing. I have lost one of my very best friends, for whom I felt a hearty regard. Other reflections arise in consequence of this sudden event, but each man thinks for himself on these melancholy occasions.

" ' Yours very faithfully,
" ' PERCY W. POWLETT.'

" ' GEORGE HARRIS, Esq., Jun.'

"*March 1st.*—Long quotations from my pamphlet in the *Leicester Conservative Standard Magazine*.

"*22nd.*—Received a note from Mr. Lee, thanking me for my pamphlet, praising it, and saying, ' I much like many of your remarks, especially those on the equilibrium in our Constitution, and I hope the book

will obtain general circulation, as it decidedly will be
useful. I most sincerely congratulate you on so good
a *début* as an author.' Spent the evening at Mr. Lee's,
and talked with him about my pamphlet, with which he
was much pleased.

"27*th*.—Saw Dr. Arnold after school chapel in afternoon, and talked to him about some books I had lent
him. He said Wilkes' 'Introduction of the History
of England' was a very curious work indeed, and he had
never heard of it before. He did not think that Wilkes
would have written a history of England.

"29*th*.—Went to Warwick on business, and stayed there
all night. The Inneses, Mr. Birch, and Mrs. Halcomb
commended much my pamphlet. Say they think it too
clever to be mine without assistance, and that if I have
so great a turn for writing, I shall not stick to law ;
may become a celebrated character ; had better either
give up writing or else law, and stick to politics. Mr.
Halcomb said it was a better pamphlet than he could
have written, and the best he had read, and he should
give a copy to Sir William Follett. Mr. Birch said I
should be going to the bar.

"31*st*.—My Mother told me to-day in general conversation that I had 'very good abilities,' and also that my
Father always said that 'my abilities were much better
than his.'

"*April* 2*nd*.—Received letter from G. W——, of
Birmingham, thanking me for my pamphlet, which he
termed 'very able and powerful, and calculated to be
of essential service to the Conservative cause.'

"6*th*.—My birthday. Spent the evening at Mr. Lee's.

"22*nd*.—Sent an article to *Standard* on South
Warwickshire election.

"24*th*.—My communication to *Standard* appeared
as a leading article.

" 28*th*.—Went to Warwick Sessions. Drank tea with Mr. Halcomb, who said that pamphlet ' showed much reading and reflection, and seemed to be the work of a much older head than mine.'

" 30*th*.—Spent the evening at Mr. Lee's.

"*July 6th*.—Spent the evening with Mr. Lee, settling holiday excursion plans.

" 16*th*.—Went to London by ' Wonder and Antelope.' Put up at Wood's Hotel, Furnival's Inn.

" 17*th*.—Spent the day at Dr. Sleath's. Went to Lincoln's Inn Chapel in the morning, and to St. Paul's with Dr. Sleath in afternoon, where I met in the vestry room, and was introduced to, Mr. Sydney Smith, who asked me if I was ' an aspirant to the mitre.' Met Mr. Macaulay, Head Master of Repton, at Dr. Sleath's.

" 22*nd*.—Went to House of Lords with Mr. Halcomb. Returned to Rugby at 7 p.m.

" 23*rd*.—Dined at Mr. Lee's.

"*August 6th*.—Called on Matthew Bloxam about purchase of etchings in his possession, by Salvator Rosa belonging to the late Sir T. Lawrence, and for which I agreed."

As regards my professional occupation at this period, I generally undertook the journeys on business and also attendance at assizes and sessions, which latter urged me on the more in the course I had resolved on of going to the bar ; and when in court I used to watch the progress of trials, and measure my own powers with those of the counsel engaged in the case. I attended also regularly to my work in the office, and did most of the conveyancing business myself.

On Monday, the 22nd of August, I came up to London with the Lees. We stopped at St. Albans in our way, and explored the Abbey Church there. Mr. Lee had settled to accompany me on my intended tour on the Continent, but after he got to London found he could not do so. On the evening of the 22nd, I proceeded to Dover, and thence by packet to Ostend, and so on to Bruges, Ghent, Antwerp, Brussels, Namur, Liège, Aix-la-Chapelle, Cologne, Amsterdam, The Hague, Haarlem, and Rotterdam.

A full account of my expedition is contained in my journal. I returned to England on the 7th September.

My great object in making the tour of the Netherlands was to see the works of art there. I had lately sketched out the design of a work which I had proposed to entitle " The Theory and Principles of the Ideal and Imitative Arts."

On the 4th of October, I delivered a lecture at the Rugby Literary and Scientific Institution on " The Connection between the Different Branches of the Ideal and Imitative Arts," the substance of which formed a chapter in my work above referred to. I also continued the composition of short essays and orations, as before.

About this time I designed what has since formed my work entitled " Civilisation Considered as a Science," and the original titles of which were as follow : Civilisational Jurisprudence, or that branch of jurisprudence which concerns and regulates the intellectual and moral condition of a nation ; its general nature, effects, and importance with the laws expedient for regulating the same.

At this time I commenced rewriting the " Treatise on Man," in a greatly enlarged shape, embodied in it the essays I had lately composed, and rearranged the topics treated on ; this occupied me mainly during leisure until the 7th of September, 1837, when I considered it as complete as I could then make it, and sealed it up, and laid it by for future revision.

1837. In February, 1837, I was elected president of the Rugby Literary and Scientific Institution, and on the 7th March, I delivered a lecture there on "The Delineation of Character and Passion in the Ideal and Imitative Arts," which has been incorporated in one of the chapters in my "Theory of the Arts."

In May of this year I subjected myself to a really strict and searching self-examination as regarded my intellectual acquirements, the books I had read in different departments, my knowledge of Greek and Latin and of history and philosophy.

In June I went to the Warwick Sessions, and finding them in want of a candidate on the Conservative side to stand for that borough, proposed Mr. B—— L—— to them, to whom a requisition was sent; but Sir Charles Douglas having come to Warwick in the meantime, it was eventually decided that he should stand, and I therefore stayed to support him and to give him Mr. B—— L——'s interest. I had several times to make speeches at meetings of our party, and indeed now longed more than ever to start as a candidate myself.

After the election was over, Sir Charles Douglas came and stayed a night with us at Rugby, and met Mr. B—— L—— and others at dinner. I obtained from him his first frank.

In July died my poor brother Stephen, who had long been a suffering invalid, but was in all respects an excellent pattern of what a person so afflicted should be.

In September I started on an expedition of pleasure for the Lakes and Scotland. A full account of my tour is contained in my journal. A small incident befell me on my setting out which had a considerable immediate, though perhaps not ultimate, influence on my destination. The guard of the mail by which I travelled from Dunchurch offered me the *Dispatch*

newspaper to read, in which an advertisement soon
caught my eye headed " Income,—£90 a year for
£350." It then described some property to be sold in
London which would realise this return. I at once
wrote to the person named in the advertisement, as it
seemed to me just what I wanted to enable me to escape
from Rugby and have an independence in London ;
and I arranged to see the advertiser in town, and
for that purpose went there by the steamer from
Edinburgh.

The property alluded to consisted of eleven small
houses in West Street, Bethnal Green ; and after some
inquiries, I agreed for the purchase of the property at
the sum named of Mr. C—— V——, the proprietor,
who lived in a good house in Highbury Terrace. The
houses in West Street seemed well built and in good
repair, and I congratulated myself on having made an
excellent purchase, even if the return was much below
what I was assured it would be. I had shortly before
purchased some premises at Kilsby for £225 ; and on
these and the Clifton house I borrowed the money for
my new purchase. I was so well pleased with my
bargain, that I immediately entered into a correspondence with Mr. V—— for the purchase of some more
property of the same kind, and I now considered myself as a man of independent property.

During the summer of this year I sent to Mr. Valpy
an article on " The Committee on Arts and Manu-
factures," which I requested him to get accepted for
me if he could by the *British and Foreign Review.*
On the 13th of October, Mr. Kemble, the editor, wrote
to him and said " the very excellent article " was in
type, and that he " wished that more such articles were
submitted to him."

Shortly before Christmas, I went to London with

Mr. Lee, and spent Christmas Day with Mrs. L——
at Findon, Sussex.

1838. Soon after Christmas I returned to London.
My journey to Findon had been one of some perplexity
and even peril ; for it being the eve of Christmas Day,
all the coaches were full, and I could only get a place
as far as Horsham.   From thence I obtained a conveyance, with some other persons who were similarly
situated, in the shape of a light cart, in which I did
manage to reach Findon, and put up at a small inn there
called the Gun.   The next morning I told the waiting-
maid to go to Mrs. L——'s and inform her that I
would breakfast with her.   She went accordingly ; and
the message delivered was, " Please, mum, there's a
mon at the Gun, as came in the middle of the night in
a tax-cart, says he shall breakfast with you."   This
of course not a little astonished my very kind and
hospitable hostess until I appeared and explained the
mystery.

On my return to London, I called on Mr. Kemble,
the editor of the *British and Foreign Review*, who gave
me a cheque for twenty guineas for my article, which
I showed to Mr. Lee.   I thought then that I should be
able to make an income by writing in addition to what
my property brought me, and I considered that my
independence was at length established.   Soon after
this I returned to Rugby, and on the 20th February
was re-elected president of the Rugby Literary and
Scientific Institution.

My brother William, who had been articled to my father,
was now out of his articles, and about to go to London
to be admitted as an attorney.   He was very fond of the
business, and very attentive to it ; and my mother
often said how much better some other employment
would suit me, something in the British Museum

or the Post Office, and that William would be a capital
person to have in the office. All this very much favoured
my design of escaping from Rugby, so one day, when
William and I were walking together, I asked him
what he would allow me to give up my place in the
office to him, and he proposed £150 a year. I afterwards told him of my ground-rent purchase, and
agreed to relinquish my share in the business to him
for an annuity of £100 a year and £800 in cash,
including the arrears due to me during the time I
had been in the firm, which were between £400 and
£500, and I to give up my Clifton and Kilsby property
which I had lately purchased, and which was worth
about £350. I told my father and mother of the
arrangement, to which they assented, the latter using
all her influence with the former to secure this, and
it was finally arranged that the proposal should be
carried out in June. I did not at first tell my father
and mother of my ground-rent purchases, but we spoke
of it as an appointment bringing in £150 per annum.
though, on settling the money part of the transaction
this was explained.

In March William went to London, and, through
my introduction, became a pupil of S——- M——,
who was a chancery barrister and conveyancer.
While he was reading in M ——'s chambers, Martin,
my tenant, called on him one day in a state of great
agitation, and said he could not possibly fulfil the
terms of his lease, that the property would not yield
the rent he had covenanted to pay, that it was not
worth £600, and that V—— had deceived me. William
wrote me word of this; and I received the letter while
staying with one of my brothers at Magdalen College,
Oxford, of which he was then a Fellow. The news
came upon me like a thunderclap. I was a ruined

man, and all my prospects were destroyed, which of
course distressed me dreadfully, although I did not
mention to any one what had happened. I still,
however, adhered to my determination to escape from
Rugby, come what might, and went up to London
to try and arrange matters. After a great deal of
discussion, I found that it was vain to attempt to hold
Martin to his bargain. I applied to V——, and threatened
him with proceedings both at law and in equity. I, however, agreed with V—— eventually to take the property
of me on lease at a rent of £100 per annum, including
the ground rent of £25, at a nominal premium of
£600; but instead of paying me cash, he was to give
me two ground rents, one of £7 per annum and another
of £21, which arrangement was eventually carried out.

Mr. Lee was elected in the summer of this year to
the head mastership of King Edward's Free Grammar
School in Birmingham. I went once or twice to
Birmingham for him on this business, and also on the
day of his election.

People in general, I believe, in Rugby thought me
very foolish for giving up so good, so comfortable,
and so respectable a berth. Lee, however, told me he
thought I should not regret it, and that it was no
compliment to tell me I was fitted for a higher occupation than what I was then engaged in. I mentioned to
him my project of going to the bar. I talked with
him also about going to Cambridge, but he thought
it was not worth while for a mere degree, unless I
could take honours, which a person would have very
great difficulty in doing when so long a time had elapsed
since his leaving school. Our honest old servant, poor
old Joe, who had lived with us ever since my father
was a youth, one day asked me in the garden, when
I was alluding to my departure, with a very grave face,

"Ah, master, d'ye think you'll better yourself ?" However, I was resolved on quitting Rugby, and rejoiced in taking my departure.   In June William passed his examination, and was duly admitted an attorney.   My last day in the office at Rugby was the 22nd of June, when I renounced all further connection with the business.

CHAPTER VII.

LEAVE RUGBY TO RESIDE IN LONDON.

1838—1839.

ON the 23rd of June, I left Rugby and arrived in London.   No prisoner ever escaped from his dungeon with greater delight than I felt on running away from my friends and my home.   We parted, however, on the very best of terms, as indeed, I have always lived with them ; and as the railroad was now about to be speedily opened which would render Rugby and London but a short distance from one another, the separation seemed but trivial.   At this time the railway was in use from Birmingham to Rugby, and from Denbigh Hall to London.   The intermediate distance was travelled by coaches and omnibuses.   It happened that the coronation was near approaching, in consequence of which there was an immense rush of people to London, so that I had as much difficulty in getting away from Rugby to London corporeally, as I had had in effecting my escape from it in consequence of my position.   At first I could only proceed as far as Daventry, where I was detained a long time ; but I eventually obtained a conveyance to Denbigh Hall, and thence by the railway to London.

On my arrival in town, I procured a bed at William's lodgings, 9, Featherstone Buildings, close to my old quarters ; and on his going to Rugby, which he did in a day or two, I succeeded to the occupation of his apartments. I now recommenced keeping a journal, which I have continued uninterruptedly until the present period, and from which I have here extracted any matters of interest.

"*July* 1st.—Perusing Aristotle's 'Metaphysics,' preparatory to revising article on 'Phrenology and Mental Philosophy' which I had written, intending to send it to the *British and Foreign Review*.

" *8th.*—Engaged principally this week in revising and copying article on 'Mental Philosophy' for the *British and Foreign Review*.

" *11th.*—Called at *British and Foreign Review* office, and delivered article on 'Mental Philosophy.' Engaged lodgings at 20, Craven Street, Strand, at £1 1s. a week, taken for three months from September."

On the 9th of August, I left London on a grand tour through parts of Belgium, Germany, Switzerland, Italy, and France, of which I have left a full account in my journal on that occasion. When I visited Mont Blanc in 1838, I wrote the following verses, the copy of which, unfinished, I lately found while moving my papers. I have since completed them, and they form a suitable adjunct to the notes of my present tour.

ODE TO MONT BLANC.

Hail, Nature's minster, in her noblest form
Of glories aptly reared, where all around
Huge mountains towering high, the silvery glacier,
The rude-cleft crag, the frowning precipice,
The smiling valleys verdant, decked with flowers ;

These, Nature's capital, her towers, and these
Around her minster stand in solemn awe.
Thou glorious dome, crowned with eternal snow,
Of spotless purity, above the clouds
And earthly shades and vapours ! Nearest to heaven
From earthly mists thou lift'st thy head sublime.
Thy alabaster pinnacles stand forth
Pointing to heaven from earth, and upward rise
High into regions of celestial light ;
While from thy choir the solemn note of praise
In the full swell of Nature's organ peals.
The roaring avalanche, the thunder's roll,
The foaming torrents ; these thy organ notes.
The birds, thy choristers, echo thy song.
All join alike in hymns of gratitude
To Him Who placed thee here, a pile sublime,
His noblest temple, in the fittest scene
To raise the sinking soul from earth to heaven.

I arrived in London again about the 17th or 18th of September, when I fixed my quarters at 20, Craven Street.

"*November* 24*th.*—Received a letter from John, who was then settled in Hull in a mercantile business, asking me to write articles for the *Hull Times.* He sent me with his letter a number of the *Hull Times*, containing a review of the current number of the *British and Foreign.*

"*December* 22*nd.*—Went down to Rugby, where I spent the Christmas holidays.

1839.—"*January* 7*th.*—Read review in *Quarterly Review* of 1810 of Gifford's 'Life of Pitt,' which I borrowed from the school library, and which Dr. Arnold recommended me to read as the most perfect article he knew, and with the exception of Macaulay's which he said he thought the best. It appears from Mackintosh's 'Life' that it was written by Canning. Arnold told me the writer was never known, and that even Murray, the publisher, could not tell who it was.

"*8th.*—Went to Birmingham to stay with Mr. Lee. Mr. Stevenson, of Cambridge, there. A discussion with Mr. Lee on mind, and also on politics and personal identity.

"*9th.*—Talked with Mr. Stevenson about my entering at Trinity Hall, Cambridge. He said he would assist me.

"*10th.*—Talked with Mr. Lee about my proposed article on 'Mental Philosophy,' sent to *British and Foreign*, the draft of which I showed to him. He said it was ingenious, and would attract notice ; but advised me to keep it by me for the present, and to read Mackintosh's 'Rise of Philosophy,' second book of Locke, and Butler's 'Analogy,' also Euclid, to improve me in metaphysics, and to study the New Testament, Dugald Stewart, and Brown. Returned to Rugby to dinner.

"*11th.*—Went to London by two o'clock train.

"*14th.*—At the House of Commons. Sir Charles Douglas took me into the House below the gallery, and very kindly said he hoped I should often call for him there, and inquired if I was settled in London. The debate a good one, on Lord Mahon's motion respecting election committees. Lord Mahon, Sir R. Peel, Lord J. Russell, Sir R. Inglis, and Mr. Bernal Osborne spoke.

"*17th.*—Accidentally led to form an idea that a small pamphlet in a colloquial style on the subject of the London University would be my best mode of expressing an opinion upon it. Reflecting on this, I thought what an excellent pamphlet of this kind might be made on the present state of affairs. Set to work and wrote 'Cabinet Colloquies : an Imaginary Conversation between Her Majesty and Certain of her Ministers,' etc., etc.

"19th.—Called with the manuscript 'Cabinet Colloquies' on Mr. Southgate. He requested me to leave it with him, and call again in an hour, when he should have read it. I did so; and he said I had given some tremendous thrusts, and he thought it would do, and that there was no fear of my losing by it; that the play upon words and light part would take with the many, and the more serious matter with regular politicians; that at first, before he read it through, he thought it was only a light, frivolous pamphlet throughout, and that the sooner it fell to the ground the better, but that now he thought quite differently. He wished me to make it the first of a series, and put 'No. I.' on the title-page.

"22nd.—T. A. James called, and said both he and his father had read 'Cabinet Colloquies' without knowing it was mine, and thought it very good.

"23rd.—Called at Mr. Halcomb's. Mrs. H. said that Mr. H. thought there was a good deal of matter in 'Colloquies,' etc. Mr. H. told me it was written in good taste.

"25th.—Went to House of Commons in evening. Sent in my card to Sir C. Douglas, who came out to me, and took me into the room where admission book kept, and entered my name for going under gallery to-morrow and next night. He told me all about the Warwick election funds dispute. I gave him four copies of 'Colloquies,' which he said he supposed was mine.

"March 4th.—Attended on Mr. Southgate, and arranged respecting publication of 'Colloquies,' No. II., and advertising and handbill. Went to Debating Society, Exeter Hall. Spoke quite unexpectedly, owing to remarks made by a speaker; felt nervous, but managed to go through several topics, and several times cheered.

"9th.—'Colloquies' reviewed favourably in *Grant's Weekly Journal*, and also reviewed in *Hull Times*.

Called on Southgate with those papers, and asked him about sale. He said sale of No. II. was a decided improvement on No. I.

" 13*th*.—Called on Mr. Southgate respecting 'Colloquies.' He told me they were 'moving rapidly,' that he felt confident above a hundred and fifty were sold, that more than seventy went off in one day, and that a bookseller in Paternoster Row ordered four dozen to sell in the city. Went to House of Commons with T. A. James (for whom I obtained an order to gallery). Saw Sir C., who approved of requisitions respecting poor law which I drew up for him, and took me into body of House. Continuation of debate on Corn Law, after a motion of T. Attwood disposed of. Fielden hardly heard. O'Connell said some good things, but not equal to his best ; hesitated considerably. Lord Sandon heard with difficulty ; his manner very bad. Harvey's was the great speech of the evening ; he was loudly called for, and listened to most attentively. House crowded. Left about one o'clock. Villiers replying, but quite inaudible. Hanson spent evening with me. Read out in manuscript No. III. of 'Cabinet Colloquies.' He said he liked it as well, if not better than, No. II. Showed me a poem of his.

"19*th*.—Saw Sir C. Douglas at the House of Commons, who had received a most quaint and amusing letter from ' R. M. C. ' (Eastbourne) about the separation of man and wife in the new Poor Law Act, saying 'it was the only part which the poor people cordially approved of, as old people wished to get a little peace before they died, which they could only ensure by having their wives separated from them.'

" 28*th*.—Went to Rugby.

" 29*th*.—Saw Dr. Arnold, and had some conversation with him.

" 31*st.*—Saw Mr. Price and Dr. Arnold, and had some talk with both of them.

"*April 4th.*—Returned to London. Called on Mr. Southgate, who gave me proofs of sheets of ' Colloquies,' No. III., and told me ' he liked it much the best, and thought it decidedly the best number,' that they continued moving, and that there had been a great many inquiries for No. III.

" *6th.*—Went with Henry, who came yesterday to stay with me, in evening to Covent Garden to see *Richelieu.*

" *9th.*—Went with Henry over Westminster Abbey, and to Pantechnicon, also to University College Debating Society in evening. Spoke. Shaw told me he congratulated me on the third number of the ' Colloquies,' which was a great improvement—more intelligible to the generality.

" *12th.*—Went this day to Windsor. Called on Mr. T——. Went over Castle, having order, and saw both public and private apartments. Also Eton College. Dined and drank tea at Mr. T——'s. Returned to London in the evening.

" *15th.*—Sent letter to Mr. Stevenson, requesting him to enter me as a member of Trinity Hall in the University of Cambridge, and offering to send caution money and certificate, etc., as required.

" *17th.*—Received letter this day from Rev. J. Power, Fellow and Tutor of Trinity Hall, stating that he would enter me at that college in Cambridge, and that he should not require certificate.

" *23rd.*—Received letter this morning from Mr. Power, informing me that he had entered my name as a pensioner of Trinity Hall, Cambridge. Notice of ' Colloquies ' in the *Northampton Herald.*

" *26th.*—Mr. T—— called this morning. Said ' he liked the " Colloquies " very much indeed ; they were very satirical, and in very good taste : that, to tell the truth, he liked them better than he expected to do.' Said they would succeed, he thought, and would pay, but required to be made known, as people would not buy them on speculation. Requested me to let him have copies to send round to masters at Eton to make them known.

" 28*th.*—Walked over to Hampstead, and dined with Mr. Ward who said they wanted draftsman to accompany the expedition which the New Zealand Company were sending out to make sketches, and asked if I knew of one. I thought I might perhaps do, but did not then mention so to him. Said they would pay expenses and keep whoever went out in that capacity, and give him £100 per annum besides.

" 29*th.*—Wrote to Mr. Ward offering to accept the office alluded to if artistical qualifications were deemed sufficient. He replied I should be 'an acquisition' to their expedition, and requested me to call on him and go to the committee meeting that afternoon at four. Did so, and showed him my sketches ; but found that a regular artist had been appointed to the office. Felt in some respects satisfied that I could not go ; a great sacrifice to leave England and London so long. Found, however, that the business required rather mechanical than scientific ability, and that I should be required to draw plans and elevations and views for engraving.

" *May* 1*st.*—Went down to House of Commons. Saw Sir C. Douglas, who put down my name for going under gallery five nights this month.

" 3*rd.*—Went to the Debating Society, Exeter Hall. Spoke in favour of proposal to abolish juries, with more fluency than on any former occasion. M —— told me afterwards that I should talk well enough by-and-bye, and that I ' had the elements for it in me ; ' that

I had got on a good deal better to-night and was less nervous ; that he wished he had my ideas ; that he perceived I spoke as I wrote.

" 4*th.*—A very good review of ' Colloquies ' in *Oxford Herald* to-day.

" 13*th.*—Mr. Grant to-day pointed out to me a short but very flattering notice of ' Cabinet Colloquies ' in the *Morning Herald* of Friday. Took the paper to Mr. Southgate, who said that ' Colloquies ' were still moving.

" 19*th.*—Conversed with C. Marriott on mental philosophy and Locke in the evening, and about phrenology. Said the latter would make a very interesting subject for an article in a review. Showed him mine proposed for *British and Foreign.*

" 21*st.*—Saw Mr. Kemble at library British Museum, who showed me some Anglo-Saxon manuscripts, including some very interesting wills. Said not a syllable decided as to contents of next number of *British and Foreign*, though part in type. Such uncertainty about everything. Charles Marriott read over manuscript of my article on ' Phrenology.' Supplied me with some extracts from Plato of his own translating.

" 25*th.*—Saw T—— W——, who told me they had got ' Cabinet Colloquies ' at Welton. Said his brother S—— was very much pleased with them, and that they said at Rugby they did not think I could have done so much. S—— W—— delighted with them.

" 29*th.*—Mr. B—— L—— called on me, and left a note for me to call on him, in consequence of death of his son from sea-sickness at Plymouth, where he was landed from the vessel on the way to Canada, and wished me to go for him to Devonport.

" 30*th.*—Arrived at Devonport about four. Called on

General Ellice, Colonel S——, etc., respecting death of young B. L——, and wrote to Mr. B. L—— thereon.

"*June 1st.*—Went by coach at 1.47 to Newton Bushell to get to Teignmouth, hoping to reach the old school in time to join dinner with pupils at one. Passed through Totnes. Streets seemed much smaller than I supposed, but recognised the town, and all its different points, and Rosemount House, which I ran round on returning while the coach changed horses, and dragged up the hill. Got to Newton about eleven, and breakfasted at a small inn. Went down by river in boat to Teignmouth. Saw the old house rising up among the trees. As I walked up to it, observed it was two o'clock, and feared family would have dined. Surprised to see a handbill on door, and bell taken away. The reality at once flashed on my mind, and I found on inquiry that proprietor had got into difficulties, school given up, and house to be sold. Went all over it, on pretence of inquiring about price: into the schoolrooms and bedrooms, and round the grounds, the latter grown over with weeds, but could trace every spot. This day the anniversary of my leaving it fifteen years ago, just half the age I now am. Walked through the town, and back to Newton.

"*2nd.*—Dined at Colonel S——'s, who asked about 'Colloquies,' and whose production they were. Said he was much amused by them, and that there was a good deal of point in them. Told me I had made a very good hit about Lord Durham.

"*3rd.*—Returned to London by packet, bringing with me the coffin of Mr. B—— L——, jun., which was put in a wooden box and placed in the hold; obliged to conceal it from the sailors, on account of the superstitious feeling against having a corpse on board. Accompanied funeral to B—— Hall, and attended it there.

" 20*th.*—Left Rugby this morning by railway at half-
past seven, and went to Blisworth, and so on to Cambridge by coach.   Arrived in Cambridge at about eight
o'clock.   Called on Mr. Stevenson, when he promised
that his son should go round with me to-morrow morning to see the lions.

" 21*st.*—Went with Mr. Stevenson, jun., round the
town, and to the different colleges.   Long vacation
had commenced, and very few in town.

" 22*nd.*—Went this morning at seven o'clock with
Mr. Stevenson, jun., by boat to Ely.   Went over cathe-
dral at Ely ; interior very fine, especially the screen work.
Saw tomb of Bishop Patrick.

" 24*th.*—Returned this morning to Cambridge.   Talked
with Mr. Stevenson, sen., about my residing in college,
the studies required, also about attending Mr. Whewell's
lectures.   Called on Mr. Power, Trinity Hall, but not
at home, so left my card.

" 25*th.*—Left Cambridge for London.   Called on
Southgate respecting sale of ' Colloquies.'   He said three
hundred and forty-four sold.

" 27*th.*—Went this evening to House of Lords.
Saw Duke of Wellington at the entrance, who seemed
very decrepit, and spoke very falteringly in the
House.   Heard the Bishop of Exeter, Lords Win-
chelsea, Lansdowne, Wyndford, Abinger, Ashburton,
Westminster, Salisbury, and Ellenborough, and Bishop
of Gloucester.   The great debate was on Malta, opened
by Lord Ripon, style very fluent and good delivery.
Lord Glenelg spoke next ; he speaks very well.
The Chancellor followed, a gentlemanly man.   Lord
Brougham was in one of his happiest moods, and
kept every one laughing ; the newspapers did not at
all do justice to his speech.   Lord Normanby followed,
and him I left speaking.   Had a good view of Lord

5

Melbourne, Lord Holland, and Lord Lyndhurst in the House.

"*July* 1st.—Critique on 'Colloquies' written by Hanson appeared in *Standard* to-day. C. Marriott called on me in the evening. Went with him to Rotherhithe, to Mr. Hutchenson's, and met Mr. F. D. Maurice there.

"4*th*.—Hanson dined with me at Bertolini's, and took wine with me. Showed him plan of my work on 'Theory of Arts.' He said it would make a very fine work, and one which would live. Showed him plan also of 'Treatise on Man.' Went with Hanson to House of Commons. Debate poor. Heard Shaw, Jackson, Pigott, Peel, and O'Connell in committee on Irish Corporation Bill. Hanson asked me if I desired to get into Parliament; thought it would be worth more to me than £100 per annum.

"7*th*.—Went to Westminster Abbey in morning. Mr. Milman preached. Style eloquent, with great flow of language and fine, moving sentences, but not much power or depth of matter. Called on Mr. Halcomb in afternoon; walked with him to inquire after Dr. Sleath, and in park. Dined at Mr. Halcomb's with Mr. Fox (afterwards Sir W. Fox), and went to Queen Square Church in the evening.

"8*th*.—Went in the morning to breakfast with Hanson and Lilly at Martindale's, and with them to see Hanson off by the *Wellington* for New York. Met Shaw also there. Went on board vessel, which was most beautifully fitted up. Poor Hanson in high spirits. We saw the vessel towed out of the docks and down the river by a steamer."

Engaged pretty frequently at British Museum in philosophical studies and researches since the commencement of the year, skimming works and reading analysis of the systems of Lord Bacon, Malebranche,

Hobbes, Des Cartes, Locke, and Aristotle, also of Freeman's " History of Philosophy " and Paley's " Natural Theology," for "Outlines of Mental Philosophy," which, however, was never published, but it served for, and is indeed embodied in, notes to "Treatise on Man," for which it also supplied suggestions. Of " Locke on the Understanding" I made a complete and elaborate analysis.

" *August* 4*th.*—Went this morning with some Rugby people to Mr. Baptist Noel's chapel, St. John's, Bedford Row. His manner good and taking ; his fluency great. Finely eloquent passages ran through his sermon, but not much matter or thought, and but little really to be learnt from them. His notions wild and latitudinarian, but a very sincere and honest man, I believe.

" *7th.*—Went this morning to Hull by the *Victoria* steamer. Notice of the ' Colloquies ' in *Hull Times* of to-day, with extract from letter to Lord J. Russell and Queen's speech.

" *19th.*—At Hornsea, with John and his family. Commenced this morning the composition of my work on ' The Theory and Principles of the Ideal and Imitative Arts,' as I then entitled it.

" *21st.*—Called this morning on Mr. Quin (the editor of the *Hull Times*).

" *September* 4*th.*—Wrote article on change of Ministry for *Hull Times.* John said Mr. King had inquired, ' Could they not persuade the author of " Cabinet Colloquies" to take the editorship of the *Hull Times* in Mr. Quin's place ? ' to which Mr. Quin said, ' A very good idea ! '

" *5th.*—Mr. King asked me if I could contrive to make arrangements to take the editorship of the paper, and that it would be very desirable, which I said I would arrange to do if it was wished, and of matters could be so effected. Mr. King and Mr. Scott both pressed me to take it, and consulted with John. I agreed to return £100 out of the £300 salary if appointed until the paper paid."

CHAPTER VIII.

A NEWSPAPER EDITOR.

1839—1840.

"September 11*th.*

" THIS morning I was duly elected editor of the *Hull Times* in the place of Mr. Quin, at a salary of £208 per annum, to be increased should profit of paper amount to £2 per week for six months. My appointment to commence on 1st October.

" 17*th.*—Went to London by train.

" 23*rd.*—Returned to Rugby, and so on to Hull.

" 24*th.*—Went to Hornsea with John and his family, to stay there.

" *October* 4*th.*—My first number of the *Hull and East Riding Times* appeared to-day. People seemed pleased with it. A sketch of Macaulay's life and intellectual character, and an article on his appointment to the Ministry, the principal matters.

" 18*th.*— Review in this day's *Hull Times* of the *British and Foreign Review* and of 'The Palace Martyr' and the leading article, respecting Lord Monteagle, are the best things in it. The latter was copied at length into the *Times* and *Standard*, and a letter respecting it appeared in the former, and another I received out of Scotland upon it.

" *November 9th.*—This day I concluded the rough draft of 'The Theory and Principles of the Ideal and Imitative Arts Examined and Illustrated,' which I had been at work upon at intervals as leisure permitted ever since I returned to Hull.

"*23rd.*—Went to Rugby to-day. Rode over to Cotesbatch in the afternoon. Mr. Marriott much pleased with the *Hull Times.* Frank also said Mr. M. was much pleased with it, and that he had observed ' it reminded him of what a distinguished man * once said of me when I was staying at Cotesbatch : that I was a boy of very great promise !'

" *December* 3rd.—In London.

"*4th.*—I was this day admitted a member of the Middle Temple. While in London had a conference with Mr. A. J. Heraud, the poet, and proprietor of the *Monthly Magazine*, about my joining him in it, but the proposal was not carried out. Returned to Hull on the 11th.

" *20th.*—Revising plan of great work ' Philosophical Treatise, etc., on Man.'

" *28th.*—Wrote to Mr. Stevenson, Cambridge, to inquire what residence required at Trinity Hall to keep a term, and what books studied there.

" *30th.*—Mr. John Scott told me that Mr. King said the last number of the *Hull Times* was the best that had appeared. It was enough to set a man thinking. Suppose he referred to my leading articles on the Whig Commissions and on Macaulay's Indian Code.

" *31st.*—This evening I delivered lecture at the Literary and Philosophical Institution on the different branches of the fine arts. About sixty present. A discussion after it, to which I replied.

* Archdeacon Sinclair.

1840.

"*January* 5*th*.—Went to hear Mr. B. R. Haydon's lecture on art in the evening. Greatly disappointed with it. He deprecated high intellectual culture in an artist, and to that attributed Fuseli's defects. Consider that Haydon has not sufficient genius to admire Fuseli. His lecture shockingly egotistical, and very low jokes introduced. Appeared dissatisfied with everybody and everything besides himself.

"24*th*.—Went up to London to-day by mail. Mr. Broadley, the M.P. for the East Riding, one of the inside passengers, a most agreeable, intelligent, and gentlemanly man. Talked a good deal, principally on politics. Wylie, of the Temple, whom I met at Lyons Inn Debating Society, another passenger.

"25*th*.—Dined in hall to-day, Martindale, Cameron, and Robinson forming the mess. Very agreeable, and not at all formidable. Went to Debating Society, Lyons Inn in the evening, where I met Wylie again.

"29*th*.—Dined in the Middle Temple hall to-day, completed this term, and returned to Hull by the mail.

"*February* 7*th*.—My article in *Hull Times* on a Beverley education meeting appears to 'tell,' and likely to create a sensation. John said it was 'a capital article.' Mr. Garton observed that I had indeed, as I said, 'grilled' Mr. S—— ; that the article was very good, 'piquant without being coarse.' Mr. King said it was 'a capital pill,' 'very well done indeed.' Goddard observed it was 'very strong, but not too strong.' Brookes said 'if I had a few numbers with such articles as in present one, it would establish the paper at once.' Mr. Scott said the same, and that all the clergy liked it, and it was capital; remarked that 'the best I had yet written, that a few such would very much raise me in good opinion in Hull;' and that Mr. King said 'there was more thought in this than in any article I had written.'

" 20th.—Dined at Mr. Scott's. Talking about paper, he said I had a peculiar capacity for political controversy, and for making much of a small matter, which 'Colloquies' showed ; and that Mr. King said that in two years the paper might be worth to me £500 per annum.

" 21st.—Mr. Scott said that Mr. Wanton, the rector of Sculcoats, Drypool, had been intending to give the *Hull Times* up, but said that there was such a fund of wit and humour in it that he laughed over it. Was amused with article about Thoroughgood, and read it over several times.

" *March 2nd.*—My article on 'London' in *Monthly Magazine.* Part of it copied into the *Sun ;* and the *Herald* said it was ' one which should be read by all.'

" 3rd.—Wrote an article for the *Hull Quarterly Magazine*, being an account of my visit to St. Bernard.

" 18th.—This evening I specially set apart for opening the 'Treatise on Man,' for which I have been at work good deal lately, devoting several mornings to it, and which I had sealed up in a packet on the 7th September, 1837, and laid by ever since.

" *April 7th.*—Received a letter from C. Marriott, who said he did not think it desirable to start a paper in opposition to the *Record.* The Rev. C. A. Thurlow, of Beverley, called on me in the afternoon, and said he came to thank me for what I had done respecting Warren and Sandys (the education meeting at Beverley), he told me that the articles were written 'judiciously and very cleverly,' and that they were much pleased with them at Beverley.

" 10th.—Drawing out sketches of political characters—Lord Melbourne, Duke of Wellington, etc.—for magazine. Intend to bring out some in *Hull Times* as specimens.

"11*th*.—Received a letter from Mr. Stevenson, in which he stated that he thought it would not be advisable to publish 'Outlines,' etc., in Cambridge, as the study was not sufficiently followed there, but only *moral* philosophy. He sent also letter of a Mr. Moore [afterwards the Rev. Daniel Moore, a highly distinguished preacher] on my analysis, which took the same view with regard to its publication as Mr. Stevenson did.

"24*th*.—The article in to-day's *Hull Times* on Haydon's letter to me respecting my critique on his lecture here the best I have written for some time. Hope it may attract some attention among the London press, and serve for a literary introduction for me.

"29*th*.—Went by the *Victoria* steamboat this afternoon to London.

"*May* 1*st*.—Dined in Middle Temple hall to-day. Spent the evening at Sergeant Halcomb's.

"6*th*.—My birthday. The new postage plan comes into operation to-day.—Dined in hall at Middle Temple, completing this term.

"7*th*.—Went to Rugby.

"11*th*.—Returned to London. Found letter from C. Marriott, who was not favourable to establishment of *Church of England Chronicle*, but said he would take it on trial."

I had much correspondence with different persons on the subject, but nothing resulted. The ultimate issue, I believe, was the establishment of the *Guardian*.

"12*th*.—Mr. Wells, secretary to the Archbishop of Canterbury, unfavourable to establishment of *Church of England Chronicle*. So he writes me word. Sent analysis of 'Outlines of Natural Philosophy' to Mr. Tarver, to be submitted to Mr. C. Knight.

" 16*th*.—Returned to Hull by the *Victoria* steamer.

" 18*th*.—The *Hull Times* has decidedly gained ground since I have had it, and articles, etc., noticed by London press, which was not the case before. Last stamp returns show it to be *now* for the first time equal with its rival, the *Hull Packet*.

" 22*nd*.—Occupied a good deal lately in revising ' Treatise on Man' and adding notes. It appears to me that the general design of the treatise may now be considered as complete as to all the different theories on the various branches. The outline of the design is all correct, and the shading in some parts, but it requires finish.

"*June* 1*st*.—Conclusion of article on ' London' in *Monthly Magazine*. It reads well. I hope it may help me in obtaining some literary appointment.

" 3*rd*.—Went to London by the *Victoria*.

" 5*th*.—Went in the evening to Brompton to see Mr. S. C. Hall, and very kindly received by him and Mrs. Hall. When I told him of my intention to resign the *Hull Times*, he said, ' Perhaps I can point out something worth your notice in London.' Talked to him about Haydon. He asked me if the articles on his letters were my own, and praised them very much, and said they displayed deep thought and a greater knowledge of the arts than he possessed. Showed me a proof sheet of a very complimentary letter he, as editor of *Art Union*, had addressed to me on the subject. My remarks copied into, and highly eulogised in, the next number of that periodical. He said he had given up the *Britannia*, and did not intend to return to it, and that they had been looking out for a suitable successor, but did not succeed, and no permanent arrangement made. He thought I should do.

" 12*th*.—Dined in hall. Went in the evening to the

Debating Society, Exeter Hall, where I spoke with more fluency and declamation than usual, and introduced some tolerable jokes.

" 17*th*.—Mr. Cope, the secretary to one of the committees for promoting metropolitan improvements, called on me this morning. Had a long interview with me, and pressed me to attend a public meeting to-morrow, and move a resolution on the subject, which I declined on the ground of going out of town. Thought the publication of my articles in the *Monthly* on 'Metropolitan Improvements' as a pamphlet would tend to excite an interest in the subject.

" 18*th*.—Went to Rugby.

" 23*rd*.—Returned to London. Got Robinson to write me an account of the particulars of the trial of Courvoisier for the *Hull Times*.

" 25*th*.—Left London this morning by the *Wilberforce* for Hull.

" *July* 17*th*.—Completed general revision of my 'Treatise on Man' prior to again 'laying it by.' Like it very much altogether, and hope that it may decidedly serve to establish my name as a philosopher. It wants a good deal more 'working at' before it is brought out.

" 21*st*.—Designed to-day a legal work which would be quite in my line of pursuit, and might serve to introduce me to practice that would just suit my studies : " On the Natural, Moral, and Legal Proofs of Idiocy and Insanity, both in Civil and Criminal Cases.' It should not be brought out until I am called to the bar. Lunacy cases, and defending prisoners especially on the grounds of insanity, I should like more particularly to be employed in, making, however, *politics* my grand object, and profession *secondary* to it.

" 24*th*.—Mr. Scott said the last number of *Hull Times*

very much lauded, and that it was the best I had put
out ; and that trial of O'Connell the best thing I had
written, superior to the ' Colloquies.' Said it was much
talked about and praised by Mr. Knight and Mr.
Wanton and the clergy at their meeting on Friday
The article on Oxford's trial he also said was very
good.

" *August* 10th.—My article for the *Hull Times* of
to-morrow on the railway accident I think original
and well reasoned. Would have told well as a legal
argument in defence of the Company. Perhaps it
partakes too much of that character for a newspaper
article.

" 16th.—Left by *Victoria* at four o'clock for London,
taking with me 'Treatise on Man,' 'Theory of Arts,'
and ' Outlines, etc.,' also all books of value.

"*September* 15th.—Wrote a very strong article for *Hull
Times* on the conduct of the Hull railway directors as
regards the neglect on that line and number of
accidents.

" 17th.—Letter from Lee, asking me to stay with him
at Birmingham Saturday and Sunday, but obliged to
decline.

" 18th.—Returned to Hull at half-past one by the
Midland Counties Railway.

" 19th.—A most prodigious ferment excited in Hull by
my article on the railway, which was warmly applauded
by the people in general, but the directors very angry
with it. Some of them called yesterday on G——
(one of the proprietors of the newspaper), who wrote
desiring the article to be withdrawn in the second
edition, which Mr. D—— (the sub-editor) did. The
article also cut out of the papers exchanged with other
papers, to prevent its being copied. People very angry
at this. In consequence, I declared I would resign, and

announced to Goddard, Dunn, and several others, my determination of doing so, also wrote a letter to the committee announcing such, 'in consequence of what I cannot but consider a very uncalled-for and unjust interference with the editorial department of the *Hull Times* by one of the proprietors.' Goddard said I should come out of it with great *éclat*. Gawtress (editor and proprietor of the *Watchman*, London paper) in Hull told me they had appealed to him on the subject, and that he said the article ought not to be withdrawn, and that the subeditor was guilty of a dereliction of duty if he did so. Observed that the article was a capital one, well worded, severe without being coarse. Goddard said everybody, except those connected with the railway, praised it. Another accident has occurred, also the result of sheer carelessness.

"21*st*.—Sent my letter of resignation to the committee. A letter in the London *Times* relative to the last accident stated, 'All chance of an "accommodation" with the Hull paper is now at an end.' The following remarks appeared in the *Times* of Monday, September 12th, in a leading article : 'We have been informed upon indisputable authority that in a town not very far distant from the *terminus* of a northern railway notorious for its mismanagement, some strictures upon accidents which had occurred on the line in question appeared a few weeks since in a weekly Conservative journal. No disinterested person doubted the seasonableness or the justice of these remarks ; but the railway directors, among whom were persons of wealth and influence on both sides of politics, were greatly exasperated. A body of them called on the leading proprietors of the newspaper, and prevailed on them (by what arguments we know not) not only to insist on the withdrawal of the offending article in a second edition, but absolutely to cut it out of all the copies sent in exchange to the weekly journals in town and country, lest by any means it should be extracted and get into general circulation.   We are ashamed, for the credit of the press, to say that this was actually done, in the absence and without the knowledge of the intelligent and independent editor, who of course threw up his connection with the paper on being informed of the censorship by submitting to which it had been disgraced.   This, it may be said, was a peculiar instance ; for the honour of our calling, we hope it was.'

"29*th.*—Dined at Mr. Dryden's with Frank.   Told him about the circumstances of my resignation of *Hull Times.*   He said the article was called for, and that it was the only spirited thing which had appeared for a long time, and that G—— was an overbearing fellow."

CHAPTER IX.

PREPARING FOR THE BAR.

1840—1842.

"*November 2nd.*

"TERM begins to-day, my fourth at Temple, first of my *legal career* since determining to adopt law as my main pursuit.   Commenced my law studies to-day by reading Stephen's ' Principles of Pleading,' a scientific and clear exposition of the subject.   Went to Westminster to see the courts opened.

" 3*rd.*—Reading Stephen's 'Pleading.'   He shows the science very clearly allied with that of reasoning, and quotes a passage from Quintilian, whose method of conducting an argument exactly similar in process with that of pleading.   It also very nearly accords with the 'strict process of reasoning' which I have described in the chapter on judgment in my 'Treatise on Man.'

" *7th.*—Reading ' Stephen on Pleading.' ' The capacity of detail (deprehension) is eminently fitted for this pursuit, and indeed its nature and purpose and action might be best illustrated (so far as regards the perception of the facts on which special pleading is supported) by describing it as peculiarly adapted for the exercise required in this study. Analysis assists here (as regards the reasoning process), but is not so essentially requisite as detail. Hence it is we find out why the same minds are so seldom fitted both for lawyers, for leaders, and for statesmen, the first being mainly characterised by detail, the two latter by extension (comprehension). By cultivation and exercise, these capacities become more exclusively adapted for their own particular pursuits, and less for those of an opposite nature.'

" *14th.*— Dined in hall. G. Cunningham took wine with me afterwards. Went to debate at Lyons Inn. Subject, the imprisonment of Napoleon. Wanted to speak, but could not persuade myself to do so. Meant to have argued against the justice of his exile, and to have told them that ' it was a wondrous spectacle, truly, to see Europe at large trembling and turning pale at the presence of one man ; but most pitiable was it to witness England, the greatest nation in Europe, summoning all her powers to crush one fallen and forsaken, unfortunate individual.' Determined to devote a large portion of time and attention to attaining skill as an orator, which is as necessary to my success in the law courts as professional knowledge. I am convinced that with practice if I could once thoroughly subdue the great diffidence which I always feel on such occasions, so as to retain, at all times, my presence of mind,

that I should succeed. My best plan will be to belong
to several Debating Societies, so that I may have an
opportunity when I am prepared of exercising myself
and of ensuring success by getting up the questions
beforehand.

" 16*th*.—Dined in hall, completing my fourth term
to-day. A great deal of discussion in hall, especially
as to whether a person's distinguishing himself at
a university can be regarded as an earnest of his
real abilities, which will raise him in the world.
To me it appears that it cannot, and for two reasons :
1. University honours are adapted not as a test
so much of actual *talent*, as of *diligence ;* and are
intended not as proofs of ability, but as stimulants to
exertion. The capacities of comprehension (apprehension), detail (deprehension), and analysis are those
which are chiefly exercised ; while those of a higher
nature, and the possession of which in an extensive
degree principally serve to confer great ability, are
scarcely called into action, or their existence ascertained.
2. It will sometimes happen that certain persons appear
in youth to possess great abilities, but who on attaining
mature age display no more than ordinary talent.
This is probably mainly owing to a premature
development of their faculties. The material intellectual
organs, it may be, reach maturity too soon, and begin
to decay and lose their energy at the period when the
mind arrives at its perfect state.

" 20*th*.—Dined in hall. Had coffee with Robinson.
Went afterwards to debate at Exeter Hall. Spoke, but
immediately after Creasy, afterwards a Colonial Chief
Justice, by whom my arguments were forestalled, which
upset me, and made me very nervous. Left several
sentences unfinished, did not say half I intended, and
made no point in my argument. Sat down persuaded

I never could succeed as a speaker. Talking with Robinson in the evening (who spoke capitally) about overcoming diffidence by practice in these Societies, he was convinced it might be effected, and had been done by many. He himself is an instance of the improvement which one is capable of effecting in this respect. Resolved to make another attempt to-morrow night, and recover my ground.

"21st.—Dined in hall. Introduced Mr. W. H. Adams [afterwards a member of the Midland Circuit and M.P. for Boston, eventually Chief Justice of Hong Kong]. Two bottles to-day, one given by the Bench in honour of the birth of the Princess Royal. Went to debate at Lyons Inn. Spoke on a business motion with fluency, and said all I intended. Spoke also in the debate, without hesitation, and felt much less nervous than last night.

"22nd.—Went this morning by the Great Western Railway to Eton. Attended Windsor Church in the morning with Mr. Tarver, with whom I dined, and who told me he had shown my prospectus of my 'Outlines of Mental Philosophy,' which I had lately composed, to Mr. Knight, who thought the work could not be complete without comprehending in it Kant's system of philosophy as well as that of the present day. Mr. Tarver proposed to me to meet Mr. Knight, and said we would go some Sunday and dine with him at Highgate, when I could talk the matter over.

"23rd.—Wrote to Robinson, 'If it will not be giving you too much trouble, I should be obliged to you if you would call on Mr. Dow (a great special pleader in the Temple) and inform him of my wish to become his pupil for half a year after Christmas.'

"25th.—Received a letter from Robinson stating, ' I have seen Dow, who will be happy to receive you. He has not so many pupils as usual, which will be rather an advantage to you.' A note also from Lee, in answer to one I wrote to him on Wednesday, proposing to pay him a visit on Monday.

" 28*th*.—Went to Birmingham by the 2.30 train.

" 29*th*.—Walked about Birmingham, and visited book-shops. Sat with Mr. Lee, and had several discussions about Napoleon and the balance of power, income tax, etc.

"31*st*.—This is the last day of the old year, an eventful one to me, but, I believe, not altogether an unfortunate nor unprofitable one. During the past year I have completed four terms at the Temple, effected the revision of my work the 'Treatise on Man,' and read several useful works. The final settlement of my plans as to my future career and pursuits is, however, the most important point ; the completion of grand works designed, not, however, to be forgotten or disregarded, but to occupy leisure only, and to be perfected by occasional revision.

1841.

" *January 2nd.*—If a grand parliamentary debate resembles an action between two armies, a law trial may be aptly typified by a contest at a tournament, where only a limited number on each side engage, and where the strictest rules are enforced as to the manner in which the contest is conducted, and where the interest of the spectators is intensely excited as to the skill with which the encounter is maintained. The dexterity and power of each combatant, both in attack and defence, and in gaining and maintaining his position, is alike observable in the martial and the intellectual encounter. In each case, too, offensive weapons are hurled to and fro, and the issue is contended for with the utmost zeal and animation.

" 7*th*.—Returned to London.

" *8th.*—Went to the debate at Exeter Hall, and spoke. Nervous, and had but few points to urge in the question, but contrived to speak without hesitation, and to say everything of importance I intended. I believe that getting up each question well beforehand, with a certain number of good points to urge, will be of more consequence to me, and do more to assist me in becoming an effective speaker, than anything else.

" *9th.*—Called with Robinson on Mr. Dow this morning, and fixed to go there on Monday.

" *11th.*—Term begins to-day. Went to Mr. Dow's chambers, was introduced by him to the pupil room, and commenced operations accordingly.

" *15th.*—At Mr. Dow's chambers, as usual, all day. Dined in hall. Had a discussion respecting Locke's opinions on innate ideas and conscience.

" *22nd.*—Went to Debating Society, Exeter Hall. Spoke third in the debate in favour of a coalition Ministry. Felt very nervous before rising, but prepared with several points to urge, and managed to make a tolerable speech, equal, I think, to any I have yet delivered. Said all of importance I intended, and a good deal besides. Felt convinced I should be able to do well in time. Replied to rather fully by the succeeding speaker, also in part by Creasy, whose was the best speech of the evening. The debate opened by Robinson, who spoke with great confidence and readiness, but rather too much flippancy.

" *23rd.*—Charles Marriott breakfasted with me. Went to chambers this morning. Walked afterwards with Charles down to see Parliament opened, but did not get a good view of the Queen. Dined in hall. Cameron and Charles spent the evening with me.

" *27th.*—Formed an idea to-day of writing an introductory work on the study of the law—' Principia

Prima Legum'—taking my lecture on jurisprudence as
the basis, enlarging it on several points, especially as
to the first principles of laws and as regards general
study. This would afford me full scope for bringing
out something creditable, and might serve to introduce
me—to treat the law as a grand science, and recommend its study on this ground ; also to unite with
this principles of mental philosophy and civilisational
jurisprudence. I really think I might produce something worth reading.

" 28*th*.—Went to debate at Lyons Inn. Spoke there,
being the only one, except the opener, who defended
the character of Charles I. Very nervous on rising,
and hesitated at first, but gained confidence afterwards, and spoke with tolerable fluency, and made
a good finish.

" *February* 14*th*. —Went to Whitehall Chapel in morning. Sir Robert Peel there. Sits in rather a prominent
part of the chapel. Attends without any ostentation,
without a servant, there and back on foot. Looks aged.
Not noticed by any one on coming out. An uneasy and
suspicious expression in his countenance, which is far
from agreeable.

"23*rd*.—Robinson took wine and went with me to the
debate at University College, where I spoke twice on
business motions with readiness and fluency, and also
on the regular question in debate, *i.e.* in support of
duelling. Contrived to speak with great fluency and
without any hesitation, and to say all I intended. This
I managed to do without any preparation beforehand,
not knowing the subject of debate before its commencement.

" 25*th*.—Went to Debating Society at Lyons Inn,
and spoke. Managed to lay hold of a few points which
had been urged by previous speakers, and acquitted

myself tolerably well. Not *at all* nervous, which was never the case before.

"*March 4th.*—Went to debate at Lyons Inn. Opened the question at some length. Said all I intended. Spoke also in reply.

"*6th.*—Everything goes on very satisfactorily at chambers. Hit it off very well with Mr. Dow. Find myself making progress in information and professional skill, and the time passes most agreeably.

"*7th.*—Went to St. Margaret's, Westminster, in the morning to hear Mr. Whewell. His appearance does not strike one with that idea of intellectual power I had expected. His face remarkably round and florid ; his whole contour of countenance very much like that of Sir James Mackintosh. His sermon plain, not much originality, but his points very forcibly put. He kept close to his subject, and amplified it very fully. Congregation not very large. Church full, but not overflowing.

"Commenced reading Old Testament to-day, intending to go regularly through it each Sunday.

"*16th.*—Went to debate at University College. All the speakers on one side, except the opener. Consented to take the unpopular side to keep up the debate, and managed to put down a few points while the speaker before me was on his legs, and to make a tolerable argument out of it, in defence of Queen Elizabeth's conduct respecting Mary, Queen of Scots.

"*21st.*—Went to Whitehall Chapel this morning. Sermon by Mr. Walker, evidently directed against Sir R. Peel's late discourse on science affecting religious principles. The sermon well argued, but very inconclusive, I thought. Sir R. Peel there, and seemed very attentive to it.

"*26th.*—Went to Rugby this afternoon.

" *April* 13*th*.—Returned to London. The chambers, 10, South Square, Gray's Inn, were ready for my reception, and I prepared to move my books and bookcase there to-morrow.

"*20th*.—Went to debate at University College. Found my name put down to reply to opener in favour of America being considered as rivalling European nations in civilisation. Noted down arguments of opener, to obtain points for debate. Managed to speak at some length, and with considerable fluency and point. The best speech, I think, I have yet made as regards the delivery of it. Would have done in court as respects this. I may therefore now hope (which I have more than once despaired of) to obtain sufficient confidence to acquit myself creditably as an advocate. If in debate I could once acquire a habit of speaking readily and fluently, I should soon find good points to urge. I felt very little nervous while speaking this evening, and contrived to *amplify* well several points, and managed to 'think on my legs.' Spoke quite as fluently as I could do when practising alone.

" The principles of metaphysics, and which regulate metaphysical reasoning, are too refined for ordinary use. So also of pure mathematics. The true line to be followed is that which runs between the two extremes of strict logical accuracy on the one side and the common usages of life on the other. To modify and render practical the one, and to correct and establish maxims for the other, should be the leading rules by which the principles of all laws should be construed. The greatest mathematicians are not unfrequently sceptical respecting everything which does not admit of absolute demonstration, and of which the common occurrences of life but seldom allow. Hence the most subtle reasoners and logicians are not always the first lawyers. There have been many better lawyers than Blackstone, Mackintosh, and Stephen, though perhaps but few more powerful reasoners.

"The acutest reasoners and advocates, moreover, often turn out but indifferent judges, the power of adducing arguments and of weighing arguments depending on very different faculties. A man of a very acute metaphysical mind is very likely not to make a good practical lawyer, because he will spin too finely for common perception and usage the thread of his argument. A man may also be oftentimes metaphysically right and morally wrong, or logically right and legally wrong; that is to say, his reasoning may, if strictly tested, be incontrovertible while, practically, his principles are unsustainable. Therefore, in cases of this nature, we should be careful, while testing the strict truth of the question by our capacity of analysis, to modify the severity of this test by the aid of that of sense. I think the real principle is this. First we should determine the abstract logical metaphysical truth and reason of the point in dispute. We should next modify this by the practical rules of life, so that the decision may work no injustice in the particular case. And lastly, we should correct our decision or modification here so as to render it consistent with the principles of the first-mentioned kind.

" *May* 17*th.*—Dr. Childe and Lilly dined with me in my chambers. Discussing art and metaphysics, Childe said he thought the principle of the being of the soul was best explained by that of gravitation, which was, like it, an immaterial but powerful agent annexed to matter.

" 23*rd.*—Went this morning to St. Stephen's, Coleman Street, to hear the Bishop of Winchester (Dr. E. R. Sumner). His appearance unpleasing; rather a

satirical expression. Though of evangelical sentiments, he has anything but a puritanical or fanatical
countenance. The sermon extemporary or from notes.
Matter very good, superior and striking, without being
first-rate for argument or originality.

"28*th*.—Attended debate at Exeter Hall. I opened
the question of no confidence in Ministers. Very
nervous and confused.

"*June* 8*th*.—Went in the evening to the debate at
University College. Felt very nervous, but got up,
and spoke for some time with readiness and fluency,
and urged some very good points. Managed to dilate
upon several topics.

"The subject was the expediency of a hereditary
aristocracy, in favour of which I argued.

"9*th*.—Went to the Political Institute in Holborn ;
a great many present : the chapel in which meeting
was held quite overflowing ; the debate animated.
Some of the speeches very good. Intended to have
addressed the meeting, and had got several points to
urge, but could not obtain a hearing. Repeated off
what I intended to have spoken when I reached
home. A preparation for delivering a speech is doubtless highly advantageous in arranging thoughts and
arguments, and collecting points of debate. Did not
feel at all nervous or hesitating at the prospect of
rising.

"10*th*.—Went to debate at United Law Society.
Spoke on legal questions. Nervous, but contrived to
say all I intended, and to speak without hesitation.
Spoke on the subsequent debate with energy and
effect, and urged some good points. Did not feel
nervous.

"13*th*.—Went to St. Clement Danes in morning to
hear a sermon by the Bishop of Norwich (Dr. E.

Stanley). Sermon good. Nothing very striking, profound, eloquent, or original.

"17*th.*—Opened the question at the United Law
Society—a legal one. Said all I intended, and did not
feel nervous, though rather confused at first commencing, but got righted on proceeding. Replied at
the conclusion ; did not feel the least nervous or dis-
concerted. Feel as though I could open a case in court,
and speak upon it, though probably I should feel nervous at first, but believe I should be able to go on, and
should soon overcome the feeling and acquire perfect
confidence after a very few cases.

"*July* 4*th.*—Went to hear Rev. Robert Montgomery,
author of 'The Omnipresence of the Deity,' preach a
sermon for Charing Cross Hospital at St. Paul's, Covent
Garden. He is rather a small man, I should suppose
about forty years old. Face plain and inexpressive ; very
dark. Manner affected ; voice melodious, but rather
too much like that of a Dissenting preacher. He read
a portion of the Communion Service ; very affected, and
placed very strong emphasis on words not at all requiring
it, as *maidservant* in the Fourth Commandment, and
occasionally on quite insignificant words. Disappointed
with his sermon. He preached quite extemporarily. His
eloquence forced, his arguments feeble, and his matter
commonplace. Here and there were some fine and
touching sentences ; but his eloquence seemed rather
to accompany them than to pervade his discourse,
imaginative expressions being here and there introduced, while the reasoning matter was quite ordinary.
Expressions such as 'the soul smiling back on the
body it is about to quit,' 'flitting spirits," 'damned
spirits in the darkest pit of hell,' 'leaves fluttering in
the breeze or glistening in the sun,' 'Shriek away, my
soul,' constantly introduced. Sentences short and dis-

connected. He dwelt constantly on the topic of the omniscience of the Deity, a subject with which his mind must be well imbued. Many of his remarks very commonplace, which, however, his manner enabled him to carry off. An instance certainly of the advantage of self-confidence to an orator, as he never seemed at a loss or confounded. One of Mr. Montgomery's statements respecting St. Paul's assertions about charity was that it was 'the most glorious expression that ever proceeded from the *mouth* of the Holy *Ghost.*' At the conclusion of the sermon he covered his face with his white pocket handkerchief, and remained so for ten minutes, until nearly all the congregation had dispersed.

"*August* 12*th*.— The best way of showing the advance and present state of science in each department of knowledge would be by a map divided into portions corresponding with those different branches and marked so as to show the point of discovery attained in each. Thus logic and law, which are fully cultivated, and admit of being thoroughly explored and known, would resemble Europe, every portion of which is well explored and investigated, while, on the other hand, metaphysics and chemistry, of which but little certain has been discovered, would represent those but partially examined regions, such as the interior of Africa and parts of America, of which our knowledge is very imperfect. Each science would be divided into districts, as territories are, and names given to each portion or branch, as to towns in countries ; and, as these are numerous, in both instances so is the degree of knowledge attained.

"14*th*.—Came down by the five o'clock train to Rugby.

" 30*th*.—Went by the afternoon train to Birmingham, to stay with Mr. Lee.

" 31*st*.—Reading Lord Brougham's speeches. The argument in some of these defending in libel cases

undertaking, or I declare I would do my utmost to attempt it. Could you not take it in hand ? Anything I could do in the way of throwing in hints I would ; besides, the work is of that nature that it would best be written at different intervals, as ideas sprang up. I should dearly like to be associated with you in such a work, with the Atlantic rolling between us. Am I not romantic ? Besides, the wild scenery of America would wonderfully aid your descriptive and imaginative powers for such a purpose. The work might appear as an Indian tradition, or as the researches and wanderings of a spirit through the universe. I have lately been revising the work of which I showed you the plan, but do not intend to bring it out for years. I have others in embryo, if I can find time and opportunity.'

" 16*th*.—In morning engaged in arranging completion of my proposed work, ' On the Natural, Moral, and Legal Proofs of Idiocy and Insanity,' etc., which I first contemplated last year, and which will admirably suit for study with ' Treatise on Man.'

" 21*st*.—A letter from Trinity Hall, saying they were ' very much surprised ' at not hearing from me respecting my residence there, and sending my account, amounting to £22 15s.

" 25*th*.—Wrote to Mr. Marsh at Trinity Hall, saying I had not quite determined yet what to do, but would write again when I had seen a friend (Phillipps), whom I expected in town very shortly.

" 31*st*.—In afternoon walked to the Tower, to see the fire there, which was still raging. No flames visible, but volumes of thick smoke rising up from the ruins. The amount of building destroyed appears prodigious, and to extend a vast way. Crowds of people about on Tower Hill, and every part which commanded a view

of the Tower. A great many carriages, several of
noblemen among them ; quantities of cabs. The scene
resembled a great fair, people shouting and moving
about, and numbers of eatables on sale. The crowd
seemed to be increasing when I left, about four,
although the rain was coming down pretty sharply.

" *November* 13*th*.—This evening Kelly and O'Dwyer
had cocoa with me, and went with me to Coger's Hall.
Tried several times to get an opportunity of speaking
early in the debate. At last got a hearing. The toast
proposed was the healths of the Duchess of Kent and
the Duke of Sussex, that of the King of Hanover
being studiously excluded. The preceding speakers had
grossly attacked the King of Hanover, and lauded the
Duke of Sussex, and denounced hereditary succession.
Addressed the meeting at some length, and with energy
and fluency. I spoke on the opposite side, and it being
very near twelve o'clock, concluded with thanking the
meeting for the kindness and attention with which they
had heard me, and sat down much applauded, though
the majority was decidedly against me. I spoke for
about a quarter of an hour. Warmly congratulated by
my two friends, one of whom heartily shook me by the
hand. Both told me I had spoken capitally, that there
was a great deal of point and argument in what I said.
I spoke with great readiness, and without hesitation.
This by far the best speech I ever made. Feel convinced now that I shall succeed as an orator. I spoke
without any notes.

" 28*th*.—Went in the afternoon to St. Paul's, where
Sydney Smith preached. His manner and appearance
anything but reverential or dignified. He is a stout
man, with ruddy complexion and humorous expression. He sat down during the anthem, but nodded
very composedly to the notes. His voice, manner, and

gesture, and everything about him, fully characteristic of his dry, cool humour. The subject of his sermon was the government of the heart, which he treated as the seat of the animal feelings and affections. Some of his remarks very striking ; his language very eloquent,—eloquence of a deep and profound nature, of the highest order,—very different from that of the Montgomerys, Macneils, and Stowells.

1842.

"*January* 13*th.*—Wrote to Mr. Marsh, Trinity Hall, and told him I had finally determined to take my name off the books of the University.

" 14*th.*—Went down to Rugby by the five o'clock train.

" 16*th.*—At church morning and afternoon. Mr. Moultrie preached in afternoon a very powerful sermon on the New Year. He observed that no ideas which had once entered into the memory were ever entirely effaced from it, and that probably at the day of judgment each person's memory would be to him a counterpart of that possessed by his Maker, so that he would at once remember all the sins of which he had been guilty, and thus stand self-convicted. This doctrine appears to me to have been adopted, if not actually copied, from S. T. Coleridge.

" 18*th.*—Returned to London this morning. Dined in hall with W—— M——, who told them at dinner that I followed very exalted studies (alluding, I suppose, to my 'Outlines of Philosophy'), and that I should either be a first-rate, or make a dead failure of it. He afterwards spent the evening with me at my chambers. Said I was of a very active mind, and that I should be 'aut Cæsar, aut nullus.' Showed him my article on the arts in the *British and Foreign* and articles in the

Monthly. He praised the style of them, and said it was forcible and pointed, and that I ought to write history.

" 19*th.*—A letter to-day from Mr. Holme, asking me when I should be called, and whether I intended going to the Salford Sessions. Feel doubtful which sessions it will be most desirable for me to attend, whether the Hull and East Riding, or the Salford and some other. On the whole, however, I feel inclined to join the Salford Sessions, and, at any rate, may as well go down there some time and see how matters look, paying my *patron* a visit on the occasion.

" 21*st.*—Dined in hall with Hawkins (afterwards a judge of the Court of Queen's Bench) and Nicholson.

" 22*nd.*—Dined in hall with W. H. Adams.

" 30*th.*—Took a long walk in the afternoon through the City by Cripplegate, looking at St. Giles' Church, where Milton was buried, and through Bunhill Row, where the famous John Bunyan lies. A rather tumultuous funeral party, teetotalers, were going to inter a poor woman, a member of their Society, who had destroyed herself—not a very encouraging end for the members in general to look forward to or a very flattering specimen of their party.

" *February* 1*st.*—Cranmer's is, I think, the most *uniformly* base and contemptible character which stains the page of history—a hypocrite in religion, a bigot without even sincerity, a persecutor without honesty of purpose, the highest dignitary in the Church, and the most degraded minister of the vices and caprices of others. His Popery was unredeemed by any of the sacrifices or self-denials which atone to some extent for its deformities ; his Protestantism was defaced by all the cruelties and intolerance of Popery ; and his martyrdom, which might have atoned in some measure for his life, served only by his apostacy to consummate the baseness of his character, and to raise a monument of eternal infamy to his memory.

"*24th.*—Went to the debate at the United Law; the subject for discussion, the perpetuation of copyright. Spoke on the negative side. Spoke for about five minutes, from notes of speeches on the opposite side; felt rather nervous, but urged several very good points, and managed to amplify pretty fully. Went to Coger's Hall. Spoke for about ten minutes with fluency and point, equally well, I think, to my first speech there. The subject for debate, Sir Robert Peel's new scheme of taxation, which I supported. About one hundred present.

"*March 2nd.*—Went in the evening to the University Debating Society. The subject for discussion, the right of the State to require oaths in courts of justice from persons not specially exempted from swearing. Spoke first on the negative side—in favour of the right. I contended that the question resolved itself into the two points of protection to the State and private liberty of conscience to individuals; that an oath was the only binding process to get at the truth; that no ample substitute could be found for it; that abolishing it would lead to endless frauds; that many who would not solemnly call their Maker to witness would dare to tell a lie to serve important purposes; that a distinction existed between persons whose ruling principles forbade them to swear, and whom our laws exempted, and mere common persons who were swayed by ignorance or mistaken feeling; that conscience was liable to err, and often led men wrong, as instanced by Locke; that allowing every one to act just as his conscience impelled him struck at the root of society, some objecting to contribute to maintain laws, and some objecting even to prosecution altogether; that the laws did not now, as formerly, require an oath on every trivial occasion, as observed by Paley ; and that when men entered into society, they each gave up a portion of their liberty, of which liberty of conscience was doubtless the deares and most valuable.   Rather more nervous than usual before rising, and did not speak with very great fluency, but this owing to the abstruse nature of the subject. Felt composed while speaking, urged every point I intended, and amplified fully.

"23rd.—At this period I think it desirable I should record exactly my own views as regards my capacity as an advocate and my general success as an orator.   I believe, indeed, that I am, on the whole, more capacitated as an advocate than a lawyer, that I can deal better with facts than with points of law, and that I shall fail in arguments *in banco* where abstract questions of law are involved, though occasionally I may assist in proceedings of this description.   I expect to succeed best in cases of libel, seduction, breach of promise, and Crown cases, lunacy, treason, assault, parliamentary practice, and political and criminal proceedings.   My main point, therefore, must be to attain eminence as an advocate in these departments. to commence my efforts progressively by practising at sessions and on circuit.   I think I may determine to adopt the Midland as my circuit, and to attend the Warwick and Birmingham Sessions.   I have every reason to hope and feel confident that with practice I shall acquire confidence and composure and readiness and fluency in speaking.   On the whole, I trust fully that, both as regards my own powers of mind, and the professional and general cultivation of them, I may fairly anticipate success in my career.

"To what extent it is of course impossible to determine, but I would specify some second-rate judicial office, such as the Chief Barony, Mastership of the Rolls, or Chancellorship of Ireland, and which, I believe, my abilities may enable me to attain. My name I also hope to establish by the works which I have in progress.

"31*st.*—In a notice in to-day's *Times* of Lord Campbell's speeches, it is observed, 'Cicero trembled, grew pale, and faltered at the commencement of his most splendid harangues; Erskine was obliged to soothe his irritable nerves by an opiate; but John Campbell's Northern nerves, unlike Macbeth's, were never shaken;' so far consolatory to me as regards my own diffidence, which the former great orators also possessed, and also overcame. The above writer observes that the finer sensations of the soul, keen sensibility and feelings, and vivid imagination, are essential to an orator, though acting as described in Cicero and Erskine.

"*April* 10*th.*—"Went in morning to Christ Church, Newgate Street, to hear a sermon by the Bishop of Chester (Dr. J. B. Sumner, afterwards Archbishop of Canterbury). The Bishop has an unpleasant countenance, expressive, as I think, of deficiency in greatness of mind. I consider his manner bad and wandering. There was very little in his sermon in any way, either as regards matter, point, originality, eloquence, or power; and, on the whole, I thought it very commonplace.

"17*th.*—Went in the evening to St. Sepulchre's Church. Mr. Dale preached. A very crowded congregation. The secret of Mr. Dale's great popularity as a preacher appears to me to be that he contrives to make himself remarkably clear, and to put common things in the most forcible light. What he says is not only intelligible to each, but to each is *striking*. He is never deep, or profound, or sublime, but always forcible, and illustrates what he says by the commonest allusions. His eloquence is seldom of a very high order; his manner is affected and pompous. He scarcely deals at all in argument. By baptism, he contended very energetically, we were only admitted into the visible, and not into the spiritual, Church of Christ.

" 21st.—I went down to Westminster to hear an appeal case before House of Lords. Wilde spoke as counsel in it. Very powerful, but too diffuse, I thought, and left some strong points untouched, it struck me. It was observed the other day in Hall that Follett is often very concise in his speeches, and that Romilly seldom exceeded a quarter of an hour. Dr. Franklin used to say that twenty minutes was sufficient for any speech, which quite accords with my theory in matters oratorical.

" 25th.—Went this morning to a public meeting at the Freemasons' Tavern respecting a memorial to Dr. Birkbeck, Lord Brougham in the chair. Lord Brougham spoke with great eloquence and effect; manner rather slow; language graceful and correct; accent strongly Scotch. Lord J. Russell also spoke; matter and manner both commonplace, I thought. Hume I liked better. Brougham's remarks in reply to a speaker who differed from the resolutions proposed very sarcastic and ironical, and provoked some laughter.

" 27th.—In speaking at Societies like the United Law and Forensic, while there is sufficient to intimidate you equally with a court of justice as regards the observation and criticism of those about you, and while there is the want of excitement and stimulus to sustain you and to lead to great exertions, you feel as though you could not make any grand effort. Attempting to make a grand oration at one of these Societies is something like trying to swim in a mist, where, though you have all the obscurity of water to overwhelm you, you have none of its bulk and weight to sustain you.

"*May 2nd.*—Went down to Westminster. Sat a short time in the court. Heard Sir F. Pollock, Attorney-General, move for a criminal information against editor of *United Service Gazette* for a libel. His manner is hesitating, and irregular, and not very clear in the mode of expression or enunciation, but he generally manages to bring out the most forcible points in the case, I believe. Sir W. Follett, who next rose, a great contrast to him in the former respect. His voice very melodious, his manner regular, accent particularly clear, language fluent ; and he always speaks forcibly and clearly. Went afterwards into the Election Committee Rooms, the Southampton and Penryhn ; remained during the day in the latter. The cross-examination of the witnesses by Mr. Austin and Mr. Cockburn very fine indeed ; paid particular attention to this ; the mode in which information is elicited from witnesses by circuitous questions which had been denied when the question was put directly, and the sifting all the parts of the story to test its consistency, deserve the closest observation. A knowledge of human nature of the utmost importance here, especially as regards the mode of operation and power of memory, the feelings, and the intellectual faculties, etc. In this respect my study for 'Treatise on Man,' which, though the work is a theoretical one, has been of a practical nature, will prove very valuable to me. Parliamentary practice is one of the departments I have marked out for myself, and should hope to succeed in, so far as regards the examination and cross-examination of witnesses ; a valuable preparatory exercise.

"Dined in hall at the bar table. Discussion about Dr. Johnson. I contended that he had left no really great work behind him, that his dictionary was one of mere labour, that ' Rasselas' was his grandest production, that his law arguments were the best things in Boswell, and that he owed his celebrity in a great measure to his eccentricities.

"4*th*.—At Westminster. Attended Election Committee Rooms. Watched the examination of an adverse witness. Counsel tried hard, but could not extract any favourable testimony from him, though he put several circuitous questions to him.

" Dined in hall with Dowling,* Archibald,† and Murphy.

"6*th*.—My birthday. 1 am to-day thirty-three years old, and have not yet established myself in a profession, and have to commence my progress in the world, though, on the other hand, I have done more than many have effected at my age in the two works which I have framed, and in the foundation which I have laid as regards my professional career, both as respects legal and general attainments.

" Many of the brightest and most sultry days are ushered in by a mist. During my past year, I have done much as regards the completion of ' Treatise on Man,' the works I have read, my progress in rhetorical effects, the completion of my professional studies, and the settlement of my plans, which are now, I hope, mature and straightforward.

" How often men who have gained very high honours at the university, and passed off for persons of first-rate talents, do nothing afterwards, and seem to sink to the level of ordinary men. This can only be accounted for by considering them to be endowed merely

---

* Afterwards a colonial judge.
† Subsequently a judge of the Queen's Bench.

with the talents for acquiring knowledge, so as to obtain the possession, but not the power to use it. Success in academic honours frequently depends on acquirements without capacity for exercising it. Thus the large possession of comprehension and detail (apprehension and deprehension) most conduce to the former, and go to make a great university scholar or tutor, while without judgment and genius he could do little as a reasoner or orator.

" 13*th*.—Very much shocked indeed by the arrival of a letter this afternoon informing me of the sudden death of Dr. Arnold yesterday morning, at seven o'clock. A sudden announcement of this nature takes entire possession of the mind, and seems to transfix it to one subject for a time, and quite to obstruct the current of ideas. I was obliged to put aside everything I was engaged in after the letter arrived, and could not draw my mind off the subject the remainder of the evening. I do not know any man for whom I have so high and so unfeigned a respect, or whom I believe so thoroughly honest, honourable, and in every respect disinterested. He has, in fact, been a martyr to his disinterestedness and nobleness of soul. He might, had he chosen to be the slave of his party, have ere this obtained the highest preferment, and would probably for many years have lived in luxury and ease. Because he would not be subservient to party interests, he has fallen a slave to the labours he incurred in the conscientious discharge of his duties, and a sacrifice to his efforts to benefit mankind. He was one of the three greatest men of the Liberal party of modern times. Great men in the highest and truest sense, Brougham, Mackintosh, and Arnold, form the glorious trio, who have at once (by belonging to them) ennobled and rendered (by the treatment they have received) ignoble their party. Arnold's works are, unfortunately for us survivors, left unfinished. Possibly, as regards himself, enough remains to establish his fame as an original and eloquent writer, to carry out his peculiar views. After all, perhaps, his ephemeral productions— his pamphlet on the Catholic question, his sermons (and the introduction to the last volume), and his lectures on history—will do most to establish his fame. Only on Thursday I called on Mr. Ward. Had I found him at home, I should probably have dined with him on Sunday and been at his house when the sad news arrived. The following is the letter I received from home :—

"*Sunday evening.*

"'My DEAR GEORGE,—We have been very much shocked and grieved to-day by the sudden death of Dr. Arnold, which took place at seven o'clock this morning, after an illness of only two hours. He was quite well yesterday, and slept till five o'clock this morning, when he was seized with spasms at his heart. He was quite sensible that his end was near, and in a most delightful state of mind, repeating portions of the Psalms, etc., and quite longing to be gone. We all observed how very ill he looked at the speeches on Friday, but little thought we should never see him again in this world. It is, indeed, a most sudden blow to poor Mrs. A. and his family. Jane and Matthew are at Foxhow, but will soon be here. I write in great haste.

"'Your very affectionate mother,

"'C. HARRIS.

"'G. HARRIS, Esq.'

"17*th*.—This morning, at eleven, I attended Dr.

Arnold's funeral, together with my father, Tom, and William. We all go into mourning for him. A great many people there. The Bishop of Norwich, Mr. Justice Coleridge, Dr. Hawkins, Provost of Oriel, Sir Gray Skipwith, and a great many old Rugbeians followed. Moultrie performed the service with a great deal of feeling, and several times much affected. Mrs. Arnold and the family also there. In the afternoon I met Matthew Arnold, and shook hands with him. I also met Mr. Ward, who, with Mr. Justice Coleridge, was going down to the station.

"19th.—At Rugby. Attended the parish church in morning. Moultrie preached, and alluded touchingly to Dr. Arnold's death. In the afternoon Grenfell preached one of Dr. Arnold's sermons from 1 Corinthians xv. A fine simile in it, comparing the soul to a foreign plant which in our clime cannot attain perfection, but which from its nature is evidently fitted to do so in another and more genial region.

"27th.—A paper was found on Dr. Arnold's table, which was written the evening before he died, containing reflections on his birthday, which would have been on the Monday, and expressing regret that he had not done more good, and saying that now he had more mortified all ambitious desires.

"*July 7th.*—Left Rugby this morning in carriage for Birmingham, on our way to Kynnersley. We dined and stayed all night at Mr. Lee's. Lee seems to have made up his mind not to stand for Rugby in Dr. Arnold's place.

"28th.—The meeting to-day of the trustees of the school, when Mr. Tait, of Balliol [afterwards Archbishop of Canterbury], was elected Head Master in Dr. Arnold's place. I cannot understand why he was preferred before so many abler and more distinguished

competitors, unless it was because he seemed most of all
to resemble Dr. A. both intellectually and morally,
and especially in his great general knowledge (though
far inferior to him), and therefore seemed the best
adapted to carry out his plans, but which I should
doubt if an inferior and less original mind could do.*

" *August* 4*th.*—Went in the evening to the House of
Lords. Saw the Duke of Wellington, who seems very
much aged and worn, but not infirm, ride down. Several
people following him and taking off their hats, which
he acknowledged in his cool manner. In the House
I heard Lord Monteagle, Lord Fitzgerald (a fluent,
pleasant, and very efficient speaker), Lord Campbell,
Lord Brougham, and Lord Radnor (a very awkward
and dull orator indeed). I also heard Lords Beaumont
and Wharncliffe.

" 21*st.*—At Oxford. Went to St. Mary's in the
afternoon. The congregation very small. The curate
read prayers. Very little singing and no chanting.
Looking about for Mr. Newman, I recognised him
(from the portraits of him) sitting very near me—on
the seat next behind me. Expression very reflective,
with a scornful character about the lip, which is not
pleasing ; habit very spare ; neck remarkably thin ;
countenance seems deeply thought-worn ; hair dark ;
he wears spectacles ; eyes nearly closed ; voice and
manner very gentle ; nose rather large and aquiline ;
height about the middle size. He preached a sermon
on the character of Josiah ; very simple, unaffected,
and plain, but striking. Liked him exceedingly. Very
much in Dr. Arnold's style, a great contrast to the
Stowells, and Macneils, and Montgomerys. He appeals
to the reason rather than to the heart, but also in some

---

* He turned out a failure as a schoolmaster, but a great
success both as a bishop and archbishop.

degree to the latter, to the finer and higher sensibilities at least. Dined with Tom in his own room at Magdalen College.

" 22nd.—Went to see the Martyrs' Memorial. Very elegant, and chaste, and beautiful, indeed. I told them that as they had put up a monument to Cranmer, I should expect next to see one to Judas Iscariot, a sentiment which was much applauded.

" 23rd.—This morning I spent in the library of Magdalen, which is a very excellent one. Referred to several works. Dined in the Fellows' committee room with Tom and John Bloxam and Henry.

" 24th.—Returned to London by railway.

" 25th.—Left at eight this morning by the 'Vivid' for Hull.

" *September* 18th.—At Rugby.

" 25th.—At St. Matthew's Church in evening. Mr. Alford, the incumbent,* preached. He spoke of the Gospels as containing a less perfect system than the Epistles, which were delivered when Christianity was more matured, which is surely a strange argument, as the precepts of the former were addressed mainly to the Apostles and disciples themselves, the latter to heathens and new converts.

" *October* 26th.—Called on Dr. Tait, Head Master of Rugby, respecting Catlin, at Mr. Lee's request, to whom he promised to grant the great school. Very young-looking, countenance pleasant and intelligent, but not very clever-looking ; manners stiff; says very little.

" *November* 13th.—In London. Wrote to Lee, saying what I had done about Catlin. Dined at Dr. Sleath's. Went to St. Paul's in afternoon. Sydney Smith preached a very able and effective sermon on ' Using the things of this world as not abusing them.'

* Afterwards Bishop of Victoria, Hong Kong.

He pointed out the different pursuits, occupations, and recreations which are good used moderately, but pernicious in excess.

"28th.—At opening of the Temple Church. The building exceedingly beautiful, especially the east windows and ceiling ; the chanting very good, and service finely performed ; the crowd very great, but all accommodated with seats. Mr. Benson preached. Sermon argumentative and powerful, exemplifying the doctrines of the Church contained in the Liturgy as a guide to Christian duty, and generally stating the grounds on which the present restoration and decoration of the Church was right and reasonable, but the sermon was considered as adverse to them on the whole.

"*December* 24th.—Staying at Mr. Lee's at Birmingham, with whom I had a good deal of chat about my professional prospects. Told him I intended to go to the Birmingham Sessions, and he said that he would exert all the influence he had for me. Talking about public speaking, Mr. Lee said he always spoke from notes, and that the great thing was to have plenty of facts on which to ground a speech. In cross-examination he said the only way to test the truth was to make the witness give a full account of a transaction, and thus try its consistency. Told him I should feel rather awkward at first appearing at Warwick, but he said I must not think anything of that."

CHAPTER X.

1843—1844.

1843.   "*January* 14*th*.

" THIS day, being called to the bar yesterday, beholds the consummation of the hopes of a most important period of my life, and turns into reality visions which I had long eagerly revelled in, scarcely daring even to indulge the hope of their actual realisation. I am called to the bar. Now more than ever do I believe myself calculated for that walk of life I have so long and so ardently desired to have open to me. As regards my intellectual capacity, my endowments, and my prospects of professional success, I believe I may fully confirm the opinions I adopted in the memorandum of 23rd March, 1842.

"I may here specify the completion so far of my grand work, the 'Treatise on Man,' which I again looked through to-day, and confirmed good opinions respecting it; afterwards sealed it up and laid it by.

"Having been yesterday duly called to the bar, I attended to-day in hall in full costume to be sworn in. Messrs. Moxon, Martindale, Robinson, Hanson, and four others, and Archibald, afterwards dined with me in hall.

"*February* 1*st*.—Attended all day at the Old Bailey. The trial of the Rev. Dr. Bailey for forgery. The prisoner was a distinguished and leading member of the Evangelical party in the Church, and some time ago got up a chapel at Tunbridge Wells to oppose the 'Puseyites.' A good-looking man; middle size; dark

and round face; age thirty-six, but looked fifty; head
bald; not much expression in countenance, but a bad
look about the eyes. The result proved that he had not
only forged a note for £2,875, but supported it by
perjury, and hired several others to do the same. He
seemed quite unmoved and unaffected throughout the
trial.

"Mr. Gladstone, the Vice-President of the Board of
Trade, was examined in court to-day. His countenance
certainly does not indicate his power of mind, and is
chiefly expressive of great amiability and unaffected-
ness. Nothing of his deep thought and vast capacity is
portrayed.

"28th.—This morning I made my *début* in court on
a prosecution case at the Old Bailey. The prisoner
was defended by Ballantine [afterwards Serjeant, and
a very eminent advocate], and the case specially fixed
to come on at the Central Criminal Court first this
morning. I had to address the court in stating the
case, and to examine one witness. Managed quite as
well as I could have anticipated. Said all I intended,
did not at all hesitate, and made myself quite clear.
Not very nervous, not so much so as I have been at
the Forensic. Successful too. I have at least no
longer to apprehend that my diffidence and nervousness
will be an insuperable obstacle.

"*March* 4th.—All to-day and yesterday at Mac-
Naughton's trial, at the Old Bailey, for the murder of
Mr. Drummond. Very interesting to me as connected
with the jurisprudence of insanity. The prisoner a
mild, amiable, young-looking man. His eyes seemed
glassy, and his countenance flushed and melancholy;
and every now and then he gave a slight start; but
there was nothing else to lead to the supposition that
he was different from other people. Follett made a most

lucid and argumentative opening. Seemed to have fortified every point which might be attacked on the defence. Cockburn,* for the prisoner, made a very eloquent, effective, and argumentative speech, not a grand effort, but parts very beautiful and touching, and as a whole, very telling. His manner and appearance much against him. The court densely crowded. The insanity of the prisoner clearly proved by the medical testimony. Made a sketch of the prisoner, which Sir W. Follett pronounced to be very much like him.

"21*st.*—Leicester. Here I find myself this evening in very comfortable lodgings, having just arrived for the purpose of joining the Midland Circuit. I have not any prospect of business, but I thought it better to commence here than at Coventry or Warwick, where I might be supposed to have an attorney connection. On Friday I conducted a case for Burbidge in the Secondaries' Court. Spoke without feeling at all nervous, and with fluency, and examined two witnesses.

"27*th.*—At Coventry. Felt nervous on going into court, and on being recognised by some attorneys I had known; but this soon wore off, and I was quite at home. Had two briefs: one from Bloxam, the other from W——. In the former case the prisoner pleaded guilty, so that I had nothing to do. The latter came on before Alderson. Did not feel nervous, and opened without hesitation; but felt difficulty in examining witnesses. Omitted some points, and put one or two questions irregularly, which was corrected by the judge, who consequently put a great many questions himself. Prisoner not defended, and was found guilty.

"At Warwick. Came from Coventry in a chaise with

---

* Afterwards Chief Justice of England.

Eardley Wilmot [afterwards Sir Eardley Wilmot, Bart., and M.P. for South Warwickshire] and Hayes [subsequently Mr. Justice Hayes, of the Queen's Bench].

"28*th.*—A letter from Henry, informing me he had been publishing a pamphlet entitled 'Trust and Reason,' the object of which, he says, 'is to show how we may make use both of Church authority and our own reason at the same time by following the proper dictates of our own nature.' The president, he says, applauded it, and said he thought it was a very fair position, and, as far as he could see, rightly conducted. Charles Marriott, Henry says, told him the same, though he seemed to think too much was given to reason. Read the book, and like it very much; style clear, closely reasoned, and philosophical. Some of the reflections are profound and fine. The observations at pages 33, 34, on the different conclusions which different persons may arrive at by the same process of reasoning, the mode in which they are influenced here, that 'to-day's casual thought may turn the balance of our decision in future years,' and how reason may sometimes lead us wrong all at once, are beautiful, philosophical, and profound. Something of Dr. Arnold's style and mode of thinking in many parts.

"*May* 13*th.*—Concluded reading Aristotle's 'Politics' (Gillie's translation), a most masterly, profound, philosophical, and able treatise on the first principles of government. Like it better than any other work of his that I have read; it contains more thought, and reflection, and practical observation, a great deal of the latter fully applicable to the present times. His views are very enlarged and comprehensive, and, at the same time, accurate and based on facts. Throughout, his reasonings and deductions are all drawn from nature, and yet his arguments are deep and philosophical. He has all Montesquieu's information as regards nature and the practices of other countries, with far more acuteness, and depth, and comprehensiveness, and power.

"31*st*.—Attending court each day at Nisi Prius sittings. Noting down the points on each side which I think may be urged, marking those which the counsel engaged in the cause take, and what points which I omitted they originate. This, I think, is very improving mental exercise for this branch of the profession.

"*June* 15*th*.—The last day of term. To-day I had two motions to make in the Bail Court—my first effort in Westminster Hall—to make rules absolute : the one was from Robinson, the other I held for Shaw. The first came on in the morning. Felt nervous before getting up, but not so when on my legs. The second came on quite late in the day ; did not feel nervous before bringing it on, and was quite composed and at home while speaking, and expressed all I intended.

"21*st*.—Attended both to-day and yesterday the trial of Gregory *v.* Duke of Brunswick and another for conspiracy in creating a row at Drury Lane Theatre, to drive plaintiff from the stage. Intense interest excited. Several noblemen on the bench : the Earls of Erroll and Belfast, Lords A. Fitzclarence, W. Lennox, Gardner, Beaumont, and the Duke of Brunswick. Shee, for the plaintiff, made a very good, powerful, but ineloquent speech. Great laughter excited by the examination of some of the witnesses, especially the Irishmen from St. Giles' who had assisted in the row, but the leader of whom persisted he did it out of pure patriotism. Talfourd made an excellent speech for the defendants, passages of fine eloquence in it, and great tact displayed. I noted down the points which I thought might be urged for the defendants.

" Having to defend in such a case as this would suit me as well as, or better than, any parliamentary opportunity that could be afforded, as here I should be the sole performer on the stage, and have the entire design and conduct of the case.

" *26th.*—Attended Warwick Borough Sessions. Only three prisoners for trial, and, with myself, only three barristers. The chief difficulty I feel is in making a good start, in doing common and ordinary cases decently, so as not to excite ridicule by putting irregular questions or omitting proper ones. I find some of high ability, who are capable of great things, fail here, though largely endowed with genius and judgment for originating good points and speaking eloquently, and who, forcibly endowed with extension to take an enlarged view of the subject, yet fail in minute points and commonplace essentials from deficiency in detail (deprehension) and comprehension. This I feel to be my own case, and this accounts, I believe, for many not getting on at the bar at first, until some grand opportunity offers and allows them to display their power and ability.

" *27th.*—At county sessions. Had two briefs. There appears to be but very little opportunity afforded here for exhibiting power and capacity in any way, though in some defence cases I may.

" *July* 19th.—At Coventry Sessions. Had three briefs from H—— and S——. One of the cases to be defended by Hayes, but the grand jury threw out the bill. In another case prisoner pleaded guilty. Conducted the third case, and had several witnesses to examine. Held also a brief for A——, and had a brief from T—— and L——, of Coventry, making four here, so that I had plenty of exercise in examining witnesses, and got through it well and satisfactorily, and without any

difficulty. About five o'clock M—— asked me to hold
a brief for him.   Found unexpectedly that the case was
a very long, intricate, and difficult one.   The prisoner
defended by A——.   Had not any time to read my brief
before the case began, and I did not know the points
on which the evidence turned.   Did not therefore
attempt to open the case.   Examined witnesses from
the brief at great length, but not understanding the case
or in which direction the drift of it lay, much at a loss ;
and the attorney, R——, very angry, and constantly
interfering and wanting me to put all sorts of irregular
and leading questions.   However, I got out from the
witnesses, I believe, all the important facts, re-examined
witnesses, and cross-examined those for the defence
with more readiness than I should have expected, and
suggested some good points.   Prepared to make a reply
which would have been pretty efficient and telling, as I
thought, but M—— came in and took the brief before
my time for this arrived.   Disappointed at this.   Felt
much perplexed, and confused, and annoyed, but got
through the case as well as I could have expected.
The attorney said it was a case which required at least
two hours' study beforehand, and that it was impossible
I could do justice to it in that hurried way.   He said
the case had taken him great time and trouble to get
up.   I fear that the bystanders who did not understand
how I was circumstanced thought me very stupid, and
that I made a sad mess of it, though many perhaps
would not think this.   M—— told the attorney that
the said case was a very difficult one before it came on.
At all events, it was a capital exercise for me in conducting one.   The trial excited intense interest, and
lasted three hours and a half.   I feel now more decidedly
confident than ever of success.   In conducting the
common cases to-day I did not feel at all nervous.

" 24*th.*—In London.

" 25*th.*—Went to the exhibition at Westminster Hall of the cartoons of paintings for the new Houses of Parliament. The general defect of the English school is visible in these, in want of expression, character and feeling, while the drawing and grouping are correct enough.

" 28*th.*—At Coventry and Warwick Assizes. There seems to be very little scope or opportunity of doing anything, of 'coming out,' or evincing talents. The generality of prosecutions require no ability, and afford no room for display. If I could get a good defence or be retained to undertake a leading nisi prius case, I should hope to do myself some good. I have heard six cases during the present assizes, either of which would have suited me well for this purpose.

" 29*th.*—My father had a letter from Mr. Lee the other day, in which he said, ' I have lately wished the new trustee of my marriage settlement should be appointed, and I much wish your son George (whom I much value as a friend) would undertake the office. For him, as regards integrity, kind feeling, and good sense, I have much regard.'

" *September* 21*st.*—Agreed to-day to take the chambers at No. 9, King's Bench Walk, Temple. Got Burbidge lately to lay prospectus and plan of ' Natural, etc., Proofs of Insanity,' before Mr. Richards, the law bookseller. Sent him a letter containing a general description of the work, and in the plan gave the heads of the contents of each chapter ; but he declined it, principally on the ground of its not being a sufficiently practical work.

" *November* 4*th.*—A case I had from B—— was heard in the Exchequer this afternoon, before Lord Abinger and Barons Parke, Gurney, and Rolfe. Court full at the time. Felt nervous just before it came on, and on first rising, but became composed soon after. Spoke for some time, cited and commented on several cases, and argued every point I intended. Went over the several grounds of the case. Got on altogether better than I expected. King told me I did it very well indeed, but too quick. Did not, however, succeed. B——, who was against me, had a case later than, and dead against, those on which I mainly relied, not referred to in Archbold or known to Mr. Dow, who very kindly lent me his aid in going over the case this morning, and said he thought me pretty safe in the cases I relied upon. I quite thought I had succeeded when I sat down, and Lord Abinger seemed all along in my favour. B—— replied to me on each point at some length, and there was a good deal of talk about the case in the robing room after it was over. Some of the men said they thought when I sat down I had made out a good case, but W—— seemed to think that I was quite on the wrong side. Disappointed at not succeeding, but glad on such an occasion to have acquitted myself so well. Several of the counsel about me very kind on this occasion. Jervis, the Q.C. [afterwards Chief Justice of the Common Pleas], handed me up two or three cases, and W—— and K—— did all they could to assist me in this way.

"*9th.*—Saw Mr. Dow to-day, who told me he was quite satisfied I should not succeed in my case in the Exchequer, and that he thought it had been decided against me quite rightly.

"*23rd.*—Some of the cases in Banco I find suitable to me. The other day, in a case of application for a new trial, Stone *v.* Dunlop, two points struck me which I thought might have been made a good deal of. The principal witness as to the identity of a person was a little girl. Much might have been said as to the great value of a child's testimony (1) from peculiar power of observation in children; (2) because a child is quite unprejudiced and disinterested.

" *December* 2nd.—Attended yesterday at the Old Bailey to hear Wilkins defend in a murder case. Very eloquent, some really very high flights indeed, but manner not good. Part of the defence rested on insanity, which I felt I could have worked up well, and made much of, more than he did. Also another point relating to anatomy, which he missed, I should have tried a good deal at.

" 11th.—The following principles I have endeavoured to lay down respecting the conduct of cross-examination. The main points elicited thereby will of course form points for reply in defence. They are applicable both for civil and criminal cases.

OBJECTS.

1. To elicit context of story. 2. To ascertain actual knowledge of witness. 3. Test consistency. 4. Probability. 5. Ascertain prejudice and interest. 6. Character and credibility.

MODE.

I.—1. Obtaining re-narration of whole story. 2. Following out the collateral points. 3. Sift the weak points. 4. Elicit qualification of assertions in chief. 5. Remodel questions before put. 6. Elicit explanation of omissions. 7. Bring out favourable testimony. II.—Show positive statement exceeds positive knowledge. Ascertain limit of knowledge. What points obtained through others. As to identity : (1) length of acquaintance; (2) whenever doubtful; (3) grounds of belief; (4) light and nearness. 5. Accuracy of memory : details; whence impressed; where memory fails, and why; exact expressions. 6. Elicit where witness is doubtful. III.—1 Circuitous questioning. 2. Re-narrating whole story. 3. Contradictory facts, etc. 4. Variance from depositions,

conversations, etc. 5. Detail collateral circumstances. 6.
Remodel sentences. 7. Invert order of events. 8. Repetition
of set phrases. IV.—1. Conduct under circumstances unusual, unnatural. 2. Recollection of particular facts only. 3.
Extreme supposed disinterestedness. 4. Absurdity of case.
V.—1. Reward for conviction. 2. Quarrel, etc., with prisoner
or defendant. 3. Duty to convict—police. etc. 4. Strong
opinion on case. 5. Opinion of prisoner's character. 6. One-
sidedness of testimony. 7. Manner of witness, object. VI.—
1. If ever convicted, or testimony repudiated. 2. Implicated in
present case. 3. Inaccuracy, previous mistakes. 4. As to
skill : experience ; ability ; education ; similar case before.

1844.

"*March* 28*th.*—Drew a pen-and-ink sketch of
G——, which was much like him, and greatly
admired and laughed at, and handed round the court.
H—— said it was perfect, and claimed it for his collection, and declared he must show it to T—— [the
Chief Justice]. Made a very good one of G—— also
for A. A——, and several other sketches of G——,
T——, W——, M——, etc. Humfrey said he should
sit to me, and did not know I was such a wit.

"30*th.*—On the circuit. Junior with Mellor in a
prosecution for arson, which came on first to-day, and
was the principal criminal case at Coventry.

"*April* 25*th.*—Composed exordium and peroration
for a speech in defence of a case which appeared
some time ago in the papers, and which I like on the
whole as well as any I have made. Less eloquent
perhaps than some, but contains more matter; and
argument and eloquence better entwined together.
Much longer and fuller than any of the others. Most
writers and orators, I believe, who feel a deep interest
in the subjects they pursue, and who are intense
thinkers, have some one subject of paramount interest

and importance to themselves, towards which all their currents of thought flow, and which forms, as it were, a sort of intellectual ocean, that absorbs all minor streams, and to which, in whatever quarter they originated, they all tend.

" In each of the compositions of either kind which I have attempted, as in the above, I find human nature, the study and investigation of which has formed my chief and choicest pursuit, to be the ocean towards which all the other currents of thought, from whatever topic springing, ultimately diverge.

" *May* 23*rd.*—Went down this morning to the House of Lords. Committee of Privileges on Sussex case. Wilde opened. Much power, points well put, language good and elevated in style, but nothing of high eloquence.

" *July* 5*th.*—Dined at the dinner given to Mr. C. Knight at the Albion. Lord Brougham in the chair. The Tarvers and several friends there. I sat between Dr. Dickson and J. Mellor. Lord B. spoke well, with a good deal of point and humour. M. D. Hill also made an eloquent and powerful address.

" *August* 10*th.*—It is certainly very vexatious being circumstanced as I am, feeling within me full power, and capacity, and resource, for doing great things as an advocate, and yet having no possible opportunity of coming out. But this is what every ambitious man has to go through, and these emotions are the surest sweeteners of success when secured. Follett felt great despondency as to success for a long time, and made no way. Cockburn was many years before his talents as an advocate were discovered, and encountered great pecuniary difficulties. So also with Eldon, Lyndhurst, and many others. I have no doubt of ultimate success, and I must have ample opportunities eventually of coming out. I feel within me full talents, and resources, and oratorical power, for all I require, and that a few fair opportunities and vigorous and rightly directed efforts would establish my reputation at once.

"One reason which I lately heard given at the Temple why some very able men, as Cockburn, do not get on for some time, was that though they were very well fitted for leaders, they were not adapted for juniors, and so had no opportunity for displaying powers. Lord Eldon's diffidence seems to have been as bad as mine. His love of conveyancing and being well grounded in laws of real property must have been advantageous. Long before he obtained any business of importance, and though he had several defences on the circuit where he mentions how few are the opportunities of doing anything to display ability, yet it was five years before he obtained a regular opportunity of 'coming out,' and soon after that he rose rapidly. He appears, however, to have had several chances soon of doing something before the House of Lords, and in defending prisoners; and, considering his peculiar adaptation for the profession, it seems singular he did not 'come out' sooner than he did; he rose through no one great cause, but through a succession of them. A good hit in the way of a joke he seems to think as conducive to success as anything. Yet with his entire and sole devotion to his profession, and great power, and the reputation, both general and legal, which he possessed in his own circle, it does seem extraordinary he made no more rapid progress at first.

"My three works, 'Civilisation Considered as a Science,' the 'Treatise on Man,' and the 'Theory of Arts,' suit well together for contemporaneous study. 'Treatise on Man' embraces man as a whole, and forms

the foundation of the other works, and indeed of all
other studies. Out of this, in one direction, springs law,
which is founded on a knowledge of man's nature and
actions, and is formed by his faculties of reception and
judgment. The 'Theory of Arts' and 'Treatise on Man'
must be taken together. In the latter man is considered
as an individual ; in ' Civilisation,' in the aggregate.

" *October* 20*th*.—Went to Birmingham in evening,
and had a walk and dined with Mr. Lee. Mr. Yorke,
the new rector of St. Philip's [afterwards Dean of
Worcester, and brother of Lord Hardwicke], staying
with him. Lee asked me, or rather recommended me, to
bring out a Life of the great Lord Hardwicke, similar
to H. Twiss' Life of Lord Eldon, and said he would
give me an introduction so as to obtain the manuscripts from Lord Hardwicke. They once, I believe,
wanted Lee to do this.

" *November* 2*nd*.—First day of term. Business prospects very gloomy. Feel sometimes very much dis-
pirited, and afraid I shall not succeed ; but, like many
around me, drag on miserably, never advancing beyond
what they did the first year. This, too, the case with
many who seem well qualified for their profession, and
with those who work hard at it.

" *8th*.—Composed an ode to the Winter Assize,
a satirical poem. Showed it to H——, S——, M——,
W——, and others, who praised it up, called it
capital, exceedingly good, very clever, and some asked
for copies, and recommended me to send it to *Punch* or
the *Times*. Sent it off to the former, with a note.

" *9th*.—This morning manuscript of lines on Winter
Assize returned to me from *Punch*, with a note saying
the editor 'regrets that want of space compels him to
return them,' so I sent them off to the *Times*. C——
told me they would be too long for *Punch*, without my

telling him of this. Directly I got into court to-day,
H—— called out to me for the copy of them which
I promised him, and laughed very much, and handed
them about to others."

CHAPTER XI.

LAW AND LITERATURE—COMMENCEMENT OF LIFE OF
LORD CHANCELLOR HARDWICKE.

1844– 1847.

" *November* 24*th.*

"FEW men who have been either very great or very
good have been free from the affliction of adversity,
the effect of which must be admitted to be in many
respects, both intellectually and morally, very extensive.
As regards the former, it refines the soul, purges it of
gross thoughts, inculcates reflection, and to a great
degree, calls forth its resources. As regards the latter,
it leads us to self-examination and contemplation, and
engenders religious feeling, dependence and care, which
might otherwise become extinguished.

"The greatest characters in both these respects, both
in sacred and profane history, and in ancient and
modern times, have been largely purged and refined in
the furnace of affliction.

"I do hope even now for ultimate success, and that
speedily; and I trust yet to have some happy days,
for which I am by no means unadapted. At present those at Rugby, from which I so vigorously tried
to escape, are, I think, the most so, if I except the
two years I spent in London after my clerkship. How
many, however, whose early career is one of unin-
terrupted success, have their latter period darkened by
the reverse. Few have the same run of fortune through

life. Mine may yet be changed, though, at the same
time, I have many advantages and possessions I should
highly prize and be grateful for. My days of late have
indeed been most miserable, and at night I have been
constantly disturbed and lain awake reflecting despond-
ingly on my situation.

" Skimming lately Sir Humphrey Davy's Life. Very
interesting. Resembles me in one point : the power
I have to get possession of the contents of a book (as
I have done with this) in a very short space. The
general matter I can glean from the 'contents,' and read
fully only the particular points.

" Dr. Arnold once told me he never took more than
a quarter of an hour to read any review ; and Lord
Brougham is said to have acquired his immense knowledge through this power. Scott and Southey also
possessed it.

1845.

" *January 7th.*—At Birmingham Sessions. Stayed
at Mr. Lee's. He urged me strongly to bring out Lord
Hardwicke's Life ; said that it would do me good, and
that there were quite enough materials for it, which
are, however, more scattered than I supposed, and less
in the present Earl's possession, many of the letters,
etc., printed in Coxe's ' Memoirs.'

" *17th.*—Mentioned on Monday to W. Moxon my
plan of bringing out Lord Hardwicke's Life, and asked
if his brother would join me in it. Thought he would
very likely bring it out himself. Saw him again on
Tuesday, when he said he had mentioned it to his
brother, who liked the idea of it, and wished to have
published some other biographies.

" *18th.*—Called on W. Moxon to-day, and asked him
what his brother had determined, and he said he

thought that he would accept my terms, and asked me to call upon him about it, which I accordingly did this afternoon.

"*21st.*—Wrote to Mr. Lee, informing him of above, and asking him to procure for me a sight of the papers at Wimpole, and sent him a sketch of the materials.

"The difficulty in Lord Hardwicke's Life is to make it at once interesting and a good sound book.

"*March 8th.*—Dined to-day at Mr. Lee's, and called on Mr. Yorke. The former said he should expect a great deal from my Life of Lord H., and the latter said he should look for it with much interest.

"Received to-day a letter from Lord Hardwicke, sent on to me from London, in answer to the letter I wrote to him in February, informing him of my intention to write the Life of the Chancellor, and asking permission to be allowed to see the papers in his possession. In this letter, which was dated from Wimpole, Arrington, Cambridgeshire, March 4th, 1845, his lordship said, as I had determined to undertake a work of great interest to him, viz, the Life of his ancestor the Lord Chancellor Hardwicke, I should have all the assistance he could give.

"He would be in London on the 15th, in attendance on her Majesty, and would reside at Patterson's Hotel, Brooke Street, where he would be glad to see me any morning at nine that I might please to call.

"W. H. Adams dined with me at the Junior Athenæum Club. He told me he wondered I did not go into the equity courts, and that it was hardly worth my while to go down to sessions and on circuit; too much bustle and row for me at Nisi Prius. Thought me better suited for chancery and conveyancing than common law. I fail only for want of nerve and

physical defects, which practice will be the surest and
most efficient mode of remedying.

"*April 30th.*—Last day of April.   A good month for
me in point of business.   Made this month twenty-six
guineas.   In excellent spirits lately, and really happy
now.

"*July 26th.*—Had a visit on Thursday from Mr. Eliot
Yorke, brother of Lord Hardwicke and M.P. for
Cambridgeshire ; and on Friday morning, by his
recommendation, I called on Lord Hardwicke, whom I
saw, and had a walk and a good deal of chat with
him.   Found him very civil and kind, and he asked me
to go down to Wimpole in September.   Said, however,
he should make two bargains with me : (1) to be
allowed to see and revise the letterpress, which I
hardly know what to think of, and which may be very
annoying if I am to have any one who is to interfere
in the work ; (2) to refer any points that may
arise as to the conduct of the Chancellor, to two
of Lord Hardwicke's friends for their advice.   Lord
Hardwicke asked me if I had before been concerned
in any literary work, and seemed rather, I thought,
to hesitate as to my qualifications, etc.

"*31st.*—Wrote a long letter to Lord Hardwicke,
sending him epitome of the Life, etc., telling him I had
consulted Moxon, whom I saw on Tuesday, and agreed as
to what he wished, and was desirous to meet his wishes
and feelings in all respects ; that I was determined to
make the work one of a leading character.   I told him of
the literary undertakings I had been engaged in, viz. :
'Prospects of a Republic,' etc., of which I sent him
prospectus containing criticisms, articles in *British
and Foreign* and *Monthly*, and offered to produce a
testimonial from Lee as to qualifications for the
undertaking.

"*August* 19*th*.— A letter from Lord Hardwicke, beginning 'My dear Sir,' and saying he was quite contented I should go on with the Life of his great-grandfather, and should have all the assistance he could give me. He added that he should be at Wimpole about the middle of September, when he should be glad to see me there.

"*September* 13*th*.—Wrote to Lord Hardwicke to-day, asking him to inform me when it would be convenient for me to go to Wimpole, and saying I would run down any day on hearing from him, but that if not convenient to him to see me there now, I hoped he would postpone my visit. Told him I had written a rough draft of the three first and part of the fourth chapters, which I hoped to have the pleasure of submitting to him.

"17*th*.—Had a brief at the Old Bailey. A prosecution for highway robbery. The trial came on before Justices Wightman and Erle, and the prisoner was convicted and transported for ten years.

"22*nd*.—A letter from Henry, with the chapters of Lord Chancellor Hardwicke's Life which I left with him. He begins by saying, 'I have read through your manuscript, and think it very interesting and well written, and improving both in interest and style as it goes on.'

"28th.—A letter from Lord Hardwicke, saying that owing to the death of his wife's mother, he is detained at Ravensworth Castle, and will not at present be at Wimpole, but will write to me as soon as he is settled at home.

"*October* 2*nd*.—Sent manuscripts of portion complete of Lord Chancellor Hardwicke's Life the other day to W. Moxon, and asked him to look through it for me, and write me word his opinion on it, which he agreed

to do.   Told me to-day he thought I had treated it
in rather a masterly manner.

" 15*th*.—Busy all day about railway cases, etc.   The
whole town intensely excited by them.   The sole
subject of conversation everywhere, and London quite
full all the vacation.   All the upper stories over shops
seem converted into railway offices.   All the newspapers blocked up with their advertisements.

" 22*nd*.—Went to Birmingham on Saturday, and
stayed with the Lees until Monday, that I might
inquire about my railway shares, etc.   Have now, by
being on committees and applying for shares, become
entitled to above eight hundred.

" My father told me the other day that Mr. James had
admired an opinion of mine which I wrote some time
ago on a point involving some suspicious circumstances
on the face of a will.

" 23*rd*.—Called on W. Moxon, who told me Lord
Campbell was bringing out ' Lives of the Chancellors,'
and now intended to bring it down to end of George IV.,
and so would include Lord Hardwicke ; but Moxon
does not think he will injure my work, as his will be
necessarily a very brief notice of Lord H.   He said he
thought mine was very ably done, especially the dissertation in the first chapter, and that I only wanted
ampler materials.

" 30*th*.—Left London by the two o'clock train for
Cambridge, where I obtained a fly to carry me on to
Wimpole.   I arrived there about half-past six, and
found Lord and Lady Hardwicke waiting dinner for
me.   Dressed as quickly as I could, and made all the
apologies I was able.   Most kindly and hospitably
received by them.   Mr. and Mrs. Eliot Yorke also
staying here.

" 31*st*.—Hard at work yesterday and to-day in the

muniment room looking over papers and letters. Found some respecting Walpole, Atterbury, Jack Sheppard, and several of interest.

"Lord and Lady H. appear much pleased with my undertaking, and evince great interest in it. Lent Lord H. the manuscripts of what I have written of the work to read. Lord H. said he thought the remuneration I was to have for the work very inadequate, and that I could have got more, but trusted I should make the book as perfect as possible, and a really great work, which I told him I should hope to do. He said he thought I should do it well. He and Lady H. particularly agreeable, friendly, and kind. Like the whole family very much. The house a most comfortable one. Everything seems to conduce to comfort, and in the most perfect style, without the least display. The park and grounds, where I got a good walk this morning before breakfast, very delightful.

"Wimpole is really a fine place, with a large park and extensive pleasure grounds belonging to it. The house is very large, the roof covering two acres of ground. The estate was purchased by the founder of the family, Lord Chancellor Hardwicke, of the celebrated Earl of Oxford; but though Lord Hardwicke told me that the rental of the estate was about £20,000 a year, it is wholly inadequate to keep up the establishment, which he considered requires £100,000 a year. He regretted that the Chancellor had ever bought Wimpole, and wished that he had kept Hardwicke, in Gloucestershire, from which the title was taken, and which might be maintained without difficulty.

"There is an extensive library and a very valuable collection of historical manuscripts, as well as several interesting pictures of the time of Lord Chancellor

Hardwicke, including fine portraits of several of his distinguished contemporaries.

"A chapel is attached to the house, in which the family assemble every morning for prayers, read by Lord Hardwicke."

1846.

"*January 3rd.*—Lord H. told me yesterday he liked the preface to Lord Chancellor Hardwicke's life very much, and that my plan of rendering the judgments intelligible and of interweaving them and the speeches with the general matter was very good. He also approved the plan of introducing narratives from newspapers. Said he should like to show the preface to Mr. Croker, but should not wish him to interfere in my plan of the work, but thought he might be of use to consult on some points or make suggestions.

"To-day Lord Hardwicke read Chapter I. Told me he liked it very much. Said my observations on legal education were very good, contained excellent reasoning. At dinner Lady H. told me she thought a person like me, who took up the work from having a real interest in the subject, much more likely to do it well than one who merely did it for profit, or as a regular professional writer. Lord H. to-day said he should treat me as a friend, and therefore be quite straightforward with me and talk to me in his blunt way, and so hoped I should stay over Sunday and see the church and monuments.

"*4th.*—Attended the service this morning at Wimpole in the family gallery of the church. Several coats-of-arms of the Yorkes in the windows which have been collected. Some of them very old, in painted glass; show an old and a gentle genealogy. Several monuments of the family in the church, and one to the Chancellor.

9

That to the late Lord H., by young Westmacott, very fine ; the repose of the recumbent figure admirable. The church rebuilt by the Chancellor.

" 5*th*.—This morning I left Wimpole, having had a most agreeable and in every way satisfactory visit. Before coming I occasionally felt some misgivings as to how I should get on ; but I could not have wished for matters to turn out better. As I did not take leave last night, or have any opportunity of seeing Lord and Lady Hardwicke this morning, I left a note for the former, saying I could not quit Wimpole without thanking him and Lady Hardwicke for their extreme kindness and hospitality during a visit which had been to me one of great pleasure as well as of deep interest. I asked Lord Hardwicke to let me have an account of the purchase of Wimpole for the Life, and for permission to dedicate the book to him. Returned to Rugby by London.

" Found a letter at my chambers from Savage, saying I was threatened as one of the guarantees for Rugby and Swindon Railway. A great fuss at Rugby about this line. Provincial committee all written to, and £200 demanded as their share of expenses. In terrible consternation.

" 13*th*.—Mr. Savage told me I was sued, with five others, for £500 on a guarantee for money owing by R—— and S——. Authorised him to appear for me. General meeting of committee to-day to consider our desperate and frightful position. Only £3 10s. more of capital paid. Provincial committee refuse to contribute.

" 31*st*.—Another letter threatening proceedings against me for £600 bill in which I joined with the ordinary committee. Called on Savage about arranging it.

" *February 2nd.*—A letter from the solicitor of a Captain R——, demanding £1,200. Three of the city aldermen are said to have bolted.

" 'This dreadful worry and annoyance of railway and pecuniary matters keeps me in a perpetual turmoil.

" *9th.*—The other day I wrote to Lord Hardwicke and sent him an extract from a speech of Lord Chatham on the importance of supporting the agricultural interest and the superiority of that to the manufacturing, which I told him I thought peculiarly applicable to the present times. This morning an answer came thanking me for it, and saying I should see he had soon made use of it.

" *18th.*—At Rugby. Every morning now, as regularly as breakfast itself, some annoying letter arrives about the railways. Almost callous now, and look for these arrivals as a matter of certainty. Saw in the Cambridge paper to-day an account of Lord Hardwicke's speech at a Cambridge meeting, in which he introduced my quotation at length, and with great effect, and which was much cheered.

" *21st.*—The excessively depressed state of the share market at present is as unnatural as its former exalted condition, and the only hope of its reviving, if merely from the necessity of a reaction taking place, is in some measure pretty certain.

" *May 6th.*—Reading account of suicide of poor Haydon, with whom I had a controversy in *Hull Times*. His feelings, and apprehensions, and sleepless nights and disquietudes, how like mine now. It is a horrible condition, but I hope in my case I have some prospect of relief eventually.

" *July 6th.*—At Coventry Wednesday and to-day. Had four briefs. Junior in a heavy prosecution with Miller against a Dissenting minister at Rugby for burglary. He also carried on the business of a cooper, and had stood very high in the town, but had gone down of late. He was convicted and suspected of several other robberies.

"*September* 5th.—Wrote the other day to Lord Hardwicke, whom I hope to visit at Wimpole this month, when I shall obtain papers, etc.

"12th.—Matters monetary are growing worse and worse, and are now almost as bad as they can be. A letter from Lord Hardwicke asking me to go to Wimpole in October.

"21st.—A letter from Lord Hardwicke, who says he has seen Prince Albert, who consented to allow the dedication of my Life of Lord Chancellor to him.

"*October* 18th.—This afternoon a letter from Lord Hardwicke, which is in every way most satisfactory and kind. He asks me to go to Wimpole at once, and says of my proposed form of the dedication of the Life of the Chancellor to Prince Albert, 'It is excellent. Do not let any one induce you to alter it. It is short, expressing all that is necessary, devoid of absurd flattery, and speaks truth. Yours most sincerely, Hardwicke.' Wrote to him, and told him I would go to Wimpole on Thursday. Put off going to London to-day.

"22nd.—Came to Wimpole to-day. Arrived at Wimpole about half-past five. Lord Hardwicke came to me in the drawing-room, and we had a long chat together, principally about political affairs, before dressing for dinner. A great distrust of Disraeli appeared at this time to exist among the Tory party, as I gathered from the conversation at Wimpole. But Lord Hardwicke much liked Sir R. Peel, and said he was sure he acted quite conscientiously when he changed his opinion about the Corn Laws.

"Lord Hardwicke told me that once, when he contested the county of Cambridge, Sir E. Sugden contested the borough, and that he and Sugden stayed at the same hotel, where he found him excellent company and very agreeable, though he was reputed to be very dry and dull in conversation as a mere lawyer. Lord Hardwicke told me that on one occasion Sir R. Peel asked him, during a debate in the House of Commons, to go home and dine with him, and that he wanted Disraeli to meet him. During dinner Disraeli said something that put Peel out, whereupon Peel gave him such a dressing as never man had. Told him of his ambitious feelings and taunted him with want of principle, and with acting contrary to his convictions. He said that Disraeli appeared quite cut up by the attack, and to this incident he (Lord Hardwicke) attributed the severe animosity in after-times between Peel and Disraeli.

" 28*th*.—Working away very hard at the manuscripts each day, Lord Hardwicke several times telling me how very closely I worked copying papers, never before seen; discovered some few new ones. Proposed to Lord Hardwicke to sort and catalogue papers for him, which he said he should like. Would pay me, so that I should be no loser, at any rate for time I was about them, and I am to let him know what my avocations are. Said he should be at Wimpole during the winter, and glad if I would stay there, if I liked the accommodation and to be treated as an old friend.

" *November* 6*th*.—Each day working hard at Wimpole papers, copying letters of Lord Bolingbroke and narrative of C. Yorke's death, etc. Made good progress in materials. Lord Hardwicke said he should be at Wimpole after the beginning of December all the winter, if I would stay with them the same as I am now doing. Lord Hardwicke also proposed to me to pay a visit to Lord Ripon's to see papers there, and said he would write to Lord Ripon to invite me. He further suggested that I should visit the Cambridge libraries, and offered to give me an introduction to heads of houses, so that I should dine in college; also to see library at Windsor, and to give me an introduction to the librarian there; also to visit the library at Paris, and to give me an introduction to the Marquis of Normanby, his brother-in-law, who was ambassador there.

"When I was at Wimpole last year, Lord Hardwicke asked me what I was to receive from Moxon for the 'Life of Lord Chancellor Hardwicke,' and said he particularly wished to know; and when I told him he observed that he thought it very inadequate, and that I might have got more, but wished me not to consider that as my remuneration, but make the work as perfect as possible, and I should find I was well remunerated for doing so, and be no loser.

"Prince Albert wishes to have the proof sheets sent to him, which I am glad of. Lord Hardwicke said that the Prince was entirely free from party and political feeling, and that he never showed the least animosity towards him on account of his differing in politics from the Ministry in office. Even though he voted against the large annuity proposed to Prince Albert, the Prince never evinced any ill-feeling about it.

"Lord Hardwicke told me that in early life he had been very poor, and that when he and Lady Hardwicke married (before he came into his titles and estates), they feared they were utterly ruined on the bill coming in for making the marriage settlements.

"Lady Hardwicke's sister, Lady Barrington, is a regular correspondent of the Queen, and seems to be her favourite among the family, but Lord Hardwicke is regarded as *the friend*, among the nobility, of Prince Albert.

"*7th.*—Returned to London on Tuesday, leaving Wimpole Monday morning. Lord and Lady Hardwicke going out on a visit. Obtained leave of Lord Hardwicke to bring away seven volumes of Lord Chancellor Hardwicke's note-books of cases while he was Chief Justice and Chancellor, at which cases I am now working each day, and am making good and steady progress.

"*26th.*—Yesterday last day of term. This term I have only made altogether 10s. 6d. by signing a plea. Entirely occupied by Lord Hardwicke's Life. Not having been down in court friend B—— asked me quite seriously if I had not given up practice at the Bar altogether.

"*December 8th.*—A letter from Lord Hardwicke yesterday, requesting me to postpone my visit to Wimpole, where, according to arrangement, I was to have gone to-morrow for a week.

"Obtained yesterday, through Moxon, Lord Campbell's 'Lives of the Chancellors.' Annoyed and alarmed on first perusing to find Lord Hardwicke's Life so fully treated in it. Nevertheless, on the whole I do not think his book will injure mine. Without the Wimpole manuscripts mine much more perfect, not only as to length, but variety and completeness of points embraced, and my dissertation more full and varied. With the manuscripts, and original letters, and notes of trials, and diary, I may hope to place my performance considerably above Lord Campbell's. Lord C. says in his preface, 'The copious materials which existed for the Lives of Lord Chancellor Hardwicke and Lord Chancellor Charles Yorke have been improved by several interesting documents transmitted to me

by their distinguished descendants." I am sure he
has had nothing from Wimpole, and there is no
allusion by him to the papers there, but he has
evidently got some materials I do not know of, as
there are new facts in his work of which I have not
heard.   There must be additional papers somewhere
in the family, and yet the story about C. Yorke's death,
which the family are most anxious to clear up, remains
uncontradicted as before.   If they had sent Lord
C. papers, they surely would have insisted on this
being done.

   " 9*th.*—Searched at Doctors' Commons for wills of
family of the father of Lord Chancellor Hardwicke,
but could not find them.   May have been proved at
Canterbury.   My great fear as to the effect of Lord
Campbell's book on mine is that it may lead people to
say there is no necessity for another Life of Lord
Hardwicke, and that everything of importance that
could be said about him has been stated by Lord
C. and that the present is only an attempt at
book-making.   On the other hand, the publication
alone of the original letters of Bolingbroke and
others to Lord Hardwicke, and of his own diary, is sufficient to justify the work, and so great a character
cannot be undeserving a separate and full account of
his life.   Contradictions of errors, in many ways both
numerous and important, which his papers afford,
would, in my opinion, alone justify, if not demand, the
work.

   " 11*th.*—Wrote to Lord Hardwicke.   Told him I
should be sorry to intrude at Wimpole when inconvenient, but would hold myself ready to resume my
researches at any time.   Referred to the Lord Chancellor's 'Lives of the Chancellors.'   Told Lord Hardwicke
that some misrepresentations which are in it required

correction, and that the story about the death of C. Yorke had been reiterated.

"*23rd.*—A letter from Lord Hardwicke on Monday, asking me to go to Wimpole at once, and saying I should 'have a hearty welcome,' which I did and had yesterday.

"*31st.*—At Wimpole. Very pleasant indeed. Working hard at papers. Arranging and sorting them, putting aside all of use to me in ' Life of Lord Chancellor Hardwicke.' Found several interesting original diaries and letters of Lyttelton, Chesterfield, Duchess of Marlborough, etc., etc.

"Mr. Eliot Yorke and Mr. Henry Yorke mentioned to me that they thought it would be a great advantage to me Lord Campbell's work having come out before mine, and that the points to contradict would be of great use to me; and Lord Hardwicke says he has asked Mr. Croker to meet me here next month, and will request him to review my book in the *Quarterly.* Very pleasant here indeed. On Christmas Day most convivial. Venison and champagne for dinner, and charades in the evening acted. Lord and Lady Hardwicke, Lord Royston and the children, Mr. Eliot Yorke and old Mr. Schedtky amongst the performers. Capital."

1847.

"*January 10th.*—Still at Wimpole, where everything has passed most agreeably and satisfactorily. Hard at work every day at the papers, selecting materials for ' Life of Lord Chancellor Hardwicke.' Have now obtained enough for whole, having examined all the papers of importance, and taken out and put aside whatever I considered useful for my proposed work. Arranged with Lord Hardwicke to allow me to take away a portion of the papers up to 1745. He said he should place the fullest reliance on my honour and judgment as regarded them and all matters connected with the work. Believe I shall now have ample materials to go to work upon, but I shall have to alter a good deal, and very likely to subdivide some of the chapters.

"Sent portion of manuscripts containing preface and chaps. i. and ii. to Mr. Henry and Mr. Grantham Yorke to read. The latter said he should like to talk to me about it ; the former said that there was too much disquisition in the first chapter, and that some of the sentences were too long.

"12*th*.—Left Wimpole and returned to London to-day.

"Yesterday evening talked with Mr. H. Yorke about 'Life of Lord Chancellor Hardwicke,' which he said he and Mr. G. Yorke liked with the exceptions he had stated, and that the arrangement of it was particularly good.

"30*th*.—Hard at work all the week at Hardwicke manuscripts ; completed chap. vii. (1742—1745), which is a long one, from them. Matter interesting. Business now almost extinct, but I hope the work which has driven it away will more than compensate for the loss of it."

CHAPTER XII.

VISITS TO WINDSOR.—INTERVIEW WITH PRINCE ALBERT.

1847.

"*February* 3*rd.*

"WENT down to Windsor, with letter of introduction from Lord Hardwicke to Mr. Glover, Queen's librarian, to inquire after any manuscripts in royal library, as Prince Albert told Lord Hardwicke he thought there might be, but Mr. Glover said there were none. Left with Mr. Glover my draft of the dedication of the ' Life of Lord Chancellor Hardwicke ' to lay before the Prince, and talked with him about sending proof-sheets to Prince, which he asked Lord Hardwicke for, but which Mr. G. thinks he would not really require, and that I should find it very troublesome.

" 4*th*.—Called on Lord Ripon with a note from Lord Hardwicke to ask him for some papers respecting ' Life of Lord Chancellor Hardwicke,' but he has none of importance. Very civil, pleasant, and chatty.

" Have some doubts and misgivings, after all, as to success of ' Life of Lord Chancellor Hardwicke.' The *personal* materials are very barren, especially in domestic matter, prior to 1734, so little to illustrate his private life and habits, and even up to that time the general correspondence very scanty; that most valuable portion of every biography and that to which the most popular of biographies, Boswell's ' Life of Johnson,' owes all its interest, the personal recollections and descriptions and domestic anecdotes of the man, is entirely wanting here.

" There is much that is interesting, but it is not personal, and much that is personal that is not interesting, at least not to persons not otherwise caring about it. The latter parts of the biography may be better off in this respect ; the correspondence is more copious, and of more general and extended interest."

Went to Wimpole on March 15th, returning to London on 22nd. Lord and Lady Hardwicke appeared to be devoted to the Queen and Prince Consort, and gave me an account of the visit of Queen and Prince to Wimpole soon after they were married. Said the

Queen and Prince gave them very little trouble, and were very easily satisfied, though some of their attendants were very different. The Queen said all she required was a comfortable, plain bed and a table on which to lay the miniatures of her children. The principal expense was having a band from London. Lord Hardwicke would not allow any reporters to attend, and dismissed one from the house very unceremoniously. He said he would not allow any one to go into the walks about the house, where the Queen and Prince used to take a stroll every morning before breakfast, as they wished to have the walk to themselves.

Lord Hardwicke told me that it was a great mistake to suppose that being in office was a source of emolument, and that the expense far exceeded the pay, as when he was not in office he only came to town on special occasions, and lived at his club, whereas when in office he was obliged to take a great mansion, bring all his family to London, and give large entertainments.

Some members of the family gave a very unfavourable character of Croker, whom they seemed much to dislike. Said he treated Lord Hardwicke with great deference, but snubbed all the other members of the family, as also several persons that he met at Wimpole, particularly an American gentleman, to whom he was overbearing. Returned to London.

" *May 7th.*—Left Rugby, where I had been on a visit and came to London, and so on to Wimpole.

" *8th.*—Lord Hardwicke mentioned at dinner the following anecdote of the Duke of Wellington, which he had from Lord Fitzgerald. When the Duke was about nineteen or so, Lord Mornington, his father, observed one day at a party at his house that all his

sons appeared to be getting on in the world well
except *poor Arthur*, and he did not know what was to
become of him, but they hoped to get him some
appointment in the Excise. That he was a loiterer
about Dublin when the Lord Lieutenant became
jealous of him in relation to his mistress, and obtained
him a commission in the army.

" 13th.—Still at Wimpole. Lord Hardwicke went
to London on Monday to take part in the debates.

" Enjoy myself here very much. Lady Hardwicke
most agreeable and kind, and also the children. Mrs.
Gillespie Smith here, who is writing the Life of her
grandfather, Sir Robert Keith, and whom I assist to
discover manuscripts. Lady Hardwicke and Mr. Henry
Yorke reading chaps. vi. and viii. of my work ; seem
pleased with it ; both say it is very interesting, but
think I go from one matter to another rather abruptly,
and that style wants finish and working up.

" Lord Hardwicke used to tell other very amusing
stories of the Duke of Wellington, whom he knew
intimately, and whom he could imitate in manner.
Once, when Lord Charles Wellesley came home from
school, the Duke suspected that he had been doing
something wrong, and would not allow him to ride any
of his horses. But eventually he found out that he
was mistaken, and Lord Hardwicke took off his way
of accosting his son when he told him he had been
wrong, and that he was quite at liberty to use any of
the horses.

" 17th.—Arranged with Lord and Lady Hardwicke
to send them proof-sheets, and to commence printing
on 1st June. Lord Hardwicke to write to Croker to
review the whole in the *Quarterly.* Told Lady Hardwicke I must get it out before November, as it was so
serious an interruption to my professional pursuits.

Returned to London with Lord Hardwicke. Called on Moxon in evening, and arranged to send him manuscripts of work. He thought it would not do to extend the work to three volumes; that Lord Hardwicke's life was not of sufficient interest—no correspondence with great literary men; that the part relating to rebellion referred rather to the times than to the life of Lord Chancellor Hardwicke; and that substance of it had been published in other works. As I came to London with Lord Hardwicke, while talking about Lord Campbell's book, he observed on the great difference between speaking and writing, and said that several who could write well never could succeed as speakers, owing to diffidence, and were always absorbed with the thought of their audience instead of their subject, and experienced that extraordinary sensation of the drying up of the saliva and the tongue sticking to the roof of the mouth, sensations which I have experienced. I thought that his observations might be intended to apply to me, and as a hint of his opinion of me.

"*August* 16th.—Elections going on lately. At one time hoped, if my book had been published and I had "come out" well, through it to have been a candidate for a seat in Parliament at this election, but perhaps I ought to become more established in my profession. Hope, however, when next election comes, to be ready for it. A long letter from Lady Hardwicke, written in the kindest way, saying she hoped I should take her observations as well meant, and saying she thought there appeared a repetition and redundancy in the early part of work, and proposing I should read it out to a friend. Several of those suggested by Lady Hardwicke have been made in the revised proof. Wrote to her, telling her so, and thanking her for her kind letter.

"*September* 16th.—Printing of vol. i. completed.

Wrote to Lord Hardwicke, informing him of this, and proposed deferring sending anything to Mr. Croker until whole completed, as other volumes were of more general interest.

" 22*nd*.—A letter from Lord Hardwicke says, ' I think it as well to forward the *whole* work to Croker as soon as printed, and I wish you would be so good as to take care that the first copy issued is sent to him.'

" *October* 19*th*.—Much gratified to-day by hearing of Lee's appointment to the bishopric of Manchester, his prospect of which we discussed when I was staying with him, when he promised me I should be his chancellor if this happened. Fear, however, I am not qualified for this, not being a D.C.L., which is requisite in a layman, or it might be just such an appointment as I want. My sole reliance is on success as an advocate.

" 30*th*.—Saw Lee on Wednesday, and drove with him to the Paddington station, on his way to Windsor Castle. Talked with him about the appointments he should make of secretaries, etc. He said, ' I have been with my cousin, Dr. H——, about the Chancellorship,' to which I made no reply, and did not ask if he thought of appointing me, but said afterwards, ' I shall be a candidate for a registrarship if you have one to give away,' to which he merely replied, ' A registrarship !' and said he had promised no appointment, and should not until he had been elected and consecrated. Met Lee yesterday morning, as he asked me, at the Paddington station.

" He seemed greatly delighted with his visit to Windsor. Much less state than he expected. Had three quarters of an hour's talk with the Prince before dinner on Thursday, and with the Queen after dinner. Talked on theological matters and state of parties in

the Church, and about education of Prince of Wales.
I told Lee I had thought of applying to him for the
Chancellorship, but found I was ineligible, to which he
said, 'Yes ; it must be a Doctor of Laws.' I then said
'I should ask for the registrarship if he had no one in
view. I supposed there would be several applications
for it, and probably B—— would apply.' He said
'he had no one in view, and should not appoint B——
if he did apply, which he had not done ; but he thought
he should be a good deal fettered in these appointments,
that many of them which had had good perquisites
attached to them would be now only compliments, and
that he should be obliged to give away certain offices
to leading professional men in Manchester to strengthen
his position there.' I did not urge anything further,
except saying that the 'principal registrar was usually
resident in London, and a man of standing, who was
responsible to the Bishop, as the deputies, who resided
in the diocese and did the business, were to him, and
that I hoped he would bear me in mind if he could.'
He merely said then that 'the Bishop of Chester had
promised to send him an account of all these appointments and the emoluments attached to them.' Nothing
more on this subject passed, and soon after we parted.
Considering Lee's friendship for and connection with
me and the desire he has always expressed for my
promotion and my obtaining an appointment of this
kind, I shall not think that he is acting as he ought if
he does not give it me, provided, of course, he can
fairly and rightly do so.

"*November* 1st.—A letter from Lord Hardwicke,
saying he should take ten copies of the work, and
asking me to forward two first volumes at once to Mr.
Croker. Called on Stevens and Norton, who thought
the book would not have a large sale ; might run out the

edition. They were disappointed in not finding more anecdote about the men of the time, but in other respects liked it, though in former details less interesting than Lord Eldon's Life.

"*December* 1st.—A letter from Lord Hardwicke, saying, in reply to suggestions of mine, that he has asked Lord Brougham to review my work in the *Edinburgh* and that when I present the work to the Prince, it will be desirable to show him some of the manuscripts. Old P—— strongly advised me not to lose the opportunity.

"*6th.*—A great many friends calling to see the manuscripts and plates, and every one I meet full of the subject of my book, and inquiring about it. A great contrast to Rugby, where no one cares about it. My father, indeed, did *once* enter into conversation with me about it, but in letters from home it is not even alluded to.

"*8th.*—A letter in the evening from Lord Hardwicke, asking me to call on him on Monday and settle about the presentation to the Prince.

"*10th.*—Called on Lord Hardwicke this morning ; very cordially received by him, and he appeared much pleased with the book. Said with respect to replies to Lord Campbell and to my remarks on death of Mr. C. Yorke, 'It is uncommonly well done indeed.' He ordered altogether twenty-one copies, some to be sent to Sir R. Peel, Lord Stanley, Lord G. Bentinck, Mr. Disraeli, Mr. Lockhart, Lord Ashburton, Lord Campbell, etc., etc. Asked me to go to Wimpole next month, and promised to write to the Prince about my presenting the dedication copy. B—— told me he liked the book very much.

"*28th.*—Went to Birmingham, and spent the day with Lee, and presented him with a copy of my book.

10

He cut the leaves of it, looking through each page as he went on, and at the conclusion praised it very much ; said he liked it ' exceedingly ; ' a good arrangement, and variety of interesting matter.

" I returned to Rugby in the evening. My father and mother both reading my book, and express themselves greatly pleased with it. On my return I found a letter from Lord Hardwicke, saying he had Prince Albert's commands for me to wait on him at Windsor Castle to-morrow, at half-past two, to present my book in person. I accordingly left Rugby by the midnight train, and came to London, sleeping, or rather going to bed, at the Euston Hotel.

" 29*th*.—Called at my chambers for some of the manuscripts to take down to Windsor.

" Went to Windsor by the one o'clock train. At the Castle I saw Mr. Glover, and asked him about the ceremony of being presented to the Prince, and said I doubted whether I ought to have appeared in a court dress. He replied, ' O Lord, no ! the less ceremony the better ; none is required with Prince Albert ; you will find him very affable and courteous.' I waited in a small room until a quarter past three, when an attendant announced that His Royal Highness was ready to see me. I was shown into a moderate-sized room, with a library table in the centre, and took the books and papers with me. The Prince was standing about the middle of the room ; he was quite plainly dressed in a dark frock-coat. When I came in, the servant announced my name. The Prince bowed twice, and I did the same, and after a brief pause His Royal Highness said, ' Mr. Harris, I suppose you have come to present me with your book.' I replied ' I had the honour of presenting the work to him, and had the more pleasure in doing so as His Royal Highness was

now a member of the same profession as myself;
that I hoped the contents would prove interesting,
that the part about the rebellion of 1745 would, I
thought, be so ; and that there was an original description of the battle of Culloden by Colonel Yorke, a son
of Lord Chancellor Hardwicke, who was aide-de-camp
to the Duke of Cumberland, and to whom the
Chancellor wrote frequently, giving an account of all
that was taking place, and to whom the son wrote in
return, describing the transactions in Scotland.'

" The Prince asked some questions as to the office held
by Colonel Yorke, and as to what part of the work the
account of this was contained in, to which I replied,
and then said, 'There are several matters of interest
relating to the royal family, especially conversations
recorded by Lord Hardwicke in his diary and letters
both with King George II. and also with Prince
Frederick and King George III.' I then read His
Royal Highness the dedication, which he took up
and read to himself, and I told him that 'I felt that
the only merit and force of the dedication was in
its truth, which not only I, but all the profession
to which I belonged, felt to be the case.' His Royal
Highness bowed, but made no remark. I then showed
him the plates. The portrait of Lord Hardwicke he
said he had looked at, and he read the autograph letter.
I then said that 'I regretted, owing to His Royal
Highness having had the kindness to honour me so
early with an interview, I had been unable to present
the work to him in a more handsome binding ; that I
had intended to have had it bound in red morocco in a
suitable manner, but found that, owing to its having
been so recently printed, it would not admit of that.'
The Prince remarked, 'I suppose, as it has been so
lately printed, it would not do to bind it.' I replied,

'No, sir ; I am informed it would spoil it, and bring
the ink off to the opposite page.' He then said, ' O
Mr. Harris, I look to the inside of a book, and not
to what is on the outside,' and praised the general
appearance of it. I then proceeded to show His
Royal Highness the manuscripts, and first gave him a
letter of Garrick's, which he read through, but made
no remark upon except 'Ha! ha!' and smiled, and
ooked pleased ; and in the same way he afterwards
read some of Lord Chatham's, President Montesquieu's,
and David Hume's—including the one about the
' court ladies,' whom Hume says King James termed
' a dangerous kind of cattle '—but His Royal Highness
made no remark.

"He afterwards glanced at other letters by the King
of Poland, Duke of Newcastle, Dr. Dodd, etc.

"I showed him Lord Chancellor Hardwicke's last
note-book of chancery cases, which he looked through,
and made some observations about a name which I
did not catch. I then read the concluding entry about
Lord Chancellor Hardwicke's giving up the Great Seal,
which he had held for nearly twenty years. I afterwards showed him some of the judgments. He asked
me ' how I managed to put them in the work, and if I
had given much of them.' I replied ' I had put them
at the end of each chapter, according to the time at
which they were delivered, so that any one might read
them or not as they liked, without the narrative being
broken.' His Royal Highness replied, ' That was a
very nice way.' I then said ' I had made the
Chancellor tell his own story as much as I could from
his own letters and diaries.' His Royal Highness
asked ' if there was any of his diary.' I replied
' there was.' He then asked ' if all the materials I
mentioned came from Wimpole.' I replied that ' they

did,' and said I believed that in different noblemen's houses in this country there was a rich collection of materials for history. He then said, 'I believe the Duke of Buckingham has the finest collection.' His Royal Highness then asked me 'how long I had been about the work.' I replied, 'Just three years.' He said, 'Oh, that is not very long.' His Royal Highness then said, 'Why, Mr. Harris, how is this? All the lawyers are writing history! There is Lord Campbell's book, and there is Lord Hardwicke's Life, and Lord Malmesbury's.' I bowed, and after a brief pause, he then took up the three volumes, and said, 'I thank you much, sir, for your present,' and bowed, and again said, 'I thank you, sir,' and again bowed, and left the room, and so the audience concluded.

"He is very pleasing, but his manner and accent are very foreign, much more so than I should have expected. Indeed, sometimes I could hardly understand him, and doubted whether he understood me.

"During our conversation he also asked some questions about Lord Campbell's 'Life of Lord Hardwicke.' I said 'I had contradicted several of Lord Campbell's statements from Lord Hardwicke's papers; that Lord Campbell had accused Lord Hardwicke of neglecting Dr. Birch, to whom he had given, or been the means of his being presented to, no less than nine livings; and that Lord Hardwicke had been accused of neglecting the poet Thomson, but who I had shown was writing against, and a political opponent of, the Government of which Lord Hardwicke was a member,' to which His Royal Highness merely replied, 'Indeed!'

"*31st.*—Went to Rugby. All much pleased with my agreeable interview with the Prince. Wrote on Wednesday evening to Lord Hardwicke, to inform him of the satisfactory termination of the interview with Prince Albert. In reply, he asks me to go to Wimpole on Wednesday, and says, 'I am glad the presentation went off so well.'"

CHAPTER XIII.

UPS AND DOWNS.

1848.

"January 6th.

"LEFT Rugby and came to Wimpole yesterday, calling at my chambers as I passed through London for the Hardwicke papers, which I brought down with me to Wimpole. Talked about book, but nothing said as to how it is liked or about reception by Prince. This morning I returned the papers to Lord Hardwicke. He said muniment-room was closed, and he could not let me in, as there were secrets there, which he afterwards laughed at, and explained to mean some presents he intended to give to his children in the evening, this being Twelfth Night. A grand banquet is to take place, and there are to be games in the evening. At my re-entering Lord Hardwicke's study after luncheon, he stopped me, and said there were such secrets, I could not be admitted. Some of his children with him, and all laughed very much. Possibly something is intended as a surprise on me by a present at these games, as I am invited the day before, and it seems odd nothing should be said if this not intended. Owing to illness of Lady Hardwicke, Christmas festivities were all postponed until to-night. A large party at dinner, and a grand display of plate, etc. We dined in the large hall. I was placed near the top, close to Lord Hardwicke. My health proposed by Lord.

Hardwicke, among other toasts, as a gentleman to whom they were much indebted for writing Life of the ancestor to whom they owed all their wealth and position. Returned thanks; spoke fluently; said undertaking very arduous, that the merit of my performance owing to value of the materials, and chief pleasure derived from kindness evinced by Lord and Lady Hardwicke, and proposed health of latter. A play acted in the evening, and lots drawn; mine a purse, but quite empty.

" 7th.—Lord Hardwicke out in the morning, but in the study with me all the afternoon. Read me a letter he had from Lord Campbell, who said he had read my book with great interest, and asked him to thank me for the handsome manner in which I had treated him whenever his name occurred. Talked with Lord Hardwicke generally about my book, which he thought very correctly printed, and that the character of the Chancellor much raised by it.

" 8th.—Lord Hardwicke at Cambridge all the morning, but returned in the afternoon, and came into his study for a short time, when I gave him up the key of the muniment-room, and told him I had put by all the papers. Never before at Wimpole was I so low, or even ever low; and this I fully anticipated to be my happiest visit !

" 10th.—Had a conversation with Lord Hardwicke in his study about papers just before leaving Wimpole; he wished me to complete sorting the papers soon. Returned to London to-day.

" 11th.—Dreadfully distressed at my poverty-stricken state. I have not a pound now left, and all sorts of demands on me. Called on G——, but he was out of town, also on B——. Wrote to Lord Hardwicke fully, as proposed, and applied to him to appoint me to the clerkship of the peace for Cambridgeshire when it became vacant.

"12*th*.—Awake during great part of every night lately, and horribly distressed thinking of my condition, and this morning meditating an abandonment of all my ambitious hopes, taking to conveyancing until I can get some appointment; but this afternoon more composed, Moxon said they sold twelve copies yesterday. All this has rather revived me after being all day down at Westminster, not so much to get briefs as to avoid duns.

"14*th*.—Congratulated by several barristers on the favourable notices of my book. Mellor to-day told me he thought I had 'no right to be dissatisfied with the way in which it had been reviewed.' H—— said newspaper reviewers hardly ever read the books they criticised, and that Sydney Smith used to say that was the only way to be impartial. B—— said Mr. S——, editor of the *Law Review*, approved of my dissertations and observed of remarks on legal education that 'though he did not agree with them, he thought book very ably done.'

"16*th*.—In the *Observer* of to-day a capital review of my book, in which they say that the work is worthy of the subject, that I have performed my task well, and that mine is not only the best Life of Lord Chancellor Hardwicke, but the best compilation of history relating to his times. Long extracts given from my original remarks. Greatly pleased at this, and hope now work in a fair way of success.

"17*th*.—Terribly dismayed this morning by a letter from Lord Hardwicke expressing astonishment at mine, and refusing to appoint me clerk of the peace, as he means to put in a leading solicitor. Thus my hopes of preferment and relief from pecuniary embarrassments are brought to the ground. What am I to do ? It is impossible I can remain in London, even as a conveyancer.

" 18*th*.—This morning a very favourable notice of my book in the *Law Times*, in which they commend my ability and accuracy, also a review in *Economist*, generally favourable. This evening B—— sent for me, saying he had a letter from Lord Brougham to show me. Mr. S——, the editor of the *Law Review*, some time ago wrote to Lord Brougham to ask him his opinion of my book. In a letter from Lord Brougham to S—— he omitted to refer to my book, but answered, S—— said, every other query, at which S—— was disappointed, but only hoped B —— was taking full time to consider. Yesterday S—— received the letter from Lord Brougham which he sent on to B——, entirely devoted to me and my book, in which he says it is very interesting ; he points out different portions of it, and comments on them. Says it is the most important work which has appeared for years, but thinks I commend Lord Hardwicke's oratory much too highly. Considers the materials used of great value, but says the book is also well done as a literary composition. B—— promises he will get me the original letter if he can.

" 20*th*.—Book does not sell at all. Moxon said not moving, and Stevens only sold one copy. No business of any kind. What am I to do ? Indeed, I have no London business at all. Quite distracted, and unable to settle to any kind of study.

" 22*nd*.—A good review of my book in the *Hull Packet*, and also in the *Britannia*.

" Wrote to Lee, who is to be consecrated Bishop of Manchester to-morrow, apologising for my non-attendance, congratulating him, telling him of success of book in reviews and of correspondence with Lord Hardwicke. A very satisfactory review of my book in the *Morning Chronicle* of Tuesday. A retainer to-day in a Nis Prius case at Derby, my first retainer.

" 29*th.*—Called on the Bishop of Manchester this morning. Found him just going to send off a letter to me, which he gave me, and in which he says, 'The book is well done. I wish I could review it, but time is, I fear, not to be had. On Thursday I did homage and stayed at the Castle. Nobody could be kinder than her Majesty and Prince Albert. If Lord Hardwicke employs you as his legal adviser, I hope that may lead to good. I expect more from him *indirectly* than directly as regards the book.'

"I showed the Bishop Lord Brougham's letter, in which he says, 'I have run over Mr. Harris's volumes with the greatest pleasure. It is a very valuable book, and he deserves (as well as Lord Hardwicke) great praise for so important a contribution to legal history.' He then criticises some of my remarks, and concludes by saying of the book, 'It is the very first in value that has for a long time appeared. However, I say nothing against its execution being good.' It is indeed con- solatory, and, in fact, now matters are quite changed as regards my apprehensions and misgivings which I felt on Tuesday, January 11th, and even now, should I be attacked and abused in some quarters (as the Bishop of Manchester told me I ought to expect), I need not be dismayed.

"A review of me in the *Law Magazine*, strongly condemning Lord Hardwicke as a very commonplace character, whom I have very unworthily extolled. They, however, say of me, 'Mr. Harris, we would fain hope, has talent for the composition of a far more stalwart work than this.' A favourable review in the *Tablet*, in which I am complimented for fairness. My work is termed a 'pleasant biographer,' and the book is generally commended. Also a favourable review in the *New Monthly.* In the *Law Review* I am noticed in a long article, generally favourable, and several original portions are extracted, but I am said to be too fond of the sublimities of commonplace ; it remarked that there are several pages of truisms, and that I am in some observations behind my age.

" *February* 3*rd.*—The abject misery and wretchedness I have lately gone through is past the possibility of all endurance. Lord Hardwicke and the book sustained me for some time ; now my last hold has given way, and down I am plunged. Some course I must adopt : either take at once to literature and make an income by that, or give up chambers and retire to Rugby, practising conveyancing.

" *7th.*—Moxon said Disraeli had talked to him about my book. Said it was almost the last book his father had read ; that he had been much pleased with it, but disapproved of the introduction of the parts about Jack Sheppard ; that materials very interesting, but not skilfully used ; that the book should have been not a Life of Lord Hardwicke, but 'The Hardwicke Papers,' comprising a history of the time. This, however, would never have satisfied Lord Hardwicke or the publishers, or done for me. It would have been like an architect building a church or town hall on a gentleman's estate when he was instructed to build a mansion. There are doubtless great defects in writing the work, especially in length, owing mainly to the manner in which I was obliged to compose it, not seeing any of the Wimpole papers until so late, then being only allowed a glance at them at Wimpole, instead of having them all before me, and only during the last half-year being allowed to take them away, and then merely a portion at a time.

" 17*th.*—A letter from Harrison Ainsworth this morning, saying he hoped to see me to dinner when I returned from the circuit and to make my acquaintance, when we could arrange about my becoming a continuous contributor to the *New Monthly*.

" 8*th.*—Passed a most dreadful night, hardly any sleep, but lay in a sort of doze, fancying I was flying from persecutors, who were hard after me, now and then awaking, and tortured by reflecting on my miserable condition.

" A very good, copious, and complimentary review of my book in the *Morning Herald* of yesterday, extending over four columns, and announcing that it is to be continued.

"31*st.*—At length reduced to the lowest desperation. Practice lost ; book unsalable ; purse penniless. Passed a most horrible night. Awoke between two and three, and unable to get to sleep again until near five, then dozing and dreaming about executions and wretched state. Thinking all day of the disgrace I should incur and the severe loss I should sustain if my books should be seized for debt, books so carefully selected and full of my own notes and works and choice engravings. It is most distressing. I really am now quite on the brink of ruin, and worried most acutely, and how to obtain relief God only knows. Mr. Grantham Yorke told me to-day that the family were much pleased with my book, and that he thought the character of the Chancellor never stood so high before, but wished me to introduce as an appendix a memoir of the late Lord Royston, which the Bishop of Manchester mentioned to me yesterday.

" *April 8th.*—On Monday went to Warwick to hear

Guttridge's trial for libel on Bishop of Manchester, and saw the Bishop.

"A capital review of my book of twenty pages in *Blackwood*, in which they say, 'The biography is vigorous, intelligent, and remarkably interesting,' and that it is essential to the historians of George II.'s time, though with one or two observations they find fault.

" 12*th*.—Dreadfully annoyed this afternoon by a letter from G——, my clerk. Wrote to my clerk, saying I would be in London to-morrow.

" 15*th*.—First day of term. How different a day from what this is usually with me.

" 18*th*.—Felt in morning much revived after a good night's sleep, which I have not had for some time, and am rejoiced in prospect of relief by some help from my father, but annoyed on calling on Moxon to find him in a great stew about my book. Says he quite despairs of its succeeding, as I almost do of my own success. I never on the whole at any time felt so desponding as to my future career as I do at present. A general shipwreck of all ambitious hopes seems to have occurred.

" 22*nd*.—Feel disposed to adopt real property law as my main professional pursuit and go into House of Lords and Chancery on appeals, etc., and drew out plan of course accordingly.

"26*th*.—Dined at Lord Denman's ; a small party : Mr. Justice Erle, Mr. Warren, Mr. Taylor, Mr. Joseph Brown, Lady C. Lindsay, Mrs. Opie, and Lord Denman's own family ; very pleasant. Lord Denman came up to and sat by me and chatted when I arrived. Talked about Guttridge and the Midland Circuit, etc., but did not allude to my book. Almost as low now as I can be, and I suppose the lowest grade is inevitable—

that of throwing myself upon, and living on, my friends.

"*May 6th.*—I this day enter on a new year of my life, and commence the fortieth of that; and Saturday is the day of the week on which I was born. The year past has not been an uneventful one, though, on the whole, undoubtedly unprosperous. Nevertheless, one step in my progress has been made.

"Lord Chancellor Hardwicke's Life has been completed, and published, and reviewed, and, on the whole, I believe my reputation has to a considerable extent been established by it, which was the grand point, after all, to be gained. Called on Moxon, who said Wordsworth's works were hard to move at first, but in time they sold every copy.

"*14th.*—Dined at Mr. Harrison Ainsworth's, who was very civil, but nothing passed about my engaging in any literary work for him.

"*July 8th.*—A favourable review of Lord Hardwicke's Life in *Westminster Review*, in which they extract several passages of my original remarks, and say 'considerable ability' in some of them.

"*August 3rd.*—At Coventry Assizes yesterday and to-day. Had three briefs: one from B——, in which prisoner pleaded guilty, and two from W——, for robberies.

"*4th.*—Had one brief at Warwick from W—— and S——, in which the prisoner pleaded guilty. Held a junior brief in a Mint case, with Sir Eardley Wilmot. Not nervous at all."

CHAPTER XIV.

MARRIAGE AND MARRIED LIFE.

1848.

"*August 6th.*

"FOR a long time I have been deliberating within myself whether to resolve to remain a bachelor for life or to marry.

"My first determination when a youth was to marry as soon as I could, and I then thought there was no real happiness to be had without it. But as ambitious desires arose, and I determined to quit Rugby and go to the bar, I was obliged to relinquish these hopes as interfering with my prospects of rising in the world, resolved to remain a bachelor for life. Recently, however, I have felt some indecision on this point, and my general determination has been to marry as soon as I could afford to do so, if it would be no hindrance to my professional and general prospects, and if a suitable person could be selected. The want of a companion and confidential friend I have much felt of late, and am persuaded I should still more experience it if I had a residence in the country, as I desire. I do also greatly feel the want of a house of my own, and an associate to whom I can always resort and enjoy society with.

"Matters being arranged, I have become more than ever desirous of settling myself; and the present period seems the most fitting. On Whit Sunday (June 11th) I surveyed amply, and very fully deliberated on, my whole condition and prospects, and after due examination and consideration I resolved that if this could be attained, I would marry at once, and that Elizabeth

Innes, being morally and intellectually well suited to
me, of cultivated mind, good principles, excellent disposition, and companionable habits, and also of agreeable person, moreover possessing fortune enough to
prevent our union being any hindrance to my prospects, should be selected as the object of my choice.
This resolution I adopted, entered on my journal,
but afterwards abandoned. I, however, each day until
the 22nd of June, deliberated fully upon it, when I
finally resolved to carry out my design. On Tuesday,
June 27th, Miss Innes paid a visit to Rugby, and spent
part of the day with us, when I walked with her to the
railway and confirmed fully my resolution during the
time I was with her. On the 29th of June I wrote
her a letter, telling her that I was now desirous of
being settled in life ; that I knew of no one to whom I
should so much desire to be united as herself, who was
in all respects suitable to me ; that the Bishop of Manchester and some of my own family had observed this.
My own income, I told her, was small, though I hoped
increasing, and I offered to settle her own fortune
entirely on herself; and in case my offer was not accepted,
I begged it might be kept secret. In a few days a letter
arrived, expressing surprise at mine, thanking me for
my proposal, but declining it as unable to meet my
wishes. As it appeared undecided in its terms, I
wrote again, but another reply, still more undecided,
coming, though still negative, I proposed to return
the correspondence and close the matter irrevo-
cably. This was acceded to, and my letters were
sent back, but with a long one accompanying them so
undecidedly expressed that I wrote again after a few
days, on the 12th July, and again pressed my
suit. A new correspondence then ensued, the proposal being declared worthy of consideration, and a

change of mind to some extent announced, several very candid and friendly confidential letters passed. One morning I breakfasted by invitation at my lady's house, and spent two hours with her alone, and by arrangement in the evening met her at Mrs. W——'s, and afterwards had tea at her own house, when we talked over matters fully, and she invited me to tea on a subsequent evening. Then, subject to a few conditions which I know can be fulfilled, more especially the consent of my own family to the union, the matter was arranged between us, so that I am now at last in effect and morally a MARRIED MAN.

" I really solemnly declare that I know of no one in all respects so entirely suitable to me as Elizabeth Innes, who has so many of the qualifications I require, and so few disqualifications ; and of all those I can think of she certainly on the whole seems the most desirable for me, the most perfectly adapted to me, and a union with whom promises to be fraught with permanent advantage and prosperity, and also real comfort and happiness. This is the greatest event of an eventful year, or which has for very long, or indeed ever, befallen me. In a professional point it will make no difference, except that I shall now be able and shall determine to carry out to the full my long-resolved course of proceeding.

" *7th.*—Lunched and spent an hour with Elizabeth Innes. She said the Bishop of Manchester had proposed the matter to her, as he had done to me, and that some of the Warwick people accused her of looking after me.

" *12th.*—Wrote on Tuesday to Elizabeth. On Thursday I had an answer, intimating that she consented to become my wife. For the comfort of married life and the society of a suitable companion I do much long, and would willingly give up the luxuries of club and Temple and bachelorism for this.

"Appointed a commissioner for inquiring into exchange of Elborow charity lands for some of Mr. Boughton Leigh's, and at work in perusing abstracts, etc., which will enable me, I hope, to pay off a large portion of pressing liabilities this vacation.

"*14th.*—Proposed taking a house on Hampstead Heath, which I had looked at ; the house has a nice garden at the back of it, so that here I do think I could obtain nearly all I want in a country house, and with a certainty in income and an intellectual companion with whom I can enjoy confidential and social intercourse, I ought to be as happy and comfortable as I could desire. The way in which the matter has been conducted ensures, too, the fullest consideration of comfort and permanent advantage being promoted by it ; for match-making at forty is very differently conducted and considered from match-making at fourteen. But, after all, the former mode is the most rational if permanent happiness and comfort are sought.

"*September 23rd.*—Wrote a letter to my mother, to be delivered after I am gone to London on Monday, informing her of my intention to be married, 'which,' I said, 'has not been resolved on without the fullest consideration and deliberation, and which will, I trust, be productive of the happiness that it promises.' I also said that E. 'appears to be in every way most suitable to me,' and that I hoped she and my father would on reflection approve of the step I am about to take.

"*26th.*—A letter from my mother, saying the announcement has given her and my father 'the most *entire* satisfaction,' and that she thinks I am 'very fortunate in having engaged the affections of one whose good sense and Christian principles' she has ever most highly valued, and that she shall *most cordially* welcome her as a member of our family.

" 30*th*.—Met E. at the Euston station yesterday, and brought her on to Ashbury, the rectory of my uncle, the Rev. W. Chambers, B.D., where we have passed our time together most agreeably and satisfactorily, and find her in every respect all I could wish, and we appear to suit in our plans and notions exactly.

" *October* 2*nd*.—At Ashbury, walking about with E. over the downs, etc., talking together and settling our plans. Find her all I could wish. In our views and notions about my rising in my profession, having a house out of town, going abroad together in the summer, and in all other respects we seem to suit exactly.

" 5*th*.—Left Ashbury on Tuesday and came to Oxford, staying at Magdalen College with Tom and Henry. E. gone to Bath to stay with the Millses.

" 23*rd*.—E. received a letter from the Bishop of Manchester, saying he would marry us, as he promised her he would do before I proposed to her, if ever the marriage did take place.

" *November* 11*th*.—Returned to London. Thompson told me at dinner that Sir Frederick Pollock was staying with Sir Robert Peel during the long vacation, and that Sir Robert Peel told him (the Chief Baron), on his retiring to bed rather early, that if he wished to amuse himself he should read Lord Hardwicke's Life, which he gave to him, and in which he said he had been much interested. Lord Hardwicke, I know, sent Sir R. Peel a copy on its being published. Sir R. Peel also told Sir F. Thesiger he had been much pleased with the work.

" 23*rd*.—No reply having come yet, F. tells me, from the Bishop of Manchester fixing the day, I wrote to him to-day, saying, ' We are all most anxious to hear that the proposed *happy day* will suit with your numerous engagements, for I do assure you I look forward with great pleasure and satisfaction to meeting you on that occasion, and it will be very gratifying that so important a ceremony, and one through which I am hoping for so much happiness, should be performed by one from whom I have long been in the habit of receiving so many marks of personal kindness.'

"*December 9th.*—In a letter which I wrote to E. to-day, I told her that as this was probably the last letter of our correspondence that I should address to her before we were united, I could not conclude it without assuring her how greatly in *every* respect my opinion of her had been raised by her letters to me, and of the sincerity of my devotion to her, the truth of which I here solemnly avow, as also my determination to fulfil to the utmost the solemn and sacred duties on which I am about to enter, in the contemplation of which I must also bear in mind the implicit and unreserved and unhesitating confidence which Elizabeth has placed in me in thus giving herself entirely to me and the sacrifices in many respects of ease and comfort which she must make in doing so, and at which no murmuring or repining on her part has been uttered. I believe her to be thoroughly and sincerely not only attached, but devoted, to me, and it surely ought to be by no fault of mine that our union does not produce all the happiness that it promises.

"*11th.*—Came this morning from Ashbury with my father and mother, Edmund and my uncle, to Bath, preparatory to the wedding, which is to take place to-morrow morning, in Bathwick Church, at half-past nine, my uncle officiating for the Bishop of Manchester, who is prevented from attending.

"*13th.*—The marriage was duly solemnised yesterday at the Bathwick Church, my uncle, Mr. Chambers, officiating, and my father and mother, and Edmund, and Mr. and Mrs. Henry Mills, and Elizabeth's cousin, Miss Hazeland, being present. Henry Mills acted as the bride's father, and Miss F. Hazeland as bridesmaid. Nothing could go off in every respect more satisfactorily or more happily than did this eventful day ; and soon after the ceremony, we, 'the happy pair,' came to Ashbury, where we are enjoying ourselves until to-morrow, when my uncle is to return, and we are to proceed to London, thence to Hastings for a week, then to Mrs. Liptrott's at Findon, and after that, I suppose, to London, where I must resume, with all the ardour and assiduity I can summon, my professional duties according to *course*. A letter of apology yesterday morning from the Bishop of Manchester to me, saying it was quite out of his power to be at Bath, and assuring us he much regretted it, and was heartily vexed at the disappointment. Arrived at Hastings on Friday. Much enjoy the sea and the scenery. Talking with E. about myself and the opinions people have entertained of me, about which I have often been puzzled, and as to whether I was considered clever or dull and wise or foolish, but from which I glean that I have been generally regarded as clever, but very frivolous and volatile. E. said she told the Bishop of Manchester, when he proposed to her to marry me, that 'she did not think I had one grave thought in my head.' Others have remarked that they thought there was more below the surface than what appeared. And yet I, who have been thus regarded as frivolous and addicted only to trifling pursuits, have during the period I acquired this character been really engaged in the gravest and most serious studies and reflections and preparing my grand work, the 'Treatise on Man,' as well as other treatises of deep thought and reflection, for publication. This proves to me at least how little people really know of other persons character and turn of mind.

"At church in the morning, and received the Sacrament with E., and truly grateful for the many favours and blessings which now surround me. Our Christmas dinner we ate by ourselves, but could not have wished for better company to enjoy our plum-pudding.

"*30th.*—Came to Worthing on Wednesday, and stayed with Mrs. W—— until Friday afternoon, when we came on to Findon to Mrs. Liptrott's, where we now are most kindly and hospitably received by both."

CHAPTER XV.

ON CIRCUIT AND AT HOME.

1849—1852.

"*January 4th.*

"WE returned to London in the afternoon, very glad to get settled, though we have enjoyed our trip and the hospitality of our kind friends very much. All my epistles are congratulatory, and several of them speak warmly, and I believe I may now say from experience truthfully, of my great good fortune in having got such a wife.

"*6th.*—Went about a house in Queen Square, which I like the look of, and it is of sufficient importance and character to give me a standing. It is better to have one quite convenient as regards the Temple and Westminster, as we must defer having one out of town, until I can purchase a rural retreat.

"*February* 10th.—Agreed on Monday for the house No. 19, Queen Square.

"11th.—My experience of wedded life is now mature,

and I really think I may say I have gained all I could
hope for, and have experienced hardly any of the
drawbacks I apprehended. Our real love for each
other increases day by day; and I am sure it is much
greater than the day we married, though I believe
I then distrusted rather myself than my wife. My
condition is, indeed, now most satisfactory, and I trust
I am grateful, as I ought to be, for all this to Provi-
dence.

"*March* 10th.—Went to Northampton for the
assizes in the evening.

"12th.—Letter from E., who has been as good to
me as a correspondent as she has been in every other
way. Wrote to her, and told her that 'I assure you I
do not in the least doubt your determination to do
everything to make me happy, and feel myself most
fortunate in having got such a wife.'

"20th.—Went on Wednesday to the Coventry
Sessions. Had only one brief, which was from H——
and S—— against a prisoner for robbing the poor's
gardens at Rugby, and in which case I had great
doubts of succeeding, but the evidence came out well.
I elicited more than in brief, and was successful. A
little nervous and anxious about this case. Immediately
after it ended on Thursday, I went to Warwick to the
borough sessions, where were four cases for trial, out
of which I had two briefs. M—— observed to-day at
breakfast at Coventry (where I came yesterday for the
assizes), 'Since Harris has been married he has taken
to the profession in real earnest, and there will be no
standing against him!' A great libel case, Lord Leigh
against Griffin, which would have suited me well to
have led in on either side. W——, Q.C., who appeared
for the prosecution, singularly ineloquent and tame.

"During progress of trial drew a caricature entitled

'Ye Ghost or Apparytyon of Mystress Sarah Small-bones,' being a portrait of an old woman who spoke to the terrible disclosure made by this worthy before her decease. My sketch much laughed at, and handed about. Composed also during the assizes the following distich, which was handed about the court and much laughed at: 'Addition to Porson's "Devil's Walk"' (on seeing M—— hand a sandwich to B—— in court):—

> " ' When he saw old M——, with a look so kind,
>   Give to old B—— some meat and some bread,
>   The devil smiled, for it put him in mind
>   Of Elijah by ravens fed.'

"Dined on Thursday with E. at Mr. Justice Patteson's. The Archbishop of Canterbury (Sumner) there. E. sat by him. Very unassuming and retiring, but much more like a Dissenting preacher than a prelate.

"*July 8th.*—On Monday I went to the Warwick Sessions. Had no brief that day, but on Tuesday morning had one. The borough sessions in the afternoon. Four prisoners for trial. I had three of the cases. At Coventry had two cases. Had also some briefs to hold: three for Sir E. W—— and one for Spooner. Got well through all the cases, though the last one was of considerable difficulty, and the brief only put into my hand just before the trial came on. Not nervous, or more so than in general conversation in a large party, beyond which I hardly hope to get. It was mentioned at dinner at Warwick by Mr. P—— that he recollected Lord Lyndhurst at sessions, but that he never did much either there or on circuit, *he was so nervous.* My best sessions; made nine guineas.

"At the Leicester Assizes. Sent a paper to the circuit court entitled 'Mr. Pips, his Diary,' being an imaginary journal of a visitor to the assize court here,

containing a description of each of the leading counsel.
It was read out by the Recorder after dinner, and took
very well indeed, exciting great applause and laughter.
The thanks of the circuit were voted to me for it, and
it was ordered to be copied into the record book.
H——, Q.C., said it was the best presentment that
had been made for twenty years. Several copies of it
taken.

"'Mr. Pips, his Diary.*

"'*Julie* 25.—Atte Leicester this daie. Offe to ye
Assizes betymes. A valliant arraye of Counsellors
aboute ye Courte, whose hungrie lookes and greedie
cravings after ye briefes that are handed aboute doe
well betoken ye barrennesse in ye law that now pre-
vaileth. Among ye Counselle I noticed a most grave
and reverende manne, one Mister W—— ; and besyde
him satte another of goodlie aspecte, butte of fierce
demeanour and speeche, named H——, whose loude
tones doe startle betymes ye slumbering juryman from
his dreames.

"'But ye choyce wonder of ye Courte this daie was
ye greate Sir Frederick T——, from Londonne, a most
brave speaker, with a marvellously noble aspect and
bearinge, and who did looke arounde him and on his
adversaries lyke a bayted lyon. Among ye herde who
do frequente ye Assizes in these partes, and there was
pointed out to me a right cunninge and most wary
counselle, one M—— ; but ye onlie flowre that he doth
grinde is much flowre of speeche ; and his action, too, in
his vocation, doth ofttimes betoken his trayde, as when
one grindeth atte a handmill. Soe marvellous albeit is
his subtletie and addresse, that no longe tyme agoe he did
fullie persuade ye unwarie Jury at Warwicke Sessions
that a poore Ducke, which a hungry clowne had stolen

and slayne, did of its owne accorde and free-will com-
mitte suicide, insomuch that ye simple Jury did return
a verdicte of *felo de se* agaynst ye Ducke, instead of
guilty agaynst ye Clowne. Nighe unto this M—— satte
one M——, whom my Ladie, in her wantonnesse, did
nickname Mister Fayre-speeche, and of whose smyles
I did overheare my giddie daughter remarke that they
would bewytch ye hartes of a female Jury right sure.
Mister M—— was ofttymes prompted in ye case by one
B——, a ladde of goodlie promise. But itt did some-
tymes fall out that these two were opposed in their
pleadings one to ye other, and thence ye conteste did
make me thinke on ye combatte betwixte Goliath of
Gath and ye shepherd boye David. Of ye Dignytaries
that minister aboute ye affaires of ye Courte, one
H——, ye attorney-generall of ye Circuitte, is ye
chiefe, a right merrie and conceited manne, and fulle
of myrthe and gladdnesse. Ye Chaplaine of ye Circuite
is ye reverende Mister F——, concerninge whose
sermonne respecting ye rich manne and Lazarus I did
heare much commendation; butte methought ye subjecte
ill-tymed, toe preache on such a grievouse topicke, when
there appeareth soe little feare of riches besetting ye
poore followers of ye Barre. Two counsellors of
wondrous bignesse satte over agaynste where I did
stande; yette such plumpnesse, I trowe, dothe butte ill
accorde with ye barrennesse of ye times.'

"31*st*.—At Coventry Assizes on Saturday. Had
two briefs, one for arson. Conducted the case before
Baron Parke. Not at all nervous. Case clear, and
prisoner convicted. In the other trial the prisoner
pleaded guilty. Only twenty-four cases; about twenty-
five barristers. At Warwick yesterday and to-day. I
had two briefs. In one of the cases I had to prosecute
three gipsies—a wedding party, being the bride and

bridegroom and a third lady, a bridesmaid, I suppose—
for stealing a couple of fowls on the morning of the
wedding to supply the wedding dinner, and which were
being cooked in a lane, when a policeman ungallantly
came up and took the fowls out of the pot and the
bridal party into custody.   The head of one of the
chickens was discovered in the bridegroom's breeches
pocket.   They all pleaded guilty, and were sentenced
to spend the honeymoon in *Bride*-well.   In the other
case, which was a *capital* offence, being for stealing a
hat, the prisoner pleaded guilty.   My belief is that I
shall ' come out ' well in a suitable case some day or
other, and so establish myself at once, in order to
do which I must be thoroughly fortified and well
prepared to maintain my ground when I have once
occupied it.

" *August* 18*th*.—After the Warwick Assizes came to
Oxford, and met our Rugby party at dinner at Magdalen,
with Tom and Henry.   Proceeded from Oxford to Brad-
field, and stayed a few days with John Marriott.   Came
to Ashbury on Monday last.   Occupied lately in designing the plan of my proposed domain near London,
for which I have gathered hints of great variety from
places recently visited, and of which I have made a
sketch.

" A review in the *Leamington Courier* of the 18th
of last month of my ' Life of Lord Chancellor Hardwicke,' extending to nearly two columns.   Praise it
much, and extract from my original matter, particularly
my winding up at the end and the character of Lord
Somers.   Commend style and descriptive powers.   A
letter the other day from Charles Hume, in which he
says with reference to my Life of Lord Hardwicke,
' I really feel entire satisfaction in your very full and
interesting biography of the great Chancellor ; it seems

to possess that true mark of perfectness that neither
addition nor change can find place in it.'

"A note the other day from Mr. Justice Patteson,
thanking me for my Life of Lord Hardwicke, which
I sent him in the summer, and telling me that he
'took it with him into Devonshire during the vacation,
and read every word of it with the greatest satisfaction.'

"*November* 12*th.*—My three great works are now
all written. The first treats of *man* as an *individual*,
the second of the development through *art* of his
highest faculty, the third of *man* in the *aggregate*
and his perfection through *civilisation*. The last
serves to unite the others with my professional studies.

1850.

"*March* 6*th.*—Came to Northampton on Tuesday
morning. I had not any brief, but this afternoon,
about five, as I was going away, F—— asked me to
hold a brief for him for the defence of two poachers.
Delighted to have such a case, though not time to read
the brief before the case began, which was called on
before I had the brief. Sir E. W—— for the prosecution. I cross-examined the witnesses pretty effectively,
and addressed the jury with some spirit in a short
speech, making several points, and without any hesitation, and Parke, in summing up, adverted freely to the
points in my argument. A dead case, and prisoners
convicted, but fully satisfied with my efforts and very
glad to have got so well through this my first defence
case.

"23*rd.*—Wrote a leading article for B—— on
proposed abolition of trial by jury, entitled 'The Last
Attack on our National Privileges.'

"30*th.*—Had one brief at Leicester. Prisoners

pleaded guilty, but I had to make a short address to
my rival biographer, Lord Campbell, on recommending
them to mercy. At Coventry Thursday, Friday, and
to-day. Had six briefs there. Three of the briefs
important cases for three burglaries against three
prisoners. Conducted another case, a common
robbery in a shop, before Baron Parke, well and
successfully. Next case was the principal burglary;
a great many witnesses; got pretty well through the
examinations, though the judge interfered several
times, and expressed his opinion that the evidence
was very slight, and directed an acquittal against two
of the prisoners. The third was convicted of stealing
only, as Judge thought evidence of burglary not
sufficient. The second case conducted in the same
manner, and with the same result, though against the
Judge's wish, who said when I proposed to go on with
it, as I thought the case stronger than against the
acquitted prisoners, 'Why didn't you put your right
leg foremost?' In the third case I obeyed Parke's
intimation, and declined to offer evidence.

"In both cases the evidence came out well and
stronger than in the briefs. Conducted another case
before Lord Campbell for stealing barley, the principal
witness being a labouring man, who was stupid and
confused. The evidence, however, was deemed sufficient, and the prisoner was convicted. Not very
nervous in either of the cases, though the two burglaries
really perplexing, especially from having the judge so
decidedly against me.

"*April* 13*th*.—Came to Warwick for the assizes on
Monday, the 1st inst. Had only one brief, which was
for another burglary. Conducted the case, which was
undefended, before Lord Campbell. The evidence
came out well, and prisoners convicted of the entire

charge. Held a brief in a defended case for a highway
robbery belonging to H——, which Sir E. W——
gave me. R—— defended. I opened the case
briefly, and got well through it, but prisoners convicted
of a common assault only.

"In a case sent me by Archibald, as there appeared
no possibility of successfully defending it, I recommended the prisoner to plead guilty, much against my
interest, as it would have been a capital case for cross-
examination and for an address. But the course I
adopted was the surest mode to save him from transportation, and by this he got only a year's imprisonment. So my conscience, instead of my reputation,
was accommodated here. On Tuesday we dined at the
judges' chambers, when H—— introduced me specially
to Lord Campbell, who shook hands with me very
cordially, and said, 'I believe we have met before on
another arena,' and asked me to take wine with him at
dinner—the only junior he invited. He was remarkably courteous in court to all the circuit.

"On Wednesday I was at the Coventry Sessions.
Had two briefs. Both rather doubtful cases, but convicted in both. In one case the prisoner was a quack
doctor, and his crime consisted in picking patients'
pockets who had taken, not too much medicine, but too
much ale. Yesterday I went to the Birmingham
Sessions. Had one brief. The prisoner defended by
M——, but convicted for obtaining goods under false
pretences, so this ended well my circuit and sessions
career for this time, by which I have made a little more
than twenty guineas, and a little more than paid my
expenses.

"*24th.*—B—— told me to-day that my article on
'The Shuttlecock Ministry,' which appeared in the *Bucks
Herald*, was 'received in Aylesbury with uproarious

applause.' Wrote him another in the same style, entitled ' Bulletin of the Ministry,' comparing its condition to that of a dying man.

" *May 6th.*—In the prospectus contained in the advertisements of the *Quarterly Review* of Lord Campbell's ' Lives of the Chief Justices ' is a long extract from my review of it in the *Britannia*—the only critique quoted.

" 12*th.*—To-day I went to the Roman Catholic church in St. George's Fields, to hear Dr. Wiseman preach on the Pope's supremacy as contrasted with the royal, in reference to Gorham's case. Not so eloquent as I expected, but very argumentative and subtle. A 'Te Deum' was afterwards sung for the Pope's return to Rome. The interior of the cathedral, especially about the altar, very magnificent. In his sermon Wiseman said there were now two grand causes of rejoicing : the Pope's return to Rome and the disruption of the English Church. The question of baptismal regeneration, he argued, was a cardinal point of the faith. He read extracts from the correspondence between Mr. Maskell and the Archbishop of Canterbury, and said he wished the former had asked the Archbishop his opinion of the royal supremacy, and alluded to the constitution of the Judicial Committee of the Privy Council. He concluded with a peroration in which he declared that, like an earthquake, the late revolutions had shaken to their centre the Powers of Europe, but Pope Pius IX., like St. Peter, had his prison burst open and his chains shaken off, and walked forth, uninjured by this convulsion, out of his prison, while the Church of England was not only laid prostrate, but had her arms chained to her side.

" My first article on ' The Threatened Universities Commission ' appeared in to-day's *Britannia.* Composed

two others to follow, which are more effective
and telling, I think, especially the parts parodying
Macaulay's description of the proceedings of James II.'s
commissioners at Oxford and the account of the
Bedford property which, stolen from the Church, and
charged with the Government estimates, was never
paid.

"*July 2nd.*—At Warwick Sessions yesterday and
to-day. Had two prosecutions. A person from Birmingham brought a brief to me, and inquired for
O'Brien, who does not attend these sessions, and
afterwards asked me to take it. It was to defend a
prisoner for stealing a gun. Several of the barristers
who read the brief thought I could not succeed in it.
F——— prosecuted, and opened the case very fairly. My
brief contained merely a copy of the depositions, but I
cross-examined with some effect, and addressed the
jury with spirit and fluency, never hesitating for a word,
and dwelt on each point I intended quite as well as I
could have done in a speech by myself. The Chairman,
Mr. Dickens, in summing up, alluded to the points I
had dwelt upon, and said he thought the case too
doubtful to convict upon, on which the jury acquitted
the prisoner. My most important case, and my best
conducted.

"*6th.*—At Coventry Sessions Wednesday and
Thursday. Had three briefs. Much shocked this
week by the melancholy death of Sir Robert Peel,
whom I often saw, and who of late looked younger than
formerly.

"A review by E. on 'Common Sense for House-
maids' appeared in the *Britannia* to-day. It reads
well, is really very sensible, and is racy and piquant.

"*August 3rd.*—At Leicester Tuesday, Wednesday,
and Thursday. Had nothing to do, but was appointed

attorney-general of the circuit court during Haye's absence, and acquitted myself, I think, well. Conducted two State prosecutions before them. Sent in a present-ment, which was much cheered, and drew up a bur-lesque report of the convivialities. At Coventry Assizes yesterday and to-day. Had two prosecution briefs. About eighteen prisoners and thirty bar-risters.

" 18*th.*—At Warwick until Friday morning, but had only one brief, which I conducted before Platt.

" *October* 12*th.*—Proposed to offer my ' Legal Evidence of Idiocy and Insanity both in Civil and Criminal Cases ' to Cox to print and divide profits, and to offer him also 'Historical Gleanings' for the *Critic*, if he will pay for it after *Law Times* rate.

" *November* 9*th.*—Wrote an elaborate and, I think, conclusively reasoned article, which appeared in the *Law Times* to-day, respecting the illegality of the maintenance of the Pope's jurisdiction in this country and its liability to punishment by law. It is the best thing of the sort I have done, is quite in the judicial style, and revives all my lately damped ambitious professional aspirations.

" 30*th.*—The Professorship of Common Law at King's College is now vacant, for which E. wants me to become a candidate. I should much like the appoint-ment. Had a long chat with the Bishop of Manchester about my offering to hold the professorship, which he seemed to think unadvisable on the whole, as it would lead to nothing, bring in nothing, and occupy so much time.

" *December* 12*th.*—I am now in all respects as com-pletely comfortable, happy, and well off as I could fairly hope or desire. Every day I see more and more to value in her whom I am so truly happy and fortunate as to call my own, and whose genuine high principles, excellent disposition, and superior mind, render her to me of 'a price far above rubies.'

" 14th.—Cox told me the other day that my article on the Supremacy had been read out from beginning to end at the great Protestant meeting in Liverpool ; and that one of the county newspapers had copied it at length, and others extracted from it. He thought the law was quite correct as laid down by me.

" 23rd —In an article I wrote for the *County Courts Chronicle*, ' On the Union of the Functions of Adviser and Advocate,' I introduced the story of Thelwall sending a note to Erskine just before his trial came on to say he should conduct his own case. Erskine wrote back, ' If you do, you will be *hanged.*' Thelwall replied, ' Then I'll be hanged if I do.'

" 24th.—Paton the other day in a letter to me describing his visit at Wimpole told me, ' In the evening the conversation occasionally, or rather I should say often, turned on my labours, or on the Lord Chancellor Hardwicke, or on his biographer Mr. Harris, amidst which the esteem in which they held you was every way discernible. The Countess talked of you frequently, with evident feelings of respect.'

" 28th.—The *Law Times* of to-day mentions that Sir E. Sugden's opinion on the Roman Catholic question, as delivered at the Surrey meeting, exactly agrees with and confirms that of Mr. G. Harris contained in their columns.

1851.

" *January* 4th.—At Coventry Sessions. In a case which I conducted, the prisoner being defended by F—— —evidence very slight—was acquitted. F——

made a vehement attack on an unfortunate schoolboy on account of a variance in his testimony, from which I vindicated him. Mr. W—— told me I should speak as well as F—— if I had a bottle of wine in me. They all say I want brass and pluck.

"*April 20th.*—I wrote lately, while at Rugby, to Lord Brougham suggesting that in the Bill for giving equitable jurisdiction to the county courts the administration of small trust estates under deeds and wills might advantageously be placed under the control of these courts, especially as to the investment of trust funds, and that a certificate of the county court judge approving of such investment ought to be made to discharge the trustees from all personal liabilities.

"The letter I have embodied in an article in the forthcoming number of the *County Courts Chronicle*, entitled 'Projects for the Extension of the County Court System.' On my return to London I found a letter from Lord Brougham, in which he requests me 'to accept his best thanks for the very useful suggestions in his [my] letter.' He promises to forward me a copy of the Bill, that I may see how far my views are met by it and may make suggestions upon it, and he alludes to the passage of and opposition to the Bill in the House of Lords. He concludes, 'Lord Brougham takes this opportunity of thanking Mr. Harris for the great pleasure and instruction which he received from reading his most valuable and interesting Life of Lord Hardwicke.' Several of my friends urge upon me to apply for a county court judgeship, for which they think I have a fair chance, and might obtain.

"Went to a large party at Cox's on Wednesday evening, where we met the foreign commissioners of the Great Exposition. Had much conversation with

those from the Roman States and Bavaria, and the one
from America, I believe. The Roman commissioner
invited me to visit him at the Exhibition, and offered to
get me a private view of it before it opened. I accordingly
went there yesterday, taking Sir Eardley Wilmot with
me, and we were much gratified with all we saw,
especially the works of art, mosaics and sculptures
from Rome, and with which the Queen and Prince
Albert had been much pleased. The Roman commissioner, Signor Tredi, much taken with the young
Prince of Wales, whom he said he lifted up to see the
works of art, just as he should one of his own
children. The Duke of Wellington, whom he had
become acquainted with some years ago in Italy, had
also paid him a visit, and was very affable. My
knowledge of art and having been on the Continent
enabled me to converse with the commissioners very
fully, and Signor Tredi had the choicest works un-
covered for our inspection.

"*May* 3*rd.*—Wrote again to-day to Lord Brougham,
thanking him for his letter to me, and saying I wished
the Life of Lord Hardwicke was followed by the
publication of his 'Judgments,' the manuscripts of
which are at Wimpole, and copies of some of which I
offered to send him. Forwarded to him also the
present number of the *County Courts Chronicle*, in an
article in which I have embodied my suggestions.

"24*th.*—On Monday went with E. to the Great
Exhibition, where we spent the day. Went without
our dinner in order to feast our minds to the full on
the rich repast there offered.

"Some good sculpture from Austria, but not equal
to our finest by Flaxman and Bacon. No really grand
work of art there. Saw the Queen and the Duke of
Wellington.

"*June* 21*st.*—Lord Denman the other day, in a letter to Lord Brougham on the present state of the law, said that the barristers must now turn their heads to some other occupation, as the bar as a general profession was gone.

"*November* 17*th.*—Wrote a humorous letter in the *Times* last week respecting the deficiencies of the catalogues at the British Museum, headed 'Hunting Extraordinary at the British Museum,' commencing 'Were you ever at a rat-hunt?' to which I compared hunting for a book there.

"22*nd.*—This afternoon E. and I called on Mr. Wright, the celebrated aurist in Duke Street, St. James' who told us some interesting anecdotes about Napoleon and the Duke of Wellington. He said on one occasion he was at Calais when Napoleon was First Consul, and had occasion to go and see him at Boulogne; that he found him walking on the pier, and that he overheard some ladies say how they should like to see him, and so he turned round directly, and took off his hat, and introduced himself; that while he was walking on the pier a shot was fired from an English frigate which was in the bay, and which was aimed at him, but fell at the foot of the pier into the sea, being intended rather as an insult than an attempt to kill him; that he immediately went to the battery and desired them to return the salute, when the ball fell into the sea about half the distance, on which he exclaimed at once either that the powder was bad or there was an insufficient charge, and that there was some peculation going forward in the provision of it; that he insisted on part of the next charge being given to him, which he analysed straight, and found it very defective. On this he went up at once, to the commanding officer of the fort, tore his epaulette from his shoulder, trampled upon it, and ordered him immediately into custody.

"The Duke, Mr. Wright said, had never seen Napoleon, and once took him to look at two portraits he had got of the Emperor to know if they were good likenesses. He said the Duke often sent for him in a great hurry and then said he was too busy to attend to him, but if he got on some political topic, would keep him talking for an hour; that he swore a great deal and wrote very bad English, but very good French. Lady Hardwicke once told me that the Duke never knew a good egg from a bad one; said he could not perceive any difference in the taste.

"*December* 22*nd.*—Sir E. Wilmot mentioned to me the other day that he thought it would be well worth my while getting into Parliament, and that it was now the only hope of doing anything or obtaining anything, and that £1,000 would be well spent by me in so doing. Quite agree with him, though I do not feel inclined to go beyond £500, even to secure a seat.

"31*st.*—Quite decided on standing for some place at the General Election.

"Brought out lately a pamphlet entitled 'The True Theory of Representation in a State; or, The Leading Interests of the Nation, not the Mere Preponderance of Numbers, Proved to be its Proper Basis.' The title shows the line of argument I adopted. It was published at sixpence. The criticisms of it to be alluded to best explain its nature and the mode in which the subject is treated.

1852.

"*January* 15*th.*—H—— called yesterday, whom B—— fixed on to write the notice of my pamphlet in the *Britannia*. He says he thinks it hastily written and wanting arrangement, but considers it the best thing of the sort. That it reminds him more than anything of Bolingbroke's 'Patriot King,' and that it contains an immense deal of originality. He marked several passages in his copy as particularly good and suitable to extract, but decided on the parody of Fox's description of the House of Commons.

"24*th.*—A neat and satisfactory criticism of my pamphlet in the *Law Times*, in which they say, 'Mr. Harris has treated a question at this moment of paramount importance with the knowledge of a constitutional lawyer, as well as with the calm reflection of a philosopher,' and that 'there is a great deal of extremely interesting and profitable reading in this timely pamphlet.' A notice of it in a leading article of the *Standard* of to-day, commencing, 'Mr. Harris, a gentleman of great learning and ability, has squandered a considerable portion of both upon a pamphlet,' etc., and saying that it is useless to write pamphlets, as nobody reads them, and that the Whig fallacies do not even deserve refutation. The pamphlet they term an 'able essay,' and say that 'it is ably and learnedly written.' A very good critique of it in the *Newcastle Journal*, in which they state that 'the author felicitously ridicules the notion of mob-law and mob-rule,' and 'the shallow sophistries of the Manchester school are exposed in the happiest vein of irony.'

"28*th.*—Two long leading articles in the *Morning Advertiser* of Wednesday and Thursday alluding to my pamphlet, which they term 'well written and scholarly,' but endeavour to confute my arguments very elaborately. F. Y. L—— told me that some of his friends thought my pamphlet very original.

" *February 6th.* — This morning I received a satisfactory and important letter from Mr. A. G. Stapleton, to whose pamphlet I referred, cordially approving of mine and proposing that measures should be adopted for carrying out the plan suggested. I sent his letter on with a note, asking what I should do, to Lord Hardwicke, and a copy of it with the pamphlet, also asking his opinion, to Sir F. Thesiger. A letter from Sir F. Thesiger this morning, thanking me for mine and the pamphlet, and saying he agreed with Mr. Stapleton, but thought it at present premature to put forward any antagonistic plan to the Ministerial one, but that when the time for doing so came he should probably ask for a personal interview with me.

"Sir E. W. called again to-day about a seat in Parliament. Said that only £100 required to be paid down and the expenses of the poll only before the election. Shall probably speak to Lord Hardwicke about it and be guided by his advice and direction.

" *13th.* — Letter from Lord Hardwicke this morning, approving of Stapleton's suggestions, but saying he is only now reading my pamphlet. Sent him Sir F. Thesiger's letter and his to Sir F. Thesiger. Cox asked me to take up the subject of representation of the law for him according to my 'Theory' in the *Law Times*, which I have commenced upon.

" *14th.* — Lord Hardwicke returned me Thesiger's reply, but with no comment upon it or upon my pamphlet. 'Many thanks ;' nothing more.

" *26th.* — Went on Tuesday to the Northamptonshire Assizes. Had one brief, which was from H—— and S——, a prosecution against a man for cutting and maiming a woman whom he courted. But as it came out on cross examination by O'Brien that after the commission of the atrocity prosecutrix and prisoner regaled

themselves on gin together and afterwards slept in the
same bed, and that the surgeon was not called in until
three days after, when his aid was only resorted to to
doctor the case against the prisoner instead of to cure the
prosecutrix, the trial was stopped by Chief Justice Jervis.
It made the most talk of any at Northampton, and occasioned great laughter in court.   A report of it appears
in the *Times*, which I prepared for Bittlestone to send.

"*April* 23*rd*.—Went with Charles Marriott, who is
staying with us this evening, to the House of Commons.
Obtained orders for the Speaker's gallery.   Heard Milner
Gibson, Ewart, Disraeli, and Cobden in a debate on
the repeal of the newspaper stamp duty.

"*28th*.—Mr. Stapleton came to dinner at my house.
A remarkably gentlemanly and agreeable man.   Sir E.
Wilmot, J. Smith, and Dr. Child dined with us as well.
Stapleton talked with great enthusiasm of Canning,
whose private secretary he was.   Said he made extensive
preparations for his speeches.   Described their effect on
the House of Commons.   Said that relating to America
and his summoning a new world occasioned such a
sensation in the House that the members all simultane-
ously started up exactly as he recollected the boys
doing at Rugby from an electric shock.

"Locke's ' Essay on the Understanding ' appears to
me a far higher, more profound, and more philosophical
production than Newton's ' Principia,' judging only
from what I have heard and read of the latter in the
translation and summary of it which I have been lately
studying.   But I have compared the two closely on the
greatest of all subjects—the nature and evidence of
God—and the fittest for philosophers to concentrate
their powers upon.   The concluding passage in Locke's
chapter on our knowledge of the existence of God,
which describes His incomprehensibility to our finite

minds, is truly magnificent. Newton's being so much more considered than Locke is probably owing to his having engaged rather in affording us knowledge of physics than of metaphysics. Men in general care little for mind and discoveries about it in comparison to what they do for matter. Bacon has been far more valued for the discoveries he made in matter than for those he made in mind.

"*June* 1st.—A petition on the subject of the Representation, drawn up by Mr. Stapleton and myself and influentially signed, was presented by Lord Harrowby on Thursday evening to the Lords. Lord Derby admitted the justice of the principle, but expressed doubts whether it could be carried out.

" *30th.*—I begin to think the jury system obsolete. It was very well in Alfred's time, and indeed much later, when jury and court were on an equality as regards intelligence, but does not do now, when the jury are so far below the court and counsel in acquirements. At any rate, a superior order of men ought to be selected, men who are at least a fair sample of the intelligence and knowledge of the age.

" *October* 28th.—An article in the *Edinburgh* on parliamentary representation, in which they place my True Theory of Representation, at the head of it with another pamphlet, and discuss my plan generally, though without quoting from the pamphlet.

"*November* 18th.—To-day I witnessed the Duke of Wellington's funeral. Never saw London in such a bustle or so visibly excited in all parts as on this occasion. E., with the Sayers, secured a seat opposite St. Dunstan's Church, and I hired a seat in a window near, but on going to take possession found the house belonged to some swindlers who kept a betting house, and that the seats had been sold over and over again,

and were filled by the first claimants among the many
who had bought tickets.   However, I got a very good
standing place in Fleet Street, and saw everything well.
Most of the windows had been fitted up with seats.
We went to Fleet Street about eight.   The procession
commenced about half-past ten.   The effect of the
military music very fine indeed.   The funeral car
heavy and gaudy and not effective.   Perhaps the old
horse of the departed Duke, led by its old groom, was
the most touching part of the spectacle.   I have often
met the Duke on horseback and been honoured by a
salute from him in return to the one I tendered.   The
last time I saw him was at the Great Exhibition, where
he was a frequent visitor."

CHAPTER XVI.

RESIDENCE IN QUEEN SQUARE.

1853—1859.

." *March 5th.*

"WENT with E. on Saturday to see Apsley
House, the last day on which it was shown
by tickets.   Very plainly furnished altogether.   Some
good paintings, and the china and plate very fine,
especially the Dresden china, and the Wellington shield
given by the City to the Duke.   Among the paintings
some interesting portraits of Napoleon at different periods
of his life, also of Pitt, Sir Thomas Picton, and several
of the public characters of the Duke's time and of his
contemporary generals, both British and Continental.
The library in which he usually sat and the secretary's
room, where he dined when alone, were exhibited

exactly in the state he used them, and the box there
in which the Duke carried his papers and on which he
wrote his despatches all through the Peninsula.   His
bedroom, a very small, dismal apartment, very like a
lumber room, with the doors at opposite sides, and a
small tent bed on which the mighty warrior slept ; a
colossal statue of Napoleon by Canova at the foot of
the staircase : the figure naked, very fine.

  " 12*th*.—At Warwick Borough Sessions yesterday.
Had two briefs.   One a case against a man for stealing
hay, of some difficulty, and which lasted a long time,
the prisoner being defended by B——, but I obtained
a verdict much to my satisfaction.

  " 15*th*.—Came to Leicester yesterday morning to
breakfast.   Junior in an ejectment case which came on
to-day, and I had to open it, but it was undefended.
A report of it, however, appears in the papers, as it was
the first trial of the sort under the new Act.

  " 17*th*.—A letter from Stapleton the other day, enclosing a plan of parliamentary reform according to our
scheme, and asking me to be one of a committee on the
subject, with Lord Harrowby, Sir B. Brodie, Mr. G. A.
Hamilton, M.P., Sir J. R. Murchison, himself, and others.
Replied to him, consenting, and added, 'On one or two
points, however, it strikes me that some alteration in
your plan might be desirable, or at any rate should be
open for discussion.   There is a difficulty, I think, in
giving representatives to the Wesleyan, Baptist, and
Independent denominations and excluding the Unita-
rians and Roman Catholics.   Indeed, I do not see
how such a plan could be supported *on principle*,
even by those who deem it practically desirable.
There is, I think, also a difficulty in giving direct
political power to any bodies who only exist as antago-
nistical to regular and legally constituted institutions.

Might not this be obviated by giving representatives to certain of the religious societies which include both Churchmen and Dissenters of different kinds ? It further strikes me that it would be more in accordance with the principles of representation to give members to the naval and military colleges, than to retired officers of those forces.'

" *April 23rd.*—Went with E. this afternoon to see the magnificent buffet designed and executed in oak by Messrs. Cook and Sons, of Warwick, whose exquisite taste and genius produced the famous Kenilworth Buffet in the Great Exhibition of 1851. It is shown in the Dudley Gallery at the Egyptian Hall, Piccadilly. The present is a more elaborate and a more beautiful work than the former one, and is adorned with highly finished carved panels and figures emblematical of English field sports, admirably executed.

" *May 28th.*—On Wednesday morning I attended, by Stapleton's invitation, a meeting at Lord Harrowby's, in Grosvenor Square, to discuss our reform scheme. Lord Harrowby, Lord Calthorpe, Sir B. Brodie, Mr. G. A. Hamilton, M.P., Mr. Adderley, M.P., Mr. Vincent (whom I once met at Wimpole), Stapleton, and some others present. The discussion rather desultory, and Stapleton, I think, goes too much into detail, and too little regards principle. Lord Harrowby very sensible and practical. Had some pleasant chats with Lord Harrowby at the end of the meeting, and entered pretty fully into the discussion which took place on Stapleton's suggestion. Great laughter was excited by Stapleton's declaring during the discussion that of all the corrupt constituencies in the empire most open to bribery was Liverpool, for which Lord Harrowby so long sat. On Thursday I sent to Lord Harrowby a copy of my ' Life of Lord Chancellor Hardwicke,' with a note begging his acceptance of it, and saying I thought it might prove interesting to him as containing matters respecting his ancestor Lord Chief Justice Ryder. A note from Lord Harrowby, thanking me for my Life of Lord Hardwicke, and saying, 'My earliest leisure will be given to its perusal. When next I have the pleasure of seeing you, I will take the opportunity of asking you further about the papers connected with Sir Dudley Ryder. I have in a drawer the whole of his brief on the 1745 case, with his notes during the trial and some of the intercepted letters.'

"*June 8th.*—Late this afternoon Stransom called, and brought me the particulars of a hundred and twenty acres at Northolt, near Harrow and Hanwell, nearly all grass, which seems very eligible if it can be got upon reasonable terms. On Thursday the Prices, Sir E. Wilmot, Professor and Mrs. Maurice, Mr. and Mrs. Grubbe, and J. J. Humfry dined with us. We asked the Bishop of Manchester, who did not get the letter in time, but called on us to-day when we were out.

" *17th.*—Went to Northolt to look at Iselipps. Much pleased with it on the whole, and consider it exactly suitable. The country round charming, and some fine views from parts of the estate. The village of Northolt a quiet, retired, pretty little place, and the view from it of Harrow delightful. The house at Iselipps small, but in a very good state. The land, which is nearly all grass, stands high, and is gradually undulated, with plenty of young timber on it. On the whole, I think Iselipps as a decidedly desirable and suitable property as I am likely to meet with, and am determined to buy it if I can obtain it on fair terms.

" Dined yesterday at Stapleton's. Went with F. D. Maurice.

" A valuation of the property at Northolt by Stransom.
He estimates it at £6,560, but thinks it may go much
higher.   If so, it is out of the question my buying it.

" Went to the sale of the estate at Northolt, which
was put up at £3,500, and finally knocked down to me
at £5,500.   Much pleased with and congratulated on
my bargain, as is also E.   We think of not raising the
rent, but arranging instead with the tenant for being
allowed rooms there and for having vegetables and fruit
from it.

"*July 2nd.*—At Lord Harrowby's on Wednesday
at another reform meeting.   Present—Lord Harrowby,
Lord Calthorpe, Sir R. Murchison, Mr. Adderley, M.P.,
Mr. Grove, F.R.S., Mr. Colquhoun, and Stapleton.   I
proposed editorship and authorship as an educational
qualification to vote, but, after much discussion, it was
not assented to, on the ground that all such persons
would be included in the members of some of the institutions proposed to be enfranchised.   Lord Harrowby
told me he had read a great deal of my Life of Lord
Hardwicke and was much interested in it.

" A project came into my mind as I was walking
alone one Sunday evening to bring out a plan for an
Act of Parliament to regulate trusteeships, and which, it
appears, might really be very useful as well as serviceable.   Framed it in my mind, and on Tuesday morning,
between eleven and one, reduced to writing the introductory part.   The heads of the clauses to the Bill I
can very well occupy myself in preparing while on the
circuit.   Propose to entitle it 'Suggestions for framing a Bill to Promote the Due Administration of Trust
Estates and the Relief and Protection of Trustees;'
to have it printed for private circulation only; to send
it to Lord Brougham, the Lord Chancellor, etc., etc.;
to write with it saying, ' I am interested in the subject

as a trustee for several persons, and have thereby had
considerable experience in the working of it, as also
from having my own property vested in trustees who
having felt difficulties as to investments, have also
acquired a knowledge of the law by writing a treatise
upon it, and the pamphlet sent will show my efforts
to effect an amelioration of the law.'   Revised it
on Thursday from my articles on the liabilities of
trustees and my advocacy in the *County Courts
Chronicle* of the measure I submitted to Lord
Brougham.

"On Wednesday went with E. to Iselipps to make
arrangements with the tenant about his continuing,
which I settled for on his allowing us to go and
stay in the house occasionally to do what planting we
wanted and sending us game and vegetables to Queen
Square.   I do not care so much about the house being
a good one as the land being quite suitable for a future
residence and grounds such as I propose, and for this
I believe it is everything I could wish for.

" 30*th*.--At Coventry Assizes on Thursday.   Came
to Warwick with Field (a future judge,* I am sure) and
E. Manly Smith.

" *August* 15*th*.--In the autumn of this year we made
a tour on the Continent, visiting Bruges, Ghent,
Brussels, Liege, Bonn, and the Rhine, also the Moselle,
returning home by Brussels, Amiens, and Boulogne.

" 22*nd*.--At Bonn, on the Rhine.   Called on S——
this afternoon.   I had heard of him through the female
Jesuit.

" *October* 25*th*.--At Chastleton.   Miss Whitmore
took us over the house, a very curious old place, a sort
of English schloss Elz, with tapestried rooms, and an
old hall, and carved bedsteads, and oak-panelled rooms.

* Now a judge (1881).

"*November* 16*th.*—A letter from C. Marriott this after-noon, enclosing an introduction for me to Mr. M——, a writer in the *Times.* Charles tells him that he begs to introduce his cousin George Harris, who had, he thought, met me with him in London, a funny fellow, though a thoroughly good fellow, and an occasional correspondent of the *Times,* who wants to have some talk with him.

1854.

"*January* 17*th.*—Thought on Thursday evening that the outcry against Prince Albert would afford me a good opportunity of bringing out a good sound consti-tutional essay respecting his right to attend the councils of the Queen with her. Doubted whether to put it in the form of a pamphlet or an article in the *Law Times,* but determined on the latter after seeing Cox, and com-pleted it roughly on Saturday. I think it reads well and is soundly reasoned.

" 21*st.*—To-day my article in the *Law Times* appeared under the title of 'Has the Prince Consort a Legal Right to be Present with her Majesty at her Councils?' A note from Sir E. Wilmot to-day, saying he had read my paper in the *Law Times* and liked it much, but wants me to bring it out as a pamphlet. Mentioned also, 'I was writing to Colonel Bouverie at Windsor, and said that a very able paper had been written *by you* in the *Law Times* on Prince Consort. He had referred to the attack in a former note to me.' In a second note he tells me that he has ' been reading a second time, with great care, the article in the *Law Times,* and thinks it would *do you a great deal of good* if you were to enlarge it and bring it out as a pamphlet.' I do not, however, feel inclined to do this, and cannot see that it could be more serviceable than in its present form.

" 28*th.*—Wrote to Lord Brougham on Thursday,

saying I should be happy to wait upon him, suggesting
that if the business of the Bankruptcy Commissioners
was transferred to the county court, the former tribunal should be made a court of trusteeship.   Or, should
it be thought more desirable to introduce the system at
first only experimentally, jurisdiction might be given to
county court over matters not exceeding £500 value.

"Lord Campbell, in his speech in the House of
Lords, took exactly the same view of Prince Albert's
matter as I have done, resting the defence solely on the
marital right, and not, as all the other apologists have
done, on his being a Privy Councillor.   This is most
satisfactory to me as confirming the soundness of my
legal judgment.

"*February 22nd.*—A visit from Mr. Hearne yesterday, who said he had been talking to Lord John
Russell's brother-in-law, Mr. Eliot, about my scheme
of representation.   Gave him a copy of my 'True
Theory.' Lord J. Russell's Bill admits my principle
in giving members to the Inns of Court and London
University and of giving votes in right of degrees and
money qualifications, as also in the disfranchisement of
the small boroughs.

"The death of Martin, the historical painter, in the
papers this week. Dined with E. to-day at Mr. F.
D. Maurice's. Rather dull, Mr. M. having so little
to say in company (as is the case with many great
thinkers), though so very agreeable with a select few
congenial minds.

"*March 4th.*—Wrote to Lord Brougham to-day, and
sent him some notes relating to my suggestions, in
reply to the objections which might be urged against
them—that the Trustee Relief Act provided for the cases
I proposed to meet, and that the expense under that
Act is very small.

" The Bishop of Manchester called here on Thursday, when he and I had a very cordial greeting and an agreeable chat. I gave him my 'Suggestions for a Trustee Act.'

" 25*th*.—Went to Leicester for the Assizes on Sunday night, and returned on Tuesday morning. At Hayes' request prepared a Presentment for the Circuit, which I entitled 'Assize Intelligence, 1884,' Mellor* coming as Chief Baron, and Bittlestone as a puisne judge to Leicester thirty years hence. Described them as arriving very late at night, and making a great noise on entering the town. The Presentment was very well received indeed, and rapturously cheered at the end of each sentence. At the conclusion of it, Macaulay moved that it be entered at length on the Circuit Records, and that the thanks of the Circuit be given to me for it.

"Applied to, to write a memoir of Mr. Justice Talfourd, embracing more especially his literary character, for the *Critic*, which I composed accordingly.

" *April* 8*th*.—As regards my feelings and state of mind, I every day come more to the opinion that the weather and the conditions of the atmosphere are after all the leading regulating influences as regards our condition in this world, respecting far more than, though not independent of, external circumstances and the digestive functions, which indeed they very much control.

" *May* 27*th*.—Informed lately that a Bill for establishing a Court of Trusteeships, on a plan very similar to mine is being brought into Parliament by S. Gregson, M.P. for Lancaster. Wrote to him on the subject last week, offering to call on him to give him my assistance.

* Afterwards a Judge of the Queen's Bench.

"*July 29th.*—Read through this week my essay written in 1833, 'On the General Nature of Man,' which forms the germ of my large work. Very curious to see what it is like, and whether it possesses any merit, as I have not read it since 1837, when I expended it into the present work. The style quaint and stiff, but the general matter good and sound. Several of the leading principles in the large work developed in the essay. Several of the notions, however, I have abandoned as quite contrary to those which I now hold.

"*August 3rd.*—During August and September and October this year, we made an excursion on the Continent to Belgium, the Rhine, and Baden-Baden, the account of which is recorded in the journals kept by both of us.

"While at Heidelberg I called on the Chevalier Bunsen; a young gentleman, one of the Chevalier's sons, came to me and said his father was walking in the garden if I would go to him. He accordingly conducted me there. The Chevalier came up to me and shook hands very cordially with me, and asked me if I were just come from England, and said, almost directly, 'Have you seen Maurice lately?' I told him I was a near neighbour of his, which he said he had perceived by my card. He afterwards asked me, as did Madame Bunsen, if I saw much of him, and I told him that he dined with me the day the Chevalier left England, and went from my house to his. He said there was nothing at all in the College Library at Heidelberg of MSS. of interest beyond the Law Papers. Told him I knew his son formerly, also Dr. Arnold and the Bishop of Manchester, who he said was one of the best bishops on the bench. Said how admirably he managed the school at Birmingham, and that he knew him when he was with Dr. Arnold. Told him I knew B. Price.

He asked me what he was doing, and said it was a pity he left Rugby. I told him he wrote in the *Edinburgh*. He said, 'Ah, we shall soon have another number out. He asked me if I was a barrister, and how the new law reform worked. I said, 'Very well for the public, but not for the barristers;' at which he laughed very much, and said, 'Oh, but you get some good places out of them.' I told him of my Trustee plan which I had submitted to Lord Brougham, and he said something of the sort was much wanted; and also to settle the responsibility of partners and joint stock companies in England. Asked me about my travels in Germany.

"Told him of my having published Lord Hardwicke's life from the Hardwicke papers and MSS., and dedicating the book to Prince Albert, and having showed the Prince the Hardwicke MSS.; but he did not make any observations on this. When we had two or three more turns we went into the drawing-room, where coffee was on the table, and one of the Miss Bunsens asked me to take a cup, which I did. He then told Madame Bunsen I knew Maurice, and offered to take anything to England, but they said their son, Henry, was coming in about a fortnight and would return straight to England. His manner was most cordial and kind throughout. On my taking leave he said, 'Give my best love, or my warmest love (I forget which), to Maurice,' who he thinks is at Bonn, where I told him we were going on Saturday.

"Asked me what walks I had taken about, and said I ought by all means to go to the Augenheim. I told him I had taken a sketch of his house to show Maurice. One of the Miss Bunsens was making a water-colour drawing of the view from their window, with the autumnal tint of the foliage very well given. A proof of an article in the *North British Review* had just been

sent to him he said, but without stating the writer.
He shook hands most cordially with me when I left,
and wished me a good voyage to England. Very much
pleased at meeting with so good a reception from so
distinguished a man, more especially as we were told
he snubbed one man who was the near relative of
a distinguished person in England, and that to several
he carried himself very stiff. Manner very kind, but
short. House quite plainly furnished, though hand-
somely so. He was dressed plainly in a frock coat,
and had on a straw hat while we walked in the garden.
Seems to have some difficulty in speaking English,
and in comprehending all you say. He appeared
the very picture of happiness and contentment with
his smiling and intelligent family around him, though
it is said that his retiring salary is only £150 a year.
Certainly, however, he looks very unlike a disappointed
or fallen man.

"*October 16th.*—Returned to London to-day.

"Prepared pamphlet under the following title, 'Reasons for urging the Necessity of and Suggestions for
framing an Act to provide for the due Administration
of Trust Estates, and the Relief and Protection of
Trustees.' I believe fully that this scheme is not only
practical and complete, but will one day be sanctioned
by Parliament and adopted. The country cannot do
without it; there is no safety for men of property or
men of honour, unless it becomes law, which has
already been sanctioned by the men best able to appre-
ciate it. I have had considerable correspondence with
the leading authorities on the subject, and it has been
several times brought before the members of the Law
Amendment Society. Several of my proposals have
been adopted, and most of them have been well
supported by men of influence and high standing; but

great opposition to the scheme has been offered by the Chancery Bar and the Profession generally.

1855.

"*January 2nd.*—Wrote a letter to the Lord Chancellor to-day respecting the Trusteeship plan of a pamphlet which I lately framed, and which embodied the form, and asking him if he would support the measure or adopt it, and proposing to submit the plan to him for his approval.

"*20th.*—Called yesterday on Mr. Gregson, M.P., was with him upwards of an hour talking over my Trustee plan, which he seemed much interested about and to take up warmly, and seemed quite at home in my pamphlet on the subject.

"*26th.*—Sent in the plan of my Trustee Bill to the Chancellor.

"*27th.*—A letter yesterday to me from the Lord Chancellor's secretary, returning the Trustee Bill plan, and saying the Lord Chancellor was too much occupied to attend to it; but that I was at liberty to pursue any course that I wished.

"*February* 15th.—Had a long talk with W. Massey, M.P., about my Trustee Bill, which he consents to introduce.

"*March* 15th.—A letter from Sir Eardley Wilmot yesterday asking me to sit for him as Deputy County Court Judge of the Bristol District at the end of next month. I wrote and told him that I should have great pleasure in sitting for him.

"*28th.*—At the Warwick Assizes attended the trial of an action of libel against Samuel Carter Hall, the Editor of the *Art Journal* formerly the *Art Union Journal*, and whom I used to know some fifteen years ago when he was editor of the *Britannia*, and for

whom I wrote an article or two in the *Art Union*.
I talked to Mr. Hall during the trial, but did not
remind him who I was. Sat by Field who was junior
counsel for Hall, and made several suggestions and
took notes for him part of the time. The action was
by a Jew picture-dealer in Birmingham, who was
alleged to have 'pickled' pictures to a large amount,
and to have cheated several considerably, and whom
the *Art Journal* had exposed. Verdict for the plaintiff
with forty shillings damages.

"*April* 21*st*.—Went on Thursday afternoon into the
City to see the Emperor and Empress of the French
returning from Guildhall after the presentation of the
address to them. The crowd not very great, nor the
cheering of Napoleon and his spouse very vociferous.
The applause more hearty in favour of the Duke of
Cambridge, who followed with Prince Albert in the
next carriage. The Emperor put his head close to
the carriage window, and kept bowing backwards and
forwards steadily all the time; only saw him in profile—a
grave, disagreeable, designing-looking man. A placard
respecting Victor Hugo was exhibited at one window;
but the mob took part against the exiled poet, and in
the presence of the Emperor smashed the glass to
pieces.

"Went with E. to-day to Bristol, and on to Sir
E. Wilmot's house at Woodcote, to take his County
Court for next week.

"24*th*.—Attended the Court yesterday and got well
through my work, and did not feel nervous; was able
to lay down the law, and delivered judgment in each
case offhand.

"28*th*.—Attended the Court on Tuesday and had
quite a heavy day, and unable to rise before nine
o'clock. A Bar attended the Court Tuesday, and to-day,

and several of the cases were conducted by counsel. One very important case against the Bristol and Exeter Railway for a nuisance, which seemed, as was urged by the counsel for the defendant, more proper for the Assizes than for the County Court. I did not feel any difficulty in deciding the case at once and delivering judgment after looking into the authorities, but it was suggested that I ought to have taken a view of the premises before doing so, which view I took on Wednesday. Did not find any difficulty in any of the cases, or in ruling at once as to points on evidence to be received, and really got on considerably better than I expected. Put questions to several of the witnesses as occasion required. Took some pains in preparing my judgment in the Railway case, which I did yesterday morning, and which I hope to get reported both in the *Law Times* and *County Courts Chronicle*. It is, I think, a good one, and well reasoned, analyses the facts, and balances the points one against another fairly and logically. A new point on each side I have suggested, which appears to me more important than any which were urged. On Thursday morning I delivered the judgment in a full Court, the parties on both sides attending; I read it audibly and did not feel nervous while doing so. The newspapers at once applied for a copy of it, which I allowed. Sir E. Wilmot strongly advised me to try and get into Parliament and take rank, and thought that by that means I should ensure obtaining some good promotion. He also recommended my calling on Lord Brougham about the County Courts' improvement plans and those respecting trusteeships.

"*May* 3*rd.*—To-day E. and I returned to London, having had in every way a most satisfactory expedition.

"26*th.*—Wrote a letter to Lord Brougham, and sent

it off at the beginning of the week, asking him, as Sir E. Wilmot had suggested, to recommend me for a County Court judgeship, on the score alone of my fitness to fill the office from having so long written the law articles in the *County Courts Chronicle*, and made so many suggestions respecting County Court legislation, and from my having sat as a Deputy County Court Judge at Bristol.

"11*th*.—Wrote a letter to Lord Brougham to-day in reference to the debate in the House of Lords about additional circuits, and proposed to him to put the County Court judges in the Commissions of Assize, giving my reasons for it, a plan which I some time ago suggested in the *County Courts Chronicle*.

"15*th*.—Came to Hitcham, to Professor Henslow, where we were most kindly received. A thorough wet day, so his village horticultural fête obliged to be put off until Thursday. Had some interesting chat with the professor in his study about points in natural history, especially as to new plants being produced when earth was brought up from mines. Said he did not believe in the existence of animals generated by electricity.

"Had some more chat to-day and yesterday with Professor Henslow on natural history topics. Talked of the various diseases in vegetables, the necessity to vegetables of light, heat, cold, moisture, etc., and on several other matters. Said he once met Prince Albert, who sat by him when he presided at the Suffolk Natural History Fête. The Prince told him that the English nobility in general could talk of nothing but horses, dogs, and politics. Went out to-day with the professor hunting snails and other insects, which he finds under pieces of wood laid about his garden.

"Do not get so much out of the professor as I

intended ; he is nevertheless very communicative, and likes to be talked to on natural history points ; but he seems to have turned his attention more to the practice than the principles of his pursuit. Has an astonishing knowledge of all the different kinds of plants and animals, but does not appear to have deduced any leading theories as to the nature and constitution of them.

1856.

"*January* 12th.—The accounts of my father represent him as declining and getting weaker, as though his valuable life was gradually ebbing away.

" Decided to go to Rugby to-day, which I accordingly did, and stayed there until his death on January 17th.

" 23rd.—My father's funeral took place this day at twelve. The service was very feelingly performed by Mr. Moultrie, who has been most attentive to my father throughout his sufferings. All the principal shops in the town were closed, and there was quite a crowd to see the funeral procession. The pall-bearers were Mr. C. M. Caldecott and Capt. Senhouse, Rev. W. James and Mr. James Butlin, Rev. W. Tait and Mr. Matthew Bloxam.

" *February* 12th.—Attended the general meeting of the Law Amendment Society yesterday evening. Mr. G. Hastings introduced me to Lord Brougham, who shook hands very cordially with me, and said he wished much to have some talk with me, and should be glad to see me any day that I would call ; but that he was very much occupied and went every day to the House of Lords. I told him I would call at any time most convenient to him, and he then fixed Saturday at two o'clock for my doing so. He afterwards took the chair at the discussion, and made some very dry and humorous observations.

"18th.—Went this evening to the meeting of the Law Amendment Society. Lord Brougham shook hands very cordially with me. I told him I thought there was required some summary remedy for cases of small trusts, and that I often heard of persons being robbed by their trustees from the want of such a tribunal. He said he had often letters complaining of this. He then proposed we should refer the matter to a general meeting of the Law Amendment Society.

"23rd.—A meeting this afternoon of Law Amendment Society, Lord Brougham in the chair. At the conclusion of the meeting Lord Brougham alluded to the provisions of the Bill which I am preparing for him, which he said would both punish fraudulent trustees, and afford relief to those who had performed their duty.

"*March* 3rd.—Attended the meeting this evening of the Law Amendment Society, Lord Brougham in the chair, and read my 'report' on Lord Brougham's observations 'of the Committee.' I afterwards addressed the meeting at some length in support of the proposed measure, and spoke without any hesitation. The report was ordered to be printed, the speech to be published in the *Law Amendment Journal*.

"*May* 22nd.—On my going to Chambers to-day I found a note from Lord Brougham, dated Grafton Street, 21st *May*, 1856, in which he says that 'you may rely on my doing what you wish, though I do not believe that my interposition will be of much service to you. He signs himself, 'Yours sincerely, H. BROUGHAM.'

"*June* 28th.—Received on Wednesday from A. Mills, M.P., a present of his book on 'Colonial Constitutions,' which appears to be well and fairly done, and is, I think, a valuable work, and one that is really much wanted. Wrote two brief notices of it to this effect in the *Critic* and *Law Times.*

"*July* 10th.—Yesterday went to Iselipps with a view to planning a house, and on the whole think the best course will be to add to the present house, laying out the ground about it, which is nicely undulated for the purpose, and planting it.

"*22nd.*—Staying with John at his house at Bramcote, near Nottingham.

"W. H. Adams spent the afternoon and dined at John's to-day. He declared I was very idle and thoroughly indolent generally. I told him my contributions to the law periodicals would alone redeem me from this charge. My chief occupation is, however, what the Germans call *working underground*, in the preparation of my large works, the labour of which cannot be doubted, though the process is invisible. Several of the professional men whom I have lately seen in London have said, 'How very hard you work at the law contributions;' and some have said what 'drudgery' it must be; others, as also the correspondents of the *Law Times*, have pronounced them very valuable.

"*30th.*—At Ilkley in Yorkshire. The evening we spent with the Forsters * at Wharfdale, with whom we drank tea; E. riding on a donkey which I had to propel with the end of my umbrella. Discussed with Mr. Forster a great variety of legal and general topics, including the Denison case, in which we both agreed as to the expediency of allowing the same latitude to all parties that was conceded by the Gorham case, and as to the persecuting intolerant spirit evinced by the evangelical

* The Right Hon. W. E. Forster, M.P., late Secretary of State for Ireland; Mrs. Forster was the eldest daughter of Dr. Arnold, of Rugby.

party. Mr. Forster told me he is a contributor to the *Edinburgh Review*, and gave me an article on 'Maurice's Theology,' which he had written for the *Westminster Review*, but which not being inserted he had printed for private circulation.

"*September 6th.* Yesterday evening we drank tea and supped with the W. H. Adamses, who are staying near here. To-day we were to have gone to Scarborough, but as the morning was very wet I occupied myself in colouring a plan I had lately sketched in pen and ink while at Ilkley for laying out the grounds at Iselipps, and adding to the house so as to make a good country residence of it ; to throw a meadow into the grounds with two fields near the house, and plant round the paddock so formed,—which would consist of about twelve acres,—and to have a drive to the house. Walks through the plantations to be carried round the paddock, and the whole to be laid out on the basis of the plan for Glengrove, but to call the house by the name of 'Iselipps Manor.'

"*September 13th.*—On Thursday I wrote out the draught of a letter to Prince Albert which I intend to send him with copy of my new edition of 'Theory of Representation.'

"*October 18th.*— Sketched out designs lately formed in my mind for the invention of certain new orders of architecture, taking for pattern forms in nature, and entitling them accordingly the 'Holly-leaf' order,' and the 'Scollop-leaf,' 'Oak-leaf,' 'Privet,' 'Vine-leaf,' 'Piscine,' 'Thistle-leaf,' 'Lime Forest' orders, etc. I really think that some of them might serve well for the purpose and be advantageously applied.

"*22nd.*—This morning I sent a letter to the *Lord Chancellor*, with the Report of the Law Amendment Society on criminal breaches of trust, containing the

outline of my trustee bill, which report I told the
Chancellor was drawn up by me at the request of the
Society, and which I begged to lay before him in case
the Government should contemplate the introduction of
any measure of this kind during the ensuing session.
Told him that Lord Brougham deferred his bill on
account of the Attorney General having introduced
a measure, but which was not proceeded with. I also
told the Chancellor that I was the more encouraged to
persevere in my efforts for the amendment of the law
relating to trusteeships as one part of my proposal
in my 'Suggestions,' viz., empowering the courts in
certain cases to supply the omission of powers of sale
and leasing and certain other powers had been carried
out in the valuable measure framed and introduced by
his lordship last session.

"Sent to *Sir G. Grey* my supplement to the outline
of a bill for regulating the sale of poisons, containing
a complete list, twenty-nine in all, of those which
should be placed under regulation, and some additional
clauses to the bill. Also a somewhat lengthy epistle
defending the different provisions of the measure.

"*November 4th.*—Attended the opening meeting of
the Law Amendment Society. Lord Brougham in a
letter to Lord Radnor refers to the report which I
prepared for the society on breaches of trust, and says
the Government mean to persevere this session in their
measures of law reform.

"*21st.*—Still rather hankering after a seat in *Parliament*, and feel half inclined to offer my services to
Finsbury, on the principles declared in my 'True
Theory of Representation in a State,' and 'Civilisation
as a Science,' delivering addresses on the subjects before
the electors. Saw in the *Morning Star* of to-day an
account of a meeting of the electors of Finsbury

about choosing candidates in the place of present ones, and so called on the secretary of it, Mr. Watts, and told him of my wish to get into Parliament, and settled to write a letter to be laid before the Committee.

"He said they wished for a resident in the borough, a person of respectability of the middle class. I proposed myself to him and settled to write him a letter, explaining my sentiments, to be laid before the Committee, which I composed this afternoon.

"*22nd.*—This morning I wrote out, and this afternoon sent my letter to Mr. Watts, detailing my political principles, mainly as contained in my 'True Theory of Representation,' and ' Civilisation as a Science,' and told him I would meet the Committee if desired. I do not expect a great deal will come of it, and until it is known whether Duncombe as well as Challis will retire, there would not be an opening for me, as Mr. Brown would be the first candidate.

"In the afternoon met Mellor who asked me to walk with him as far as his house, and in the course of conversation asked me how I was getting on at the bar, and whether I should like a colonial judgeship, which he was in a position to offer me, having been asked by the Secretary of State for India to nominate one. I said I should prefer an office of £1,000 a year in England. He then said, if I wanted his interest at the Home Office, a Recordership for instance, he should be glad to be of use to me. I told him I should be much obliged to him if he could assist me in obtaining a *Police Magistrateship*, which he said he might do through his intimacy with Waddington, whose recommendation would have great weight, provided Sir G. Grey had no one of strong political interest to appoint. He thought testimonials of little use, but that Mr. J. Patteson's would serve me. He added, as we were parting, ' I can recommend you with the greatest satisfaction.'

" 29*th.*—To-day I took Mrs. Tolme, her cousin, a German, and Mrs. Sutton's niece, Miss Bullock, an American lady, over Newgate, having obtained an order to view it through D'Eyncourt. Very much like other prisons, though more strongly built. We saw what used to be the condemned cells. Also the door through which prisoners have to pass to the gallows.

" Several of the culprits had most felonious countenances, enough to ensure their conviction of any crime. The prison very clean and comfortable and even cheerful. Indeed, almost too much so as being not only very superior to a workhouse, but to the dwellings of most, if not all, of the prisoners. An English prison is to a pauper's dwelling what a club house is to the house of a man of small means, and though it may be morally, it is certainly physically no place of punishment.

"*December 28th.*—Mr. Hastings told me that he stayed with Lord Brougham during the vacation, and met Dr. Tait there, then Dean of Carlisle,* with whom he had a good deal of conversation, and was impressed with the notion of his being a very deep thinker. I remember once taking up a volume of his sermons, and being much struck with the reflection they displayed, and for which I had not been at all prepared from the character he bore at Rugby. Hastings told me they hoped to hold the Law Amendment Congress at Manchester during the exhibition there, and wishes me to take up the manuscript question there, and make it the subject of a paper to read at one of the meetings.

* Subsequently Bishop of London and Archbishop of Canterbury. 1857.

1857.

"*January* 10th.—The Bishop of London and Mrs. Tait called during our absence, so we did not see them. A letter from C. Dickens, to whom I sent a copy of my 'Theory of Representation,' saying the differences in opinion between us are so wide that he will not attempt to explain them, and expressing his dissent from my use of the word 'mob,' as calculated to give offence. Wrote to him in reply that I did not mean to use the word offensively, and that, 'although I like calling things by the right names, and thoroughly dislike the cant of the present age in attempting to annex aristocratic terms to occupations of every degree, as though gentility was essential to respectability.' I must admit the force of his remarks.

" Told him also that I should be glad to have briefly stated the reasons for his objections.

"*February* 7th.—A letter on Monday from Prince Albert's secretary acknowledging the receipt of my book,* 'which H.R.H. has much pleasure in accepting, and for which he desires me to express his thanks. H.R.H. regrets, however, that the further object' (Manuscript Inquiry) 'you have in view, as explained also in your letter of the 21st, is not one in which it seems possible for him to assist.'

" A letter, thanking me for my book, from Mr. Gladstone, who says : 'I have already been able to gain some acquaintance with its contents, and I cannot but anticipate benefit from an attempt to excite attention to political truths, which the events of our own day and its habits of thought have tended unduly to throw into the shade. Such, so far as I have seen, is the scope

* " Theory of Representation."

of your work, and I sincerely trust its object may be attained.' Mr. Walpole says: 'The importance of the subject, and, if I may be permitted to say so, the sincere respect which I entertain for its author, will induce me to read it with great interest.'

"A long review of my work in *The Illustrated London News* of to-day, stating fully the whole plan and commenting upon it, condemning some parts, but commending others. Of the book they say: 'This is a very thoughtful publication. Its views are original and comprehensive. The various arguments are all ingenious, well sustained, and perfectly free from party spirit. Indeed, the frank, truth-seeking, and dispassionate tone of the whole book renders its perusal a real pleasure independently of its learning, logic, and earnestness.'

"A notice of my book in the *Morning Star*, in which they say it is 'likely to receive attention,' but dissent from my principles and conclude: 'We should not have considered such a mongrel plan as worthy of notice at all, were it not argued out by Mr. Harris in a way which proves him to be a severe student of the science of politics.'

"21st.—Yesterday evening at the meeting of the Law Amendment Society. A full attendance and very good discussion. Among those who spoke were Lord Brougham, the Bishop of London, Lord Ward, Lord Robert Cecil, the Lord Mayor, Sir Stafford Northcote, Mr. Liddell, etc.

"Had conversation with the Bishop of London, and thanked him for calling upon us. As we were talking outside the room he said to me, 'It is very extraordinary, but I'm afraid I've lost my watch.' We hunted about on the ground for it, and I then went back to the room and looked under the chair where he had been sitting, when Mr. Hawes said he saw him put it in his pocket just before he left the room. When I got back the bishop had found it. As the subject for discussion was the reformation of juvenile offenders, it was re-marked that it would have been a good joke against the Society if the bishop's pocket had been picked at the meeting.

"*26th.*—In a work I was reading the other day it is mentioned that 'almost every author of celebrity has had great difficulties to contend with in getting his works before the public, which have formed dismal episodes in his history. That society has had narrow escapes of losing many great works, and has been indebted only to accident for several. That W. Howitt has declared that authorship gives poverty as its reward, and abuse as its fame. That authors are only baited by the public and made martyrs of, and that even Cowper's poems, when they were first published, were loaded by the critics with the most scurrilous abuse and condemned to the butter shops.

"*April 16th.*—Read the other day in a review of Wordsworth's life that the conviction which sustained him through life was, that posterity would settle accounts fairly as to his reputation, and that all will secure fame who deserve fame. I must say that I have great confidence in the truth of this convic-tion, and that I find it very consolatory to me often during my cogitations as to the success of my own works.

"*May 21st.*—The Government Bill to regulate the sale of poisons introduced this week. Some of it precisely what I had suggested, and other parts different. Wrote a letter to the *Times* about it; and the next day a leading article appeared noticing the points I had urged, and raising objections which would have been obviated had more of my plan been adopted. The

Government *Trustee Bill* also introduced, which simply punishes trustees for defaults, but without affording them any relief as I proposed.

"25th.—This evening I read my paper *On the Constitution of Juries in Criminal Cases*, at the Law Amendment Society, tracing the origin of juries generally, reviewing the operation of the different tribunals of which juries form a part, and advocating a special jury in all capital cases. A very good debate on my essay followed it.

"The chairman, Mr. Pitt Taylor (author of the work on Evidence), in summing up commenced by saying: 'But before I proceed to offer my opinion on the subject before us I must beg to express my sentiments as to the very great value of the paper which has been read by Mr. Harris.' He also coincided to a considerable extent in my views.

"27th.—A good outline of my paper on Juries in the *Post* of to-day.

"*June* 5th.—Attended the meeting of the Criminal Law Committee of the Law Amendment Society, on my paper on Juries. Took the chair. Determined to apply to persons of note for their opinion. A rather lengthy review, containing several extracts of my 'Theory of Representation,' in the *Press* of to-day, which is said to be edited by Mr. Disraeli, to whom I sent a copy of the book. The *Press* styles it a 'philosophical tract,' a 'thoughtful but incomplete tract.' They term the analysis of interests 'too arbitrary' and 'inconsistent.' What I say of the professional they declare 'well worth notice,' and that there is 'vigorous logic' in the application of some of my principles, but the development of my plan they call 'a most wild proposition,' and add that 'the system is too crude, although a certain portion of truth may be assigned to it.' They conclude, 'The importance of the subject, and the ability shown in some parts of this philosophical treatise, have thus induced us to criticise this production.'

"18th.—Lord Brougham, in the debate on trusteeships in the House of Lords, alluded to the report on the subject of the Law Amendment Society, which was drawn up by me.

"20th.—Made an analysis to-day for Sir E. Wilmot, of the Bankruptcy Act of 1849, for his edition of 'Lord Brougham's Acts and Bills,' and which he has promised to mention in the preface as my production.

"24th.—At the Law Amendment Society on Monday, Lord Brougham in the chair. The debate was on official trustees, and was opened by Mr. Edgar, who alluded pointedly to me ; and so I spoke after him, and with some point and effect, I think, for about five minutes. He afterwards asked me for notes of my speech for the *Journal,* which I sent him.

"*July* 21st.—Had a great deal of talk with W. H. Adams, M.P., with whom I drank tea, and by whom I sat at dinner, about his House of Commons life and his speeches in Parliament, with the reception of which he seems much pleased, and urged my getting into Parliament, which I told him I was ready to do for a moderate sum.

"31st.—A circular, calling a meeting at Lord Brougham's, to consider about a congress of the Law Amendment Society at Birmingham, in October. Wrote to Hastings, saying I could not attend the meeting from being on the circuit, but would attend the congress, and read a paper, as proposed, relating to the application for historical purposes of the manuscripts in this country.

"Lord Brougham, in his speech in the House of

Lords on Tuesday evening, alluded again to my report of the Law Amendment Society on breaches of trust. To-day I had a note from Hastings, saying that the meeting at Lord Brougham's went off well, and that they should be glad of my paper.

" *August 7th.*—Called on Hastings, and settled with him to read my paper at the meeting at Birmingham, the title of it to be ' The Manuscript Treasures of this Country, and the Best Means of rendering them Available for the Purposes of Education, History, and Legislation.' A very kind note from Lord Brougham, saying my article in the *County Courts Chronicle* ' is most ably and usefully done,' and that he is extremely obliged to me for it, and my ' kind letter.'

" Made a tour on the Continent this year with E., during August, September, and October, visiting the Loire and the interesting towns on going up it and in the neighbourhood, of which we kept a full account in our respective journals, and also made numerous sketches, as usual.

" Returned home on the 8th of October.

" Invited to stay at Mr. Gifford's, head master of Prince Edward's School, Birmingham—Lee's successor —during Social Science Congress. Mr. Gifford only returned home in the evening from Brighton, and we went to the inaugural meeting at the Town Hall together. Lord Brougham read his address, which appeared inanimate, and was not well heard. He was much cheered, as was Lord J. Russell, who spoke with much spirit and effect, and was quite audible. Mr. Cowper, Sir F. Kelly, Sir C. Hastings, Mr. Commissioner Hill, and Lord Stanley also addressed the meeting.

" The last was vociferously applauded. Great applause was also evinced on the mention of Mr.

Maurice's name, as also on that of the Bishop of London, while a slight hiss (very bad taste) greeted that of the Bishop of Oxford. A round of applause greeted Bright's name, and a letter from him was called for and read at length. Lord Brougham, in his address, alluded to the move for the representation in Parliament of intelligence and education, which he said (erroneously) originated with the late Speaker of the House of Commons.

" I dined to day at Mr. Ryland's, to meet Mr. Macready—invitation suggested by Council of Association—and had much conversation with him on the subject of my paper, the reading of which he promises to attend ; but says he is too nervous to take part in the discussion ; that he never speaks in public without trepidation or without previous preparation. Had much chat with him also about Rugby, and we walked home together.

" Mr. Gifford said Lord Brougham was very entertaining at the party at the mayor's yesterday, and told them anecdotes about Queen Caroline's trial, and said that they (the Counsel) had great difficulty in getting their fees. Lord Stanley seems most popular.

" I attended the Jurisprudence room in the morning, and made a speech on legal education. Read paper containing general account of various manuscript collections, historical, biographical, and ecclesiastical in this country, and pointed out the important uses which might be made of them. Lord Brougham came, as did also Hastings, Symonds, Mr. Gifford, Mr. Macready, Dr. Bach, Mr. Yorke, and his son, and a very full attendance, which I did not expect. Mr. J. Pakington proposed to take the discussion of it with the other papers of a different nature, to which I strongly objected, and which was overruled by the meeting. The first speaker who got up complimented me very strongly, and was emphatically cheered by Lord Brougham, who during the delivery of my address several times stopped me to ask questions, which showed his interest in it. Mr. Hastings, Dr. Bach, Symonds, Lord Brougham, and several others spoke upon it, and complimented me in the most gratifying manner, and a resolution, proposed by Mr. Hastings, was carried for referring the question to the committee as to the best means of carrying it out. At the conclusion of this Lord Brougham came to me and shook me warmly by the hand, and said, he must 'thank me for the' compliment I had paid his old friend Jock Campbell (in my address), but which was quite undeserved, he said, as he cribbed from other writers, instead of using the manuscripts themselves. After my paper had been read, Lord Brougham asked me publicly several questions about the manuscripts in Germany and France. I told him what the Chevalier Bunsen had informed me respecting those at Heidelberg, and what I had made out respecting those in the towns on the Loire. Before the reading of my paper commenced, Mr. George Dawson said, " Oh, you are not likely to get any discussion on such a subject as that !"

" *October* 15*th.*—To-day I dined with Mr. Gifford, and we had some very pleasant chat about the Bishop of Manchester, state of the Church, etc. He says the Bishop of Manchester's prose composition in writing is not remarkably good, which he thinks is the reason why he has never produced anything.

"16*th.*—Lord Stanley, they say, takes great pains to prepare beforehand when he has to address any meeting, and generally writes out his speeches. He said the other day that nobody ought to want more than three hundred pounds a year to live upon.

"*December* 10*th.* – Reading lately 'Tom Brown's School-days,' a most perfect and vivid description of school life under Dr. Arnold, the portraiture of whom is excellent, as also of Cotton. Still I maintain, as I have always done, that the result of Arnold's system was only to make great *boys*, not great *men*. Indeed, it appears singular that not one really great man has ever been brought out of Rugby School. Not even an archbishop, chancellor, or chief justice. The two nearest approaches to great men are Macready and Landor, with both of whom I have been lately in correspondence.

"11*th.*— Dined at Dr. Croley's. He contended that Demosthenes' eloquence did not support his reputation as an orator, but he thought Cicero's did. I said I thought that Demosthenes' orations did not as a whole, but that particular passages did. Dr. Worthington said that Brougham assisted him in an edition of Dante, and that the soundness of his criticism was extraordinary.

1858.

"*January* 19*th.*—A letter from Lord Brougham to-day, written from Cannes on January 15th, in which he says : 'I am much obliged to you indeed for your most able and useful writing, which gives you the greatest claims to promotion, even if you had no other. I hope to be in London at the beginning of next month, and shall then ascertain how matters stand with respect to those subjects and to the department of justice which must also be arranged early in the session.—Believe me ever, most sincerely yours, H. Brougham.'

"*February* 22*nd.*—Attended the meeting of the Law Amendment Society, and read a paper 'On the

Appointment of Auditors of Trust Estates,' which was ordered to be printed. After the meeting was over, Lord Brougham called me to him and shook hands with me very cordially. I offered to be of any use to him as regards his bankruptcy bill in obtaining information.

" 23rd.—This evening I delivered at Mr. Humphry's request, at the St. Martin's Working men's Library and Institute, a lecture on ' Ancient Manners and Customs.'

" At work in court on a book which I projected some years ago, to be entitled ' Principia Prima Legum,' and to contain an analysis of the first and leading principles of law of each kind without reference to cases, through citing cases where these support, illustrate, or enunciate a leading principle. The work would really be a valuable one if well carried out.

" *April* 1st.--Working each morning at my ' Principia,' and completed the leading principles of several of the sections.

" 12th.—Came to Birmingham to stay at Mr. Wills' to deliver a lecture in the theatre of the institute. About one hundred and fifty people present, which considered a good attendance.

" My paper on ' Auditorship of Trust Accounts' was copied at length from the *Law Amendment Journal* into the *Solicitors' Register.*

" Designed a graphic descriptive lecture on ' The Great Plague in London,' picturing some of the most vivid scenes as though we were eyewitnesses, and which, if effectively done, with some good illustrations to it, will I, think, tell well.

May 6th.—Appointed a member of Serjeant Woolrych's Committee on Official Trustees.

" Delivered the first part of my lecture this evening

at the St. Bartholomew's Working men's Institute, Gray's Inn Road, terming it 'Habits and Pursuits of the Ancient Britons,' and using diagrams. A good attendance, and lecture appeared to take and to be taken in better than it has done before. Several distinguished persons among their lecturers, including Lord Bury, M.P., Mr. Mackenzie, M.P., Professor Westmacott, and Mrs. Holcroft.

"10*th.*—E. and I dined at Sir Adam Bittlestone's to-day. I showed him what I had done of my 'Principia,' of which he highly approved, and said he thought it would form a very important work, though it would be a most laborious undertaking. Had two notes from Mr. Wills, of Birmingham, father of the 'Judge,' and author of the book on 'Circumstantial Evidence;' in which he says:—'I hope you are advancing with your book of Elements; it is a thing much wanted, and I liked the little that I had the good fortune to see of it. I hope it will not be long before your book of "Principles" comes out. It cannot but be a valuable one. It is a much-wanted introduction to legal science.'

"*May* 13*th.*—Went with E. to the consecration, in Westminster Abbey, of Dr. Cotton as bishop of Calcutta. The sermon by C. Vaughan, in parts very good, but much too long. Saw Tom Burn who is to be Cotton's chaplain. The Bishop of London officiated. The crowd great.

"*June* 7*th.*—At the Law Amendment Society in the evening, Lord Brougham there. Mr. Hastings told him about our requisition for a Commission on the Manuscripts, and he promised to take charge of it.

"28*th.*—At the meeting of The Law Amendment Society in the evening; Lord Brougham came to me in the room where we had tea, and we talked about

Serjeant Jones' case. He told me the Chancellor had introduced a bill respecting the County Courts for altering the circuits that evening, in which it is proposed to remedy the evil in Serjeant Jones' case.

"*July* 3rd.—Went to the annual dinner of The Law Amendment Society. Saw Lord Brougham, and twice had a chat with him, as also with the Attorney-General, about some papers I had sent him from my brother John on the Bankruptcy Bill, and on which he said he should be glad to receive suggestions, especially about October, when the final measure will be settled. We were to have had the dinner at Greenwich as usual, but the present foul and unsavoury state of the Thames rendered that impossible. It has made ill all who have gone there to dine.

"7*th*.—Wrote on Monday to the Lord Chancellor sending him a clause which I proposed to add to the County Courts Bill, enabling the judges to appoint their registrars to sit for them in certain cases. This proposal was eventually adopted.

"31*st*.—I drew up a presentment for a circuit court at the Leicester Assize, though not till after that held at Derby. Hayes pronounced it 'very good indeed.' It was termed as follows :—

"Select extracts from the 'Confessional Register of the Reverend the Chaplain,' with his own suitable reflections on certain passages, and particular observations touching the demeanour and apparent moral condition of some of the penitents.

"This autumn during August, we made a tour on the Continent, visiting the Rhine, Heidelberg, Stuttgart, Friedrichshafen and parts of Switzerland:

"*September* 29*th*.—While at Meyringen, a peasant directed me to a point where I could see the peak of the Wetterhorn rising up between an opening in the mountains. It runs quite to a point. and is extremely elegant in form, the most beautiful object indeed of the sort that I have seen. Of this I made a sketch, and have copied it on glass for the window in my dressing-room. At night, nevertheless, a still more beautiful object was visible in the comet which I first saw one evening at Zürich, about sunset, when it appeared just above the horizon, its tail apparently about a foot in length ; but I had not seen it again for some time owing to the cloudy weather. This evening we observed it to great advantage, the sky being quite clear, and no moon to deaden its lustre. It was a striking and splendid object, has greatly increased in size as well as brilliancy, and would seem to measure, if viewed as an object near, four feet.

"*October* 3rd. —I walked up the hill behind Interlachen in the evening, and obtained a beautiful view of two lakes near, just before sunset, the mountains around which are extremely bold and picturesque. The comet, which we have not seen since we were at Meyringen, was most brilliant in the evening, and appeared from six to ten feet in length, but it soon sank below the horizon, or rather behind the great mountains which stand on the side of this valley.

" 30*th*.—Wrote to Lord Brougham, sending him the manuscript memorial, and asked him to obtain Lord Campbell's signature.

"*November* 9*th*.—Called this morning, at Hastings' suggestion, on Lord Brougham, and saw him for a few minutes only. He said he was going to the dinner at the Mansion House to-day. Should see Lord Campbell, and would ask him to sign the memorial to Lord Derby.

" 29*th*.—At the Law Amendment Society this even-

ing. During the debate Lord Brougham, who was in
the chair, gave me the memorial signed by Lord
Campbell, who, he said, put his name to it at once,
and cordially supported the measure. I then got Lord
Brougham to authorise me to put his and Lord
Campbell's name to the new memorial instead. He
said we must get some more names, which I told him I
should certainly do.

"*December* 4*th.*—This week I have been fully occupied in the afternoons in obtaining signatures to the
manuscript memorials. By calling upon them obtained
several names.

"In answer to letters and memorials which I have
sent out, I have received many replies :—

Lord Chancellor Cranworth, writing on 3rd December, 1858, returns the memorial, to which he subscribes
his name, and adds he shall be glad if anything can
be accomplished tending to throw light on our legal
constitutional social history.

Sir Richard Bethell from Lincoln's Inn, December 2nd,
wrote that he thought my suggestion a most valuable
one. He adds :—" It must be clear to everyone who has
attended to the subject at all, that such an investigation
as you suggest would tend more to give certainty and
accuracy to history, remove false impressions and errors,
as well in history as in biography, and generally give
more assistance to the student of the laws, the institutions
and progress of the people, than anything that can be
suggested. Private repositories will be found better
stored with materials of great interest and instruction
than even the public records, which are now being
investigated, with so much utility, under the direction
of the Master of the Rolls. I may mention as an
example that I, and I believe many others, laboured
under very erroneous notions with regard to the real

political sentiments of Mr. Pitt with respect to the war with France, until the recent publication by the Duke of Buckingham of the Greville correspondence. If pecuniary want had not led the Duke to publish those letters as a means of getting money, many unfounded opinions would still have been prevalent. But it is lamentable to think that the true materials for real history should be taken such little care of, and exposed to such contingencies. The duty of inspection will no doubt be a very delicate one, and I am afraid the expense attending it will, in these times, be an insuperable bar. Pray add my name to the memorial which, as requested, I return to you. I take this opportunity of again thanking you for the instruction and pleasure I have derived from your 'Life of Lord Hardwicke.' "

" 11*th*.—Made great progress with the manuscript memorial this week, and obtained many signatures and letters of several leading men. Lord Macaulay wrote from Holly Lodge, Kensington, December 8th, 1858, saying ' that he returned the memorial which he had signed, though not without some misgivings. He feared that the inquiry which he proposed to be instituted is far too extensive to be useful. He will not, however, set his own judgment against that of men so distinguished as some of those whose names have been already obtained ; and he assures me that, though he does not hope much from the undertaking, he sincerely wishes it well.'

" A note from Pitt Taylor, saying that he sent the memorial to his cousin, Lord Stanhope, ' but he has declined to sign it, stating that, in his opinion, the scheme will be regarded with great jealousy by the proprietors of manuscripts, and that the superabundance rather than the scarcity of such family publications may of late years be deemed a matter of complaint.'

"This afternoon I called on Sir F. Madden, at the British Museum, and had a long talk with him. He said that it would be impossible for him to undertake such a scheme, as he and those in his department had already on their hands more than they could get through ; but that it might be for the consideration of the trustees of the museum, whether they would appoint officers to carry it out. He thought that an unpaid commission, consisting of such men as Lords Stanhope and Macaulay and Sir D. Dundas, would be the best way of carrying out the plan ; but he recommended to limit the inquiry, in the first instance, into the contents of college and cathedral libraries, before endeavouring to inquire into private collections. He spoke very highly as to the value of the scheme, and the important matter which would thus be brought to light, and thought something ought decidedly to be done.

" He considered £2,000 a year would be sufficient for the expenses of the commission. He also said that we ought to have a definite plan before going to Lord Derby, and that the best way would be to communicate privately with him beforehand if we had any means of access,—and which I could do through Lord Hardwicke.

" 14*th*.—Called to-day on the secretary of the Genealogical Society to confer with him on the same subject, and he promised to assist me. Told me he knew of a gentleman, Mr. Staunton, of Longbridge (the documents were unfortunately burnt in the fire of the Birmingham Library), who had the original roll belonging to Knowle Abbey, which contains a great deal of information about Warwickshire families ; and that the same person had a diary commencing in the year 1400, and continued for several generations, part of which refers to the invention of printing.*

"18*th.*—Made good progress this week with the manuscript memorial. A note from the Archbishop of Canterbury, authorising me to add his name to it. I wrote to Mr. Percy, asking him to sign it, and to apply to the Duke of Northumberland, Lord Beverley, Lord Bagot, Lord Warwick, and Lord Leigh to do so. In his reply from Guy's Cliffe, dated December 16th, 1858, Mr. Percy returns my papers, and expresses that he is much 'flattered that I should have wished for his name. 'Frankly,' he adds, 'and in spite of the distinguished men who memorialise Lord Derby, I do not think it in the least a matter in which the Prime Minister has, or ought to have, any concern. A commission to call for or examine private papers is, I think, very objectionable; as, though the communication of them would not be *legally* compulsory, it becomes to a degree morally so; and the whole tendency of modern legislature being to override private rights, I should be sorry, for a reasonable indulgence of curiosity, to lend myself to anything tending in that direction. Pray remember me very kindly to Mrs. Harris, I regret that I cannot wholly sympathise in the object of your movement.'

"26*th.*—Sent to the Lord Chancellor (Lord Chelmsford) this evening a copy of the memorial, with the principal signatures, including all the legal ones, to it, accompanied by a letter, saying that, though from his position I could not ask him to sign it, yet I hoped he would regard it with a favourable eye, so many of the leaders of the profession having signed the memorial and taken a deep interest in it.

* This document was also unfortunately destroyed in the burning of the Birmingham Library.

" The following reply came from the Lord Chancellor's secretary :—

" 'Sir,—I am desired by the Lord Chancellor to acknowledge the receipt of your letter of the 20th inst., and to assure you that, although he does not sign the memorial you forwarded, he quite agrees in the utility of such an undertaking as that proposed by it. His lordship desires me to convey to you his best thanks for the " Life of Lord Hardwicke," which you have been good enough to send to him, and which he read with much pleasure some years ago, at the express desire of the late Sir Robert Peel.

" 'I am, etc., etc.,

" 'WM. CARMALT SCOTT.

"'GEORGE HARRIS, ESQ.'

" Mr. Thomas Carlyle has added his name to the memorial, and Vice-Chancellor Sir W. Page Wood* wrote to me, and Cardinal Wiseman wrote to me as follows, with his signature.

" The following is the letter of his Eminence :—

" '8, YORK PLACE, *December 23rd*, 1858.

" ' Cardinal Wiseman presents his compliments to Mr. Harris, and begs to say that he fully agrees with the purpose of the memorial to Lord Derby, but feels obliged to adhere to the principle uniformly observed by him, of not taking part in any public matter unconnected with his official duties.'

" Mr. Hallam also sent me his signature.

" Spent Christmas at Ashbury, where we enjoyed our visit. Yesterday Mr. and Mrs. Hearne came, by invitation, to meet us, and this evening I delivered a lecture on the ' Manners and Customs of the Ancient Britons and Anglo-Saxons " in the large room of the inn

---

* Shortly afterwards Lord Chancellor.

at Ashbury, which was quite full, and the people were very attentive and expressed themselves as much gratified.

1859.

"*January* 1*st.*—The following letters came to me respecting the memorial :—

"' 16, CHATHAM PLACE, BRIGHTON, *December* 27*th*, 1858.

"'Mrs. Jameson presents her compliments to Mr. G. Harris, and has added her signature to the enclosed paper with much satisfaction. She cannot doubt of the utility of the plan proposed. In Italy, where the family archives are preserved with great care, they form an almost inexhaustible as well as invaluable treasury of dates and documents for the use of the historian.'

"' NEYDON HALL, WANGFORD, SUFFOLK,
"'*December* 31*st*, 1858.

"' Miss Agnes Strickland presents her compliments to Mr. G. Harris, and has much pleasure in adding her signature to the distinguished names of those who have united in the memorial to the Earl of Derby. No one can coincide more heartily in recommending the object of the memorial than herself, having derived the most important assistance in both series of her royal female biographies, the "Lives of the Queens of England" and the "Lives of the Queens of Scotland," from the evidences furnished by unpublished contemporary documents. In proof of this assertion it is only necessary to mention the affectionate and reverential letter of Margaret, Countess of Lennox, Darnley's mother, to her unfortunate daughter-in-law, Mary Queen of Scots, recently brought to light, and published in the fifth volume of Miss Agnes Strickland's "Lives of the

Queens of Scotland," with a facsimile of the original,
fully verifying Mary's assertion "that her mother-in-
law was on terms of the most friendly and confidential
correspondence with her, and fully satisfied of her
innocence of the crimes that had been laid to her
charge."

" ' Again, one of the letters of the Earl of Shrews-
bury, edited by Lodge, proves that Darnley's servant,
Thomas Nelson, who was taken alive out of the ruins
of the House of Kirk of Field, was in Lady Lennox's
service at that time ; therefore Lady Lennox must have
been in full possession of the facts, and would not thus
have written to Mary, unless thoroughly satisfied that
she was innocent of all the violations of wifely duty laid
to her charge. Such are the important evidences in
controverted cases that are to be found in unpublished
letters. Miss Agnes Strickland is much gratified by
the opinion Mr. G. Harris has expressed of her historical biographies, and has to apologise for the delay in
acknowledging his letter and returning the memorial as
requested, but this was unavoidable as she only received it by to-day's post.'

" 10*th*.—Returned to London to-day.

" 14*th*.—Sir E. Wilmot, in his plan of 'Parliamentary Reform,' which was noticed at length in
the *Times* of yesterday, refers to 'the ingenious
theory of Mr. Harris, who has both thought deeply
and written ably on the representative system,' but
disapproves of scheme as establishing class representation.

" 25*th*.—Attended a meeting at Cox's and Plumptre's
chambers of the Public Reading Society, for reading
works of amusement to the lower classes, on the
committee of which I have been nominated, and to
which I obtained the Bishop of London's consent to be

one of the patrons. The Rev. W. H. Brookfield, whose reading at the South Kensington Museum originated the project, the Rev. Mr. Bellew, the Rev. Mr. Watson of Queen Square, and some others, were present.

" The Duke of Newcastle wrote me word, respecting the manuscript memorial, ' I shall be very glad to attach my name to the memorial of which you have sent me a copy, and to promote its object in any way I can.'

" At the Tolmes' in the evening met Mr. and Mrs. McCullagh Torrens, M.P., there, who gave me some valuable advice about the proceeding with regard to the ' Manuscript Commission.'

" *February 7th.*—Went this evening to the opening of the Public Reading Society. Mr. Brookfield read a scene from the *Merchant of Venice;* very good, indeed perfect. Mr. Bellew too theatrical and ranting, but the humorous parts excellent. Cox and Plumptre also read.

" 15*th.*—Lord Robert Cecil, M.P. (now Marquis of Salisbury) wrote to me, stating that he had the honour to return the memorial to Lord Derby signed as I desired, and, ' with the most hearty wishes for your success in the praiseworthy undertaking.'

" The reply of Dr. Whewell, Master of Trinity, dated from Trinity Lodge, Cambridge; February 13th, 1859, intimated that the object of the memorial seems to be good ; but as he had no opportunity of consulting those who have signed it, or of ascertaining all its bearings, he declined to sign it.

" 19*th.*—Lord Robert Cecil writes word : ' I regret that I have been prevented so long by a press of other business from answering your note. I am afraid that my engagements will hardly permit of my undertaking to join in such a deputation as you propose' [to the Premier].

" Mr. Dilke, the proprietor of the *Athenæum*, wrote to me from 76, Sloane Street, February 15th, 1859, that he cannot in conscience put his name to the memorial. ' There is no doubt,' he says, ' that, among the archives of particular families there are important manuscript documents of historical interest ; but how would a commission find them out, when, as you say, their existence is, in many cases, unknown even to the possessor ?' [I have not said their *existence*, but that their *value* is not known to the possessors.] ' When known, is it not fair to assume that the family object to entrust them to strangers for examination. Every one who has signed the memorial could probably illustrate this by reference to cases of direct application and direct refusal. A commission would, in my opinion, only lead to a waste of public money and to public disappointment.

" Sir Thomas Phillips wrote to me from Haverford-west, February 16th, 1859, to say that he remembered the correspondence at Birmingham, and now thanks me for the plan and list of supporters ; he adds, ' may I beg to ask which of all these nobility and gentry have *first* set the example of depositing their family records in the British Museum ?'

He would be glad to keep the plan of the proposition.

" Wrote him and told him that it was not intended to ask any one to give up their papers, and that the inquiry was to be quite a voluntary one. Offered to show him the correspondence and to give any explanation he desired.

" A note from J. W. Parker, junior, the publisher, to which I replied thus :—

"'I do think your literary friends rather unreasonable. If they will only read the memorial they will see that it is not contemplated in any case to *compel* owners of manuscripts to open their collections. Although I have been in correspondence with all the largest possessors of papers, not one of them has objected to the commission, and several of them have signed the memorial, which has now attached to it the names of nearly every author of eminence in the kingdom. I do not, therefore, think that any additional signatures can give it more weight.'

"21st.—Had a chat with Lord Brougham. He said that my memorial had 'succeeded completely.' Laughed about the charge for obtaining money—a penny—under false pretences, preferred at the Bow Street Police Court against the Reading Society, on account of no one appearing to read in Leicester Square on Friday evening. A leader in *The Morning Post*, which parades all our names. Great blundering in the general management.

"26th.—From the following, letters respecting the manuscript memorial have been lately received. The first from Mr. Buckle, the author of the 'History of Civilisation,' says:—

"'I have such strong feelings against any interference or even any recommendation from Government respecting literature that I cannot honestly sign the memorial which you have sent to me, and which I now return. I am sensible of the honour you have done me in giving me an opportunity of coupling my name with those of the eminent men who have already signed theirs; and I trust that you will do me the justice of believing that I do not withhold mine from any affectation of singularity. I am obliged by your courteous expressions respecting my history.'

"The next was from Mr. Grote, the historian of Greece, and late M.P. for the City of London. Mr. Grote wrote from Saville Row, February 22nd, 1859, stating that he was favoured by my note of the 19th, enclosing the printed copy of a memorial intended to be addressed to Lord Derby respecting manuscript historical documents in the hands of private families. He approved of the general prayer of the memorial, and would be 'ready to sign it,' along with those other gentlemen whose names were appended.

"This afternoon I called on the Attorney-General, and left with him a copy of the memorial, with all the signatures, and a note saying that, although, from his position as Attorney-General, I feared I could not ask him to sign it, yet I ventured to hope that he might be induced to regard with favour the object aimed at by the memorial. Pointed out to him how many leading members of our profession had signed it. Offered to call upon him to give any explanations, and said I should be particularly obliged to him if he would favour me with his sentiments as to the best means of laying the memorial before Lord Derby. I then repeated what I had said to Lord Hardwicke as to the objections urged against the commission.

"*March* 1st.—Opened the adjourned debate at the Law Amendment Society. Spoke from notes, and said all I intended. Met Lord Brougham after the debate was over.

"5th.—Have received the following letters lately respecting the manuscript memorial. The first is from the Attorney-General, Sir Fitzroy Kelly, in reply to mine to him, and is, I think, very satisfactory.

"The Attorney-General who wrote from 32, Dover Street, W., March 3rd, 1859, said he had signed the memorial, and sincerely wished it success. He added,

'I think your better course will be to forward your memorial, when the signatures are complete, to Lord Derby with a letter from yourself, requesting him to receive you and any two or three of influence who will accompany you as a deputation to explain the objects of the memorial and the means by which they may be attained, but be well prepared to state exactly what you wish his Lordship to do.   If I have an opportunity, I will mention the matter to Lord Derby between this and next week, before which time I suppose you will hardly be ready to wait upon him.'

"The following is Sir Thomas Phillipps's reply to my letter to him :—

"Writing from Haverfordwest, February 13th, 1859, he said, in reply to my letter, ' that the idea is excellent, and I wish it had been adopted a hundred or two hundred years ago.   But, to make your plan successful, Lord Brougham must pass an Act of Parliament that no document deposited in the British Museum shall ever be brought forward as legal evidence in any claim to an estate.   This enactment will fill the Museum with old deeds.   But perhaps you may better say no deed prior to a hundred years ago.   Without some such law nobody will let you look at his title-deeds except fools.   If the law of entails was done away with, it would set many deeds at liberty.   If you get any commission for your object, take great care that nothing *tyrannical* is inserted in it, or you will destroy more deeds than you will save.'

"I particularly told him in my letter, we should not want to inspect title-deeds at all.

"*7th.*—A notice of my ' Theory of Representation' in the *Constitutional Press.*   They say of it that ' Mr. Harris's theory is so perfectly *ingenious*, and so elaborately worked out, that it deserves to be carefully studied

as the production of a thoughtful man, who believes
that our present system of parliamentary government is
organised on a wrong basis altogether. . . . All the
subjects are discussed with candour, ability, and fairness. . . . Mr. Harris's scheme ought to be well
considered by every politician, and deserves respectful
attention from all constitutional publicists.'

" 21st.—I came to Warwick this morning by the
11.35 train from Rugby, for the purpose of calling at
Guy's Cliffe should Mr. Percy be there, which I found
to be the case, and accordingly I walked over there.
I discussed the memorial question with him and Mrs.
Percy very fully, and explained my plans in detail, in
order to obviate the objections contained in Mr. Percy's
letter to me on the subject. Mr. Percy said I had quite
taken the sting out of the measure, and that he thought
there could be no objection to it, if only those who offer
the papers for inspection are to have their documents
looked into, and if the greater part of the commission
is to consist of the proprietors of manuscripts. Mr.
Percy said he hated commissions of inquiry as a general
rule, and did not expect much would come of this, as
most of the collections of value have been pretty well
sifted. I must excuse his frankness with me. I told
him that I really felt much obliged to him for it, and
that I thought his arguments, very fair and reasonable,
were most forcibly urged in his letter, and that several
other people had raised objections, though not any of
them in so comprehensive a way as he had done. I also
discussed with Mr. Percy the reform question and my
' Theory of Representation.' After I left the house Mr.
Percy came running after me to ask me to dine with
them to-day, which I promised to do, and accordingly
did. Lord Somerville, Mr. Dickens, Mr. Dugdale, and
several others whom I did not know were there. Mr.

Dugdale told me that all the papers of his ancestor Sir W. Dugdale had been given to the Ashmoleian Museum, the founder being a relative of the family.

"23rd.—Dined with the judges. Had a barristerial party at my rooms in the evening to look at my diagrams of the Plague, which they said should have been produced at the judges' dinner had they known of them.

"*April 6th.*—Came to Warwick to-day for my 'Reading on the Plague.' The audience was above the average, and very attentive. I exhibited all the diagrams at once. The reading lasted just an hour and a half.

"*9th.*—There is a brief notice of my 'Reading on the Plague' in both the local papers of to-day. In the *Warwick Advertiser* they speak of it as 'abounding with interesting facts, couched in a forcible and pleasing style.' In the *Leamington Courier* they term it a 'celebrated imaginary stroll through the streets of London during the dreadful Plague,' etc., and say that the subject was treated with the gravity and solemnity it deserved, and which attracted the deepest attention.

"An Oxford journal forwarded to me containing an ample review of my 'Theory of Representation,' in which they say, 'There are many valuable and original suggestions, to all of which, however, we cannot give our adherence. On the whole, the work is extremely valuable, especially at this particular moment, and every class of the community, from the highest to the lowest, may read it with advantage, and gather much from it. The subject is treated in a most masterly manner, and no point connected with the representation of the kingdom . . . has been overlooked. The style is clear and lucid, the arrangements are powerful, and the earnest and manly spirit which pervades the entire work clearly shows that the writer feels a deep interest in the subject, and has brought ability, judgment, and experience, and a well-stored mind to bear upon it in a manner eminently successful.'

" 19*th*.—Went to the Law Amendment Society, and saw Mr. Hastings, who had been talking with Lord John Russell about the manuscript memorial. Lord John thought it would not do to grant the commission, though he has signed the memorial, at which Mr. Hastings was much surprised.

" *May* 16*th*.—At the Law Amendment Society this evening. A question on commitments by the county court judges, whom I defended. The report of my speech appears in the *County Courts Chronicle*. After the debate was over I read a paper ' On the Present Position of Executors and Trustees,' suggesting, as an initiatory measure for their relief, that the Chancellor should make an order for the reference to officers of trust estates, where the parties desired an investigation. to some master or registrar, who should report thereon, The paper was ordered to be printed, and was much commended by some, and Edgar said the other day that he thought it was the most rational and practical plan that had been proposed. A report of the proceedings, and of my speech and paper, in the *Post, Standard, Herald*, and *Morning Star*.

" 19*th*.—The public reading for the Reading Society took place at the Eyre Arms, St. John's Wood.

" 24*th*.— Mr. Ingham, Q.C., M.P., Mr. W. H. Adams, M.P., and Mr. and Mrs. Hastings dined with us. Some warm discussion after dinner between Ingham and Adams as to what will be the issue of the approaching session of Parliament. Adams said that Bright told him some time ago that he expected to be prime minister, and that he would not serve under any lord.

Mr. Hastings said that he knew that within the last few days a proposal had been made to Mr. Bright by Lord J. Russell to join his Ministry in case he came into office, and that Mr. Bright had consented.

"*June 6th.*—At the meeting of the Law Amendment Society. Showed Lord Brougham the manuscript memorial with the signatures to it, with which he expressed himself much gratified, and promised to be one of the deputation to present it. He said he thought Miss Strickland would find it very hard to clear up the character of Mary Queen of Scots.

"Sent the memorial to Mr. Gladstone, who returned it with his signature, but without any reply to my note to him.

"13th.—Came to Hatford on Saturday to Mr. Hearn. Delivered my lecture 'Manners and Customs,' etc., at Faringdon to-day.

"14th.—Gave the same lecture this evening at Hatford extemporaneously on my diagrams before quite a select party, Dr. Wordsworth [afterwards Bishop of Lincoln] and his family and two other clergymen and several ladies being present. Showed Dr. Wordsworth the manuscript memorial, and got him to sign it. He appeared much interested in the matter, and offered to show me the documents belonging to the Dean and canons of Westminster. Walked some time with him, and had a good deal of conversation, particularly on the theory of representation, in which he quite agreed with me.

"24th.—Delivered a lecture on Napoleon at Barns-bury Hall this evening. The attendance respectable, and extremely attentive and appreciative.

"28th.—Delivered lecture on Napoleon this evening at the St. Bartholomew's Institute. The evening wet, but a tolerable attendance.

" 30*th*.—This evening I delivered second lecture on Napoleon at Barnsbury Hall.

"*July* 2*nd*.—Dined to-day at the Law Amendment Society's dinner at Greenwich, an agreeable one. Lord Brougham came up to me just before dinner and talked about the manuscript memorial, and at parting inquired, ' Have you heard anything from Campbell ? '

" Wrote to-day to Lord Palmerston, asking him to appoint a time for receiving the manuscript memorial.

" 4*th*.—The letter which is next referred to I received from Sir Edward Bulwer Lytton, the celebrated novelist, and late Secretary for the Colonies.

Writing from Knebworth, July 2nd, 1859, Sir Edward says, " I have very little belief in the chances of obtaining the access to private family documents through any steps which it would be in the power of a commission to take ; but I could not object to add my name to those of Lord Brougham and Lord Macaulay in the memorial."

"5*th*.—Attended to-day by appointment the meeting of the Historical Society to see Lord Ellesmere and obtain his signature to the manuscript memorial, which I did ; addressed the meeting, and explained all the proceedings, and replying to observations. Lord Ellesmere agreed both to add his name to the memorial and to allow it to be mentioned as one of those of the proposed commissioners.

" Delivered my second lecture on Napoleon at the St. Bartholomew's Institute. The audience very attentive, and seemed especially pleased with the caricatures. In reply to what the chairman said, in proposing vote of thanks, about my having drawn too favourable a character of Napoleon, I added that if I had erred I had done so on the right side, and in a way characteristic of the generosity of our country.

" Lord Macaulay writes to me from Holly Lodge,

July 5th, 1859, begging to be excused from being a member of the commission which is to report on private collections of manuscripts. It would be impossible for him to attend the meetings of the Board ; and he must be permitted to add that, though he signed the memorial which I submitted to him, he did so with much hesitation, and from deference to the judgment of others.

" The inquiry he thought would be best conducted by persons who entertain a confident hope that it will lead to important results ; and such a hope he frankly confesses he does not feel.

" I went this evening, having a card of invitation, to the meeting of the Historical Society, which was held at Lord Ellesmere's, at Bridgwater House, in the gallery. The paintings looked very well by gaslight. One of the speakers, Lord Bateman, denounced our commission as intended to pry into titles to estates ; but I thought it better not to reply to so absurd an accusation, which is easy to refute should it ever be necessary.

" 7th.—A letter from the Bishop of St. David's (Dr. Thirlwall), saying that the 'only objection I feel to letting my name be placed on the proposed commission is that in general my sojourn in London is confined to about a couple of months in the first half of the year. If, taking that fact into account, you should still think it desirable, I shall be willing to be a member of the commission.'

" 8th.—A note from Lord Ellesmere, who says, ' I undoubtedly think that your proposal if carried out under some precautions will be beneficial. I have hardly, however, given the scheme sufficient consideration to enable me to sanction it so far as accompanying the deputation to the Minister would involve. I regret therefore to be obliged to decline.'

" Received also the following :—

"'*July 8th*, 1859.

"'Lord Shaftesbury is fearful that his many engagements will not allow him to attend the deputation or serve on the commission.'

"9th.—Lord R. Cecil writes me from 21, Fitzroy Square, W., July 9th, 1859, saying he is afraid that engagements will preclude him from joining the deputation to-morrow. He will be very happy to be nominated on the commission if there is any one of superior rank, but not otherwise. In consequence of other duties, he has so little chance of giving to it any considerable portion of his time, that he would not like to appear in any conspicuous position in the matter.

" Dr. Wordsworth writes word, 'I fear that I am as little qualified by knowledge of the subject as by opportunities of leisure for being a member of the commission of inquiry, but I heartily wish well to the design.'

"Attended at Lord Palmerston's house in Piccadilly to present the manuscript memorial. I explained to and discussed the matter with Lord Winchilsea and Mr. Cunningham till Lord Palmerston came in, when Lord Winchilsea began to talk to him about it, but did not get on very well, and at last said, 'Mr. Harris, perhaps you had better read the memorial,' which I did throughout, including the names. I then explained the matter to Lord Palmerston very fully, speaking extemporarily for about a quarter of an hour, and read through and commented on my plan of operation for the commission. We then discussed the different points together, especially matters of expense, which I calculated at £2,000 per annum, including £600 a year for the secretary ; and at the foot of the list of those willing to serve on the commission I put my own name as secretary *pro tem.* Mr. Hugo and Mr. Hastings made a few observations occasionally. Lord Palmerston said the matter was a very important one, and that no doubt a great deal of valuable information would be brought to light if the commission was granted, but there were other people he must consult before giving an answer. He was very courteous, and seemed particularly attentive, without any attempt to throw ridicule on the matter, as had been anticipated by some. He shook hands with us all as we came away. When I got out, Hugo said to me, 'I don't often compliment people, but your speech was so forcible and argumentative, it could not have been better, and Lord Palmerston paid marked attention to you.' Hugo says he is sure the commission will be granted, and Lord Winchilsea told me he thought that it would be. I was rather afraid I might be thrust into the background, but there was no attempt at this. Mr. Hugo said he thought we had done a very good morning's work, and that he should long remember the 9th of July.

"Wrote to Lord Brougham, Lord R. Cecil, the Bishop of St. David's, W. N. Massey, and Forster to tell them of the presentation of the memorial. The commissioners mentioned to Lord Palmerston were the Earls of Winchilsea and Ellesmere, the Bishop of St. David's, Lord Brougham, Lord Robert Cecil, M.P., Sir G. Ramsay, Bart., Mr. W. N. Massey, M.P., Mr. G. Bowyer, M.P., Mr. J. G. Phillimore, Mr. J. Forster, Rev. T. Hugo, Mr. W. T. M'Cullagh Torrens, M.P., and Mr. Matthew H. Bloxam.

"11*th*.—Mr. Joseph Parkes, whom I met at the Law Amendment Society's dinner on Saturday week, told me that on the Sunday before Palmer's trial Lord Campbell called on him to borrow Donellan's trial.

"12*th*.—At the meeting of the Law Amendment Society this evening, Lord Brougham, who was in the chair, as soon as I got into the room, said ' he was very sorry he could not go to the meeting on Saturday, but he

was obliged to be out, and hoped it went off well.' I told
him it did, and that Lord Palmerston received us very
kindly. He said £2,000 was a very small sum for the
object, and that he quite thought the commission would
be granted, and that he was sure Lord Campbell would
support it. My paper on executors and trustees was to
have been discussed, but on my own motion, as another
stood before it, it was postponed until the next meeting,
in November.

"28th.—At Sutton, Nottinghamshire. Went to meet
the Leicestershire Archæological Society at the church,
among whom I found Matthew Bloxam, who introduced
me to Mr. Nicholls and Mr. James, of Peterborough,
with whom I had some conversation about the manuscript memorial, and gave them copies of it. We
afterwards proceeded to Kingston, and inspected the
church there and the interesting monument to the
Babingtons, where Lord Belper met us, and pointed out
the objects of main interest, and afterwards took us to
his residence, politely showed us the gardens and
grounds, and gave us a lunch of fruit and cake and
wine, laid out in the hall. He then led us into the
library and conservatory. I gave him one of the
manuscript papers.

"*August* 1st.—Received a courteous letter to-day
from Lord Eversley, the late Speaker of the House of
Commons, respecting the manuscript memorial. It is
dated Heckfield Place, July 29th, 1859, and says :—
'On looking over my papers I find the enclosed memorial,
which, I am sorry to see from the date of the note which
accompanied it, has been waiting for an answer for many
months. I am afraid it is now too late to request you
to add my name to the list of signatures, or I should
be happy to do so, but I must beg you to accept my
apologies for my apparent inattention to your request.'

"One of the papers to-day gives a report of Mr. Albert Smith's farewell address to his audience, in which he tells them as follows with regard to lecturing, 'This finally led me to a very terrible conviction, painful to an intelligent mind to contemplate in this age of progress and high-pressure intellect : that my audiences did not care one straw for more instruction, unless it slipped into my lecture under cover of a joke or allusion, but they came here entirely to be amused.' This confirms the views I had formed from lecturing experience, and is not very encouraging to those who, like myself, wish to afford information of value, and not merely amusing trash. A good lecture should indeed, as I told my last audience, contrive to combine entertainment and information together.

" 3rd.—Wrote to Lord Eversley to acknowledge the receipt of his letter respecting the manuscript memorial, which I told him I was much gratified by receiving. Mentioned to him the presentation of the memorial and the names of the proposed commissioners, and concluded, ' I shall be very glad to afford your Lordship any further information on the subject, and hope that we may calculate on your Lordship's powerful support. As soon as Lord Palmerston has announced his determination, I will communicate the result to your Lordship, and I will also mention to him your willingness to have your name added to the memorial.'"

CHAPTER XVII.

1859---1860.

PROGRESS OF MANUSCRIPT COMMISSION.

" I MIGHT yet, I believe, retrieve my failure at the bar, but in one way only, which would be a desperate effort; and that is by obtaining a seat in Parliament and taking rank, so as to obtain employment in leading cases suitable to me and to strive to come out as an orator. As soon as I get into Parliament, I shall make all due efforts to get into practice, especially in the Divorce and Probate Court and in the cases I selected originally as suitable to me, and shall bring forward some professional questions in Parliament, especially a measure relating to trusteeships. I should also deliver some popular lectures on 'Theory of Representation' and 'Civilisation as Science.' To the title of the latter I should add, 'enunciating the Principles of Legislation essential for its Complete Accomplishment.'

" 10*th*.—Wrote to Sir Thomas Phillipps, sending him a copy of the memorial, and told him of my calling on him, and asked if I might add his name to those proposed to Lord Palmerston to act on the commission. Wrote to Sir R. Bittlestone, telling him I was greatly perplexed what to do, and that on the whole I thought I should really follow the advice which Wilmot and Adams, among others, had often given me, and try and get into Parliament, and which seems to afford the only hope of rising or, failing that, of obtaining some appoint-

ment. Said I had but two courses : either to do this
and make every effort to get on professionally, or else
to retire quietly from the profession altogether. Told
him I thought my 'Principia' would be of use to me
if I obtained standing. Said that 'if I am to sink I
do not like to do it without an effort.' I also told him,
'The Thames has been stinking very badly this summer,
of which the Parliament complains ; but from the dis-
closures of the election committees, it would appear that
the Parliament is quite as foul, and corrupt, and stinking
as the Thames, so it need not complain.' "

During the autumn of this year, in August, September, and October, we made, as usual, our tour on
the Continent, visiting Guernsey, Jersey, and Brittany,
and returning home by Paris. Wrote a full account of
all we saw in our journals, which may be interesting
and even valuable to refer to in times to come, when
so much that we observed has been swept away, and
the accomplishment of which seems even now to be
in rapid progress.

"*October* 12th.—We reached home on the 12th of
October, having had, as I recorded, 'an interesting,
enjoyable, and satisfactory tour on the whole.'

"13th.—Wrote to-day to Lord Brougham to ask him
if he would apply to Lord Palmerston for his determination respecting the manuscript commission, or to
the Chancellor, or whether he thought I had better
write to Lord Palmerston.

"19th.—At Winchester. Called on Mr. C. Bailley,
the town clerk, who enters fully into the manuscript
commission, and promises me leave to inspect the
Corporation documents.

"26th.—Applied the other day to Canon Jacob for
leave to inspect the cathedral manuscripts. He called
on me, and I wrote him an official letter, 'asking if,

in the event of a commission being granted and duly qualified persons appointed as inspectors, leave would be granted to me to inspect the documents belonging to the Dean and Chapter of Winchester, not including title-deeds, the report to be submitted before publication to the Dean and Chapter.' He gave me the key of the cathedral library, and I looked over the books, but the manuscripts are locked up. Some old law and divinity of the seventeenth century, but the additions of the last hundred and fifty years would not, I should think, cost above £5. Returned to London this evening.

" A note from Mr. Wickham, saying he had just met Canon Jacob, who desired him to express the feeling of the Dean and Chapter as to my application respecting the manuscript commission. 'They can foresee no difficulty in giving permission to your inspectors to search their manuscripts whenever they may desire to do so.'

" *November* 15th.—Delivered lecture on Napoleon at the schoolroom in Theobald's Road this evening. A very full attendance, and good reception.

" 16th.—Wrote to Mr. Stapleton, asking him to meet me to discuss pressing forward on the Government at this time our plan of parliamentary reform. I also said, 'What think you of getting the general question discussed by some of the working men's societies, and also of trying the question by contesting some fair constituency upon it ? I should have no objection to do the latter if it could be effected at a moderate expense, and with a reasonable prospect of success. But I think a contest would do good, even if not successful, in bringing the question fairly before the public. I should like much to know your sentiments on this point.' Cox told me to-day that he had made every inquiry previous to the last election about obtaining a seat in

Parliament, but could not obtain anything under from £800 to £1,000, and did not think it possible to get into Parliament for less. He said that Mr. H. Labouchere told him that it cost him £700 a year on an average. Only those who had strong local influence could get in for less, and some of the Radicals. Cox said his last contest did not cost him above £45, but that he could not have come in without spending much money.

"21st.—Wrote to Sidebotham to-day, asking him if he could get the 'Theory of Representation' question debated at the Union of Oxford, which might serve to bring it before the university. The resolution I proposed to submit to them was as follows : 'Would the plan which has been proposed by the advocates for the educational franchise of allowing the working classes to return a hundred and fifty members to the House of Commons by suffrage, and of allowing the interests of intelligence, property, and the different trades and professions, to be distinctly represented there, secure a satisfactory adjustment of the suffrage ?' To propose it also to the Mechanics' Institute and the City Reform Association.

"23rd.—A note from Sidebotham, saying he had put the 'Theory of Representation' into the hands of a friend, but asking if an amendment on the original resolution on the reform question would not do. I wrote and told him that this would not bring the question so well before them as preparing an original resolution.

"Went to Carshalton to-day to deliver a lecture there on Napoleon. The lecture took place at 7 p.m., in the schoolroom, and lasted until half-past eight. The room quite full. Chairman, in moving me a vote of thanks, said that he was very glad to see the subject treated in so extremely temperate and judicious a manner, which he thought was of great consequence, considering our present condition as regards France.

" 24th.—I asked Mr. Ingham particularly about the expenses of a seat in Parliament, and he seems positive that they are very much reduced, and that in ordinary cases only those sums are spent which pass through the auditors' hands, and which would bring it quite within my means.

" 26th.—A note from Sidebotham, saying that my resolution had been debated as an amendment during the discussion on representation, and had been rejected by sixty-five to twenty-six.

" 28th.—At the Law Amendment Society this evening, and moved adoption of my plan for the relief of executors and trustees, but which was strongly opposed by a compact body of Chancery men, including the chairman, C——. The supporters of it were also absent, on the ground that all that is wanted has been done by Lord St. Leonards' Bill of last session, so I was forced to withdraw. Still much yet is required which that measure does not effect, and which I believe my plan would secure. I am defeated in what I believe to be a very useful effort.

" 30th.—My second lecture on Napoleon at the schoolroom in Theobald's Road this evening, which went off well.

" Received the following note this morning in reply to my letter to Lord Palmerston about the manuscript commission :—

"'Downing Street, *November 30th,* 1859.

"' Sir,—Lord Palmerston has directed me to acknowledge the receipt of your letter of yesterday's date, inquiring whether it is intended to grant a commission for making inquiry into different collections of manuscripts, and to inform you that her Majesty's Government would be better able to come to a decision on the subject if you were to forward to him the details which you mention, stating at the same time whether it is proposed that the commission should be paid or unpaid, what its specific functions and powers should be, what the probable annual expense, and what the duration of such a commission would be, and in what way the result of its inquiries would be utilised.

> " ' I remain, etc.,
>
> " ' C. G. BARRINGTON.

" ' GEORGE HARRIS, ESQ.'

" *December* 3rd.—Engaged to-day in preparing for Lord Palmerston, after laying it before a meeting of the proposed commissioners, which I have summoned for Thursday, at my house, a ' specification of the terms on which it is proposed that the commission for inquiring into private collections of manuscripts should be granted, together with the intended plan of operation,' and which I think will be satisfactory, and serve to obviate objections to the undertaking.

" 5*th*.—Received to-day a note from Lord Brougham about the manuscript commission dated Paris, December 2nd, 1859, in which he says he was extremely sorry that my note did not reach him in time to afford him an opportunity of seeing me, as he had almost every hour he was in London occupied by private business, which could not be postponed. He therefore begs me to suggest anything that I can do by letter while he remains in the South. His address he says is ' Cannes, France,' and he signs himself most sincerely yours, ' H. BROUGHAM.'

He adds that he has the memorial and list of names.

" Perusing to-day the specification, and have under consideration to alter the period of the commission from ten to twenty years, as on making a calculation I feel it impossible that the work can be got through in less time.   A note from Lord Eversley, saying, ' I am sorry that I cannot undertake to be one of the commissioners whom it is proposed to appoint for the purpose of inquiring into the various private collections of manuscripts in this country.'   This is in reply to the letter I wrote to him the other day asking him to join the commission.

" *6th*.—Called on Sir F. Madden about the commission, which he thought the Government would not grant for twenty years or for more than three or five years, and recommended us to apply for it for that time only and to endeavour to get it renewed on its expiration.   He said the record commission broke down from taking too long a time.   He thought we should have great difficulties in getting access to private collections, but was very favourable to the undertaking.

" *7th*.—A note from Lord Ellesmere about the manuscript commission, who says, ' My being in the country will prevent my attendance at the meeting at your house.   The proposal you have originated is, in my opinion, well worthy of discussion ; at the same time, I must confess I have, on further reflection, considerable doubts of the feasibility of carrying it out. At all events, I know that, having considerable manuscript collections of the kind your plan refers to, I should feel very unwilling to allow them to be unreservedly investigated by any officials named by the Government, or by any one who was not personally known to me. The motives which would actuate me, I must presume, would actuate others; but even supposing they would not, I can hardly come forward as the advocate of a scheme which I am not prepared to allow to be carried out in my own case. I shall be obliged therefore if you would, at least for the present, withdraw my name from the list of its promoters.'

" *8th.*—Wrote to-day to Lord Ellesmere in reply to his letter, asking him to reconsider his decision about withdrawing his name. I said, 'From my own experience, I am inclined to think that the great bulk of proprietors of manuscripts entertain sentiments exactly in accordance with those so clearly and so candidly expressed by your Lordship. But I cannot say that I consider the feeling at all inconsistent with the successful carrying out, or with their support of the commission. There could be no possible objection to inspectors in particular cases being appointed who were personally known to the proprietors of the papers. And I cannot but anticipate that one great good, perhaps the best result of all, of the commission will be that it will lead proprietors of manuscripts themselves to undertake the arrangement of their papers, applying to the commission for such aid in so doing as they may require in the occasional attendance of an inspector with whom they may consult.

" ' I have proposed in the return to Lord Palmerston that title-deeds of less than a hundred and fifty years old shall on no account be inspected ; that no papers shall be removed from the custody of the proprietors ; that it shall be the duty of the inspectors to put aside any papers which ought for particular reasons to be kept secret, and to communicate all matters of this sort to the family, and which are on no account to be divulged without their consent, so that this inspection will really be in cases highly advantageous to the proprietors. The inspectors are also, when the proprietors wish it, to stamp and page the different papers, so as to prevent their being on any future occasion purloined and sold.'

" To-day I sent in to Lord Palmerston the specifications, etc., with a short note, saying they embraced all the points on which information was asked for in his letter.

" 13*th.*—Wrote fully to-day to Lord Brougham about the manuscript commission. Told him of my writing to Lord Palmerston, and of his reply, and said I hoped that I might augur from these inquiries that he has some intention of granting the commission. Said I had been able, I thought, to reply satisfactorily to all his inquiries, and that if he (Lord Brougham) would now aid us with his powerful influence, I trusted that Lord Palmerston would not hesitate to grant the commission. ' In my replies I stated that the commission was to be an unpaid one, except as regards the necessary expenses of paying the inspectors and other officers. I thought it would take twenty years to complete all the contemplated work of the commission in England, Scotland, and Ireland ; but that probably Government might prefer granting it for five years at first, and then renewing it if it proved successful.'

" 15*th.*—A note from Mr. Beresford Hope in reply to one I wrote to him about the manuscript commission, in which he says, ' I shall feel myself much honoured by being appointed on the archives commission which you have so judiciously set on foot. Such an undertaking as yours would be of the utmost historical value.'

" 20*th.*—A note from Mr. Stapleton on the 'Theory of Representation' question, who says, in reference to 'trying some constituency on the cry of the educational franchise,' that 'I know of no constituency where such an appeal would be likely to be made without the chances of failure greatly exceeding those of success.' He also tells me that after the failure of the Reform

Bill, of which he is confident, 'will be our time to try our "nostrum." '

"24*th.*—Worked hard at 'Principia,' to which I have lately devoted much time, and for which my labours for the present must terminate to-day. Probably it is now half completed. If I can make it as perfect as I hope, illustrating the different principles by extracting into my work the cream of all the best judgments that have ever been delivered, it will really be a highly intellectual performance.

1860.

"*January 2nd.*—At Worthing. Called on Saturday, on Mr. Demett's recommendation, on Mr. Davey, to inquire about the manuscripts at Chichester, and showed him my memorial.

"Shocked to see in the paper the sudden death of Lord Macaulay. Talking with Sir F. Madden about him shortly before I left London, Sir Frederick told me that he (Macaulay) was sanguine as to the results of the manuscript commission, and talked much about it, which I should not have expected from his letters to me. Fascinating as was the style of his narrative, yet as an historian I fear it must be said of him what Talleyrand said of language: that he rather distorted than narrated facts.

"*8th.*—A letter from the Home Secretary respecting the manuscript commission as follows :—

"'WHITEHALL, *January 3rd*, 1860.

"'SIR,—I am directed by Secretary Sir George Lewis to inform you that Viscount Palmerston has forwarded to him the letter which you addressed to his Lordship on the 12th ult., submitting a specification of the terms on which the proposed commission for inquiring into private collections of manuscripts might be granted, and the intended plan of operation ; and I am to inform you that her Majesty's Government, after having consulted the Master of the Rolls, have come to the conclusion that it will not be advisable to issue the proposed commission.

" ' I am, etc., etc.,

" ' H. WADDINGTON.

" ' GEORGE HARRIS, ESQ.'

" I called on Mr. Cunningham, the member of Parliament for Brighton, at his house there, and talked over matters fully with him. He said Government would not do anything without great pressure, and that agitation was the only way to carry anything. I proposed to him that we should try and get the record commission extended so far as regards the cathedral and Corporation papers, which he said he thought was a very practical plan, and he promised to get a deputation on the subject of members of Parliament if I would speak to Mr. Walpole, Mr. Shirley, and Mr. W. Heathcote, and see the Master of the Rolls on the subject.

" 14*th.*—Attended the meeting at the St. Bartholomew's Institute, and proposed my resolution respecting the ' Theory of Representation' question. Spoke from notes for about twenty minutes, and pretty effectively ; but every speaker was decidedly against me. The speaking good and fluent. The question adjourned until next Saturday, when I shall have the reply.

" 19*th.*—Called on Sir F. Madden about the manuscript memorial, but he says that it would be impossible for the British Museum to undertake the proposed inquiry, and that he had consulted the late Lord Macaulay and Mr. D. Saunders on the subject. Thinks the inquiry would be of the utmost value as regards the

Corporation and cathedral papers which were not at all searched into by the record commission. Says that at Chichester the jackdaws were actually allowed to carry off some of the manuscripts and build their nests with them, and that they were afterwards picked up under the trees, so carelessly were they kept. He recommended me to call on Mr. Hardy at the Rolls Office, which I afterwards did, to ask the Master of the Rolls to undertake the duty. Mr. H. thought this could not be done, and that all the cathedral and Corporation papers, where access could be obtained, were looked into by the record commission, that none of the private collectors would allow their papers to be inspected, and that there was but little of value in them. Said the inquiry if made would prove a failure, very much the same as what the Master of the Rolls had expressed, though he denied having influenced the Master of the Rolls,—which Sir F. Madden thinks is the case,—and whom Mr. Hardy strongly recommended me to see. Mr. Hardy said that, with so many names of members of Government appended to the memorial, he did not see how they could refuse to grant the commission.

"21st.—A good and fair report of the Reform discussion in the *St. Pancras News* and *St. Pancras Times.* Attended the debate this evening. Several spoke generally against my plan, but did not appear to understand it, and much of what they said, as I observed in my reply; was entirely in my favour. I replied at length, going over the different objections, and talking to them rather than speaking. Introduced a few jokes and compliments, which told, and my reply negatived much of what had been urged, so that, though only three votes were for me, eight were against me ; the great body of the meeting did not vote.

" Wrote to the Master of the Rolls to request an interview with him on the subject of the manuscript commission, to which he consented. Received me very politely, and sent for Mr. Roberts, the secretary to the Record Office, whom he introduced to me, to be present. I went fully into the matter, and suggested that the inquiry might be conducted by the record commission and made an appendage to it. He said that the record commission was now defunct, but the proposed Board might be appended to the Record Office, if a new staff of officers was added to it, and a superintendent, which was what he, in fact, suggested to the Government in his letter to them, though he thought we should be disappointed as to the papers of value we found in the private collections. I told him that I should recommend the proposed commissioners to acquiesce in this plan, and that we should have a deputation to Government on the subject. He said it should be to Sir G. C. Lewis, the Home Secretary.

" He said there was a difficulty in asking Government to go to the expense of arranging private collections, which would be a benefit to the owners, unless the public derived some advantage from it, and that the collections ought to be thrown open under certain restrictions. Suggested that all persons, and those only, should have access to them, who produced a certificate from the established publisher or other person that they were engaged in some literary work, which would prevent unnecessary intrusions, and that some restriction of a corresponding nature was imposed as regarded the admission of strangers to Lincoln's Inn library.

" *February 8th.*—Delivered a lecture on the Plague this evening at the Institute of St. George's-in-the-East. The room was quite filled, more than there was sitting room for, and the audience appeared deeply interested throughout. Mr. Lowder, on moving me a vote of thanks, characterised it as a very interesting lecture on a dismal subject, and hoped the others would be more cheerful. I extemporised several times to-night, and looked off my paper as much as possible at my audience, which, I think, aided the effect of delivery a good deal.

"10*th*.—I wrote to Lord Brougham to tell him of the interview with the Master of the Rolls, and asked his opinion of the proposal made by him. My letter obtained a return note, dated 4, Grafton Street, February 9th, 1860, in which he said he entirely approved of the plan suggested by Sir J. Romilly, and thought it a great improvement.

"Wrote as follows to the Home Secretary :—

"'19, QUEEN SQUARE, W.C., *February* 13*th*, 1860.

"'SIR,—I have the honour to acknowledge the receipt of your letter to me of the 3rd of last month, relative to "Memorial for inquiring into the various collections of private manuscripts," and to inform you that, in consequence of that communication, I have lately had an interview with His Honour the Master of the Rolls, who informed me that although he had advised the Government not to issue a commission for this purpose, yet he had suggested that the inquiry desired might be effected by the Record Office if a new department for the purpose was added to the body.

"'In consequence of a communication which I made to Lord Brougham, whose name stands at the head of the memorialists, his Lordship writes me word that he entirely approves of the suggestions of the Master of the Rolls, and considers that his plan is a great improvement on that originally proposed. I have now the honour to inform you that at a meeting of the leading subscribers to the memorial, held this day at the offices of the Law Amendment Society, 3, Waterloo Place, Pall Mall, they unanimously coincided in the opinion expressed by Lord Brougham, and requested me to communicate to you their sentiments, with their earnest desire that the suggestion offered by the Master of the Rolls may be acted upon by the Government.

" 'I have the honour, etc.,
" 'GEORGE HARRIS.

" 'The Right Hon. C Lewis, Bart., M.P.'

"This morning I sent the Master of the Rolls a copy of Lord Chancellor Hardwicke's Life, accompanied by the following note :—

" '4, PUMP COURT, TEMPLE, *February 11th*, 1860.

" 'SIR,—May I beg your acceptance of the accompanying volumes, in the perusal of which you may perhaps feel an interest, and which may serve to some extent as an illustration of the benefits which might result from the proposed inquiry into the private collections of manuscripts in this country ? Had such an inquiry been instituted years ago as regards the Hardwicke manuscripts, I believe that I should have been able to render this work less imperfect than it is.

" 'I read with great pleasure at the time it was published the "Memoirs of Sir Samuel Romilly," and have the volumes in my library. I have heard Mrs. G. Harris' father, the late Rev. George Innes, of Warwick, speak with much interest of an evening he once spent in Sir Samuel Romilly's company when he dined with him at Warwick Castle, Lord Warwick and Mr. Spencer Perceval being the only other persons present.

" 'I am myself a member of the Midland Circuit, of which he was once so bright an ornament.

" 'Since I had the honour of waiting upon you at the Rolls House, I have received a note from Lord Brougham, who says, "I entirely approve of the plan suggested by Sir J. Romilly, and think it a great improvement."

" 'I have the honour, etc.,

" 'GEORGE HARRIS.

" 'His Honour the Right Hon. the Master of the Rolls.'

" In reply to the above letter, the Master of the Rolls wrote to me from the Rolls, February 12th, 1860, thanking me very particularly for the present of my Life of Lord Hardwicke, which he prizes very highly. He has also to thank me for the obliging note which accompanied it, and the notice of his father, which is always acceptable to him. He adds, 'with regard to the remainder of your letter and the observation of Lord Brougham, you must forgive me for remarking that I made no *suggestion* in the conversation I had with you on the subject of manuscripts in private repositories. I only answered your question, and stated what I had done on the reference to me by the Government respecting your memorial.'

" In reply to above I wrote to state that I did not at all understand the Master as making any suggestion to me, but understood him to remark, when I inquired if the proposed investigation into private manuscripts could not be undertaken by the Record Office, that in his reply to the Government he had made a suggestion of that nature."

CHAPTER XVIII.

COMPETITION FOR A PROFESSORSHIP, AND AN AUTUMN
ADVENTURE.

1860.

"February 15*th.*

" WENT yesterday to Wimbledon to deliver a ' Discourse on Ghosts,' at the Lecture Hall there. About two hundred and fifty present. Audience very attentive.

" 21*st.*—Delivered this evening lecture on the Plague at the St. Martin's-in-the-Fields Institute. A hundred and forty present. Very attentive.

"*March* 1*st.*—Delivered my lecture on the Plague this evening at Dunn's Hall Lecture Room, Newington Causeway. About two hundred and twenty present, as many as the room will well hold. Here ends the present session of my lecturing campaign, which has been a very successful one on the whole—could not well have been more successful—and I only hope that the next, in which I shall begin to turn my efforts to real account, may be equally prosperous. I do really think that lecturing is my forte after all, and in this I believe I have been more successful, and hope for still greater successes, than in any pursuit in which I have yet engaged.

" 2*nd.*—Dined to-day with Elizabeth at the Sydney Turners'. Had much talk with Mr. T. about the manuscript memorial. He also recommended me to apply to the Master of the Rolls about it, and if that did not do, to get some influential member of Parliament to go with me to the Home Secretary. Mr. Turner said that the Tailors' Literary Institute originated in 'Alton Locke,' and that he (Mr. Turner) had lectured there.

"*7th.*—At Nottingham Assizes to-day. John introduced me to Mr. Enfield, the town clerk, who promised to show me the Corporation records.

"*8th.*—Saw in the paper to-day the appointment of Creasy, who is Professor of History at University College and one of our proposed manuscript commissioners, to the chief justiceship of Ceylon. Should much like to obtain the professorship, and wrote to Elizabeth to make inquiries for me about it. It would give me a status, and be useful for bringing out my best works, also for lecturing, and in connection with the manuscript memorial. At the town clerk's office in Nottingham to-day, looking through the index of the records, which was prepared by one of the deputy keepers of the records in 1818. Several entries relating to the progress of James I. and the preparations for entertaining him, houses to be fresh-painted and roads cleared. The King was to enter Nottingham on horseback, and a short speech was to be prepared for the occasion by Mr. Pierrpoint. Among the items of the expenses are some for 'wine and sugar,' also for a 'bottleman and jester.' A reference in another part is made to the Gunpowder Plot, and to the congratulation to the King from Nottingham on his escape.

" Some references to the Plague at different times. Huts to be prepared for the infected, especially below the castle. Swine were ordered to be kept up. Dogs and cats were to be killed, and the goose fair to be held in a different part, for fear of bringing in infection. Under the head of 'Town,' there were several references to the Great Rebellion and the raising of forces, etc.,

also to Oliver Cromwell, and to Queen Anne, and the
marriage of the Princess Mary to William of Orange,
and the Revolution of 1688, the Rebellion of 1745, and
the Young Pretender.   Reference to a present to the
Archbishop of York.   Families of Pierrpoint, Bryan of
Newstead, and Clifton referred to.   A general order for
the destruction of hedgehogs.   Dates not generally
given in index.

" 10*th*.—Wrote to-day to Lord Brougham respecting
the professorship of history.   Elizabeth to-day forwarded me a note she had from Mr. Sydney Turner
about the professorship, in which he says that ' one's
general impression of the views of any English professor at the Gower Street College would be that he
was a good Whig, if not a Radical, and a very liberal
Churchman, if not a Dissenter.   But that is no reason
why, if the opportunity offered, some better infusion
should not be made.'

" 17*th*.—Received a kind note from Lord Brougham
this morning in reply to mine about the professorship,
with which I am very much pleased indeed.   Writing
from Cannes, (Vor), March 16th, 1860, he says ' I am
extremely pleased with your disposition to become a
candidate, conceiving that your accepting the vacant
professorship is of the greatest importance in the point
of view in which you put it.   I have written by this
day's post to mention how great a value I attach to
your filling the professorship.   If any others occur
to me I will write them also, but I believe the letter
I am about to write will have all the effect I can
give.'

" 27*th*.—A letter from the Secretary of University
College, saying that ' the class of history is not endowed.'

"*April 2nd.*—Received yesterday the following note

from Lord Brougham, containing one enclosed to Mr. Atkinson, which I sent on. Lord Brougham, again writing from Cannes (Vor), March 24th, 1860, hopes and trusts I have sent in my application, else what he had written would have no effect.

"'He enclosed also a few lines to the Secretary, which I was to send if the matter had not been determined.'

"A notice the other day of my 'Theory of Representation' in the *Sun*, in which they say of it, 'At this time, when the attention of the House of Commons and the public generally is so much excited on the subject of reform, Mr. Harris' comprehensive and well-written little volume will be read alike with interest and advantage. All his propositions are stated clearly and temperately, and are argued throughout with logical skill, judgment, and discretion.'

" 10*th*.—Delivered, at Mr. Short's particular request, in the schoolroom at Temple, Balsall, a lecture on ' The Pursuits and Mode of Life of our Forefathers,' illustrated by diagrams. The room quite full. Very attentive, laughed a good deal, and seemed highly pleased and quite to enter into the lecture.

" 27*th*.—Received the following from Mr. Macready, to be used, if I wish, as a testimonial.

"'6, WELLINGTON SQUARE, CHELTENHAM, *April* 26*th*, 1860.

" 'MY DEAR SIR,—It was with peculiar satisfaction I heard of your intention to offer yourself as a candidate for the professorship of history at University College, London. You may remember I was among the listeners to your interesting paper on the manuscript treasures of England, and shared with your auditors in the gratification of learning from your research

how much might be brought to light of valuable knowledge that is at present buried in the obscurity of
neglected libraries.   Much of the history of our country
is yet to be rewritten, and I feel sure your occupation of this professional chair would greatly tend
towards furnishing materials for the task.   With the
sincere hope that I may have the pleasure of congratulating you and ourselves on your election,

" ' I remain, etc.,

" ' W. C. MACREADY.

" ' GEORGE HARRIS, ESQ.'

" *May 1st.*—Went to Nottingham, and delivered in
the lecture hall of the Mechanics' Institution this evening ' The Story of the Plague.'

" *9th.*—This evening I went to a meeting at University
College of the Schoolmasters' Social Science Association, at which Lord Brougham, who returned to England yesterday, presided.   I never heard him speak
with more force, and effect, and readiness ; and the
applause was tremendous.   The great hall was crowded
in every part.   At the close of the meeting I got Mr.
Atkinson to tell him I was there, and he wished much
to see me before he went out of town again.   He
asked me to call on Sunday, between one and two.
Mr. Atkinson asked me to accompany them, and he
and Lord Brougham then went to a conversazione
in the library of the Graphic Society, where were
a number of fine water-colour drawings and paintings.

" *13th.*—Called on Lord Brougham (who was at the
Temple Church in the morning) at his house at half-
past one, but found him in a great bustle ; he said
he had been most unreasonably and unaccountably put

out by a sermon at the Temple Church of three-quarters
of an hour, which ought to have been only a quarter
of an hour, and that therefore he could only see me
for a few minutes.

"He said he was going to-morrow morning for a
couple of days to Brougham Hall, thence on to Edinburgh to be installed as Chancellor, and then he was to
take a tour with the Bishop of Oxford on the cotton
question, and should be back in London on the 25th.
I told him of the testimonials I had got, which he said
he was very glad to hear of, and that nothing would be
done at present about the election.

"I asked him about getting the manuscript memorial arranged, and he said, 'Oh, you had better let me
see the Master of the Rolls about that, which I will do
when I get back,' and which is just what I wish.   I
told him that I believed some of the clerks in the
Record Office were strongly opposed to the plan, fearing, I suppose, that they will have more work put upon
them without more pay; but Lord Brougham laughed
and said, 'Oh, the Master of the Rolls won't care about
the opposition.'

"14th.—At the British Museum. Obtained a view
of some of the volumes of the missals and other works
in the Harleian manuscripts, and was taken into a private
room for this purpose, and obtained (by getting a
recommendation signed by Mr. Selfe as police magistrate) permission to copy any of the drawings and
illuminations.   Some of these, done by the monks in
the old times, particularly about the fourteenth century,
are really most beautiful.   The drawing is not always
very correct, and the perspective is generally bad; but
the colouring is good, and the finish exquisite.   The expression, too, in many of the countenances is admirable.
The figures are in general rather stiff.   The buildings

are very well done, and serve to afford a very complete notion of the state of things at the time described. The manuscripts are in beautiful preservation, and are bound in large folio volumes in crimson velvet, and are valued at £1,000 each. The drawings are in general very small, and require to be looked at through a magnifying glass, but will serve admirably to make enlarged copies from on calico for diagrams ; and it will be very convenient doing this in a private room, where I can have my apparatus for drawing about me and be undisturbed.

"24*th*.—At work each day lately at the British Museum, copying some illuminations in missals in four departments, which come into one diagram, representing criminals being bound and taken to prison and to execution and being decapitated.

"*June* 9*th*.—Received a note from Lord Brougham, dated from Grafton Street, June 8th, in which he says he feels the importance of despatch so much, that he sent the letter [which I prepared for him] signed, with the printed paper, this morning before nine o'clock to Sir G. Lewis' private residence in Knightsbridge, and accompanied it with a private letter, strongly urging despatch and telling him how important it was.

"16*th*.—Received another letter from Lord Brougham, dated 4, Grafton Street, Saturday, 3 p.m., in which he tells me he is sorry to say that, having sent for Mr. Atkinson (Secretary to the college), he found that the report of the Senate, to whom the matter was referred, was in favour of Beasly, an Oxford man, so very decidedly, that there would have been no use in my attending the Council, which will adopt that report as a matter of course. He asked Atkinson if, from his communication with the members of the

Council, he could say that there was any doubt, and he distinctly said, " None." He is heartily sorry for this, and feels it personally a great disappointment.

" Wrote as follows to Lord Brougham in reply to his communication :—

"' 19, QUEEN SQUARE, W.C., *June* 16*th*, 1860.

"' MY DEAR LORD,—I feel extremely obliged to your Lordship for your very kind note. I will not affect to deny that I am excessively disappointed at not succeeding to the professorship, as I had formed hopes and plans of importance respecting it which are now doomed to be annihilated. As regards the manuscript inquiry also, I feel that the failure to obtain the professorship is very serious. On the other hand, I am persuaded that the Council have only discharged their duty in choosing what appeared to be the best man ; and if I can be of any use in assisting the new Professor as regards the particular department in history to which I have turned my attention more especially, my services are entirely at his disposal. I should be very sorry to be instrumental in interrupting the harmony between the different members of the college.

"' I must now also beg of your Lordship no longer to labour under any disappointment or annoyance on my account, and I can assure you that I shall ever feel deeply grateful for your extreme kindness to me on this occasion, and proud of the good opinion which you have been pleased to express in my favour.

"' Believe me, etc.,

"' GEORGE HARRIS.

"' The Right Hon. LORD BROUGHAM.'

" A new project came into my mind this evening,

which is, to have an exhibition of all my diagrams
respecting 'Habits and Pursuits,' adding to their
number from all the most interesting illuminations I
can find, and call it a 'Pictorial Exhibition,' illustrated
by a descriptive account instead of a lecture, and which
will be much more attractive than the latter, and, I
should think, sure to take ; and if it does, it may be
followed by the 'Discourse on Ghosts,' the 'Story of
the Plague,' and the 'Lectures on Napoleon.'

" *August 8th.*—This autumn we again made a tour
on the Continent, and leaving England on the 8th of
August and visiting the Rhine, Nuremberg, and the
Tyrol, of which we made ample notes in our journal.

" *September* 19th.—In the afternoon, about half-past
four, having ordered dinner to be ready at six, I went
to explore the Finsterminz Pass. The entrance
is strikingly like the Via Mala, and is most noble, a
suitable gateway to so splendid a territory. Made a
sketch of this for an etching, and walked on to near the
Finsterminz inn, where I made another sketch of the
pass running into the main one. The tops of all the
mountains to-day covered with snow, which added
much to the effect of the scenery. In returning I
stopped again near the fortifications, and made another
sketch. The scenery on the whole is most magnificent,
even sublime, and equals, if not surpasses, anything
I ever saw before, not excepting even the Via Mala,
to which it is in some respects superior, having more
rock. While I was sketching near the fort, two
soldiers came and looked over me, and observed it was
a fine prospect. I showed them my other sketches,
which they seemed much interested in, and asked to
look again at those of Linz and Salzburg, but did not
thank me for showing them when I went on. When I
had got about a quarter of a mile homewards, I met a

party of soldiers, and they stopped me, and told me I must go back with them. At first I thought they were in joke, and waited ; but they said I must march with them. Very soon a larger party from the fort, and apparently a sergeant, joined them, and walked by my side. When we got to the fort, they all came out to look at me, and there seemed to be a great commotion. They took me into a dark passage, and I was much afraid I should be detained, that poor Elizabeth would be dreadfully alarmed, and that I should not be able to let her know where I was. I also feared that my sketch-book would be taken away, as I know in France it is forbidden to sketch any fortified places. In a short time the sergeant came to me, and brought me into a room where a man, the commanding officer I suppose, was sitting at a table with papers before him. The sergeant made his complaint, and I at once showed my passport, and pointed out the Austrian visés upon it, which were duly inspected.

"He looked very suspiciously indeed at my manuscript vocabulary of German words, as though he suspected it was a list of persons I was commissioned to assassinate or of forts I was to report upon as a spy. He also looked at the papers in the pocket of the passport. He then asked me if I had not a drawing-book, which I at once gave him. He looked carefully at each picture, and the sergeant insisted that those of Linz and Salzburg were drawings of fortifications, which, with the sketches of the rocks I had just made, supplied counts in the heavy indictment against me. I told him I was a traveller, and that they were only made for pleasure, and to each of the sergeant's charges he shook his head, and said, 'Nichts!'—*i.e.*, 'Not guilty!'—and then returned the book to me, and I was permitted to return to my hotel, the officer telling me

I must not make any more drawings of the pass
about there. This detained me so long that I did not
get back until a quarter to seven, and met a man sent
by Elizabeth in search of me, who said she was much
alarmed.

" When I got to the inn, I found the poor dear
quite frantic in the street, and a crowd round her.
She fell on my neck, and I of course told her what had
happened. She feared I had tumbled down some
precipice or lost my way.

" In a short time, however, she became pacified, and
we enjoyed together a nice little dinner of boiled trout,
goat cutlets, and wild strawberries. Our inn is
comfortable, but lacks bells, so that I am obliged to
use my voice instead. We laughed over my little
adventure as we finished our half-bottle of red wine,
and it furnishes a pretty and sensational little episode
in our tour.

" *October* 20*th*.—Sent yesterday to the *Times* a full
account of my arrest in Austria, very much the same as
that contained in this journal, though rather condensed,
and omitting names. I headed it 'An Englishman
arrested in Austria as a Spy.' Did not much expect
the *Times* would put it in, so kept a copy to send to
the *Standard* and *Morning Star*. But this morning it
appears at full length, and on the same page with the
leading article ; but they have omitted the words in the
heading 'as a Spy.'

" 27*th*.—While I was on the circuit, Mundell proposed
to me to write to Lord Brougham and offer to become
his biographer, at which he said he thought he would
be much pleased. But I fear he might consider it
presumptuous, and may wish some one of more note
and standing to do it, and indeed probably he has
arranged for this already."

CHAPTER XIX.

FAILURE OF MANUSCRIPT COMMISSION AND OTHER DETAILS.

1860.

" *October 29th.*

" THIS evening I received the following note, which at once finally extinguishes all hopes of the inquiry under the manuscript memorial being instituted, the last remnant of one of my ruined castles in the air :—

" ' HOME OFFICE, *October 29th,* 1860.

" ' SIR,—In reply to your letter of the 20th inst. respecting the memorial for an inquiry into the private manuscript collections in this country, I am desired by Sir George Lewis to inform you that, after full consideration, her Majesty's Government decided not to take any steps for instituting an investigation of that nature.

" ' I have the honour, etc., etc.,

" ' B. C. LAWLES STEPHENSON.

" ' GEORGE HARRIS, ESQ.'

" Wrote as follows to Lord Brougham :—

" ' 19, QUEEN SQUARE, W.C., *October 30th,* 1860.

" ' MY DEAR LORD,—I received the accompanying note yesterday evening from Mr. Stephenson, private secretary to Sir G. C. Lewis, in reply to a note which

I wrote to him about a week ago. Considering that ten members of the present Government signed the memorial and the hopes from time to time held out, I am of course a good deal disappointed at the result. The expense which I have incurred in printing and other respects has also been considerable ; and I had anticipated that very great results of a literary nature might be produced from the proposed inquiry, to prepare the way for which I have made great efforts, and obtained promises of support and assistance from possessors of important documents in several quarters.

" ' I have the honour, etc., etc.,

" ' GEORGE HARRIS.

" ' The Right Hon. LORD BROUGHAM.

" ' To this letter Lord Brougham replied from Brougham, October 31st, 1860, saying, ' how very vexatious it was to find this refusal when the memorial was so signed, and, he believes, backed by some Ministers who signed it. He fears nothing can be done, but will speak to one or two when he passes through town in a week or ten days.'

" *November 6th.*—Sent the following letter to Mr. Fergusson :—

" ' 19, QUEEN SQUARE, W.C., *November 7th,* 1860

" ' SIR,—I have read with much interest an article in the *Quarterly Review* on Stonehenge, of which I am informed that you are the author. In that article allusion is made to the druidical remains in Brittany, and it is stated that, "except in one instance in France, not a single architectural moulding or detail exists." Last year I travelled entirely through Brittany, and paid particular attention to the druidical remains there, and visited not only the great temple at Carnac, but the seldom-explored island of Gaffir Innis, and made several sketches (rough and hasty, indeed) of the different relics, with copies of some of the ciphers to be found on them. These I should much like to show you if you will allow me to have the pleasure of calling upon you, and perhaps you may be able to furnish some clue towards deciphering them. I have consulted Sir F. Madden and others on the subject, but have obtained no satisfactory solution of the mystery. Mr. C. R. Weld, I believe, copied some of them, but I do not know whether he has attempted to discover their meaning. From the mode in which you have handled the subject of your article, it struck me that you possibly might be able to furnish some satisfactory suggestions as to the purport of the ciphers alluded to. I read some time ago with much interest your most able and ingenious work on Indian architecture, which was lent me by Mrs. Moultrie, of Rugby, who is, I believe, your sister. With Mr. and Mrs. Moultrie my family and I have had the pleasure· of being well acquainted for many years past.

" ' I have the honour, etc.,

" ' GEORGE HARRIS.'

" Went to Aldershot this afternoon, and delivered there a 'Discourse on Ghosts.' A very good attendance, and my audience very attentive.

" Received the reply from Mr. Fergusson in answer to mine, dated ' Athenæum, November 9th, 1860,' and saying he should be delighted to see drawings of the Brittany temples.

" 15*th*.—Wrote to Lord Brougham, asking for permission to dedicate to him the work ('Civilisation Considered as a Science') of which I forwarded a copy, and in the composition of which I have been for several years past closely engaged. I told him that the line which I have adopted is that education, although the

main element in the civilisation of a nation, is not alone
sufficient ; and that in conjunction with it should be
applied all those various institutions and requirements
which together constitute what may be considered the
elements of civilisation. I have therefore discussed
separately its value and influence in this respect, and
in conjunction with education, of religious influence,
cultivation of art and science, national institutions
connected with civilisation, dignities and national
distinction, national holidays and commemorations,
moral jurisprudence (including the effect of particular
laws upon civilisation as regards different forms of
government, certain prohibitions, modes of punishment,
dealing with criminals, etc., etc.), internal communi-
nication between different parts of the same country,
and intercourse of different natives one with another.
In the introductory part ('Essence') I have considered
the nature of civilisation, and in what it really consists,
and in the concluding part ('End') I have endeavoured
to point out the leading results derived by a nation from
the complete establishment of civilisation according to
the principles laid down.

"To this request I received a reply from Lord Brougham
dated 4, Grafton Street, November 16, in which he says
he was on the point of writing to me, as he wished to
see me before seeing the Chancellor, whom he had
desired to appoint a time before Tuesday, when he
left town. He asks me to call any time before twelve
o'clock on Monday morning, or before half-past eleven
to-morrow, or to-morrow at four, or Sunday at four,
when he would be at home and free. He is greatly
honoured by my proposed dedication.

"I accordingly called upon him, and I saw him at
once. He said, 'Isn't it scandalous about this manuscript memorial when so many of the Ministers signed

it !' I said that 'ten of them signed it, and several wrote to me as well, saying they would do anything to support it.' He then said, 'Have you any idea who has done it? Is it Gladstone, d'ye think?' I said 'I fancied Lord John Russell, as I heard that he raised objections to it shortly after he came into office, though he was quite in favour of it before.' Lord Brougham asked 'whether Lord John Russell had signed the memorial,' and I said he had. I then observed that 'the Duke of Newcastle had written to me offering to do anything to support it, but he had been abroad lately with the Prince of Wales.' Lord Brougham then said, 'I'm afraid nothing can be done now,' and I feared not.

" 19th.—Went to the Law Amendment Society. Saw Lord Brougham, who shook hands very cordially with me, but did not say anything about having seen Lord Campbell.

" 20th.—Received this morning a note from Lord Brougham, dated 4, Grafton Street, Tuesday morning,— saying, 'I wanted to see you for a few minutes at the Law Amendment Society, but there were too many people.' It was to mention that he had had a long conversation with the Chancellor, who much regretted their conduct in the manuscript department.'

" *December* 13th.—A note from John, asking me on what terms I would sit for Trafford as county court judge at Birmingham for two months. Wrote word I should be ready to take it on having expenses out of pocket.

" 20th.—Mr. Serjeant Jones called this morning, and asked me if I could go at once and sit for him as deputy judge of the Clerkenwell county court, which I did accordingly. Several disputed cases in which attorneys appeared, but I disposed of them all very well and without any hesitation or doubt."

CHAPTER XX.

REMOVAL TO BIRMINGHAM. ACTING JUDGE OF THE COUNTY COURT.

1861—1862.

"*January 2nd.*

"A LETTER to me from Mr. Waterfield, asking me to sit for Trafford as deputy county court judge during this month and February, to which I consented by letter in reply.

"14*th.*—An article by me appears at length in the *Law Times* to-day on the Canadian slave case, under the title of ' Extradition Case : Ought a Slave to be deemed amenable to the Municipal Laws of a Country of which he is not a Member ? ' It is, I think, closely and conclusively argued, and the point raised is quite a new one, and will, I hope, be taken up.

"Called on Trafford, at Waterfield's suggestion, and had a long chat with him. Says counsel are often engaged. Appoints me only for a fortnight now.

"22*nd.*—Came to Birmingham yesterday. In court all to-day and yesterday. Several defended cases in which attorneys were employed, and some nice points to decide, both of law and evidence, but no difficulty in doing so, and all seems to have gone well.

"23*rd.*—Heavy work to-day, and a jury case, in which Motteram [afterwards a judge of this court] was engaged as counsel on one side, and which lasted until six. I had to rule several points of law and to sum up, which I did efficiently, I think. Consider this rather a crisis in my career here.

"*25th.*—Hard at work in court till near five. Two strongly fought cases, with attorney advocates on both sides. In one I had to decide a point of law respecting a notice which put the case out of court. In the other I had to decide mixed points of law and evidence.

" *30th.*—A long case against the Great Western Railway, in which counsel on one side and an attorney on the other. Evidence very conflicting. I could have delivered judgment off hand, but preferred deferring it or giving a written judgment, both on account of the importance of the case and because by that means alone I could do full justice both to the case and to myself, and accordingly prepared one, sitting up late to do it, this evening.

"*February 9th.*—Elizabeth informs me that Blundell has called to tell her that I have been elected, he believes unanimously, a Fellow of the Antiquarian Society.

" *11th.*—A leading article in the *Times* on the extradition case, in which, referring to the opinions in Westminster Hall on the subject, they adopt to a considerable extent my line of argument in my article in the *Law Times.* This was also done lately still further by the writer of a letter in the *Times.*

" *28th.*—Called on Mr. J. Jaffray, the editor and proprietor of the *Birmingham Journal.* He said that I overexerted myself in the court in delivering such elaborate judgments.

" *March 5th.*—Delivered this evening a lecture at St. Mark's Schoolroom (Frank's parish) on ' Manners and Customs in the Olden Time,' illustrated by my diagrams. The audience a full one, and extremely attentive, and applauded and laughed much. It seemed to take thoroughly well.

" 12th.—A hard day's work yesterday, and the court sat until half-past six. A jury case, and another in which counsel were engaged.

" 27th.—At Cheltenham. Called on Macready, and gave him my testimonials for the professorship, and explained to him how it was I was not successful. Talked with him also some time about the manuscript memorial, which he seemed to think must be carried eventually, though, as he observed, measures of this sort were always a long time in this country before they were successful. Promised to dine with him on Wednesday.

"*April* 1st.—Called on Macready this afternoon, and showed him my etchings of the Tyrol and the sketches in Brittany, and also left with him Lord Brougham's letters about the professorship and manuscript commission. He said he had thought the story of Agnes Sorel, of whose burial-place I have a view in the etchings, would do well to dramatise. Talked with him about the ' Essays and Reviews.' I said very few men of moderate, but almost entirely those of extreme, opinions had condemned them, both high and low. He said that if they were so very bad, it was singular that none of the Dissenting ministers had spoken out. I said Dr. Cumming was the only one, who was another man of very extreme opinions, and that I believed what they were really most disliked for was, not any infidel opinions they contained, but the hits against both parties which they dealt out.

" 3rd.—Dined at Macready's. A very agreeable and interesting evening. Animated discussions on various topics, in which I joined, particularly the 'Essays and Reviews.' Debated the principle of identity in the Resurrection. I urged that our Lord's body must have been very different after the Resurrection from what it was before, as His disciples did not recognise Him, and He vanished ; but that, as in the case of a raised body, the primary elements were the same : also that great advantages might be possessed by a pure spirit being united to a glorified body instead of continuing in a separate state, which Dr. B—— remarked was a very important observation. I also argued that it appeared very difficult accurately to define what was meant by purely material and purely immaterial beings. Macready said he could not understand how element- ary parts of a body could be glorified, and ridiculed the idea of 'glorified gases,' and as we were coming away said to Dr. B——, 'Remember the gases.' He said he had intended to take orders, but had scruples, and so went on the stage. All the party seemed to agree with me as to the part taken about the 'Essays and Reviews' by the Archbishop of Canterbury, who has acted rather like a virulent partisan than as a mode- rator or a judge.

"*20th.*—Sometimes think of buying and rebuilding Gorcott Hall, which was early my ambition, and which has been the property and residence of the Chambers family ever since the time of Edward III. But I have no family and no one to leave it to who could afford to keep it up, and without an estate it would be a bane rather than a benefit.

"*26th.*—Held the Tamworth county court yester- day, and the Atherstone one to-day. At the latter the business very heavy, two jury cases, so that we did not finish until seven, and I only got to dinner at a quarter past ten, when I reached Edgbaston. One of the jury

cases was against the London and North-western
Railway Company. Dr. Hill, afterwards M.P. for
Staffordshire, came down especially from London for
the defendant.   It was an action for non-delivery of
forty-three geese at Christmas, intended for a goose
club.   The verdict, in accordance with my summing
up, for the defendants.

"A long extract from a judgment of mine in a
railway case, which I delivered in writing on Monday,
and lent to the attorney on the successful side, reported
at length in the *Daily Post* on Thursday.

"*May* 10*th.*—In London. This evening Elizabeth
and I went to a large conversazione at Mr. Henley's,
in Wimpole Street, on behalf of the Needlewomen's
Institute.   Lord Shaftesbury took the chair.   I thought
the shake of the hand by Lord Shaftesbury of the
Bishop of Oxford the coldest I ever saw.

"15*th.*—To-day we spent with the Gordons at
Northolt, arranging about the improvements at Iselipps, which will really, I think, make a very pretty
place as a summer retreat.   In the way of planting, I
shall be able to do nearly all I aimed at.

"Wrote a long letter to Sir A. Bittlestone. 'Are
you at all interested in, and do you hear much
about, matters relating to the Brahmin and Hindoo
traditions and natives, especially on subjects relating
to philosophy and theology ?   I fancy a great deal of
curious and even valuable matter is yet to be learnt
here.   Some of the traditions are of immense antiquity,
and, I suppose, the manuscripts also.'

"18*th.*—Called to-day on Lord Brougham. He appeared to me a good deal broken and out of spirits,
and to have lost all his usual vitality and energy.   The
cold, I fancy, affects him a good deal, and he asked me
about it.   There was a large crayon drawing in Lord

Brougham's dining-room of the late Queen Caroline
and the Princess Charlotte when a baby. The former
rather good-looking, but not handsome, in her youth.

"*20th.*—At the Antiquarian Society on Thursday
evening, and promised to exhibit my sketches of
druidical remains in Brittany.

"*30th.*—What I should like to effect with regard
to Civilisation as a Science, is to render it a leading
authority, as containing the first principles to be laid
down on the subject of civilisation, and all politics and
legislature connected with it, in a manner corresponding
with that in which Adam Smith's 'Wealth of Nations'
is appealed to in matters of commercial economy and
legislation.

"*June 7th.*—In Wales, at Gwastadcoed, near Cemmes.
Our hostess, good Mrs. G——, complained to me to-day
that her nephew was very wild. I asked her to explain
her meaning. She said, 'He swears, and attends a
Dissenting chapel!'

Mrs. E——, the butcher's widow at Cemmes, has a
son apprenticed to a butcher in London. His master
wrote her a letter, which she showed us, in which he
says, 'He is a good lad, and has done his slaughtering
a deal neater lately.'

"*21st.*—Wrote to Mr. Radford, and received a
testimonial from him in reply, addressed to the Lord
Chancellor, and stating that I am fully efficient to
succeed Mr. Trafford, and that he 'has particularly
observed the perfectly fair way in which Mr. Harris has
put the cases to the juries and the equally impartial
manner of summing up, patiently affording every
opportunity to the advocate, whether barrister or attorney, of making every point in the case.' He adds that
he here merely repeats what he has already expressed
voluntarily to others, and without my knowledge.

"A good report in the *Post* of the 3rd inst. of the last jury case, for stealing an ingot of gold, tried before me, in which they say, 'His Honour sent the matter most carefully to the jury, explaining the law as to the result of negligence on the part of the defendant as well as the plaintiff, and that the questions put by the jury were fully answered by the learned judge.'

"*24th.*—Startled this morning by the intelligence of the death of the Lord Chancellor, quite suddenly, found dead in his bedroom by his servant yesterday morning, having been quite well the evening before and had a dinner-party.

"*July 30th.*—It appears from the returns that there is an increase of two thousand cases in the court during the last six months.   If things go on at this rate, they will have to appoint another judge to assist.

"*August 6th.*—Delivered judgment to-day in a great mercantile case, which runs very long, and analyses the facts minutely, and winds up with a somewhat philosophical enunciation of the principles of evidence. Indeed, the latter portion suggested a note for 'Treatise on Man,' on the difficulty of fabricating truth, thus effecting an alliance between my law and my philosophy. A curious matrimonial case in the afternoon, judgment in which I deferred, at the request of the defendant, until reading the letters.

"*15th.*—Received yesterday the following note from Mr. Trafford : 'When I was in Birmingham the other day, I was glad to hear that your decisions had given general satisfaction to the suitors and the public, and that every one concerned was pleased with the way in which the business was conducted.'

"*September 15th.*—During this vacation I made a tour in Scotland, accompanied by Elizabeth returning home to-day.

"17*th*.—Called when in Edinburgh on Mr. Halkett, the librarian at the Advocates' Library, about the manuscript commission, and was shown their library by him. Among the papers a letter of Mary Queen of Scots; one from Charles I. when a boy; one from the Duke of York to his father, telling him he had begun to learn substantives; the original manuscript of 'Waverley,' and some valuable missals; an original of St. Augustine's 'De Civitate Dei;' and a manuscript Bible of the twelfth century.

"18*th*.—Called on Mr. Laing, the librarian of the Signet Library, who knows Sir F. Madden, and had much talk with him about the commission, and who showed me several papers; also again on Mr. Robertson, who showed me many papers of great interest: an illuminated proclamation of David I.; a disposition, in her own hand, made by Mary Queen of Scots, of her jewels and apparel in the event of her death during her confinement; an autograph of Oliver Cromwell; the address of a hundred Scotch barons to the Pope, etc. Told him of the papers at Wimpole relating to the rebellion of 1745. He doubted if the rebellion would have succeeded if Charles Edward had marched on for Derby, or whether the rebels could have held Scotland alone, as he thought the English Jacobites were not cordial in supporting the Scotch, and that the Pretender did not do enough to satisfy the Protestant feeling of the latter. Called on Professor Simpson, who thought he could get some of the literary societies in Edinburgh to take up the manuscript memorial question. He introduced me to the Master of Torpichen, who has papers.

"Wrote the following letter to Lord Brougham :—

"'County Court, Birmingham, *September* 26*th*, 1861.

"'My dear Lord,—I have much pleasure in for-

warding to your Lordship for your acceptance the first
copy of my new work ["Civilisation Considered as a
Science"], which is now ready for publication, and which
your Lordship kindly allowed me to dedicate to you.
I only hope that the book may prove worthy of this
honour, and that its contents may meet with your
approval.   It has been the occasional labour of twenty-
four years—certainly the best part of the author's life.
I am still at work here, and shall probably continue
until the end of the year, as Mr. Trafford appears to be
no better.

" ' I have, etc.,

" ' GEORGE HARRIS.

"Wrote as follows to the Emperor of the French,
with a copy of my 'Civilisation Considered as a
Science : '—

" ' I trust that an Englishman who has spent many
happy hours in France, and who has visited several of
its most attractive points of interest, may be allowed to
present to your Imperial Majesty a copy of a work
which is about to appear before the public.   Allusion
is there made to the enlightened policy as regards
'Civilisation' of the late Emperor Napoleon ; and the
author ventures very respectfully to express a hope
that, under the wise and able government of your
Imperial Majesty, the alliance between the two greatest
nations in Europe may be yet more firmly cemented by
the common desire to further the general interest of
each.'

" *October* 18*th*.—Reading an account of Napoleon's
captivity at St. Helena.   Bad as St. Helena may be,
had I been in Napoleon's place, I think I could have
made myself content there in composing a work
worthy of the theme containing the history of my

life. Had I had the opportunity, nothing I should have enjoyed more than a visit to him at St. Helena. It is surely worth while to pay a distant visit to the most remarkable man more than to the most remarkable place in the world.

" 19*th*.—Two fair and satisfactory reviews of 'Civilisation as a Science' in the Birmingham papers of to-day, each about a column in length. The *Journal* pronounces it ' a thoughtful book,' and ' as readable as history,' and says, 'Such a volume as this is always welcome, as the result, not of mere book-making, but of long and careful consideration of some of the mysteries and problems of our time.' At the conclusion it is termed ' a calm, philosophical, and thoughtful essay, written in a clear, unpretending style, and well worth the careful study of all those who are not utterly devoted to business or absorbed by the passing incidents of our busy age.' *Aris' Gazette* says that the ' arguments are urged in a spirit of frankness that does honour to the integrity and candour of the writer,' and that ' the reader will find a vein of fine philosophy running through the entire work, and a tone of high morality that cannot fail to command respect.' A tolerable analysis of the work given in both of the notices.

" 21*st*.—Delivered a lecture on ' Manners and Customs' at the Upper Norwood Institution this evening. I was asked to give another lecture, and a great satisfaction was generally expressed with this.

" The following notice of my work on 'Civilisation ' appeared in the *Observer* of Sunday last : ' In this work an attempt is made, and, we may add, with considerable success, to define the nature and essence of that somewhat uncertain and doubtful state of things which is comprehended under the term of

civilisation. The various elements which contribute
to the constitution and progress of civilisation are
pointed out with much clearness and force ; and the
author explains how in his opinion it is susceptible of
scientific treatment, and how desirable it is that every
branch of civilisation should be cultivated in order to
ensure its establishment as an entire system or condition. The work, as a whole, is calculated to have a
useful effect in directing attention to the various
systems of education, and in inducing thoughtful
men and women to examine in a philosophical spirit
those evidences or results of civilisation with which
they are surrounded.'

" 31st.—At the opening of the Middle Temple
Library by the Prince of Wales, for which I also
obtained tickets for Elizabeth. At four a *déjeuner* in
the hall ; turtle and champagne in abundance. The
ladies in the gallery. A conversazione in the library
in the evening. Met the Bishop of London, who
shook hands with me, and thanked me for my book.
Shook hands also with Lord Brougham, and introduced
Elizabeth to him.

" Wrote to the Emperor's secretary at the Tuileries,
asking him ' in what manner and to whom my book
should be sent.'

" *November 9th.*—Went to the dinner given by the
Town Council of Birmingham to the retiring mayor,
Ryland. My health as judge proposed by G. Dawson,
who said he was informed I had performed the duties
' with judgment, fairness, and temper.' I replied
pretty fluently.

" 25th.—Came this morning to Manbdeth Hall, the
Bishop of Manchester's. Very kindly and hospitably
received. No one else staying in the house. The
grounds very pretty, well wooded, and nicely undulated.

The conservatory magnificent, and a noble staircase and entrance hall. Bishop very affable, only so far proud as now and then to call me 'Mr.' Harris instead of 'George' or 'Harris,' as of yore.

" 27*th*.—A notice of three-quarters of a column of 'Civilisation as a Science' in the *John Bull.* They say of the work 'that it is remarkable, among other discussions of the topic, for the usefulness with which it has adhered to the exact province marked out by the term *civilisation,* greatly to the advantage of the precise and logical character of his treatise.' They also say that I 'discuss the nature of civilisation in a very lucid and comprehensive manner.' Have much enjoyed my visit here, and found the Bishop of Manchester most friendly and cordial. Had some talk with the Bishop in the evening about my taking the coif and trying to get into Parliament, but he does not recommend it. Nothing could have been pleasanter than the Bishop has been with me, quite in the old familiar way, and lots of joking between us, as in old times.

" 30*th*.—Returned to Birmingham to-day.

" Wrote to E. on the anniversary of our wedding day, ' May every happiness attend you, to whom I feel I owe the happiest days I have ever experienced, and am sure I would do anything I could to make your own happiness greater.'

" *December* 15*th*.—Very much shocked this morning by the intelligence of the death of the Prince Consort. On Friday was the first mention of his being ill. Yesterday there was an alarming leading article about him in the *Times.* This morning at St. John's Church, at which the prayers of the congregation were asked for the Queen and the royal family, which was the first intimation of the event, the Prince Consort's name was omitted. At the close of the sermon, the sad event was formally announced. He will be a great loss to the nation, and on various accounts, foreign and domestic; and his death must be a terrible blow to the poor Queen. The Queen, as Lord Hardwicke told me, owed much to his teaching for perfecting her education; and of the two he was always the freest from party spirit. The Bishop of Manchester remarked to me how well the Prince was up in the civil law, which, he told the Bishop, he had picked up at Bonn.

" 16th.—When the court met this morning, I alluded to the melancholy loss the nation had sustained, and said that if I were to consult my own feelings, bearing in mind, too, the Prince's repeated visits to Birmingham and his alliance to the legal profession as a member of Lincoln's Inn, I should adjourn the proceedings altogether; but considering the great inconvenience this would be to the suitors, I thought it would be better to take all the undefended cases and postpone the others until some future day. Mr. H——, who came to consult me before I went into court, then rose and, as the leader of the advocates, acquiesced in this arrangement, after speaking eloquently on the subject of the national bereavement.

" 27th.—Delivered a lecture on the Plague in the schoolroom at Northolt. Quite full, and all appeared much interested.

" A note from F. D. Maurice, thanking me for what he terms my 'careful and elaborate work on civilisation. I am glad you have done justice to Lord Brougham, whose old age we ought none of us to forget.'

1862.

"*January 4th.*—In London. We spent the evening with the Sydney Turners.

"*6th.*--Went to Norwood, and delivered a lecture at the Institute there on 'Ghosts and Apparitions.' Audience attentive.

"*8th.*—Smith, the wig-maker in the Temple, told me that he had been employed to construct a wig for the Prince of Wales to wear on the day of his being made a bencher, and that it was sent for him to Windsor, but that he declared, 'If I am to put that thing on my head, I had rather stop at home!' So they telegraphed from Windsor to the Temple to know if the benchers would dispense with his wearing it, which they consented to do.

"*21st.*—Delivered my lecture this evening at the Midland Institute on the 'Habits and Pursuits of our Forefathers.' The lecture well received.

"*22nd.*—A few lines of notice of my lecture in the *Daily Post*, terming it 'interesting and instructive,' containing 'excellent matter' and 'excellent diagrams,' and as 'graphically describing' the scenes portrayed.

"*24th.*—Addressed an appropriate letter to the Lord Chancellor, sending the dedication of my 'Principia' to him.

"Delivered a written judgment to-day in an interesting case, an action to recover money for a portrait, resisted, and successfully, on the ground of its not being a likeness, which was stipulated for expressly.

"*26th.*—This evening I presided at the annual meeting of the Birmingham Law Students' Society, and delivered an address, which was very well, I may quite say enthusiastically, received, and was much applauded by those who moved and seconded and spoke on the vote of thanks to me. In my reply, thanking them I said that Lord Coke had been adverse to lawyers cultivating literature, and had said, 'Lady Common Law must lie alone;' but I would rejoin that if she is to

'lie alone,' she is never likely to prove prolific! A
fair outline of my address, containing extracts from
the principal portions. The registrar of the court told
me to-day that my lecture at the Institute had won
for me golden opinions.

"A number of the *Sun*, containing a notice of
'Civilisation as a Science,' giving a general outline
of the work, specifying the elements, says, 'All the
several objects are treated in a spirit of moderation
and impartiality, and are examined fully and com-
prehensively; and though of course it cannot be
expected in so large and important a field of inquiry
that all readers will agree with Mr. Harris in every
view he takes and in every inference he draws, yet
every one must admire the truly liberal and enlightened
tone in which his investigations are conducted. The
division which treats of the end resulting from the
complete establishment of civilisation is one that will
amply repay perusal, and will be found of the deepest
interest alike to the divine, the statesman, and the
philanthropist.'

"*February* 16th.—Received a note from Lord
Brougham, dated from Cannes (Vor), Ch. El., February 4th, 1862, in which he expresses how extremely
obliged to me he is for the papers sent him some weeks
ago. 'Sergeant Jones' views are most useful, and are
ably urged.' Adds that what I say of the Prince Consort
receiving my new work suggests to him the expediency
of letting his acknowledgment of it be known. Was
greatly interested in reading my late proceedings at
Birmingham in a local paper which our friend the Recorder of Birmingham sent him. Hopes and trusts
that Bethel will do his duty towards me, though he is
slow about it.

"Concludes by saying 'that the settlement for the

present at last of the American affair makes it unnecessary for him to be at the meeting of Parliament.
I should very reluctantly be dragged away to encounter
frost and fog instead of the sultry summer which they
still have here.'

"*March 4th.*—Received another letter from Lord
Brougham, dated Cannes (Vor), Ch. El., February 7th,
1862, in which he says, 'the main point of law amend-
ments certainly is the addition of equity jurisdiction,
and especially as to legacies and residues to a limited
extent. But the great evil is of so arranging matters
as to leave the optional operation if power were given
to proceed in all cases within the clause without plaintiff's consent, and only to stay proceedings if opposition
were offered.'

" He also says, 'that there can be no difficulty at all
in presenting the copy of book to the Emperor. If it is
sent to him at the Hotel Meurice, Rue Rivoli, Paris, he
can, on passing through Paris, have it presented by his
friend Mocquard, his confidential secretary ; or can
write to Mocquard, having first directed the book to be
sent to him.' He concludes by informing me that when
he presents books to princes, he generally sends
ordinarily bound copies, and apologises for not having
them finer.

" I sent the following reply :—

"'County Court, Birmingham, *March 5th,* 1862.

"' My dear Lord,—I have directed my publishers
to send a copy of my work by post to your Lordship at
Meurice's, so that your Lordship may at once give such
directions as you think proper about it being presented.

" I have seen Mr. Hastings about the insertion of my
proposed article on ' County Courts Legislation ' in the

Law Review. He is desirous that it should appear in the May number, and expresses a wish that it may lead to discussion on the subject at the Social Science Conference. The points adverted to in your Lordship's letter shall be duly touched upon.

" 16*th*.—A very singular circumstance happened to me this afternoon. While taking a walk by myself, I thought I would visit the spot—a field with no road through it—about which we had a good deal of talk yesterday evening, where Treen saw the apparition of a coffin, and his relatives following it, near a spot called Dead Men's End. Just as I got to it, I met a cart, which some people, dressed in black, were following, and on looking back, I perceived that in the cart was a coffin, with a pall thrown loosely over part of it. It seems a poor man had died in a cottage near, and they were carrying his remains to Bilton. But meeting a funeral unexpectedly at such a spot, and just after talking of the spectre funeral, was a most singular coincidence.

" 22*nd*.—Delivered the first of my lectures on 'Habits and Pursuits' at the Midland Institute this evening. The audience full, and very attentive.

" *April* 4*th*.—Dined at Mr. Ryland's. A large party to meet the Recorder, by whom I sat. Very pleasant indeed, and all very affable. The mayor, Mr. Hawkes, and two others also there. L—— came and sat by me after we got into the drawing-room, and I talked to him about his prospects, and advised his getting into Parliament, but he does not think that desirable, and says he can't afford it. He has dined lately at Lord Palmerston's, and has been attending the House of Commons.

" 10*th*.—A note from Canon Gordon, who says, ' I can't refrain from writing one line to express the pleasure with which I have read, I will not say all, but the larger portion of your book on "Civilisation." I have read to page 281, and shall hope shortly to complete the whole. Your observations on national religious influence must be acceptable to all Churchmen, and what you say of Sunday being too often made a day of total idleness is most true, instead of its being the holiest and happiest of the week.'

" 21*st*.—Delivered this evening a lecture on 'Habits and Pursuits' in the schoolroom at Harborne, at the request of the vicar. A very good attendance, most of the principal people being there. The lecture was very well received indeed, and all the hits appeared to take thoroughly.

"A present from Mr. F. D. Maurice of his 'Moral and Metaphysical Philosophy,' which I shall much prize, and for which I wrote and thanked him.

"*May 2nd.*—An article in the *Law Review* of this month on my 'Civilisation as a Science,' giving a general outline of its contents, and treating it as an important work. They say of the work that 'it treats the civilising influence of Christianity with a justice which the writer of the "History of Civilisation" has utterly failed to show. Mr. Harris acknowledges Christianity to be one of the grandest elements of civilisation. There are some curious suggestions for avoiding sameness and commonplacedness of sermons, which might be put in force with advantage to those who preach and those who listen. One of the chapters contains some excellent remarks on the subject of toleration. There is an interesting discussion on the influence of war upon civilisation and the counter-influence of civilisation upon war.'

" 13*th*.—A report in the *Daily News* of to-day of the meeting of the Law Amendment Society yesterday evening, at which, they say, 'a paper by Mr. George Harris on "The Extension of the Jurisdiction of County Courts" was read by Mr. Palmer.' It commenced by eulogising the efforts of Lord Brougham in establishing county courts, and then referred to my proposals for extending the jurisdiction and promoting county court judges to seats in the superior courts. The paper was generally admitted to be of a suggestive character.

" *26th.*—At Tamworth for the county court. A hard day, two jury cases, and did not get away until eight, and the business not then all disposed of. Six actions brought by Sir R—— P—— against different tenants for dilapidations and arrears, which excited a very strong feeling, and the court constantly disturbed by cheering and clapping as important evidence on either side came out. I summed up as impartially as I could, and the jury returned a verdict against the baronet, quite contrary to the evidence. General cheering in court when the first verdict was announced, which was re-echoed loudly in the street by the crowd outside.

" *22nd.*—Walked this afternoon from Ipsley, where I have been staying with the Dolbens, to Gorcott Hall, to see how far it would be likely to serve me as a residence should I obtain the court at Birmingham. The poor old house, like the family it once sheltered, in a very ruinous, tumble-down condition, and would cost a great sum to restore ; but the grounds very pretty, and the view from it charming. Talked with the Dolbens about living there. It is only twelve miles from Birmingham and on the high-road. I feel inclined to make it my residence instead of Iselipps if Henry will sell it, either completely or only conditionally. Dr. Bloxam used to dine there in the time of my great-grandfather, who drove four greys, and went by the name of ' Old Sir,' and was one year High Sheriff of Warwickshire.

Two haunches of venison used to be cooked for one dinner, that they might get the best cuts out of each. The old gentleman usually had for his supper a bowl of cream in which the spoon would stand upright, and yet lived to be ninety. Gorcott Hall has been in the Chambers family ever since the time of Edward III.

"24th.—Dined at Dr. Gifford's (the annual school dinner to the examiners, etc.), to meet Robert Burn, who said he was reading my work on 'Civilisation,' and wished it was longer, and that I had gone more into detail under each head.

"Went to Iselipps to see the progress of the building, which is most satisfactory and well contrived. I think, when all is done, that we shall have a charming rural residence, a paradise created out of chaos. Every one, except Mr. Gordon and I, have pronounced Iselipps to be beyond the possibility of being made anything of a place of.

"Sent a copy of my 'Civilisation as a Science' to Dr. Newman, at the Oratory, Edgbaston, to whom Seager gave me a letter of introduction, which I forwarded with it. I begged his acceptance of it as a testimony of my respect for 'his great abilities, profound learning, and the noble sacrifices which he had made for conscientious motives.' I also said I hoped the book might meet with his approval.

"30th.—At my particular request, they write us accounts from Rugby each day now of our beloved mother's health, and E. offered to go over, which I could not have done, but which was declined. Each letter has told us that she was gradually but peacefully sinking, and this morning I had a letter from Edmund announcing that at about five yesterday afternoon she breathed her last. All the day she had been lying in an unconscious state, and perfectly quiet. Her manners were those of the most perfect lady, and I recollect that at Totnes, the boys said she was the most thorough lady that had ever come to the school.

" *August 4th.*—Came to Rugby to-day to pay my last respects to my poor mother by following her remains to the grave."

E. and I had a tour in the Pyrences during the autumn of this year, of which I have preserved an account in my journal. Returned home on the 25th of September.

" *5th.*—The Very Rev. Dr. Newman [now Cardinal] wrote to me from the Oratory, Brompton, July 29th, 1862, in return for my book, in which he thanks me very much for the kind present. That the book is on a most interesting subject, and will be read by him with pleasure, as well as, he is sure, with instruction. He is already somewhat acquainted with it from notices of it in reviews. At Birmingham yesterday, he did himself the pleasure of leaving his card for me at the county court, but knows I come to Birmingham for business only, which fully occupies me ; and though he would have been pleased to make my acquaintance personally, he did not expect it. My cousin Charles Marriott was a very near and intimate friend of his.

" *7th.*—Called on Dr. Newman, but he was not at home. Shown into his room, in which was a view of Oxford, with a Latin inscription over it in large letters : ' Son of man, can these bones live ? '

" *September 27th.*—A letter from the Lord Chancellor's secretary about the county court, stating his Lordship has made it a rule that the gentleman who is selected by the judge in cases of illness to act as his deputy shall not be appointed to succeed the judge for whom he acts, and adding that he is very sensible of my professional merits and hopes to have an opportunity of showing it.

"*October 1st.*—Wrote to Lord Brougham, telling him that, in illustration of the principles contained in my 'Principia,' I have made selections from different leading judgments of Lord Hardwicke, Lord Mansfield, Lord Ellenborough, and other distinguished jurists. I have also for the same purpose prepared a table containing reference to those passages in his Lordship's judgments which I intend to make use of in the same work, and which I hope to forward to him in a few days.

"The selection, if published by itself, would make a suitable accompaniment to Sir Eardley Wilmot's collection of his Lordship's Acts and Bills, in the preparation of which I assisted, and I should be obliged by any corrections or suggestions that he might think proper to make.

"*6th.*—Dined at Sir John Ratcliffe's to meet Mr. Hill, Q.C., Recorder of Birmingham. No one else there, only Sir J. and Lady and Mr. Ratcliffe. Spent a very pleasant evening. The Recorder and I told old circuit stories and jokes, and talked over old times. I also showed them my Pyrenean sketches. Dinner exquisite. Hill, in the course of conversation, expressed a very high opinion of Cockle's——now Sir James—talents, and said he only wanted confidence in himself.

"*20th.*—Received a letter from the Lord Chancellor Westbury, dated from Hackwood Park, Basingstoke, October 20th, and saying "that although he feels it to be his duty to abide by the rule he has started of not appointing the deputy of a county court judge to succeed him, yet he is very unwilling to deprive me of a situation which I have so long filled with credit, and the income of which is probably an object to me, without some equivalent. He has therefore determined to offer the vacant judgeship to Mr. Nichols, one of the registrars of the Court of Bankruptcy at Manchester, who was a Commissioner of the Insolvent Debtors' Court at the time of its being abolished, and if he accepts it, he shall have much pleasure in giving me the situation Mr. N—— now holds.   The salary of the office is one thousand pounds per annum; it is therefore nearly equal to a county court judgeship, and, he trusts, much exceeding my present allowance as deputy.   The occupation is, he thinks, much less, and that I shall have abundant time therefore for literary pursuits.   I must receive this offer as a mark of his esteem for me as a writer of merit and a man of ability and promise, and not ascribe it in any degree to the influence of the letters from Lord Brougham and others which he had, to his regret, procured to be written to him.   He pays no attention to such things.   My intended work is, he has no doubt, a meritorious one ; but the style of dedication I have sent to him is not at all to his taste. The instant he receives Mr. Nichols' answer he will write again if I tell him that the office will be accepted by me.

" To his Lordship's letter I replied at once as follows :—

" ' I beg to return your Lordship my warmest thanks for your very kind letter, and to assure your Lordship that I gratefully accept the offer of the registrarship at Manchester now held by Mr. Nichols in the event of that gentleman accepting the judgeship of the Birmingham County Court.   I assure your Lordship that the appointment now offered to me is one which is peculiarly suitable to me as affording so much more time for literary pursuits than I could possibly obtain while holding the judgeship of a county court.   The terms in which your Lordship has been pleased to convey to me the offer of this promotion have afforded me almost as much gratification as the fact of the promotion ; and I shall never cease to recur to the latter with pleasure and with pride.

" ' I have, etc.,

" ' GEORGE HARRIS.

" ' The Right Hon. the Lord Chancellor.'

" By the Lord Chancellor's direction, I went to Manchester, and saw Mr. Nichols, who had returned there, and who, on my communicating with him, at once wrote to the Chancellor signifying his acceptance of the offer of the judgeship of the Birmingham County Court, on which the Chancellor immediately wrote to me appointing me the Registrar of the Bankruptcy Court at Manchester. I, however, returned for a time to Birmingham, and acted as judge of the county court until Mr. Nichols was ready to take the office, on which I went to Manchester and commenced my duties there as Registrar."

CHAPTER XXI.

RESIDENCE IN MANCHESTER AS A REGISTRAR IN
BANKRUPTCY.

1862—1864.

" *October 9th.*

" A LEADING article in the *Gazette of Bankruptcy* on the judgeship of the Birmingham County Court, in which they say of my appointment to the registrarship that it ' is one in every way beneficial to the public, Mr. Harris being the author of many valuable works of proved capacity.' They give also a report of the proceedings on my taking leave of the court.

" 28*th*.—Came to Manchester. Wrote to Canon Gordon, telling him I intended to complete the improvements at Iselipps, which we hoped to make our future residence, either on my promotion to London, or on my retirement on my pension, when I hoped to end my days there, and therefore I should like to make it as complete and comfortable in all respects as possible.

" Received the following very kind message from Mr. Justice Mellor :—

" ' I am delighted to hear of your appointment, and if I have an opportunity, will say what you desire to the Lord Chancellor.'

" *November 7th*.—Received to-day a letter from Lord Brougham, in answer to a request from me that I might write his biography. In reply, written from Brougham, Penrith, November 6th, 1862, he says, ' that as to notes of his judgments there are none. He prepared them very carefully, and they were copied by one or other of the secretaries and given to the reporters, Mylne and Craig or Mylne and Keen. Some were by accident omitted, and were dictated to Gurney, the shorthand writer, who gave them either to one of the secretaries or to himself to correct, and then they went to the reporters. The one on the privilege question, delivered without any notes, he thinks he corrected the report of before it was printed.

" ' On the more important matter of biography, no doubt it would be a most fortunate thing for him were it to fall into such fit and friendly hands as mine. But he cannot enter into more particulars at present than to say that his autobiography is so far prepared, with the intention of an immediate publication, at least of being published while he remains alive and ready to meet any attacks and give any explanations ; that he will be able to show it to me and to confer about it as soon as he returns from Cannes, whither he goes in a week or ten days. He leaves for Grafton Street on Saturday, and will be about a week in London. When he returns, he shall come to Brougham for a week, and I could do him the favour of coming over at that time. If the Social Science Yearly Congress is held, as the council seems resolved it shall, at Edinburgh, he shall be there for a couple of days, and come to Brougham on his return. He supposes it will be at or before Easter. He adds as a P.S.—

"'The work is nearly all written, and the correspondence copied fairly out. But the time is unfavourable for publication, while the American War and distress lasts.'

"To this I replied, stating I was much gratified by hearing that the biography of his Lordship was to be written in the mode in which it ought to be done, and by which alone a really perfect work of this kind could be accomplished. I should be glad to render any service I possibly can to so valuable a work, though I fear it must be but small, and accepted the invitation of paying him a visit at the time suggested.

"*December* 1st.—In the evening I attended a meeting in London of the Law Amendment Society on 'What to do with our Criminals,' the subject being introduced by Mr. Hastings. I suggested that employment should be found for ticket-of-leave men, so that they should not be driven to vice from want, and that our gaols at present were far too comfortable, much more so than any poor person's houses, and far more so than workhouses. The Common Serjeant, who was in the chair, spoke directly after me, and commenced by saying, 'I must say that I think the suggestion of Mr. Harris about the employment of ticket-of-leave men meets a very considerable want in the case under discussion.'

" 11*th*.—To-morrow being the anniversary of our wedding, I wrote to-day to E., who is staying with the Seagers, as follows :—'I suppose, though I am such a very bad husband, and hardly ever do what I ought, that I shall not be acting altogether wrong in sending a greeting to the best of wives on the anniversary of the day on which we were joined together for better or for worse, and assuring her how truly I value and regard her, how convinced I am of her thorough devotedness to me, of her sterling high principle, and indeed of her value in all respects, and how sure I feel that I should never meet with such another all the world over. Long may she be spared to me, and in future years may we always spend this day, which I shall always regard as the most fortunate of my life, under the same roof. All that I can do to make her happy I shall gladly contribute, and I do sincerely hope that now there is some prospect of happiness before us. God bless the dear good old girl !'

" 13*th*.—A letter from my excellent wife this morning, in which she says, 'Thank you, dearest G., for your most acceptable and welcome letter of this morning. I am quite sure it is as much your wish and intention to make me happy as my every thought is for your welfare and well-being ; and surely if we only place our thoughts and wishes on the one thing needful, and strive to make our life here be a preparation for a blessed eternity, there are perhaps few blessed as we are, no cares, anxieties, and now with ample means for all the moderate wishes we can desire and power to help our neighbours, the brightest spot of all.'

" 26*th*.—I read to-day in an extract from Cockburn's 'Life of Jeffrey' contained in a 'biography of Lord Macaulay' that 'as to fame, if an author's is now and then more lasting, it is generally longer withheld.'

1863.

"*January 2nd.*—A letter to-day from Chief Justice
W. H. Adams, at Hong Kong, in a very mutilated and
dirty condition, and printed on the outside, 'Saved
from the wreck of the *Colombo*,' the mail packet lately
lost.   A remarkable man is Adams, and a striking
instance of how fully the highest offices are in this
country open to the humblest.   When a child, he was
stolen by the gipsies.   After he came to manhood he
was supposed to be dead and laid out for interment,
but a friend, coming to take a last view of him, discovered that he was alive.   Originally a compositor in
a printing establishment, he at length rose to be
a newspaper editor.   He was afterwards entered at the
Temple, where I introduced him, became a barrister,
a member of Parliament, was appointed Attorney-
General of Hong Kong, and is now Chief Justice.   He
recommends me to take the coif, not knowing of
course of my promotion.

" *8th.*—A notice of 'Civilisation as a Science' in the
Social Science Review, and which is very full and satisfactory, perhaps too complicated on the whole.   They
state that I have treated the matter 'with great care,
precision, and depth of thought.'   The introductory
part of the work they term 'a well-written chapter
throughout, sober in tone, just in argument, and pro-
gressive in tendency without violence or presumption.'
In another part they remark that 'it is not in any one
particular passage or part that the book excels, but in
the accumulation of all its parts.   There is scarcely
a social problem, great or little, that is not dealt with ;
there is not one that is not treated with sound sense,
consideration, and liberality.'   And they conclude as
follows : 'We commend this book earnestly, honestly,

to every social scholar. It is written with as much modesty as firmness, with as much fidelity of statement as courtesy, and with a philosophy as deep as its language is simple. It is the first extensive, and by far the most sterling, effort made in the present day to reduce civilisation to a science, and to push it forward safely, easily, and quickly in its magnificent course.'

" The work is analysed with tolerable minuteness, and some copious extracts from it are given, among them the remarks on the poverty of our psalmody and the concluding passage in the book. On some points, however, they join issue with me.

" 31st.—A notice in the *Manchester Courier* of to-day of 'Civilisation as a Science.' They say of it that though the subject promises to be dry, yet 'it is written in so agreeable and forcible a style, which derives additional relief from the judicious expedient of subdivision, that, so far from expecting readers to be wearied and put comfortably to sleep, we anticipate that the book will be put down with reluctance and resumed with avidity. . . . ' His work is a very creditable performance in all respects, and although a little more time for reflection might have rendered some of his views a little clearer, and some of his reasoning (from the *petitio principii* to the remainder) a thought sounder, there is but little to complain of, and a vast deal to admire. . . . The wonder is how the essayist has contrived, with the limits of rather more than four hundred pages of legible type, to present so complete a conspectus of a subject which presents itself in such an infinite variety of aspects. We do not say that Mr. Harris has exhausted the subject, nor anything like it, but he has given us a more compact and compendious view of it than any other writer of modern times whose labours have as yet come under our notice.'

"*February 5th.*—Delivered lecture on 'Manners and Customs in the Olden Time' at Pastricroft. The meeting very full, between seven hundred and eight hundred, and the audience very attentive, though the lecture lasted more than an hour and a half. Pressed to give another lecture there.

"*19th.*—In London. Delivered lecture this evening on the Plague at the City of London College, Sussex Hall, Leadenhall Street. About four hundred present, and very attentive.

"*23rd.*—Stayed at Mr. Flowers' (police magistrate of Bow Street), at Hornsea, until this morning from Saturday, after delivering my lecture there yester-evening on 'Habits and Pursuits.' The room a small one, but quite full, several of the better class. The lecture appeared to take thoroughly, and excited a great deal of laughter, and all the different jokes and points appeared to tell.

"*March 12th.*—Sent three dozen of champagne to-day to the Midland Circuit on my promotion as a parting gift, with a letter to Balguy, in which I said to him, 'Pray remember me very kindly to my old circuit, on which I have passed many pleasant hours, and with no member of which have I ever had anything approaching to disagreement or of an unpleasant character during the whole time that I was a member.'

"*14th.*—Engaged the house in Cornbrook Park recommended by the Whitelegges, and was much pleased with it. In front there is an extensive green or paddock common to the adjoining house, and the rooms look upon a lawn or shrubbery on a bank tastefully planted. The dining-room is a very handsome one, and the staircase of stone ; and altogether the house is the most commodious and suitable one that we have seen.

" 25*th*.—Received from Mr. Saxe Bannister, of London, his essay on ' The Uses of our Historical Manuscripts for the Last Hundred and Seventy-four Years,' with letters requesting I would read it and give him my opinion upon it. It affords an interesting account of what has been done in this way, and refers particularly to the efforts of Carte, who was a native of Clifton, near Rugby. It refers also to the Cheetham Society, and to the valuable guild rolls at Preston ; and it contains an allusion to my memorial. Only fifty copies of it are printed. Many members of both Houses of Parliament, right reverend prelates, and judges, many of all the learned professions and men of letters, have declared their opinion that our vast stores of such materials in private hands will be freely opened for public use if the owners see that proper inquiries into them are sanctioned by the Government.

" Thus, in our time, the matter rests on foundations that give it strength with the most enlightened men in times past ; and Lord Palmerston will do a thing worthy of his name if he advises her Majesty now to recognise the object which at the Revolution, with the warm approval of his Lordship's relative Sir William Temple, created one noble work of historical science, the ' Fœdora,' and in the last century led so many to support the Carte historical plan.

" 26*th*.—We dined to-day at the Dean's. A pleasant party. Met there Mr. Birch, the late tutor to the Prince of Wales, who gave us an account of the proceedings at the wedding.

" Wrote to T. Bloxam, enclosing my photograph, and which I told him he must ' add to those of other illustrious Rugbeians, officers in the navy, etc. But instead of being styled (as I ought to be) Admiral Harris, you can only set me down as

" Admirable " Harris. I daresay the difference won't be found out. The real truth is that, instead of being still in the navy, I am only in the (k) navy.'

" 31*st*.—Wrote to Bloxam, asking, ' Was not Carte, the historian, a native of Clifton ? Was not his father, S. Carte, rector of that place ? Is there any monument of any description to his memory ? If not, ought not the learned town of Rugby to do something in this respect ? Would not a painted window in the church there or in Trinity Church, which is on the Clifton road, be a suitable memorial ? Would not Lord Bradford, who is a proprietor in the parish and patron of the living, start the subscription ? Would not £50 do the whole thing ? '

" *April* 20*th*.—Murray, the new registrar, arrived to-day, and we had a cordial greeting as old friends. He said he was delighted when he heard that I should be his colleague, as he was sure we should work well together.

" 28*th*.—A letter from Sir Eardley Wilmot, in which he says, ' I think the title of your new work, " Principia," etc., a most excellent one, and I have no doubt the work itself will be most useful and valuable. We want the elements of the law simplified and made intelligible.'

" On moving our goods to Cornbrook Park, the iron chest containing the manuscript of my ' Treatise on Man ' miscarried, and was two days missing. What should I have done if I had lost it, the work and thought of so many years ? This is its second peril ; in 1840, it was very near falling into the Thames, when I landed from Hull.

" *May* 21*st*.—Dined at the Bishop of Manchester's. A very pleasant party, and the Bishop very cordial, and actually warmed into addressing me as ' Harris '! He

specially introduced me to Dr. Bayford, the chancellor
of the diocese, with whom I had a good deal of chat.
Met also Ryder, son of the late Bishop of Lichfield,
whom and whose father I used to know at Rugby ages
ago.   Saw in the *Times* to-day a long speech of
Walter on proposing a motion in the House of
Commons on national education, so determined to
send him a copy of 'Civilisation as a Science.'

"21st.—In London.   Attended, as a steward, the
festival of the Sons of the Clergy in St. Paul's, and
afterwards the dinner at Merchant Taylors' Hall.
Just saw the Bishop of London to shake hands with
him.

"26th.—Called this morning on Lord Brougham, but
found him in a great bustle.   One person had just come
out, and others, I suppose, were waiting to see him.
I thought him not so cordial as usual, but suppose he
was much hurried.   I thanked him again for his
kindness towards me, and asked him if he thought anything could be done about reviving the manuscript
commission inquiry.   He said, 'By G——, I think
not.'   I then asked him what he thought of an article
in the *Edinburgh* to revive the discussion.   He said,
'Ah, that would do.   You write it, and I'll make Reeves
put it in.'   I said I would write to him a letter
proposing that.   He said, 'Do.   That will be the best
way.'   I then talked about bankruptcy matters, and
said the trade assignees' plan did not work well, and
that some of them could not write their own names,
and that it led to great jobbery.   He said it was a
great mistake having them.   I then came out, as he
seemed so hurried, and he followed me to the door and
shook hands very cordially.   At first he seemed hardly
to know me, and asked if I was not at Manchester,
and whether it was not very cold out of doors.

"*June* 1*st*.—E. and I commenced our tour on the Continent, going to Boulogne and Paris, and intending to proceed to Switzerland, over the Simplon to Milan, and thence to Venice, the Italian lakes, and home by Genoa, all which we did, and successfully accomplished, returning home on August 3rd.

"*October* 6*th*.—We much like our new house, and the retirement and rurality of the garden are charming. But still I hope much to get to London in the course of three years, and to make Iselipps our main and final residence, having a house also in London for the winter.

"8*th*.—Invited Mr. Beresford Hope and Archdeacon Wickham to stay with us during the Church Congress here, which they are doing. Mr. Beresford Hope very pleasant as a companion, and a most efficient and telling speaker, and rapturously received. A vein of quiet humour, which takes vastly. Dined to-day at Mr. Callender's, meeting a party of twenty-six, among them Dr. Hook, Dean of Chichester, Vice-Chancellor W. P. Wood [afterwards Lord Chancellor], Sir John and Canon Anson, Archdeacon Denison, Archdeacon Wickham and Mr. Beresford Hope accompanying me. I sat by Archdeacon Denison at dinner, whom I found very agreeable. In the evening a long and very vehement though quite amicable discussion, after the rest of the party had gone, between Hope and Denison, which lasted until after one, though I several times moved the adjournment of the debate, and asked the Archdeacon to renew it to-morrow at dinner at my house, but which he is unable to do, as there is a party to meet him at Mr. Callender's. During the discussion Hope several times flourished a large carving-knife which lay on the table, as though he would at once cut short, not only the argument, but the career of his adversary. Very good

friends nevertheless, and addressed one another as
'My dear Hope' and 'My dear Denison,' though
the latter declared he would sooner vote for John
Bright than for the former. Church rates and Disraeli
were the points discussed. I fancy Hope is prejudiced
against Disraeli, through his brother-in-law, Lord
Robert Cecil. I urged that the same distrust and
jealousy had been evinced towards Canning and Peel,
and Burke too, that Disraeli was now experiencing.

"15*th.*—Wrote to Canon Anson, who is son-in-law
to Dean Hook, as follows :—

"'My DEAR SIR,—The papers to which I alluded
as likely to be serviceable to the Dean of Chichester
for his very valuable and interesting "Lives of the
Archbishops of Canterbury" consist principally of
some original letters of Archbishops Herring and
Secker in Lord Hardwicke's collection at Wimpole.
There are also a good many letters there of Bishops
Butler, Pearce, Hurd, and Warburton. Some of
these are well worth publishing, though perhaps they
would not come within the province of Dr. Hook's
labours.

"'When the Dean of Chichester next visits Manchester, I should much like to have an interview with
him, and would do myself the honour of waiting upon
him if he would fix a time ; and I am interested about
the collection of valuable manuscripts belonging to
Chichester Cathedral, of the contents of which Sir F.
Madden has informed me.

"'If I can be of any service to the Dean in the
prosecution of his valuable labours, I shall be most
happy. There are more papers of interest in the
library of Magdalen College, Oxford, relating to the
period of the revolution of 1688, which the late Lord

Macaulay I cannot say overlooked, but rather declined to look over.

"' Believe me, etc.,

"' GEORGE HARRIS.'

". 16*th*.—Our guests left us this morning, both expressing themselves much pleased, as they really seemed, with their visit, and both pressing us to pay them visits in return.

" 21*st*.—A long letter to-day from Sir Adam Bittlestone, in which he says, 'I rejoice that your "Principias" are progressing, but I do not think that you will find any assistance from Hindu law, which is more devoid of leading principles than any other system of jurisprudence in the world, if system it can be called. I do not wonder that your search into Sir William Jones' "Digest" proved unavailing, nor do I think you would be better off if you were to dive into the treatises of the Hindu lawyers.'

" 24*th*.—Wrote the following to-day to Lord Brougham :—

"' I take the liberty of troubling your Lordship with the accompanying proofs of extracts from some of your judgments, of which I propose to avail myself in the first part of my "Principia." These form of course a very small portion of what I intend to avail myself of eventually. If, at your leisure, your Lordship would look them over, I shall feel obliged, and shall of course be only too glad to make use of-any suggestions or corrections, and to receive notes on any points that may suggest themselves.

"' P.S.—I do not know whether there are any points in your Lordship's judgments (with which I have rendered myself tolerably well acquainted for the purpose of the

accompanying work) regarding which I can be of any
use in relation to the autobiography ; but if so, I shall of
course be very glad to be of service in any way that I can.'

" 28*th*.—Received a letter from Lord Brougham this
morning, dated Brougham, Penrith, October 27th, 1863,
offering me many thanks for proofs, which he has carefully read, and sees no correction required.   Says I
should be aware that the judgment in Wharton *v*. Earl
of Durham was reversed in the House of Lords by a
narrow majority not of law lords, and contrary to the
known opinion of Bickersteth, then at the bar, and who
was counsel for Durham, the appellant.   The cause
came on in the Lords in his absence from illness.
Shadwell, whose judgment he had affirmed, and himself
always continued to hold the same opinion.   He rather
thought the reversal was owing to Lord Devon's vote.

" *November* 3*rd*.--Received to-day letter from Lord
Chancellor Westbury, in which he says, ' I am much
obliged by your letter, your dedication, and the opportunity of reading some of the specimen pages of your
book.   I think it will be a very useful one.   Some of
my judgments kindly cited by you scarcely deserve to
be so noticed, as there is nothing new or material in
them, but there are some others which have not reached
you or been adequately reported that may occasionally
supply you with an illustration.   I wish you much
success, and I feel happy in being able to appeal to
your varied literary excellence when the appointments
that I have made are reviewed.'

" 4*th*.—To this I replied that ' I shall not fail to
attend to the suggestions that it contains respecting
the extracts from your Lordship's judgments.   Those
which I have printed contain only a small portion of
what I have selected, and are intended merely for the
first part of the work.'

"Received yesterday a letter from Mr. Beresford Hope, in which he says:—

"'I hope you will do me the favour to accept a copy of "The English Cathedrals of the Nineteenth Century," and also of some pamphlets which I have brought out. Such as they are, they are very grateful and sincere, though inadequate, expressions of thanks for the singular kindness and hospitality which you and Mrs. Harris were so very good as to show me at the late Congress.'

"Delivered my lecture on the 'Pursuits,' etc., 'of our Forefathers,' at the St. Matthias' (Salford) Working Men's Club this evening.

"17*th*.—The papers mention that Lord Brougham has lately been to Windsor Castle and had a conference with the Queen, which, I suppose, is the engagement referred to in his letter to me requiring him to hold himself in readiness to start on hearing the evening before. Probably it was about the letter to the Queen from the Emperor of the French proposing a general congress. Lord Brougham is now in Paris for a fortnight, where he will probably see the Emperor on the same subject. He is then to go to Cannes for the winter.

"30*th*.—Delivered my lecture on 'Habits and Pursuits' at the Salford barracks this evening, dining with Colonel Adams and the officers.

"*December* 1*st*.—Delivered this evening my lecture on Napoleon at Pastricroft, from the skeleton I have made lately from the three lectures, but including all the diagrams and caricatures. The lecture very attentively listened to and much applauded, and appeared to excite much interest. A fair account of the lecture at Pastricroft in the *Eccles Advertiser* of Saturday. They say of it that it contained 'as good an epitome of the life of Napoleon as need be desired for lecturing purposes,' and quote some of my observations.

"The *Tourist* goes on regularly appearing, there being an account of trips on the Continent and advice to those intending to travel.

"11*th*.—Came yesterday to Haughton-le-Skerne, near Darlington, to stay at Mr. Cheese's, to deliver a lecture to-day at the Darlington Church Institute on the 'Pursuits and Mode of Life of our Ancestors.' Archdeacon Dodson, Mr. Morritz, member of Parliament for the county, Mr. Pease, son of the late member of Parliament, and other ladies and gentlemen met me at dinner. The lecture took place this evening in the Central Hall. Between three and four hundred present, nearly all reserved seats at sixpence each. The audience very attentive, and cheered me much at its conclusion. In a brief allusion to it in the *Darlington Times*, it is termed 'a remarkably interesting lecture.'

"19*th*.—A *Durham Chronicle* sent me to-day, containing a short notice of my lecture at Darlington. They say that it was 'very interesting,' and was 'well considered and ably handled.' 'So versatile, so ready, and so bright indeed were the hits of Mr. Harris, so keen-witted were also his points, and so happy his deductions, that, notwithstanding a very unfortunate cold under which he laboured, the attention of a large audience was riveted the entire evening. Admirable diagrams assisted the lecture materially.' They allude to 'Civilisation as a Science,' of which they say that it 'treats the matter with that depth and still light handling which proves him at once an artist, a thoughtful and a cultivated man.' A good general outline of the lecture in the *Darlington Times*, but without any comment upon it.

1864.

"*February* 10*th.*—Dined to-day by invitation at the meeting of the Manchester Law Association. Proposed the first regular toast : 'Success to the Association ;' and an outline of my speech, which was very well received, in the newspapers. Asked afterwards to propose the health of the President, in the room of the mayor of Salford, which I did.

"15*th.*—To-day I consider as really and philosophically the first day of spring, reckoning the 21st of December as the centre of winter, and calculating the half of three months from that point, which brings us to the 8th of February, and then allowing seven days for the effects remaining of past cold, which continue to operate, as is the case with past heat, long after the active agent has ceased.

"According to this calculation, and allowing three months for each of the seasons,

> *Spring* commences 15*th February.*
> *Summer* ,, 15*th May.*
> *Autumn* ,, 15*th August.*
> *Winter* ,, 15*th November.*

"*March* 1*st.*—Delivered at Pastricroft my lecture on 'Ghosts, Apparitions, and Dreams,' which I have lately been revising, taking out several passages, adding new ones and descriptions of recent diagrams, particularly of the Sleep-walker, the Radiant Boy, the Spectre of Willington, Death holding his Cart, and the Egyptian Funeral. The attendance very full, and the audience very attentive indeed.

"Elected a Fellow of the Genealogical and Historical Society of Great Britain.

"14*th.*—This evening I delivered my lecture on

Napoleon at Wilmslow. The attendance was very good, and all extremely attentive throughout. Several speeches made at the conclusion.

"I went this morning to Sheffield, to the scene of the terrible calamity and devastation caused by the bursting of the immense reservoir at Bradford. A view from the railway as you approach the station over the desolated valley, and heaps of ruins and dead horses strewed all about, and the entire valley deluged with mud. I first of all visited the lower parts of the town. All the streets knee-deep in mud, and the goods and furniture lying about, chairs, bedding, sheets, and blankets all steeped in mud. The lower rooms in the houses quite dilapidated and full of mud. Proceeded next up the valley in the direction of the reservoir, which is nine miles from Sheffield, keeping near the side of the stream. This presents an extraordinary scene of desolation. Many of the houses are half demolished, some of them entirely a heap of ruins. In one spot there were six dead donkeys lying in a heap, and crusted with mud. Close by was a heap of several pigs in the same condition, and three horses were lying near, which had lately been skinned. Proceeding up the valley, beams, and rafters, and pieces of broken walls, and doors, and shutters, and articles of furniture were lying strewed about in all directions. Here and there you saw the remains of gardens, but the whole was covered with a thick coat of slime. At each of the bridges were collected large masses of beams and doors, and articles of furniture, as also trees which had been torn up by the violence of the torrent and carried down the stream, but were unable to pass through the arches. In several of the ruins, people were hard at work digging for bodies. Near a tanner's several skins were lying about of cows

and sheep, which had been carried away by the
torrent, and near a paper-mill quantities of paper.
At one of the mills they had just found the body
of an old man. It was lying on a sack in a stable,
and they were throwing buckets of water over it to
cleanse it from the mud. The scene of desolation
continued along the valley until I got to Hillsborough,
about two miles up the valley. Several of the cottages
are nothing but heaps of ruins. In some of these
spots horses and donkeys are lying, and appear to
have been entangled and prevented from swimming.
An immense house-dog is lying near one dilapidated
cottage. Round the schoolroom at Hillsborough was
a great crowd, but I, with some difficulty, made my way
into it. In one of the rooms five corpses were lying
of persons of different ages, covered, all except the
faces, with oiled white paper. Some of them were
frightfully mangled. A tremendous scuffle in the
room to get a view of them, and when I got out, I
found my watch was gone. Near this, but close on
the edge of the stream, was the ruin of a house, which
appeared to have been knocked down by the torrent.
Persons were digging here for bodies, and found four
this afternoon. One of the arches of the bridge at
Hillsborough was blown up by the torrent, and is
quite a heap of ruins, and a mill a little above it was
swept away, nothing now remaining but the great iron
wheels and some huge stones. Proceeded up the
valley towards the reservoir. It was thronged with
people the whole way, and every now and then in the
valley you still saw the ruins of a cottage. The road,
in two parts verging on the edge of the valley, has
been carried away by the torrent, and the ground is
in huge rents, as though an earthquake had occurred.
Walked to the reservoir and on the embankment

through which the water burst. It appears very
strong, but a frightful chasm remains, through which
the desolating flood rushed, and for some way below
all is a heap of rock and huge pieces of earth, like the
bed of an avalanche. The bed of the reservoir does
not seem so vast as it really is. Unable to get any
conveyance, as I had hoped, near the reservoir, and so
had to walk all the way back to the station, nine miles
each way, besides a divergence of two miles to explore
the valley. In two graveyards funerals were going on,
fifteen in one and twelve in the other. Notices in all
directions about the interment of the dead and
recognising the corpses found, just as, one might
imagine, during the great plague in London. People
looking in at the windows of two or three houses. I
found they were corpses that I saw, which looked like
waxwork, being, I suppose, discoloured by the water. I
went to the station for the train to Manchester, but a
rude mob had got entire possession of the station, and
rushed into all the carriages, without regard to tickets
or classes, the moment the train got in. I had some
difficulty to avoid being forced under the train by them,
so I telegraphed to Manchester to say I could not get
home, as the mob was in possession of the station and
filled the train, but that I should return to-night if I
could. At last I got a place by the nine o'clock train,
but did not reach Cornbrook Park until after eleven.
I would not have missed the sight even for the loss of
my watch. Seeing the poor wretches who have lost
their all, and their relations as well, sitting and looking
so deplorable among the ruins of their houses, added
much to the effect. Some of the houses are standing,
but require to be propped up with poles, one wall in a
corner having been carried away by the violence of
the torrent, leaving the whole interior exposed. The

scene of desolation was more thrilling, more real, more deathlike, than anything of the sort that I have witnessed, not excepting the ravages made by the invasion of sea tempests or the devastating effects and fury of avalanches. This, too, was so much more recent than the effects of what I had seen in other places. The inundation of the Loire was more extensive than this, and the ruin more widely spread, but the outburst was not so sudden nor so furious, and the scene presented here was far more exciting and more thrilling than anything that I witnessed in the valley of the Loire.

"*26th.*—Wrote to Dr. Richardson, as editor of the *Social Science Review*, offering him an article on the Sheffield catastrophe, and he said he should be delighted to receive it, so I sent him up one of which the above descriptions constituted the substance.

"*April 22nd.*—Wrote the following letter to Chief Justice Cockle, with a copy of 'Civilisation as a Science :'—

"'The subject may interest you as a scientific man, and in a new colony there is greater scope for carrying out my crotchets than in an old-established country like this. Nevertheless, I am strongly inclined to think that civilisation among *us* has passed its meridian, and that the present is rather an age of luxury than of civilisation. I am getting on with my "Principia," and wish much I had the benefit of your acute and logical head to aid me in the work. I hope to go to press with Part I., which will form the first volume, about the end of this month, and if I have an opportunity, will send you a copy. My work here is light, and affords plenty of literary leisure. I had a long letter from your brother Chief Justice W. H. Adams, which was fished up from the wreck of the *Colombo*.'

"A letter from Mr. W. Adams the other day with

deep black edge, and which we concluded was to
announce the death of my old friend the Chief Justice
of Hong Kong. It turned out, however, to be the
announcement of his marriage instead.

"28th.—A long letter from Mrs. Cockle to E.
She and her husband seem to think of Queensland
much as we do of Manchester; they find it complete
banishment.

"*May 3rd.*—In London. Dined with Chief Justice
Adams, and had a good deal of chat with him about
China. He said that the native authorities there had
complained seriously of the great loss to them from the
establishment of English courts of justice, as they used
to receive so much in the way of bribes to induce them
to favour particular parties and to let off the guilty.
A handsome address, with the seals of a great many
natives annexed, was presented to Adams thanking him
for the strict impartiality with which he had adminis-
tered justice. Persons sentenced to death actually used
to get others to suffer for them by large payments for
the benefit of their families and the promise of being
buried in a handsome coffin. Joked him about the food
at Hong Kong—dogs, cats, worms, etc.; but he said
the two former were fed on bread and milk to adapt
them for eating.

"Attended this afternoon a meeting of the Genealogical Society to discuss with them my plan for a
manuscript commission, into which they entered very
fully, and a resolution favourable to it was passed,
and for requesting Lord Dalhousie, as President of the
Society, to confer with the Government, of which he
was until lately a member, as to the course to be
adopted, and to urge it upon them.

"6th.—Elected a Fellow of the Anthropological
Society.

"*June* 10th.—A note from Vice-Chancellor Sir W. Page Wood, in reply to my sending him an extract of a judgment of his.

"*July* 3rd.—Saw in the paper this morning the appointment of Mr. Flowers to be a police magistrate in London, at which E. and I were much delighted, as I wrote and told him, and asked him to pay us a visit here and celebrate the event.

"12th.—A letter from Flowers, saying that 'of all I have received so kindly congratulating me none, I felt sure, was more hearty and sincere than yours.'

"26th.—Miss Henslow, sister of the Professor, left us this morning. She has been busy each day lately looking through my library, which she declared a great treat. Said that my 'Civilisation as a Science' was too deep and philosophical for the generality, and that I should simplify it and introduce anecdotes if I published a cheaper edition.

"*August* 8th.—Wrote the following to-day to Lord Brougham :—

"'You were so kind as to write some time ago that you would like me to look over the manuscript which you had prepared of an autobiography of your Lordship's career, when you proposed that I should pay you a visit while you were at Brougham.

"'On the Wednesday and Thursday in next week I have to be at Lancaster to hold sittings in the Castle on those days.

"'If convenient to your Lordship to see me on Thursday, the 18th, I could go to Penrith on that day, or if you preferred, I could defer my visit until the middle of November.

"'I am going on the Continent for my vacation about the middle of September, and shall probably be passing through Cannes during the first week in November, so

that if you should be there at that time, and it would
suit you better to see me there instead of at Brougham,
I will try and arrange to be at Cannes at that time
instead of going to Brougham next week. I shall be
extremely glad if I can be of any sort of use in regard
to the manuscript in question, and shall feel a very deep
interest in perusing it. Is your Lordship acquainted
with a memoir of your career written by Mr. J.
Harwood, which I have, and will bring with me ?
There are one or two matters adverted to by him which
I will point out, but which are perhaps hardly worth
your attention. Of course whatever time is most convenient to your Lordship to see me I will endeavour
to fix upon as the period of my visit.

"'I should also like to have some conversation with
you respecting the rumoured changes in contemplation
in the Court of Bankruptcy.

"'I have great hopes that something will be done
with respect to the manuscript commission, through the
agency of the Historical Society, which has taken it up.

"'I have, etc., etc.,

"'GEORGE HARRIS.

"'The Right Hon. LORD BROUGHAM.'

"9th.—Received in reply from Lord Brougham a
short note saying, 'that it will be wholly needless to
give you the trouble of coming now, as all idea of
publication is given up for the present, and during the
interruption of the American market by this horrible
civil war and the love of slaughter which has seized
the Yankees.' He would be most happy to see me
next week, but is to be from home. However, he
must expect us at Cannes in November. He has
engaged to remain in London over the 1st November,
when the bar receives Berryer at a grand banquet. He

(Berryer) has accepted the invitation, and is to be his guest at Grafton Street. He sets out the 2nd, and hopes to arrive at Cannes in a few days after that.'

"Lord Brougham adds, ' if you have anything you wish represented at our Congress, held this year at York 22nd to 29th September, and will mention it, I shall take care to have it stated. The department of jurisprudence is under Sir J. Wilde' (afterwards Lord Penzance).

" 19th.—Replied to Lord B., stating that I would prepare a short essay embracing the topics on the accompanying head, illustrated by diagrams painted, and sufficiently large to be seen by a considerable audience. 'On the Various Modes of Criminal Punishment Resorted to at Different Periods and their Influence upon Civilisation.'

" 20th.—Dined to-day at the Bishop of Manchester's, to meet Dr. Vaughan, of Doncaster.

" 22nd.—Received a note this morning from Lord Brougham, in which he states :—

"' I have just received your letter, and am much interested in it. The subject you sketch is most interesting and important, and I strongly recommend a paper upon it. There are rules and regulations as to the length—that is, the time allowed for reading— but of course I should be able to manage that, and the worst that can happen is your omitting portions and reading the most prominent and attractive parts. Your coming to York in person will be most propitious, and we could contrive to let you go away very early.

"' As I shall be forced to decline the Archbishop's request of making Bishop's Thorp my headquarters, I can hand you over to him, and it will serve as a compensation for my not going there.'

" 30*th.*—Wrote an appropriate reply to Lord Brougham.

" *September* 21*st.*—Skimming yesterday and to-day Adam Smith's ' Essays on Philosophical Subjects.' What David Hume said in reference to it in a letter to the author ought to be perhaps satisfactory to me as regards the neglect of my 'Civilisation as a Science.' The reading of it necessarily requires so much attention, and the public is disposed to give so little, that I shall still doubt for some time of its being at first very popular. Philosophers (to use an expression of Lord Bacon's) are the servants of posterity ; and most of those who have devoted their talents to the best interests of mankind have been obliged, like Bacon, to bequeath their fame to a race yet unborn, and to console themselves with the idea of sowing what another generation was to reap.

" I went by chance into the jurisprudence class at York, where a discussion was going on respecting the expediency of appointing a public prosecutor. I made, I believe, and as I was told, a rather effective speech, and Lord Brougham, who was in the chair. interposed some remarks on what I said. I observed that a public prosecutor was required, not to conduct prosecutions, but to decide on what ought to be instituted ; that where the offence was not one injurious to property there was a great difficulty in getting any one to prosecute. In many cases the parish officers were made the prosecutors, who were very incompetent to decide in such cases, and the police I thought very improper to act in this capacity, as if they were above taking bribes, they were not above the suspicion of it. The want of a public prosecutor was proved by the establishment of societies for prosecuting felons, by means of which a company was made to discharge

the duties of such a functionary. Many offences, such
as those by railways of burning coal instead of
charcoal, were now committed with impunity because
there was no public prosecutor to proceed and punish
the violation of the law, which was a great injury to
society at large. When I came into the room, Lord
Brougham looked very earnestly at me, and evidently
asked the secretary sitting near him who I was, but
who did not know me. After the meeting was over,
I went up and spoke to him, but he did not at all
recognise me. When I told him my name was
Harris, he shook hands very cordially with me, and
said, 'Well, you are going to the Archbishop's. I
told him to write you,' for which I thanked him, and
asked him if he was going. He said he was.

" *27th.*—The reading of my paper took place this
morning at half-past eleven, Lord Brougham being in
the chair. Before it began I had doubts whether I
should get an audience, as at one of the sections
yesterday only five were present, and even at the one
where Lord Brougham presided only thirty-seven.
Before I began, one of the assistant secretaries wanted
me to abridge it, and said they would not hear me out, as
they had stopped him in the middle the day before, and he
recommended me to omit all the parts descriptive of the
diagrams. Before I commenced, the room was crowded
in every part, even the galleries, and several people
standing. The paper was very attentively listened to.

"Dined at the Archbishop of York's. Lord Brougham,
Lord Teignmouth, Sir F. Kelly, the Lord and Lady
Mayoress, Mr. Ackroyd, M.P., Mr. Burgess, the rector
of Chelsea, and some others present. The Arch-
bishop very fluent and affable. Talked about Lord
Brougham, social science, etc. I told him about Lord
Brougham correcting a proof of ' Dante,' and said his

knowledge of the principle of law was extraordinary. He was cited the other day by the Chancellor in the great Yelverton case; and in 'Chitty on Contracts,' a most practical law book, his judgments constantly quoted. At dinner in answer to the Archbishop Lord Brougham said that he considered the greatest debate in the Commons was that on the Holy Alliance. He afterwards said that if he had had any idea that his speech on that subject would be one of those set for speaking at the Harrow speeches, no person on earth would have induced him to go there. The Archbishop said the Princess of Wales told him she was quite taken by surprise at hearing it, it so exactly applied to the present case of Denmark, the oppression of weak powers by the great. The Archbishop spoke of the Princess with much enthusiasm. Mrs. Thompson's father, a merchant of Aleppo, dined at Bishopsthorpe; he is a pleasant man. He said that his father, now ninety, and Lord Brougham were schoolfellows. The Archbishop took off Lord Brougham capitally in his way of answering a question the Archbishop put to him about Sir R. Peel's changing his opinion on the corn laws, when he said he did not think he would have had the spirit to do it, imitating capitally his way of screwing up his mouth. P—— told me that as he was walking down to the Museum this morning with him to hear my paper one of the secretaries to the other sections, a young man, came up to Lord Brougham and said in a very pert way, 'You are wanted in another section,' on which Lord Brougham flew into a great rage and exclaimed, 'Good God, am I to be torn in pieces in this way?' and hit the man a violent blow with his fist on the chest."

CHAPTER XXII.

1864.

" *October* 3*rd*.

"COMMENCED my vacation tour to-day on the Continent, visiting Germany, Italy, including Naples, Rome, and returning home by Mentone.

"*November* 26*th*.—From Mentone we came to Nice by carriage, and then by railway to Cannes, where I found Lord Brougham at home, alone, and expecting us, and had a cordial welcome from him. Dined at half-past six. Lord Brougham told me at dinner, when I alluded to Cannes being the place at which the first Napoleon landed on his return from Elba—and to mark the spot, Lord B. says, a pillar has been erected—that he (Lord B.) was in Paris in 1814, and that there were various rumours as to what Napoleon was doing at Elba, when the Duke of Orleans (afterwards Louis Philippe) told him (Lord B.) that if Napoleon were to drop from the clouds into the heart of France, the people would all rally round him, and that the royal family would have to be off to Belgium, a prediction which was remarkably verified by the event.

"Lord Brougham appears highly gratified by the way in which the dinner to M. Berryer went off at the Middle Temple, and says it was a complete success, and that the Attorney-General, Sir Roundell Palmer, made an admirable chairman, but that Cockburn (Chief Justice) made rather a mess of it in his speech. Lord Brougham said he did not scruple to call out to him during his speech and correct his observations with regard to himself. The French people, and even the Court, are much gratified by the compliment paid to Berryer.

"*27th.*—A lovely morning, not a cloud to be seen, and the prospect from our windows over the Mediterranean, and of the fine mountains to the west of Cannes, most glorious. Lord Brougham breakfasts at nine, and this, like the dinner, quite in the English style. Last night he said to Elizabeth, 'I am sorry to say I have no carriage at present, as my family have not yet come to me, but I hope you will be able to walk with me to the English church to-morrow, which is only a quarter of an hour's walk.' So at a quarter before eleven we walked together there. Congregation very full. They made room for Lord Brougham to have a seat, and we got chairs in the aisle. Lord Brougham's English manservant said he (Lord B.) had been expecting us some days, and the servant thought it was not well for him to be so long quite alone, and that the family were not expected until Christmas. I said we should be sorry to put him out of his way, but the man said, 'I defy you to do that. Lord B. would not allow anybody to do that.' The chateau stands on the side of a steep hill rising up behind it, and has a good domain of wood and heather land annexed to it. It is about a hundred yards from the road, and is approached by a straight road, through iron gates, with an avenue of orange trees on each side of the road. The house is of white stone, in the Italian style, with pillars, and a terrace before it. There is a good entrance hall and double front staircase, and the two principal sitting-rooms are on each side of the hall.

Lord Brougham's study is in one of the wings to the extreme left. Our rooms are over the dining-room, to the east of the hall. At the end of the hall over the staircase, with a black edge border round it, is the following inscription to the memory of his daughter, after whom the chateau is called :—

" ' ELEANOR LOUISA BROUGHAM.
Born 3rd October, 1821.   Died 3rd November, 1833.

" ' Mount, gentle spirit, to the sphere
    Where pain or grief none ere can know,
Yet sometimes shed an angel's tear
    O'er those who sorrow still below.

" ' Oh, swiftly dawn the blessed day
    When we too heavenward shall rise,
Casting this mortal coil away,
    To join thee in thy native skies.

" ' B.'

The floors of the rooms downstairs are inlaid with wood of different sorts and colours.   Those of the rooms upstairs are of tile.

"A piece of tapestry serves as a carpet on the landing of the staircase.   After luncheon Lord Brougham took me round the domain up the hill, from parts of which there is a fine view, and at one point, he told me, you can see Corsica at sunset and sunrise.   Lord Brougham appears in excellent health, and walks vigorously and quickly, refusing any offer of assistance, even down steep and rugged places in the grounds. The garden is well stocked with orange and olive trees, and in the grounds are aloes and cacti and several fir trees.   The heather here grows very large.   In the study is a large snake stuffed, which was sent as a present to Lord Brougham, and there are several fossils which were found in the neighbourhood.

"In the drawing-room is a water-colour painting

of the late Miss Brougham, and underneath it are some verses on her death by the late Marquis of Wellesley. Lady Brougham, the servant told me, has not been here since 1845. She is very old and infirm.

"Elizabeth and I attended the afternoon service, but Lord B. did not go, as he is afraid of the air late in the evening. A most beautiful glow in the sky after sunset. Nobody came to dinner, which is each day at half-past six. Lord Brougham talked pretty well on different subjects, but he is certainly much deafer than he was, and I have very often to repeat to him what I have said. I told him about having seen Mr. Gibson, the sculptor. He asked me if I had seen the pretended skull of Raphael at Rome, which he does not believe to be genuine. Said he showed a drawing of it which he has to Gall at Vienna, and Gall said it was not Raphael's. In the drawing-room are two water-coloured drawings framed, 'Cannes in 1835' and 'Cannes in 1863,' both taken from exactly the same point of view, and showing the progress in building here.

"28th.—A beautiful day, preceded, as before, by a glorious sunrise, and succeeded by a glorious sunset. After breakfast Lord Brougham took me a walk to see his garden and summer-house on the border of the sea, commanding a charming sea view. I gave him the memoir of himself by G. Harwood, with my notes and references to particular passages. He said it was very odd he had never seen the book before, or if he had, he had forgotten it. I said there were two or three points I should be happy to talk over with him, which was indeed the main object of my visit, and that if certain rumours, however unfounded, remained uncontradicted, in time they became to be regarded as established truths. I asked him if there was any truth

in the report which prevailed at the time that the King
and Lord Grey wished to make Lord Lyndhurst Chief
Justice and to pass over Denman, but that he (Lord
Brougham) insisted that Denman should be appointed ;
but he said there was no truth in it. There was, however, an idea of making Scarlett Chief Justice. In the
course of the morning I walked up the hill in the
grounds, behind the chateau, and made two sketches :
one of Cannes, with the island of St. Margaret, and the
other of the mountains to the west of Cannes. After
lunch we had a drive in a carriage which was lent to
Lord Brougham, and went first to see the grand new
hotel, over which we were accompanied in all due state
by the attendants. After this we drove to the spot
where Napoleon landed after his return from Elba in
1815. and to commemorate which the pillar has been
erected. A farmer showed us the tree—an olive—under
which Napoleon is said to have reposed, and there is a
large *N* cut out in the bark at the place where his
head rested. Lord Brougham thanked the farmer, and
shook hands very cordially with him. Another field
near, however, claimed the honour of having been on
that occasion the imperial dormitory. Near the place
stood a small *auberge*, over the door of which was an
inscription stating that the great Napoleon passed the
night there on his return from Elba. Another *auberge*
had been opened nearly opposite to it, which also
claimed the honour of having on the occasion alluded
to extended its hospitality to the Emperor, where
Napoleon is said to have slept. Lord Brougham
afterwards took us to an artist who is painting in oils
a large size view of the part of Cannes where Lord
Brougham's chateau stands as it was many years ago,
when there were only a few cottages there, and one of
it as it now appears. Two gentlemen dined at Lord

Brougham's to-day : Mr. Bellender Ker, of Lincoln's Inn, and Mr. Woolfield, of Cannes. Mr. Ker said he had known Lord Brougham ever since 1818, and that he first became acquainted with him through writing an article in the *Edinburgh* in reply to Canning's attack on him in the *Quarterly* respecting the Charity Commission. Mr. Woolfield said that the chateau was called after Miss Brougham, as Lord Brougham was first led to visit Cannes for her health. Lord Brougham said that before the railways were established he always used to post here from Paris in his own travelling carriage, stopping one night on the road ; but his old servant, who was waiting at dinner, corrected him and said he had never once stopped to sleep on the road, but always came straight on. He has two men servants to wait at dinner, the one English and the other French, who cannot speak English, which is the case with the housemaid. Mr. Ker said that Lord Brougham, when quite a young man, wrote a very clever article in the *Edinburgh*, denouncing and demolishing a theory on light, but which after twenty years was found correct, and that it had been predicted of him by the author of that theory that he would be a very distinguished philosopher if he were not unfortunately drawn off into politics.

" 29*th.*—After breakfast, walked up the hill in the forest of Lord Brougham's domain, pursuant to Mr. Woolfield's recommendation, to see the view, which is very fine indeed, although the day is thick and cloudy. The range of the snow-capped mountains behind Nice, of which I made a sketch, in full prospect, and of Cannes and the coast about it in each direction. A curious pile of stones at the summit of the hill, like a cromlech with one long, upright stone. Of these I made a sketch, and this pile is called the Guardian Cross,

an iron cross being fastened into the upright stone.
Before breakfast I made a sketch of Lord Brougham's
study, and after breakfast one of the chateau 'Eleanor
Louise.' I also collected some of the seeds in his
garden and in the forest, to sow at Iselipps. Lord
Brougham was much gratified this morning by receiving in an envelope from M. Berryer copies of the
photograph of himself and M. Berryer (which he told
me was an excellent likeness) in one card, one of which
he gave to me, with his autograph written beneath it.
I told him we had very much enjoyed our visit here,
which he said was a very short one. He said he had
wished very much to give Mr. Bellender Ker an autograph of M. Berryer, but had not got one. This morning, however, the photographs came in an envelope of
Berryer's directing, which he sent down to Ker at
once. Lord Brougham also received this morning a
photograph of his nephew—a remarkably good one. I
asked him what he thought of Lord Erskine's judgments, and said that I thought they laid down the
principles of law very well, but that they were not
much quoted from. He said there were very few of
them. I showed Lord Brougham my sketches, of
which he expressed his approval, and recollected the
buildings in Rome. He said that I ought not to leave
Cannes without seeing the prison on the island, which
is supposed to have been the scene of the *Iron Mask*,
but that it would take a day to go there, and the landing was sometimes difficult.

" Having seen Lord Brougham upon the stage of
public life, and been witness to some of the important
scenes in which he has played so conspicuous a part, I
had much wished to observe him in his hours of retirement, and to know something of the domestic life of
this great man. Like some noble man-of-war which

has returned to our shores victorious in many an engagement, but is now reposing in the harbour, its sails no longer unfurled, and its cannon silent, Lord Brougham is now seen reposing in the harbour of private life, his presence still serving to recall the memory of the great deeds of which he was the performer. Possibly, as a man, he appears even more majestic quietly and unostentatiously fulfilling the duties of domestic life and duty than when actively exerting himself in the field of action.

"Mr. Ker mentioned, in course of conversation with Lord B., 'It is very well known that your Lordship is preparing memoirs of yourself,' so that this is I suppose, after all, no secret. Lord Brougham is very temperate both in eating and drinking. Does not take more than two or three glasses of Moselle and port, and drinks principally barley-water at dinner. He seems very much attached to Lord Lyndhurst, who was a great friend of Mr. Ker, and to whom the latter always sent a present on his birthday, generally of some sort of wine.

"Lord Brougham at times appears very irritable. I heard him blowing up his servant in fearful style ; and on my asking him what was done with all the olives, he seemed to be quite excited, and flourished his stick, and said, 'Why, what can you suppose but to make oil of them ?' as much as to say, 'What a fool you are to ask such a question !' He is very proud of a very large and very old olive tree in his grounds, which he says is the finest within twenty miles. Mr. Woolfield says that the chateau was built for Miss Brougham, but that she never lived to reside in it. This, however, must be a mistake, as she died in 1833, and it was not commenced until 1835. Lord Brougham has the *Times* and *Globe* daily, and the *Star* occasionally. He also takes in the *Spectator*, the *Saturday Review*, and *Illustrated London News*. He is reading the 'Diary of a Working Man,' by C. Knight, and says it is very interesting, and asked me if I had read it. The station-master at the railway called him 'Monsieur' Brougham, but the French generally address him as 'Milord.' He seems to be very much pleased to hear about Gibson, but not to be aware of the great eminence he has attained as a sculptor. He supposed something would be done this session about bankruptcy reform, but did not at all know what measure would be introduced; also that it was remarkable how well the county court system had succeeded, and that he had not heard of one complaint against a judge on account of maladministration of justice.

"Lord Brougham rather complained of the style of a chateau built near his in the old French mode, with turrets at the corners, but which I prefer to the style of his own, which is Italian. When I proposed leaving Cannes in the morning at seven, he said, 'Oh, that is an intolerable time for starting!' and added that four in the afternoon was much more convenient. Several of the nobility and gentry called and left their cards at Lord Brougham's, but it did not appear that he saw them. Among those were the Duc de Broglie, Earl of Mount Edgcumbe, and Sir John Duckworth.

"We took leave of Lord Brougham, and left for Marseilles about three; and so ends a visit I have been looking forward to for some time, and cannot but regard as eventful.

"*30th.*—From Marseilles we came to Lyons.

"*December* 1st and 2nd.—From Lyons to Tonnerre. From Tonnerre we came to Paris.

"*3rd.*—From Paris we came to London direct.

"*27th.*—Mentioned my proposal for a Gallery of

Copies at Manchester lately to Mr. Baker, but he did not appear to approve of it, and said there was no room in Manchester suitable, and that the smoke would spoil the pictures."

CHAPTER XXIII.

TO CLOSE OF REGISTRARSHIP.

1865—1868.

"*January 3rd.*

" A LETTER to E. from Mrs. J. Miller, at Cannes, tells us that she often sees Lord Brougham out in all sorts of weather, with a very dilapidated white umbrella, the same that he used to take out when we were with him to shelter himself from the sun. Mr. W. Brougham and his family, she says, have not yet arrived at Cannes. This may be owing to Lady Brougham's illness and death. The papers stated that Lord Brougham's medical attendants would not allow him to come to England to be at the funeral, but that Mr. W. Brougham was there.

"*February 4th.*—My paper read at the York Congress on 'Criminal Punishments' appears at full length in the *Social Science Review*.

"*9th.*—Delivered my lecture this evening on 'The Pursuits and Mode of Life of our Forefathers,' in the Christ Church School. The audience numerous, and extremely attentive; all appeared and expressed themselves as much pleased.

"*10th.*—Delivered the same lecture this evening at the Mechanics' Institution, Accrington.

" Drew out lately my proposal for a national gallery
of copies of paintings. Called on the Dean of Manchester with it this afternoon, and left the following
note for him :—'

" ' I should much like at some time or other to consult
you about a project which I have long entertained,
and which, it has struck me, might possibly be better
carried out in Manchester than in London. The
project I have entertained for years, and had intended to make an effort to have it carried out in
London, and to solicit donations for the purpose in the
first instance, and eventually to try and obtain a parliamentary grant. It has recently occurred to me,
however, that, as there is no public gallery of paintings
in Manchester, and as there is abundance of wealth to
assist in an undertaking of this kind, it would be
desirable to ascertain what could be done here before I
made any efforts to establish such an institution in
London.'

" 21*st.*—Delivered lecture on Napoleon at the Working Men's Institute, Camden Hall, Camden Town.
About a hundred and seventy present.

" 28*th.*—In the evening I attended a meeting of the
Anthropological Society. The chairman remarked to
me that he thought there was too much speculation in
the papers read, and that it would be better to confine
ourselves to facts. I said that I thought speculation
often served to advance knowledge, and to promote
philosophical discovery. Who so speculative as those
great inductive reasoners Bacon and Locke ? All who
have really advanced our knowledge have been more
or less speculative.

" *March 9th.*—Came to Rugby to-day to deliver my
lecture on ' Pursuits and Mode of Life,' etc. It took
place in the Town Hall. About a hundred and

twenty present, all, or nearly so, people of education,
but several of them schoolboys.   It went off extremely
well, and was attentively listened to throughout.

" 11th.—A good report of my lecture in the *Rugby
Advertiser.*

" 21st.—At Manchester.   The judges of assize,
Justices Mellor and Shee, dined with us to-day.   I
wrote to Mellor when I was in London, asking him to
fix a day, and told him I should be happy to see Shee
as well, and also their marshals.   A letter from young
Mellor fixed to-day.   Mellor was very pleasant and
familiar, and just as he used to be on the circuit, and
alluded to the old circuit jokes ; Shee was also very
pleasant and affable.   I asked the Bishop to meet
them, but he declined in a stiff, formal note, beginning
' Dear Sir.'   Mr. R. Phillips and Mr. Langton I also
asked, but they were engaged.   The Dean came, and
Captain Bennett, Mr. Commissioner Jennett, Mr.
Fowler, Mr. Whitelegge, and young Mellor, the
marshal.

" After dinner we had a great deal of fun and laughing, Mellor chaffing his brother judge and the Dean as
well as me.   Mellor said that Shee took him to a
Roman Catholic establishment in the neighbourhood
of Durham, where they declared they were unable to
keep the Lenten fast because the Dean of Durham had
bought up all the fish to feast the judges with.   Shee
told me that if Victor Emmanuel gets possession of
Rome, the treasures of the Vatican will be at once sold
off to pay the Italian debt.   Altogether the judges
seemed to enjoy themselves vastly, and laughed so
heartily and made such a noise that they quite confounded my quiet household, who are not used to such
ways.   I don't know what the Gordons will say if we
have such noisy doings at Iselipps (as I told Canon

Gordon to-day), and that they have quite taken the shine out of old Cockman [an old tenant]. The Dean told me that he had consulted several people about my plan of a gallery of copies, who approved of it, and thought it might be carried eventually, as they were going to consolidate several of the institutions into one. But nothing can be done during the present distress.

" 22*nd*.—Some of the Northern Circuit dined with us to-day. A much quieter party than the judges, and seemed tame after those noisy old fellows, with their grand state liveries in attendance on them, and which were quite effective in the dining-room.

" 30*th*.—We dined to-day at Mr. Huntingdon's, and in the evening I read, by way of a lecture, in St. John's Schoolroom, my paper on ' Criminal Punishments,' exhibiting the diagrams as well. The audience large, very attentive, and seemed well pleased.

" *April* 5*th*.—Dined and stayed all night at Mr. Corser's, of Stand.

" Delivered my lecture on ' Pursuits and Modes of Life,' etc., in the Institute room. A great many present, and the room quite full, several ladies and gentlemen being on the platform. The lecture was very well received.

" I was able to stay at Mr. Corser's until Thursday afternoon to look over his valuable library, containing some good missals and other scarce books.

" *May* 2*nd*.—Sent Mr. R. B. Cobbett a copy of my ' Theory of Representation,' with a letter in which I mentioned that it has met with favour by some of all parties, as it has also been opposed by them each in turn.

" 11*th*.—Dined to-day at the Dean of Manchester's to meet the Council of the Cheetham Society.

" 20*th*.—Called on Mr. Taylor, the editor of the

Manchester Guardian, to whom, the Dean told me, he
had mentioned my proposal for a gallery of copies of
works of art in Manchester. He said he highly
approved of it, and that it was much wanted here, but
that there was no chance of its being carried, that
nothing was done now, and everything languishing.
Even the Royal Institute was turned to no account.
He said that the Dean had read my paper at a meeting
of the Society of Arts, and that it had been warmly
applauded, and Mr. Murray Gladstone in particular
praised the scheme very highly. But Mr. Taylor said
there the matter would end, and nothing would be
done.

"*June* 22nd.—At Northolt. I am quite satisfied
and very well pleased indeed with Isclipps as I have
now made it.

"*24th.*—In the afternoon went to Greenwich to the
Law Amendment Society's dinner. Spoke to Lord
Brougham about the proof-sheets. He said he had
been so much occupied, he had not written to me.
Parkes observed to me what a wreck Lord Brougham
was to what he recollected him. He had heard him
deliver his famous speech on the Queen's trial. Lord
Brougham, however, spoke very correctly and forcibly
this evening, though his utterance was at times in-
distinct, and the reporters could not follow him. He
was much affected by the warm reception given him,
and when his health was proposed and drunk standing,
he cried outright. I had some difficulty in understanding all he said. One thing he mentioned was, ' Oh, I
had such a disappointment after you left me. You
know I was expecting William and his family. Well,
they never came until a long time after,' meaning that
he should not have liked us to leave him so soon had
he not been expecting them immediately.

"*August* 12th.—Commenced our Continental tour to-day. Visited Berlin, Belgium, North Germany, including Brunswick, Pesth, Vienna, part of Hungary, including Debrezin and also Gratz. Returned home, after visiting Switzerland.

"*September* 30th.—Came to London. Always a treat to be in London, which I regard as my real home.

"*October* 2nd.—Saw Mr. Edgar to-day, and had a good deal of talk with him about my 'Principia,' with which he expressed himself much pleased. Said he liked the preface very much, which I was very glad to hear, and thought the work would be a very interesting one, and that it will be taken up for students.

"12th.—Drew out the circular respecting the grant for the establishment of working men's libraries, with a list of the books to be selected.

"17th.—Wrote to Lord Brougham, asking him to accept a copy of my new legal work, stating that the most valuable illustrations of the principles propounded, both in the present and the succeeding parts, will be found to be the quotations from his judgments, and submitting that a clear elucidation of the leading principles of law was essential as a preliminary to any codification of it that might be attempted.

"19th.— Received to-day a reply from Lord Brougham, informing me he had received the book, and heartily thanking me for it.

"25th.—Completed to-day the composition of my paper for the Anthropological Society, 'The Plurality of Races,' and sent it to the secretary of the Anthropological Society.

"27th.—Mr. Commissioner Jennett and I dined at the Law Students' Debating Society, and both had a very warm reception on our healths being proposed

"Very much pleased by hearing from Mrs. Huntingdon that the working men in their parish had been reading 'Civilisation as a Science,' which they got from the Free Library, and that they had been so much pleased with it as to wish that I should give them a lecture on the subject of education.

"*November 1st.*—Presided at the meeting of the Articled Clerks' Debating Society. Subject : the abolition of capital punishment. I said I felt doubtful whether the words in Scripture, 'Whoso sheddeth man's blood, by man shall his blood be shed,' authorised capital punishment. They referred to that relative system of punishing each offence by a penalty of a corresponding nature peculiar to the Levitical law, and which was the most perfect and philosophical of all modes, besides which Cain was not put to death. Said I doubted the efficiency of transportation from its uncertainty, but thought penal servitude in this country might be made sufficiently deterring. I advocated the adoption of special juries in capital cases and the private execution of criminals. The majority against the abolition of capital punishment.

" *2nd.*—Delivered lecture on the Plague at Whalley Bridge this evening.

" *3rd.*—A very favourable review of my ' Principia ' in the *Law Review*. They say of it, ' Mr. Harris has hit upon a very good idea ; and judging from the first instalment of his labours, we are inclined to think that he is likely to work it out with considerable success. . . . This is certainly a somewhat ambitious design, but we have no doubt that the industry and research of the author will be sufficient to enable him to cope with the magnitude and difficulty of the task. The perusal of the first part of the " Principia " has been attended with no small an amount of pleasure and agreeable interest.'

" *8th.*—Lord St. Leonards, the late Lord Chancellor, says, in acknowledging the receipt of my 'Principia,' ' When a principle is once established in theory, all decisions should be conformable to it. But the judges of the present day have not only to have regard to the principle, but also to the decisions of their predecessors. They intend to rest their decisions on principle. A later judge may think they erred, yet the law having been settled by decision, may feel himself bound to follow. It is thus that the principle is broken in upon, and distinctions are established which upon principle cannot be supported. And this is an obvious difficulty in the way of an elementary treatise.'

" The Master of the Rolls says, 'From the little I have hitherto been able to look into it, it seems to me to be a very able and useful work.' Sir Hugh Cairns writes as follows : ' Sir Hugh Cairns presents his compliments to Mr. Harris, and begs to thank him very much for the copy of the first part of the " Principia Prima Legum," a work which he hopes will prove as useful as the design of it is original and much required.'

" A long note from Herbert Broom, the law professor, thanking me for book, but saying he is too much engaged to assist me in it. Registrar Murray says, ' I have read the preface and some few of the leading chapters with much interest, and, if I may be allowed to say so, the work seems to be most clearly and logically arranged.'

" J. T. Humphry says that pressing engagements ' have prevented his doing more than observe the terse and able manner in which you state the principles. It is the kind of book he has always felt the want of and a desire to produce himself had he the ability and industry and courage for the work. The present race of lawyers perhaps need to be rather more philosophical.'

" 18*th*.— Received to-day a very kind letter from Lord Westbury, in reply to the two which I wrote to him some time before.   His letter is dated from ' Paris, November 16th.   He thanks me very much for my valuable present of a copy of the first volume of the " Principia Legum," and for the kindness which dictated the dedication.   ' By all means,' he says, ' make it the constant subject of your attention, enlarging and improving it, for it is a work much wanted, and I trust it will soon attract general commendation.'   When he has had time to examine it, he will write to me more fully.

" 20*th*.—Replied to Lord Westbury, saying, ' I shall feel extremely obliged by any hints or advice on my " Principia," acknowledging that the work is very capable of improvement, doubting if whether the arrangement, as developed in the table of contents, might not be considerably amended, and fearing that I may have omitted some leading judgments which ought to find a place there.'

" 21*st*.—Sent to the press to-day my plan for working men's libraries.   A list of their books, which I asked for, sent me by the secretary of the Whalley Bridge Institute.

" *December* 5*th*.—Dined at Mr. Crossley's to meet the Clerical Book Society.   On my health being proposed, I replied, in reference to what had been said about the Cheetham Society, that I was myself intimately connected with a ' Cheat-'em ' society if the aspersions cast upon the Bankruptcy Court were justifiable.   In my ' Cheat-'em ' society, too, we have an extensive collection of books and papers, though modern instead of ancient ; and from these the biographies of many persons are made out.   None of the members of the

Book Society had, however, contributed to enrich its annals, on which account I thought myself unfairly neglected by them, though I would not deny them my 'protection' notwithstanding if they required it.

"*7th.*—Received to-day a pamphlet entitled 'The Theatre and its Traducers, by George Harris, F.S.A.,' etc., being a reprint for general distribution of the chapter on theatres in ' Civilisation as a Science,' and by which I was much gratified.

" Dined with the Northern Circuit mess.

" *11th.* —An ample review of my ' Principia ' in the *Law Times*, in which they say, ' When completed, there will be a treatise on the law of England of a very novel character, composed of the dicta of great authorities, without the intrusion of commentary or case, and yet so neatly put together that one reads on almost unconscious that one page is made up of scraps gleaned from a vast variety of sources. The merit of the edition consists in the labour its author has devoted to the search, the knowledge that enabled him to discover in a long judgment the enunciation of a principle, and the skill with which he afterwards compounded the whole, so as to make a book of very pleasant as well as instructive reading out of materials which at the first sight might have been deemed very dry and repulsive.'

" *12th.*—Sent out some of the circulars respecting parochial libraries for working men to six different institutions, to the editor of the *Social Science Review*, and to Sidebotham.

" *16th.*—Wrote the following letter to Lord Brougham, enclosing in it one of the circulars respecting the parochial libraries for working men : —

"'COURT OF BANKRUPTCY, MANCHESTER, *Dec. 16th,* 1865.

"'MY DEAR LORD, — I take the liberty of forwarding

to your Lordship the enclosed paper, and of asking
you to favour me with your opinion upon the proposal
contained in it. You have been so great a supporter
of education, and have done so much for civilisation
generally, that your sentiments on such a matter cannot
but be entitled to the greatest weight.

"'To some extent perhaps I may be considered as
carrying out the principles on which was established
the "Society for the Diffusion of Useful Knowledge,"
of which your Lordship was the great patron, and
indeed the founder. In the selection of works I have
taken the liberty of putting down two or three of
which you are the author, and which appear to me
to be admirably calculated for a library of this kind,
as well as for the study of minds of more extensive
cultivation than those of the class for whom provision
is here proposed. I have received very satisfactory
letters from several leaders of the profession respecting
my " Principia Prima Legum," and I hope that the work
meets with the approval of your Lordship.

" ' I have, etc.,
" ' G. HARRIS.

"'The Right Hon. LORD BROUGHAM.'

1866.

"*January* 3rd.—Received the following opinion from
Stevens and Sons about the 'Principia' :—

"' In asking for our candid opinion as to the advisability
of completing the work, we think, if indeed it be not
too early to come to a decision, that the amount of sales
will not prove at all equal to your outlay, while the
credit it may bring you can be fairly looked to from the
part of the work already issued.'

"*February* 21st.—Dined at the Clerical Book Society's,
at Mr. Allen's. Met Mr. Crossley there, who told me

that Mr. J. Parkes' collection respecting Junius is to be sold separately, and that probably the papers respecting C. Yorke will be among them.

"A letter from Canon Gordon respecting Iselipps, who says that the plantations are looking well. The man who is making the road up to the house told Mr. Gordon he wondered I did not have it quite straight instead of all crooked. I had of course planned it in a waving line.

"*March* 11th.—Went to the cathedral this morning, where the judges of assize were present, and called on them afterwards at the court. Both very affable, and Mellor said I must come and lunch with them one day. To-day he was off to join Lady Mellor at Eccles, who is staying at Mr. Watkin's, the member of Parliament for Stockport. Singular that the sheriff, the mayor, and both the judges are all Dissenters. But they all attended the cathedral this morning.

"12th.—Dined at the circuit mess to-day, on the invitation of Cottingham.

"13th.—We had a dinner-party to-day of the Northern Circuit.

"*April* 14th.—Talking over literary matters with Mr. Crossley. He said that unless you got the publisher to have an interest in a book, it was not subscribed to by the other publishers, and the sale was not pushed. In fact, it amounted only to printing a book privately. He thought that the best arrangement I could make would be to get the publishers to undertake it, I agreeing to take so many copies. Mr. Crossley said that books were sold off now much sooner than they used to be, which was another reason why their sale at full price had been lessened. A further cause was that people obtained them at Mudie's and other libraries instead of buying them.

"*May* 2nd.— Called on Lord Westbury, at Nichol's suggestion, and had a long talk with him about the Bankruptcy Bill, and found him very affable.   Told him of my article in the *Law Times* and my proposals there, and he said he hoped I should follow it up in detail.

"*9th.*—Attended the meeting of the Manchester Anthropological Society this afternoon, when I was unanimously elected president.

"*June* 3rd.—A letter to-day respecting the union of Lancashire and Cheshire institutes from Dr. Pankhurst, who says, 'I am instructed to ask if you would kindly enable the Council to include your name in the list of vice-presidents. The Council feel greatly indebted to you for the very valuable services you have already rendered on behalf of the union, and hope ere long to have the benefit of your experience in the executive department.'   I consented to act in both capacities.

"*13th.*—At Mr. Mendal's ball with E. this evening. Ball said to be the most brilliant thing of the sort ever given in Manchester. About two hundred and seventy present. All the rooms thrown open, and the pictures and sculptures seen to great advantage. Dancing in the new picture-gallery. Ices in the conservatory, and a superb supper at twelve. We left about one. We had neither of us been at a ball since we were married, but this was thought too good to be missed.

"*19th.*—At the Anthropological Society this afternoon, and attended the general meeting in the evening. Showed Dr. Hunt my sketches of Celtic remains in Brittany, in which he was much interested. Called upon to take my seat by him at the meeting, and formally installed president of the Manchester Anthropological Society, the first that has been established in this country out of London.

"*21st.*—Called on Dr. Richardson, who is giving

up the *Social Science Review*, and would like the National Association to take to it. Showed me his invention in substitution of chloroform in certain cases of operation. The action of the anæsthetic is local.

"22nd. —Dined with Mr. Hastings at Highgate. He said Lord Brougham had resigned the presidency of the Social Science Association in a very dignified speech, saying he should have done so last year, but felt bound to go to York and Sheffield, as being among his old constituents, but that Manchester had no such claim upon him. An unfortunate letter from Mr. Fairburn to Lord Brougham alluding to this and asking him to stay at his house, where Lord Stanley is also to be, led him to ask Mr. Hastings, ' Who is this Fairburn ? I know nothing of him ;' but Mr. Hastings reminded him that he had known him a long time, but ' Harris will be very glad to see you at his house,' on which Lord Brougham said, ' Who is Harris ? I don't know him.' And when Mr. Hastings explained, he said, ' Oh, yes, George Harris! I know him very well.' Mr. Hastings thinks he is inclined to come to us, and said the best plan would be for me to see Lord Brougham to-morrow morning, and also his old servant Gordon, whom we could lodge very well. Hastings said if Lord Brougham and Lord Stanley were both in the same house there was sure to be a scene, as Lord Brougham would be breaking out. Gordon, he says, is a very nice man to have in the house, and can control Lord Brougham. He said to him one day, ' You are not going down to the House of Lords to sit there all that time without having your warm socks on ;' and he made him wear them.

" 23rd.—Called on Lord Brougham, but saw Gordon first and explained to him the object of my visit. Lord Brougham merely asked if my house was far from the law-courts, and said he had a letter from Fairburn, to which he was going to reply to-day. I said that I had asked Mr. and Mrs. Hastings to meet him ; but he said he thought that, considering the state of Sir C. Hastings' health, it was very doubtful whether Hastings would be able to go to Manchester. Lord Brougham this morning seemed very vigorous and clear, but on Monday evening I thought him much broken and very decrepit; but then he was fatigued by a long debate in the House of Lords and had only been able to get a very hasty dinner. On Monday evening he did not seem to recollect me at all.

"25th.—Returned to Manchester in the afternoon.

"*July* 15th.—This afternoon commenced etching in copper, which I gave up more than thirty years ago when at Rugby, owing to want of time.

"*August* 9th.—We started on our vacation Continental tour, visiting Paris and Switzerland, and on our way back through the Auvergne district.

"*September* 8th.—We returned to England to-day.

" 10th.—Came to Iselipps, where we found that none of the furniture, by some mistake, had been sent, and the handles not put on the doors. Obliged to sleep on the floor and to borrow a table and chairs of the servants in the house, but hope to make ourselves very cosy.

" 12th.—Very busy about Iselipps plans and improvements. It is a great satisfaction to live in your own house, but more especially when the place is one of your own making, and has existed in your mind as regards its principal characteristics many years before it actually came into being.

" 15th.—Commenced this morning before breakfast in the study the composition of a drama to be entitled *Joseph* by writing out some of the lives, the opening

stanzas, and some other parts. Engaged afterwards
in preparing coloured plans of the ground leading to
the house and of the flower-garden, and in marking
trees to be cut down.

"18*th*.—At work early again at *Joseph*, and planned
while dressing the closing address of Jacob, the lines
for which (sixty-nine) I composed in the study before
breakfast, and afterwards had a walk through the plantations to compose the four concluding lines. Probably
I may print the former privately as a sequel to the
work on 'Arts,' in which it is suggested, and as showing
what might be done in this way.

"19*th*.—At the Social Science Association. My paper
about working men's libraries read there. Mr. Dadley
showed me the number of the *Law Journal* for September 7th, in which, in an article on ' The Law of
Master and Servant,' they say that the principle has
never been more satisfactorily settled than in Mr.
Harris' ' admirable ' work ' Principia Prima Legum,'
from which they quote the whole of my original matter
on that subject, and also my extract from Puffendorf.

" 24*th*.—Returned to Manchester.

" 29*th*.—Asked to attend on Monday as one of the
vice-presidents at a meeting of the Cheshire and Lancashire Institutes' Union, on Wednesday to preside at
the opening meeting of the Law Debating Society, and
on Tuesday week to preside at the opening of the
session of the St. George's Public Reading Society.

" At the morning and evening meetings of the Lancashire and Cheshire Institutes. Spoke at the former
readily and fluently, without notes. I was elected on
the Council of the Society.

" Went to a lecture in the Town Hall on ' National
Self-knowledge in its Bearing upon National Life,' by
Mr. Ward, Professor of History, having a ticket for

the platform sent to me. Met the Bishop of Manchester there, who was particularly cordial.

"G. Denman came to us to-day for the Social Science Congress.

"*October 3rd.*—Took the chair at the Law Students' Debating Society this evening, and introduced Sir E. Wilmot to them, who delivered them a short but very pertinent and appropriate address. After this we went to the Social Science Congress in the Free Trade Hall to hear the president's (Lord Shaftesbury's) address. Lord Brougham, in the little he said, very effective and sensible, and the more so from his conciseness; but he is very feeble and very deaf. Wrote to him last week to fix a day for dining with me to meet Denman and Wilmot (who arrived this afternoon). Denman and Hastings appear to think him too feeble to come to us.

"*4th.*—Went to the Congress to hear Lord Brougham's address, which he got well through, and delivered with much energy. The address itself was very forcible and pungent, especially in parts, worthy of his best days. His vigour appears wonderfully to have revived on this occasion. He was stimulated to show what he could do.

"*5th.*—Read my paper on 'Working Men's Libraries' before the Social Science Congress.

"*6th.*—A very fair report of my paper yesterday and the discussion upon it in the *Manchester Guardian* of to-day, giving an outline of the former, and stating that I had received a number of letters from distinguished men and from institutions on the subject.

"*8th.*—Denman and Wilmot and I dined at Canon Birch's, of Prestwich. Went to the soirée at the Assize Courts in the evening, where E. met us.

"*9th.*—E. and I both went to the Social Science

23

dinner in the great hall of the Assize Courts. The
dinner itself a very indifferent one. The only things
not cold were the ices, which were all melting. The
music was as bad as the meat. The wine—champagne,
port, and sherry—pretty good, but a woeful scarcity of
it. The general effect of the assemblage very striking.
Nearly four hundred present, and a great many ladies.
Sir E. Wilmot made a capital speech, the best of any,
on proposing the health of Lord Brougham, and was
very much applauded. Lord Brougham did not come.

"10*th*.—This morning, before Sir Eardley Wilmot
went to London, I showed him my drawings and
paintings on glass, with which he expressed himself
much pleased. Said I might make more by lecturing
than by the registrarship. Denman left us this morning.

"12*th*.—At a meeting of the Council of the Lancashire and Cheshire Institutes' Union, I gave a
donation of £5, to be applied in two prizes of £3
and £2 'for the best [and second-best] drawing
from nature of "either a human head or figure, the head
or figure of an animal, a building, a tree, a landscape,
to be executed either in pencil, pen and ink, crayons,
or water-colours." To be open to any members of the
Society or of any of the institutions in union with it.'
Some of the Council said it was a capital idea, and
the very thing that was wanted, as they have prizes
for mechanical drawing.

"18*th*.—Delivered my lecture on 'Ghosts' at Ashton-
under-Lyne, before the Young Men's Society. About
two hundred and fifty present, the best audience they
have had. Well applauded at the conclusion.

"25*th*.—Delivered my lecture on Napoleon at Saddle-
worth this evening. The diagrams and caricatures
excited a good deal of attention.

"26*th*.—Attended the dinner of the Law Students'

Debating Society, and had to take the chair. Made four speeches, and managed to throw some humour into them. Proposed the ladies, moreover, without any notes, and quite offhand. Told them that, 'powerful as were the lawyers, the ladies were much more powerful, inasmuch as they ruled their husbands, whether lawyers or laity. On this account it was deemed by the legislature unnecessary to give votes to women, as they made the men vote as they pleased. One lady threatened if her husband did not plump as she wished, and dared to split his vote, that she would split his skull.'

" 30th.—Dr. Hunt, president of the London Anthropological Society, and Mr. Heath, the treasurer, arrived to-day. Had the Council of our Society to meet them at dinner. Dr. Hunt said my acquaintance with the old writers on anthropology, to which I have alluded in my address, would be a great advantage to the Society, as would be also my diagrams and etchings.

" *November* 2nd.—Our meeting came off this evening. The hall of the Mechanics' Institute looked quite gay with the diagrams, of which the greater part were mine, and which appeared to great advantage. I also exhibited some of the old works connected with anthropology and some of the most choice of my autographs, which attracted a good deal of notice, as did some etchings on copper, especially one called 'The Belgian Pig.' The meeting well attended. I got well through my address, and parts of it were several times alluded to by the speakers who followed me.

" 3rd.—In the *Manchester Examiner* of to-day there is a leading article on the Society, attacking it and Dr. Hunt, in which they say, in reference to the opinions on civilisation, ' Mr. Harris is an honourable exception, but he is about the only anthropologist we have heard of who did not seem possessed by an uncontrollable desire to tear a missionary to pieces.'

"*7th.*—An interesting letter to me from M. Quatrefages, Professor of Anthropology in the Museum of Natural History, Paris, who has been elected an honorary member of our Society, thanking me for the newspaper containing an account of the opening of our Society, and expressing his wishes for our success. In my reply to him I said, ' I beg to forward you herewith a copy of my inaugural address. I have alluded therein to several writers of ages past, who have treated on subjects connected with anthropology, whose works I have in my library, and which I have long studied with interest, years before the Anthropological Society in London was even thought of. Among them are the treatises of your renowned countryman Des Cartes, who suggested a good deal to our Locke. I have travelled through most parts of France, including that very interesting portion of it, Brittany, and have made sketches of the Celtic remains there, so eagerly examined by anthropologists. During the present year, Mrs. Harris and I walked through the Auvergne district, visiting Le Roy and Clermont, and exploring the extinct volcanoes. We spent a few days in Paris, where I have often been, on our return. I hope that the next time we visit Paris we may have the pleasure of personally making your acquaintance.'

"*9th.*—Delivered my lecture on Napoleon this evening at the Institution at Whitworth, near Rochdale. They were extremely attentive, and appeared much interested.

"*16th.*—Delivered my lecture on 'Ghosts' at the Bury Athenæum. The audience was very attentive, and the lecture appeared to take well.

"*20th.*—Received a letter to-day from Lord Westbury, dated from 75, Lancaster Gate, W., November 16th, 1866, in which he says he has had the pleasure of receiving a copy of a very interesting lecture of mine, and is much obliged for it. 'You are, I hope, still going on with your most useful work on the "Principia Legum." I shall probably have soon to consider the feasibility of a digest of the whole of English law and the best mode of proceeding to construct it as well as its actual form. If you have thought of these matters and will give me your views the subject, I shall be obliged to you.'

To this communication I replied as follows :—

"'MY LORD,—I feel highly honoured and greatly obliged by your Lordship's very kind letter of the 16th inst. in acknowledgment of my address to the Anthropological Society. With regard to my "Principia," the main obstacle to its completion is my being placed so far from London, and consequently not having access to the books and manuscripts which are essential in order to the satisfactory carrying on of such a work or to persons with whom it is important for me occasionally to have the opportunity of conferring. May I take the liberty of asking whether it would be possible for me to obtain a removal to London by the exchange of the office I now hold for one of a corresponding nature, either a registrarship, or any similar appoint·ment, or a county court judgeship in London or within fifty miles of it, without reference to higher emolument, as this would afford me the opportunity of properly carrying out my design ?'

"22nd.—Delivered my lecture on 'Ghosts' at Maple. About two hundred present. Very attentive.

"*27th.*—Wrote the following letter to-day to Lord Westbury :—

"'My Lord,—As your Lordship was pleased to ask me in your last letter to make any suggestions that might occur to me respecting the plan of a digest of the English law, I venture to trouble you on this subject, to which I have devoted a good deal of attention.

"'It strikes me that each department of the digest ought to commence by (1) setting forth as lucidly as can be effected the leading principles, independent of decided cases, and as deduced by reason alone, which govern this division of the law, and to which a reference may be made when points in dispute arise as to the interpretation of the directly practical parts of the digest. Such an exposition of principle might be said to correspond with the preamble in an Act of Parliament. This will be a very important part, and indeed the most critical and difficult portion, of the whole work. And the more completely it is effected, the less need will there be for enlarging the digest of decided cases. I hope that at best some portions of the undertaking may have the benefit of your Lordship's very acute mind and jurisprudential knowledge.

"'Having accomplished this, I should suggest that another section should follow, (2) setting forth concisely the leading principles which have at different periods been held by various jurists and the main reasons for these opinions. I think it desirable to have these on record for reference in case of argument as to the meaning of the subsequent and more practical part of the digest, and to show that these points have not been overlooked in framing a practical digest as to the actual and existing law of this country on each subject. (3) A digest should follow, under distinct heads, of each branch of the actually existing law, elucidating as far as possible, the principle involved, as well as the practical result of the case, and embodying the whole of the decisions referred to. A marginal reference to these cases may be appended. As I mentioned before to your Lordship, I have collected, as far as I can, all the leading cases ruling the law in each department, which I shall be glad to render serviceable here, after which any ordinary legal digest may be resorted to. I have not been able to see Mr. Field's 'Digest of the American Law,' which I hear highly spoken of, and should much like to have been present at the meeting of the Law Amendment Society the other evening on this subject, of which Sir Eardley Wilmot wrote me an account, and said that Mr. Lowe made a good speech in favour of codification. I have no doubt that Mr. Field's work will be most valuable as affording suggestions for framing an English digest, although I confess to being rather jealous of the English copying from their American brethren altogether, especially when we have such masterly jurists as your Lordship to assist us in framing a scheme worthy of this great country, so renowned for its achievements in the science of jurisprudence. There are, as your Lordship well knows, several other excellent samples of codification to refer to. Justinian's 'Institutes' are useful in this respect both as an elucidation of principles and a compendium of law, as is the Code Napoleon as a digest of practical law. The reports of the Commissioners on different departments of the law may some of them, I think, be found very useful, as may also several of our leading text-books.

"'There is another work to which I may refer,

which, although not a law-book, affords an excellent sample of what may be effected in the way of codification to reduce a complicated and extensive system into a comparatively short compass and render it intelligible. I refer to Dr. Henry Pemberton's "View of Sir Isaac Newton's Philosophy," published in 1720, which reduces the whole of his vast discoveries and numerous problems into a simple comprehension of leading principles and practical results, intelligible to every one who will take the pains to study such a work. Perhaps your Lordship may think me rather theoretical or fanciful in the scheme that I have propounded, but I have deemed it better to express my real opinion about a matter on which I have thought a good deal, and to which I have long devoted considerable attention. It will be easy, of course, to reject whatever is not practical or sound in my suggestions, and I have only to apologise for the freedom with which I have introduced what, after all, may be considered as mere crotchets. I shall be much interested, however, in learning your Lordship's opinion on the matter, and shall be always glad to do all in my power to contribute to the carrying out of so important and so valuable an undertaking, any labour in the completion of which, I can truly say, would be a labour of love.   " 'I have, etc.,

             " 'GEORGE HARRIS.

" 'The Right Hon. LORD WESTBURY.'

" 29*th.*—Delivered my lecture on 'Ghosts' this evening to the institution at Crewe. Very successful.

" *December* 1*st.*—At Charlesworth. Delivered, towards raising funds for the repair of the church, my lecture on 'Pursuits, etc., of our Forefathers.'

" 4*th*.—Dined at Mr. Crossley's to meet the Quadrilateral Society. Christie, Dr. Ainsworth, and four other gentlemen present.

· " 14*th*.— Delivered my lecture on ' Pursuits, etc., of our Forefathers ' at Stockport this evening. The lecture was well attended, and appeared to be fully appreciated by the audience.

" 18*th*.—Presided at the first general meeting of the Anthropological Society this evening.

" 20*th*.—Presided this evening at the Law Students' Debating Society. The question was the illegality of trades unions. In summing up, I said that liberty was the essential principle of the British Constitution, and that whatever interfered with that liberty violated the spirit. Liberty was of two kinds : one of action, the other of thought. On the other hand, no unnecessary restrictions were to be imposed by the State, even to promote liberty. Did trades unions interfere with the liberty of the subject ? If they did so, though the means by which they were constituted might be strictly legal, they might, through their object or operation, be illegal. Many combinations were lawful, because effected with no illegal object. As to the power of Parliament—which Blackstone says can do anything except make a man a woman—to put them down, no doubt could be entertained. As to what had been said about the necessity of assisting working men, we are all working men, certainly lawyers are.

1867.

" *January* 14*th*.—Delivered this evening my lecture on ' Pursuits and Mode of Life,' etc., at the Mechanics' Institution at Over Darwen. Lecture seemed to take very well. The different telling points fully appreciated.

Mr. J. Huntingdon, with whom I stayed, and whose firm have an establishment in Paris and connections with all parts of the Continent, told me that they found the Roman Catholics more honest than the Protestants, the French particularly so, even more than the Belgians; and that the Irish were very superior in this respect to the Scotch. A Frenchman who is bankrupt will make every effort to pay twenty shillings in the pound, which I fear an Englishman will take but small pains to do.

"16th.—A letter from Greenwood (the house agent), informing me that our poor dear old house 19, Queen Square, is sold to the Hospital for Sick Children.

"21st.—Delivered my lecture on 'Ghosts' this evening at Macclesfield, in the Town Hall. About two hundred and fifty present. On the whole, quite an educated and intelligent audience. Both the lecture and the diagrams took extremely well. The best audience and the best reception I have had, which further convinces me that my lectures are best fitted for educated people. The mayor moved the vote of thanks to me, which was seconded by the president of the Chamber of Commerce.

"29th.—Wrote to Dr. Hunt about our Anthropological Society. 'I must say how much I am gratified by the notices of our Manchester meeting in the present number of the *Anthropological Review*, which are ample and complimentary. I shall be very glad to have my paper on the " Plurality of Races " appear, because I am sure that this is a point which ought to be brought fairly before the public. I should like to correct a proof of it, and to add a note from what Mr. Heath said in his address at Manchester on this subject.'

"*February* 11th.—Attended a public meeting to form a Sanitary League. I was voted into the chair, and was asked to be permanent chairman ; but to this I demurred, as having no property in or close connection with Manchester, and having paid no particular attention to the subject. Besides, I really have already quite irons enough in the fire.

" 13th.—Presided this evening at the Law Students' Debating Society. I condoled with them from it appearing on the report that they had been obliged to come into the Bankruptcy Court (holding their meetings there), but congratulated them on being able to pay a dividend of fifty shillings in the pound.

" 26th.—Dined at Mr. R. Birley's, at the Clerical Book Society. He showed them my etchings, and said to me that they had been much admired. Sat by Canon Anson, and had a good deal of talk about the Anthropological Society. He contended for making mental philosophy a branch of the study, which I told him was exactly what I had urged in my inaugural address.

" *March* 7th.—Yesterday morning felt very unwell, but better in the course of the day. After going to bed pains came on, which prevented my getting much sleep, and after getting up this morning I felt worse. Took a glass of brandy before breakfast, which relieved me. Felt worse after breakfast, and took another glass, which did me no good. At eleven E. and I started for Southport, where I was to deliver a lecture this evening. But I got worse and worse, so determined to see a medical man, and called in Mr. Barron. He gave me some medicine, which abated the pain ; but it soon returned with much-increased violence, so that I was obliged to send word that I was too ill to lecture, and sent for Mr. Barron.

" At times I was in great agony, quite excruciating ; but a bath abated the pain, and I was able to get to sleep, and had a very good night altogether. Had a long consultation with Mr. Barron. He said I had congestion of the kidneys, and that I had long been suffering from indigestion and dyspepsia, which, neglected, had produced uric acid. He said my case required great care. We returned to Manchester this afternoon.

" 13*th*.—A bitter and most piercing cold wind to-day, and on leaving the court about three, it seemed quite to go through me, gave me a violent chill, and brought on severe pain. Went home, but got worse and worse. Obliged to leave the dinner-table, and sent for Mr. Greaves. Settled with Mr. Greaves to have a consultation on my case with Dr. Roberts. In bed all to-day, except for a few minutes when the bed was made. Did not feel so well later in the evening, and after going to bed a sharp pain came on in the loins at the back. Took medicine to relieve it, but it continued all the night, so I got very little sleep.

" 15*th*.—Not much, if at all, better. Mr. Greaves brought Dr. Roberts with him in the morning, and they both examined me. Still in constant pain, principally in the pit of the stomach.

" 17*th*.—Sent for Mr. Greaves early, as I do not feel so well this morning, though the hiccough is gone off.

" 18*th*.—Passed a very restless night, very uneasy, but felt stronger in getting up. So much better that I was able to write to Chief Registrar Miller myself my letter of resignation, instead of getting E. to transcribe it. But it quite knocked me up, and brought on a pain in the side, and I was near fainting.

" A very kind note from C. Mellor (son of the judge), saying that if we would lunch with the judges any day before Saturday, they would both arrange to adjourn their courts together, so as to meet us. Shee, J., as well as Mellor, J., particularly joined in the inquiry about me.

"21st.—A very civil letter from the Chief Registrar in reply to mine, saying that he had forwarded my letter to the Lord Chancellor, but that mine appeared more like a case for a temporary leave of absence or for exchange than for resignation. Replied to him saying I quite saw the justice of his observations; that it would have been better if I had applied for six months' leave of absence, as I had not the means to admit of giving up the registrarship unless I was sure of my pension.

"22nd.—A very civil letter from the Chief Registrar, saying, 'The Lord Chancellor quite agrees with me that the proposed certificate shows reasons merely for leave of absence or exchange, and not for retirement with a pension.'

"24th.—A letter from the Chief Registrar, saying, 'The Lord Chancellor grants you three months' absence from Thursday next, and appoints Mr. George Murray to act for you.'

"27th.—Got out of doors this day for the first time.

"*April* 1st.—E. and I came to Gresford, to Archdeacon Maclachlan's, the air of which beautiful spot seems much to have revived me.

"5th.—Wrote to Mr. Greaves and enclosed a letter to Mr. Rees, honorary secretary of the National Sanitary Reform League, resigning my membership.

"6th.—Left Gresford to-day, and came to Llandudno, near Oswestry, to stay with the Rev. W. Shorts (our late rector in London), whom we visited in 1862.

"*June* 20th.—Went to London on Thursday, but came to Iselipps this evening, bringing Mr. Seager with us, who is quite charmed with the place. Found a letter from the chief secretary, informing me that my leave of absence extended until September 28th.

"*September* 1st.—A letter from Mr. Reddie, of the Victoria Institute, Hammersmith, saying, 'I have been particularly interested with your article on the "Plurality of Races" in the April number of the *Anthropological Review*. I feel that it requires an answer especially from exegesists or interpreters of the language of Scripture. I am not sorry that there are doubts as to the meaning of certain passages, such as those you handle, for then our scientific inquiries cannot be alleged to be positively biassed when one concludes, for instance (as I do), that the balance of proof is against polygamy. You will forgive me, I am sure, when I add that although I admire the general spirit and ingenuity of your arguments, I am not convinced that all of them are *primâ facie* sound.' In reply I said to him, 'I am always glad, unfashionable as is the proceeding, to have these topics discussed in the fair and candid and philosophical spirit evinced in your letter, and hope at some time to have the opportunity of discussing the matter with you personally. I have several works of interest bearing on the subject, which I should like to show you, though possibly they may prove favourable rather to your views than my own, and I hope at some time that we may have a meeting at my house here. I have also watched the proceedings of the Victoria Institute with interest.'

"*October* 1st.—Dr. Bird, on whom I called, said he had been very much pleased with 'Mr. Pips' Diary' in the *John Bull*, which I sent to him, and which he said was better than that in *Punch*, and that I had entirely caught Pepys' spirit.

"*5th.*—Mrs. Page said she was delighted with 'Mr. Pips' Diary,' and liked it 'immensely.'

" *November 6th.*—Attended both the Council and the general meeting of the Anthropological Society yesterday evening. Dr. Hunt told me there was a vacancy on the Council, and that they meant to elect me, and recommended me therefore to resign the presidency of the Manchester society, which I accordingly wrote to-day to Mr. Plant to do.

" A present from Professor de Quatrefages, of Paris, of his ' History of Anthropology,' a handsome quarto work, and wrote to thank him for it, and said I should hope to call upon him and make his personal acquaintance whenever I visited Paris.

" *18th.*—Attended the meeting of the Law Amendment Society in the evening. Dwelt particularly on the Bankruptcy Bill. Several adverted to my speech, as did Dr. Twiss, the chairman. I told him that Lord Westbury once mentioned that to me as his plan, which confirmed the soundness of his (Dr. Twiss') observation.

" *20th.*—At the meeting of the Anthropological Society in the evening, when a paper was read on the character of the Scotch as influenced by their climate. I said, ' The true principle appears to me that climate is a collateral, but not a leading, cause in the formation of character. In Scotland, for instance, the general character of the people is the same, but the climate varies much in different parts. Then the characters of people in particular counties change, while the climate remains the same. With regard to religion, too, the supposition that particular soils conduced to particular forms of religion was contradicted by facts.'

" *December 3rd.*—Attended the council meeting of the Anthropological Society, when I was elected one of the Council, also the evening meeting, when a paper on 'Mental Philosophy' was read. During the debate on it,

I said that the thanks of the Society were due to the author of the paper, and took the opportunity of expressing my satisfaction that mental philosophy had at length been brought directly before the Society, considering this as the highest branch of anthropology, as it was indeed the first of all the sciences. Anthropology might do more for this science than could be effected by any other branch of knowledge, and perhaps anthropology had no higher aim than this. As yet, however, mental science had not assumed that rank in the department of anthropology which its importance warranted. Anthropology revealed to us the union between, and the reciprocal influence of mind and matter upon Society, and favoured attention to topics connected with mental philosophy.

"4*th*.—Wrote the other day to Mr. Grove, secretary of the Palestine Exploration Fund, sending him some of my etchings to sell first, and offering to give a lecture. A reply to-day, thanking me, and asking me which is the most telling, and saying he has sold ten of the etchings, which he says 'are very droll.'

"11*th*.—Dined and stayed all night at D'Eyncourt's, Hadleigh House, near Barnet. Talked about 'Civilisation as a Science,' which he said he was looking at yesterday, and that I was a bold man to bring out such a work, as it would only command attention if produced by some public man, and that it was impossible to get it read if the work of a private, unknown individual, although in course of time it would take its proper place.

"16*th*.—Read a paper at the Law Amendment Society this evening on special juries in capital cases. G. Denman took the chair. A good discussion, and complimentary to me.

"Sent Mr. Knight Watson, secretary to the Society

of Antiquaries, a set of my etchings, of which he says in a letter thanking me for them, 'They are uncommonly good.'

1868.

RETURN TO MANCHESTER.

"*January* 15*th*.—At a large party this evening at Mr. T. B. Potter's, M.P., to meet Mr. Bruce, M.P., Mr. Forster, M.P., and Mr. Samuelson, M.P. About three hundred present. Met a good many I know, and much gratified by the way in which they came and congratulated me on my return, seeming really glad to see me back. The Dean said they were a very warm-hearted people. Mr. Clay, whom I met at Mr. Potter's, said he thought my plan for parochial libraries valuable, and that it ought to be tried.

"*March* 14*th*.—Wrote to the Chief Registrar to say, ' I should be glad either to be allowed to retire at once on a pension, or to appoint some one to act for me in the registrarship.'

"*April* 21*st*.—Received a letter from the Chancellor's secretary, informing me, ' The Lord Chancellor has this day learned from the Treasury that they will concur in his granting two-thirds pension (in the words of the statute) from the discharge of your duties.' To this I replied, ' It will afford me great satisfaction if, notwithstanding my retirement, I can be engaged in any employment in London where I may be useful, and for which I should regard my retiring pension as ample remuneration.'

"25*th*.—We came this afternoon to Mr. Purcell's at Charlesworth, and in the evening I delivered my lecture on ' Ghosts,' for the benefit of the Church Fund, in the schoolroom. Attendance very good.

24

" *May 6th.*—Attended by invitation a meeting of the Manchester Ladies' Literary Society to discuss a paper by Miss Becher, the president, on the 'Intellectual Difference between Men and Women,' on which I delivered an opinion, when called on, stating that the difference was a material, not a mental, one, there being no difference in souls, but that no grand efforts in philosophy, poetry, painting, or history had emanated from females. I alluded to the difference caused by sex in animals, and the capacity evinced for rule by female sovereigns."

CHAPTER XXIV.

RESIDENCE AT ISELIPPS—RURAL LIFE IN RETIREMENT— LATEST LITERARY EFFORTS.

1868—1875.

" *May 11th,* 1868.

" **R**EAD in the newspapers to-day of the death of my great patron and firm friend Lord Brougham, who passed peacefully away, after a life of intense activity and of great results, at his beautiful chateau at Cannes, where we visited him. Born before the French Revolution was even thought of, of what events has he not been the witness, and of what vast social and moral revolutions has he himself been the cause! For eloquence he had no equal, for energy no rival, and in the practical results achieved no one approached him. His speeches are probably the best records of his achievements, the finest portrait of his soul, that could be produced. His autobiography will be his noblest monument. His partiality to me I prize

above every distinction I could attain. His letters to
me I shall ever preserve as the proudest trophies I
could possess. The photograph which he gave me of
himself, after writing his autograph beneath it, on the
day of our leaving Cannes, I shall ever regard as the
most valuable of my pictorial possessions. For some
years he has been lost to the world, a wreck of his
former self, a distorted shadow of the vast being which
for more than half a century acted so grand a part on
the world's stage. It is satisfactory, however, to me to
reflect that I knew him in his vigour, and that I was
thought worthy to aid him in some of those great
achievements which contributed to render his name
what it is. To me he has proved ever the firmest of
friends. I have always found him true to the core,
sincere to the very utmost, saying the same of me to
others as he did to myself, the grasp of his hand
characteristic of his warm feeling and energetic action.
Still now for ever lies that majestic form, once so active
and untiring, and ever engaged in some grand undertaking. Still for ever is that tongue which so long has
pleaded the cause of civilisation and progress and
benevolence. Hushed for ever is that deep voice,
whose tones entranced the thousands who have
listened with admiration. To him I feel that I owe
everything, and that debt must never remain uncancelled
so long as I can do anything to uphold the honour
of his name or to shield his fair fame from aspersion
or calumny.

"Delivered at Durham this evening my lecture on
'Pursuits and Modes of Life,' etc., in the schoolroom
at Dr. Holden's. Most of the boys present, and
several families from the town whom the Holdens
invited, and the masters of the school. Canon Temple
Chevalier also came. The lecture was very well

received and attentively listened to. Dr. Holden, the head-master of the school at Durham, with whom we have been staying, has been reading lately my article in the *Anthropological Review* on the 'Plurality of Races,' with which he expresses himself much pleased, and is going through it a second time.

"*20th.*—Met Mr. W. Lockey Harle in the railway carriage from Tynemouth. I well recollect him as the leading debater at the Society at University College thirty-five years ago, and I have his book 'A Career in the Commons.' Three men I used to meet at debating societies have recently sprung into notice : Cairns (now Lord Chancellor), Brett (now Solicitor-General), and Archibald (now a judge). The last is the only one of them I ever became intimate with. Cairns (the Lord Chancellor) used to take immense pains in preparing his speeches, but evinced no brilliancy, and gave no tokens of his future eminence.

"*23rd.*—This morning, at 9.30, we left Manchester for good.

"*25th.*—I mentioned in a letter to Lord Westbury that, having taken a deep interest in the commission for a digest of the law originated by him, I should be very glad to be of any service in the carrying out of the undertaking. 'What I should most prefer would be the selection of leading cases in different departments and the effort to lay down leading principles applicable to various topics in the same way that I have attempted to do in my "Principia."'

"*June 4th.*—Called at Law Amendment Society to inquire what is being done about Lord Brougham, following up the proposal to remove his remains to England and have them interred in Westminster Abbey at a public funeral. This undoubtedly ought to be done, and many who have deserved it far less have been so honoured. Indeed, it seems to me with regard to the public monuments in Westminster Abbey much as we are told it will be in heaven, where our double wonder will be to miss so many we made sure of meeting there and to meet so many we never supposed would be admitted. The papers describe Lord Brougham's funeral as a most shabby affair, and the coffin is said to be only of deal. Robinson, the secretary to the Social Science Class, said they would like me to write Lord Brougham's memoir. I said I would if Sir E. Wilmot entirely gave it up, and I should be glad of his assistance and that of Mr. Hastings.

"21st.—An admirable and very long letter from Sir F. Pollock respecting Lord Brougham's career on the Northern Circuit, of which I shall make ample use, and for which I wrote and thanked him.

"*July* 1st.—An interesting letter respecting Lord Brougham from Mr. Ingham, describing more particularly his career on the Northern Circuit. Edgar, whom I saw to-day, said they meant to make my article on Lord Brougham the principal one in the *Review*, and to place it first. Complimentary.

"3rd.—A second and most capital letter from Mr. Ingham about Lord Brougham, describing his career on the Northern Circuit, and his conduct of Williams's trial at Durham, and the Yorkshire election. Mr. Edgar told me that my 'Life of Lord Hardwicke' was much quoted from lately by an American writer, as well as by Jesse.

"*August* 7th.—A very pleasant, friendly letter from Sir F. Pollock, in which he says, 'Brougham was a man of exhaustless energy and indefatigable industry, of great ambition and desire for fame, and for being talked about, but he had good qualities which do not often accompany ambition. He had no malignity in

his composition. He had not bad feeling enough to
" keep up an enmity." . . . Brougham was, I think, ever
ready to do a good turn to anybody, and he bore no
malice. I think in a former note that I mentioned
he talked with any one, and his conversation was as
good with Deacon or Archbold (two very dull men on
the Northern Circuit) as with Scarlett or Sydney Smith.
Are you aware that he wrote and published a novel (as
well as Lord Erskine)? It was anonymous. He
endeavoured to suppress it, and Panizzi told me only
three or four copies existed; one of course is in the
British Museum. It was called " Albert Lunel; or, The
Chateau of Languedoc," and was dedicated to Rogers,
the poet; and the dedication is worth reading, more
than I can say for the book.'

"18th.—The *Law Journal* of Saturday contains a
notice of the *Law Magazine*, in which they say, ' This
number opens with a long and ably written biographical
sketch of the life and career of the late illustrious Lord
Brougham.' In the *Morning Star* of to-day they say,
'The *Law Magazine and Law Review* for August contains an able paper on the character of Lord Brougham,
viewed from a legal standpoint.' Extracts from my
memoir have appeared in the *Law Times* and *Stamford
Mercury*, as well as the *Morning Star* of last week.
But I have not seen the papers generally.

"26th.—The following, relating to my 'Memoir of
Lord Brougham,' appeared in the *Lincolnshire Chronicle*
of 14th August: 'The quarterly number of the
Law Magazine is noticeable for its lengthy memoir of
the late Lord Brougham, in which will be found
numerous vigorous and picturesque bits of description. Alluding to the veteran peer's last appearance
at the social science gatherings, we are told how he
seemed

> " ' But a shadow of his former self,
>   Majestic, though in ruin ! '

Feeble and tottering he was led about, reminding one
of Turner's magnificent picture of the old *Temeraire*,
which had braved many a battle and many a breeze,
being towed to its moorings. It is a most interesting
paper.'

"Received a letter this morning from Serjeant [now
Mr. Justice] Hayes, in which he says that, having
been sworn in as one of her Majesty's judges, he is in
a condition to return thanks for the congratulations of
his friends, and has sincere pleasure in thanking me
for mine. 'It is,' he says, 'truly pleasant to receive
the hearty good wishes of so distinguished a member
of that distinguished body the old Midland Circuit,' and
from one whom he used to regard as a sort of disciple
in the art of making jokes, good, bad, and indifferent.
Touching the 'Principia,' he suggests that the title
is rather too recondite for the general legal public, and
that an intelligible English name would probably
promote its circulation, such as 'Leading Principles of
Law,' or something like that. He wishes us a pleasant
journey in Spain, where I may have a chance of picking
up some sketches of Madrid law, 'but pray keep clear
of any treason against Queen Isabella.' The *Law Times*
says of Hayes that he is the wittiest man at the
bar.

"*September 22nd.*—Started to-day for our Continental tour, visiting different parts of France, including
the battle-fields of Agincourt and Cressy, portions of
Normandy, and Paris.

"*November 19th.*—Returned to England to-day.

"*27th.*—I have lately fully determined to take up oil-
painting as a recreative pursuit, and which has been
a question of debate with me for years past, when

I had not the leisure I now possess, and which I was induced to abandon, fearing it would interfere with my literary undertakings.

"*December* 10th.—Dined at the inaugural dinner of the Junior Athenæum. One hundred and thirty present. I returned thanks for the bar, and proposed the health of Mr. Roberts as architect to the Club.

"17th.—Called on Mr. Grove and talked with him about going to Palestine. He recommended me to Mr. Gaze at Southampton.

"18th.—Lunched with Mr. Murray, and returned to London in the afternoon. Dined at the Vivians'. Took them 'Pips' Diarie' and the etchings of my captivity and of Cannes. The former served to amuse them much. The view of the Mediterranean Mrs. Vivian pronounced charming.

1869.

"*January* 12th.—Called on Mr. Baillie this morning, by Messrs. Powell's advice, and had a long talk with him. He appears to effect painting on glass exactly in the way I wish to do it, and his partner, Mr. Mayer, has been a good deal on the Continent, and made sketches there of costumes, which have been copied on glass. He thought I had better do all the drawing and shading, and they would supply the colouring and burn it in, as different colours have to be used from what they appear after burning. As he said, I should do all the artistical part of the work, and they would supply the mechanical.

"14th.—Commenced this morning painting on glass in the regular and proper way at Messrs. Baillie and Co.'s, Wardour Street.

"28th.—Arranged to-day with Baillie as to the terms on which they are to instruct me in painting on glass, which are to be ten shillings a day for every day I receive instruction, including materials also, a fair and reasonable arrangement.

" *30th.*—A long, interesting letter from Sir F. Pollock, giving a general outline of Lord Wensleydale and his career, for my proposed memoir of him in the *Law Review.*

" *February* 21*st.*—Occupied myself for some time past on Sundays, commencing when I was at Manchester, in comparing the lessons for the day from the Old Testament with the Septuagint Greek version, and resorting to a lexicon to look up doubtful words. Some interesting light thrown on certain passages by the Septuagint, as, for instance, the death of Ahab. From this it appears that Jehoshaphat was taken for Ahab because he put on Ahab's robes, not his own, as stated in our version. And the transactions respecting Naboth are fuller in the Septuagint than in our version. There is a Psalm added to the Septuagint by David, taken from some other part of the Bible. Some of the chapters are differently arranged from what they are in our version.

" *March 8th.*—Left Iselipps and came to Sidmouth. Find the town very little altered indeed, and recognise the different spots and houses where we lodged, just the same as in 1814, Russell the baker's just where it was, and the tartlets in the windows look as if they had been there ever since. The rocks called the Parson and Clerk still standing, and the Sid still running. Paid a visit to Myrtle Cottage, standing in a garden leading into the High Street, where I lodged for a time with Aunt Emma, and where I had my picture taken.

" 13*th.*—Received six copies of my ' Rationale of Primogeniture.' There was a very good debate upon it (at the Law Amendment Society, at which I was too ill to attend), which is printed with it. Sent a copy to Locke King, M.P.

" 19*th.*—A note about my ' Rationale of Primogeniture' from Blundell, whom I had not heard of for years, written from Guernsey. He says, ' Your paper advocating an alteration in the law of primogeniture in England has—or rather the account of it in the *Daily News* has—attracted much notice in the Channel Islands, where, as you probably know, the laws which regulate the descent of land are peculiar, and, I believe, such as would find favour in your eyes, if modified a little to suit the exigences of Great Britain. One of our principal Guernsey gentlemen, the author of the pamphlet which I send you by this evening's book post, is very anxious to see your essay if it be published and you would let him have a copy in return for his own.'

" 25*th.*—Left Sidmouth this morning and came to Torquay.

" *April* 9*th.*—Our landlady at Torquay recollects Napoleon being in Torbay in 1814, and went out in a boat to see him, and had a very good view of him when he showed himself at a window. She said he was about my height, rather stout, and inclining to baldness. Several people drowned owing to the crowding of the boats. Another old woman, Mrs. Broad, also recollects 'old Bony,' as she called him, being brought to Torbay, and says her husband was one of the sailors on board the vessel. The avenue leading to Torre Abbey, she said, was illuminated in honour of the event.

" 17*th.*—Saw to-day in the newspapers that the Government have actually granted the manuscript commission, the members of which are appointed, Lord Romilly, with whom I had an interview and corresponded on the subject of the memorial in its favour, being the chairman. I shall write to him offering to be of any service that I can in the matter, sending him a copy of the memorial with the signatures, and alluding to my efforts in and origination of the matter.

" 18*th*.—Addressed the following letter on the manuscript commission to Lord Romilly, the Master of the Rolls :—

"'I do think that it is due to me that some recognition of my efforts should be made. I should be satisfied with either being on the commission, where I should like to be the working member, or with being a sort of honorary secretary.'

" 21*st*.—Called on Sir Thomas Phillipps, of Middle Hill, with whom I corresponded about the manuscript memorial at the time that it was in agitation, and took him a copy of the memorial. He said he had heard of the commission, but had had no communications on the subject. He desired me to say he should be willing to aid them if consulted. He was very cordial, and promised to visit us at Iselipps when he goes to London.

" 28*th*.—Received the following letter to-day respecting the manuscript commission :—

> "'HISTORICAL MANUSCRIPT COMMISSION,
> "'ROLLS HOUSE, CHANCERY LANE,
> "'*April 22nd*, 1869.

"'SIR,—I am desired by Lord Romilly to acknowledge with thanks the receipt of your letter of the 20th inst. relative to this commission, and to say that he will with much pleasure bring it to the notice of the commissioners at their next meeting.

> "'I am, etc.,
> "'W. GEORGE BRETT,
> "'Secretary.

"'GEORGE HARRIS, ESQ.'

" *May* 1*st*.—Yesterday we returned to London.

" 19*th.*—Called at manuscript commission office and saw the secretary, Mr. Brett, who was extremely polite, but equally reserved. He said they were getting on very well, and that I should certainly hear from them as to my assisting in the work. Several told me I ought to have been put on the commission, and which I quite think. But it is not too late for this.

"*June* 2*nd.*—At the Council of the Anthropological Society in the afternoon. Attended the evening meeting and read my paper, written for the British Association last year, 'On the Distinctions, Mental and Moral, arising from a Difference in Sex.'

"9*th.*—To-day we had a large out-of-doors party of the Council of the London and Middlesex Archæological Society, whom I invited to explore the objects of interest in this neighbourhood, and to partake of a cold collation on the lawn afterwards. Everything went off capitally, and the whole thing was a great success. In the dining-room I had out for inspection my Rembrandts, the engravings of London and Middlesex, etchings, and foreign sketches; in the study my autographs, manuscripts, and rare books; and in the breakfast-room hung up my diagrams.

" A letter from the secretary of the Historical Society of Great Britain, saying I had been elected a member of the Society and, subject to my willingness to act, a member of the Council.

" 26*th.*—A long letter from Professor de Quatrefages, thanking me for a letter I wrote to him containing an offer of hospitality, but fearing he will not be able to go to England at present, where he has already received an invitation to visit the Earl of Devon during the meeting of the British Association, for which he has thanked him without being able to accept it. He has been for some time engaged with other members of the Anthropological Society of Copenhagen. Says he hopes to be able to send me the result of his studies with Darwin. Regrets that he was absent when I was in Paris, but still hopes to make my acquaintance.

"At the Harrow speeches, to which we were invited by Mr. Steel, to whose house we went, and partook of a cold collation there afterwards. Called on Matthew Arnold and asked him to come and see us, which he promised to do. In the evening at the South Kensington Museum, a very brilliant affair, and the company very great, all in full dress.

"*July 9th.*—Presided, at Sir E. Wilmot's request, for him as judge of the Marylebone county court. A heavy day's business.

"*August 3rd.*—Called at the Palestine Exploration Society, and had a long talk with Mr. Besant, the secretary. He told me that a select party, headed by the Dean of Canterbury, was going to Jerusalem in the spring, and which I may perhaps be able to arrange to join.

"*4th.*—We drove over to Willesden, taking an early dinner at Mrs. Wharton's, and returning in the evening.

"We passed by a house at Kingsbury said to be haunted, the ghost, a female form, appearing in the daytime, and in a part of the house quite new. The story appears to be well authenticated.

"*31st.*—Tour to Palestine not being possible, we made one on the Continent this autumn. Started to-day, visiting parts of Switzerland.

"*October 12th.*—Returned to England this day.

"*November 19th.*—Wrote to Professor de Quatrefages, 'I was sorry to miss seeing you in Paris, but hope you may be induced to pay me a visit, when it will afford me great pleasure to introduce you to the members of the Anthropological Society, and then you might determine respecting the translation of your work.'

" 26th.—In the *John Bull* of to-day appears the second of my letters headed 'Communications from a Continental Tourist,' signed 'Iselipps,' giving an account of the railway passage over Mont Cenis, as the last did of Aix-les-Bains. The next and concluding one is to contain the story of my robbery.

" Called last Sunday on poor Hayes, who was lying at the Westminster Palace Hotel, and who died on Tuesday, having held his judgeship for a very short time only.

" 31st.—At the Marylebone court all day. A jury case, a railway case, and a trial between two artists.

" *December* 3rd.—Went to Iselipps on Saturday, and returned to London this morning for the Marylebone county court at 10.30. One heavy case, a jury case with counsel, in which I summed up, and disposed of several points of law.

" 17th.—A hard day at the Marylebone county court, the last day of my sitting there. Six months would, I feel sure, kill me. Mostly contested cases to-day, which I like better than those where only the parties appear. Several good points of law, which I also enjoy.

" 23rd.— We dined yesterday at C. J. Plumptre's. Had a heavy day in court, and did not get there until after seven instead of half-past six. Much fatigued, and felt quite knocked up this morning, but luckily a light day. Yesterday an action against Lord Vivian, in which I had to deliver judgment with reasons, and which I got through well. So many cases from the superior courts to the county courts ; they ought surely in return occasionally to promote the judges of the county courts to judgeships in the superior courts.

" 24*th*.—A notice of 'Theory of Arts' in the *Birmingham Daily Post* of yesterday of about a quarter of a column, containing nothing of either praise or censure, but giving a short description of the work, quoting largely from the preface for the purpose. It terms it 'an exhaustive investigation,' and says that a practical turn is given to it by applying the principles enunciated to the laying out of pleasure grounds and to furniture and dress.

" 27*th*.—A letter from C—— this morning, informing me of the death of the Bishop of Manchester. She says she got to Manchester the end of last week and found the Bishop very much exhausted by a rural deans' meeting the day before ; but he consecrated his hundred and thirtieth church on Saturday, and went into Manchester on Tuesday. He was very much exhausted, and became worse on Thursday night. Friday morning the medical man called, and told him he was in danger, and wished for a second opinion. This he declined. He was very calm, and said he could trust himself in God's hands. It was pure exhaustion. He died at ten o'clock Christmas Eve, p.m.

" Poor Bishop of Manchester ! I should think few lived so little beloved or died so little regretted. And yet he had a great many good and noble and amiable qualities, such as might have endeared him to every one. His great failing was his love of arbitrary power. He could not brook resistance or contradiction of any kind from anybody. But to those who chose to obey him in mind as well as body he was a most kind, steadfast, and real friend.

" His pupils and servants all adored him. He was probably the best schoolmaster and the worst bishop of the day. His capacity for acquiring knowledge and for imparting it also was very great. His information was prodigious and astonishingly accurate. His reasoning was acute, and his taste exquisite.

"In the House of Lords he was a mere cipher, though he might have shone so conspicuously. Indeed, he said of himself that as head-master of Birmingham he was somebody; as Bishop of Manchester he was nobody, and met with nothing but opposition.

1870.

"*January* 14*th*.—A capital review of my 'Theory of the Arts' in the *Manchester Guardian* of the 18th of November, extending to six and a half columns, and thoroughly going into the whole matter (informed it was by Tom Taylor, an able art critic). They say of it, 'This work will command attention by the importance of its subject, the wide culture it indicates, the earnestness it reveals, and the comprehensiveness of treatment which is exhibited in every character.' They also term it 'a very masterly and deeply interesting work.' In an Edinburgh paper, *The Scotsman* of the 23rd of November, there is also a review of it (two and a half columns). They term it 'a solid, sensible, judicious, and comprehensive book, inspired throughout with a high ideal of art in all its forms.'

"15*th*.—A letter from Mr. W——, giving some particulars about the Bishop of Manchester. 'Just ten days before the Bishop's death he had his meeting of rural deans. He was then very infirm, and unable to walk from one room to another without some one's arm, but he did not appear to be worse than he had been for some months. The change which had taken place was most remarkable. His legs seemed as if they had lost all power, and at a confirmation he was obliged to be supported as he moved to and fro along the altar rails. His mind, however, was as clear and active as usual. On the Saturday before his death he consecrated a new church. He attributed his last illness partly to the overheated church, and, indeed, it was very hot. The next day (Sunday) he fainted several times, but on Tuesday he was well enough to go to the Registry. On the morning of Friday he was informed by his medical man that he was in danger, but declined other advice. He died certainly in harness. His is a curious character to look back upon. Certainly he was one of the cleverest men, if not the cleverest. But withal he lacked common-sense, and was one of the unwisest of men. He improved somewhat as he grew older, and we had even got to like him.' Mr. W—— said he could not pretend to explain his conduct towards himself. He seemed to draw in from all but necessary social intercourse of late years, and others of his friends probably thought that he slighted them.

"A long letter from Professor de Quatrefages, thanking me for my work, which he says is 'very interesting' and 'worthy of deep consideration.' Thanks me for the continuation of my review of his book, but says it will be impossible for him to go to England this year.

"*29th.*—A review of my 'Theory of Arts' in the *Saturday Review* of two and a half columns, in which they say of it, 'This "Theory of the Arts," though not absolutely new, may be accepted as a timely arrival in English literature.'

"*February 5th.*—A letter from Professor de Quatrefages, in which he says, 'I have seen my friend Mr. Charles Blanc, and have spoken to him about your book, telling him how well I think of it.'

"*17th.*—Wrote to Professor de Quatrefages, thanking

him for his two last letters, and telling him I had directed a copy of my work to be sent at once to Mr. Charles Blanc. Said I hoped to be in Paris next autumn.

"*March* 3rd.—Two numbers of the March number of *Colbourn's New Monthly Magazine* sent to me. A review of my 'Theory of the Arts' in an article headed 'Fine Arts.' It is termed 'an able and comprehensive treatise,' and it states that 'Mr. Harris's philosophical analysis and exposition of the arts will enable the reader to spend agreeably many a recollective hour.' The article concludes, 'Meanwhile we welcome heartily the contribution which Mr. Harris has so honourably made towards rendering instructive to us in the present day the treasures of art which we have inherited from the past,' and quotes a portion of the concluding passage of my book.

"Mr. and Mrs. Matthew Arnold, Mr. and Lady Ellen Gordon, and a few others dined with us. Arnold said the young Duke of Genoa had been much excited about the proposal to make him king of Spain, and quite cried about it. Indeed, he was so depressed and affected, after his interview with the commissioners from Spain, that they had a bottle of champagne at dinner to inspirit him, probably the only occasion, as Arnold said, on which the resignation of a kingdom was so celebrated. Arnold recognised the portraits of my father and mother and grandfather, and said that when a child he and his brothers and sisters were once carried in a sedan chair to drink tea with the last, whose monument exists in the admirable description of him by Moultrie in his poem 'The Annals of my Parish.'

"*April* 20th.—A long letter from Professor de Quatrefages, thanking me in warm terms for my review of his work in the *Anthropological Review* of January,

which he says he has only just read. He particularly
thanks me for the lines which terminate my article. He
concludes by saying that he is 'translating my peroration
to send to his aged mother. She will be very pleased
at this judgment passed upon the work of her son.'

"*May 23rd.*—Two of Sir A. Bittlestone's sons came
to me in the Marylebone court on Friday, while I was
engaged in trying a long jury case sent from the
Queen's Bench, and told me that their father had
returned to England the evening before. So I wrote
and sent him my hearty congratulations on his return
to England. Sent him a copy of a memoir of Hayes.

"*25th.*—A note from Prowett about 'Theory of Art,'
who says, 'I am glad to find that your book (though necessarily addressing itself to a select few) is so successful. I
mentioned it to Delane some time ago as a good subject
for review, but he has taken no further notice of the
matter since. The reviewing of the *Times* is almost
at a dead lock at this time of year. But when things
get a little easier, and the gooseberries begin to show,
etc., I will try him again.'

"*27th.*—Wrote to Professor de Quatrefages and
asked him to meet the Council of the Anthropological
Society, whom I have asked, with some others, to spend
the day here, on Wednesday, June 22nd, the anniversary of our buying Iselipps.

"Wrote to Mr. Justice Mellor, enclosing a copy of
my memoir of Hayes.

"A note from Robert Burn, in which he says in relation to my 'Theory of Arts,' 'I ordered your book on
the Arts for our college book club some time ago, and
though I had only time while it was in my possession
to glance at a few things, I got several very good hints
from it, and found it much more solid reading than
Ruskin's books on the same subjects.'

"Sent Matthew Arnold my paper on 'Education,' with a note asking his opinion upon it. In reply he says he has read the paper with interest and much agreement. Teaching by rote is the bane of the system introduced by the revised code; and if I look at the forthcoming Blue Book of the Committee of Council, I shall see that this is his opinion as strongly as it is mine. And it is most true that what education our school children get they do not follow up; parish libraries would do something to cure this, and it would be well to institute them; but the horrible pell-mell, overcrowding, and utter misery of our social state at the bottom of society, is what in truth pulls people down, and to deal with this is an immense matter.

"*June* 10*th*.—At Marylebone county court. A jury case, and one from the superior courts. Nine cases from the superior courts waiting for trial at the Marylebone court.

"22*nd.*—Had our rural fête to-day, given to the Council of the Anthropological Society, and several other friends invited to meet them. The day fine, but intensely hot. Had an exhibition of old works bearing on anthropology in the study; of autographs and etchings in the drawing-room; of Rembrandt's etchings, views of London and Middlesex, and my foreign sketch-books in the dining-room; and of diagrams in the breakfast-room; besides the usual objects of interest in the hall. The company assembled about two. The luncheon was served under the walnut tree on the lawn at three o'clock. Mrs. Maclaren, who, as a sister of John Bright, excited much interest and attention, and Mr. Squier, the New York President of the Anthropological Society, were present.

" *29th.*—Wrote the following letter to Professor de Quatrefages :—

" ' I beg sincerely to thank you for your interesting article from the *Revue des Deux Mondes* on the Congress at Copenhagen, and also for your valuable work on Darwin, both of them important contributions to the literature of anthropology. Great regrets were expressed that you were not at my party on the 22nd, which went off extremely well in every respect.'

" *July 27th.*—In London for the day to pay a visit to Mr. Squier and see his drawings and photographs of objects of interest in Peru, principally buildings, carvings, and pottery.

" *August 29th.*—A letter from Mr. S. C. Hall, F.S.A., in reply to one I wrote to him, in which he says, ' I rejoice to hear you are going to Ireland, and to Killarney more especially, all-beautiful Killarney. I know every stone and tree and shrub, I think, there. I have not a copy of our book, or I would send it to you, but you will get it at any of the book-stalls *en route*. Go across by Dublin ; it is the only way unless you love what I do not—a sea voyage. Visit Cork, I pray you, to see its beautiful river ; and if time be not an object with you, go round by way of Bantry, Glengariff, and Kinmare. But you must "bar" it if you do, and do not fancy there is danger. Saxon though you be, you are safer upon any of the roads than you would be driving to Brentford, unless indeed you are going to buy land and eject tenants in possession. You will find our name very useful to you at Killarney. Especially fortunate you will be if you get as your guide my friend Stephen Sullivan. I do not know what hotel he is now attached to, or if to any. And Mickey Sullivan and his brother are gems of drivers. I could write you a volume. Indeed, I have done so. I envy you your trip. We have just returned from Brixton. Accept our kindest regards and best wishes.

"*October 1st.*—Made a tour in Ireland this year in August and September.

"*4th.*—Presented to the school of design established in Rugby School my 'Theory of the Arts,' and also Flaxman's designs from the *Iliad* and *Odyssey*, his lectures, and Sir Joshua Reynolds' lectures, to form the nucleus of a library. Offered also to give £5 for three prizes for the three best drawings from nature, the same as I had done at Manchester, but to be given in books on art. Talked with Mr. C. Elsee and Mr. T. L. Tupper on the subject, but have misgivings whether I shall be able to get art taken up as I wish as a branch in conjunction with classical education, as I have urged in my work, and fear they treat it as too mechanical, not as an intellectual pursuit.

1871.

"*January 6th.*—Saw in the *Times* to-day a letter from Mr. Hodgson Pratt respecting the Workman's Circulating Library; so I wrote to him, sending him copies of my paper before the Social Science Association in May, the paper on 'Working Men's Libraries,' and a prospectus of 'Civilisation as a Science.'

"*11th.*—Delivered lecture on 'Napoleon' at the Staines Institute yesterday evening. Weather wet, and the audience small, but remarkably attentive, and the lecture appeared to give great satisfaction. Prepared for it lately a map of part of the Continent, showing the dominion acquired by Napoleon, which is marked red.

"*24th.*—A long letter from Mr. Hodgson Pratt, saying he has gone through the paper which I read before the Social Science Association and that relating to parochial libraries. He says, 'Illustrations of the truth of what you say meet us at every corner. . . . The village library plan has been thoroughly worked of late in France, and the Government have made great efforts to supply books according to your plan, rewarding village schoolmasters who show energy in instituting and working such libraries. We are behindhand in everything that has relation to true education.'

" *March* 23rd.—Delivered my lecture on ' Pursuits and Mode of Life,' etc., at the Sudbury Working Men's Hall, at the request of General Crawford, who took us to it in his carriage, as also Colonel Gill, whom we met there. A very good attendance indeed. The lecture very well received. Asked to deliver another lecture there, which I promised to do. If I had had the opportunity when at the bar of delivering a speech in a great leading case suitable to me, and had acquitted myself as well as I do as a lecturer, I am sure that I should have succeeded to the full extent of my ambitious aspirations, as recorded in my journal just thirty years ago.

" *April* 18th.—Attended Council and evening meeting of the Anthropological Institute. A paper proposed by me on Ireland not accepted, Sir J. Lubbock informing me that the referees were extremely complimentary respecting it, and pronounced it a very good paper, and said they quite agreed with me, but that it was too political for the Society, in which, as I told him, I coincided, and quite thought this would be the result.

" *May* 16th.—At the Anthropological Institute council meeting in the afternoon, and in the chair at the evening meeting. A paper on 'Apparitions and Dreams,' by Dr. Callaway, was read, on which a warm discussion took place. Some went the length of urging that the age for believing in spirits and spiritual influence had quite passed away, that the times were much too scientific for such subjects, and that this question ought never to have been allowed to come before the Anthropological Institute. In reply I said that the entire disbelief in spirits and spiritual influence, in spite of all evidence, was as shallow and un-philosophical as the credulity with regard to them two centuries ago, that the majority of cases were no doubt the result of delusion or disease, but that certain cases could not be so accounted for, and that what the Society ought to do was to institute a strict test to prove the reality or falsehood of such cases, a test which I had prepared, but which the Society declined to receive. I said also that all our greatest philosophers—Bacon, and Locke, and Newton—believed in the reality of spirits and in spiritual influences. Evidently a strong material bias exists among the members generally, which seems to me to be the characteristic feature of the age, and displays itself alike in art, in poetry, in painting, and in law.

"*June 22nd.*—Had our annual garden-party to-day, which was in part artistical, in part anthropological, and in part of old Midland Circuit men to meet Bittlestone. Everything went off well and pleasantly, though, owing to the rain, there was no getting out. They seemed much pleased with my books and prints, and there was no lack of talking or of life.

"*28th.*—Received from Professor de Quatrefages a copy of his 'La Race Prussienne,' reprinted from the *Revue des Deux Mondes*, for which I thanked him.

"*July 8th.*—Commenced to-day writing out my 'Scientific Suggestions,' being plans for mechanical contrivances of different kinds, some of which I first thought of when quite a boy, and which have from time to time occasionally occupied my mind. Propose to insert them in a new periodical. Some of them are, I

have no doubt, practical. Others may afford suggestions to practical men which may be built upon and
carried into effect. The 'flying machine,' plan for
'preserving corn,' and 'water organ' I devised when
quite a boy of fifteen or sixteen. I also, on visiting a
camera obscura at Rugby when at school, felt sure that
by the process of the action of light the shadows might
be imprinted on the surface on which they were reflected,
which is the principle of photography, since reduced to
a science. Shall complete and write out my suggestions
as I recollect and can collect them.

"*August 2nd.*—At Manchester, which we left this
morning, and came to Edinburgh, for the meeting of
the British Association.

"*3rd.*—Went to the British Association meeting
(anthropological department) this morning. The section
was much crowded indeed, the room quite overflowing.
The attendance here far exceeded that in the other
sections, except to hear Dr. Hooker's address in the
geographical department. I had a very good audience
for my paper on 'The Comparative Longevity of Animals of Different Species and of Man, and of Probable
Causes which mainly conduce to promote this Difference.'
It was very well received. Exhibited some of my
etchings to some of the members in the committee
room, and at the conversazione, where they excited a
good deal of attention, as also 'Pips' Diarie.'

"*8th.*—My paper on 'The Descent of Qualities' came
off about half-past twelve, second on the list. The
paper was well received, and Mr. Flower, Dr. Christison,
Dr. Crum Brown, Dr. Tyler, Mr. Kain, Dr. Brown,
and Mr. Jack spoke upon it. I said, in reply to Dr.
Christison, that I agreed with him that facts were the
foundation on which to base our proceedings, but facts
alone were not sufficient, for theory and speculation

should be grounded upon them. Some who boasted about facts cited facts which were contradictory, and their conclusions were at variance with their facts. I replied also to the other speakers.

"*9th.*—Most hospitably and kindly entertained by Mr. Ingham, Q.C., M.P., at Westoe, who has done everything to make us enjoy our visit.

"*September 2nd.*—Very agreeable conversation with Mr. Ingham, especially about barristerial friends. Lord Denman and several judges and distinguished barristers and members of parliament have stayed with him, and he is full of anecdote about the House of Commons and the Northern Circuit.

"*November 17th.*—In the evening read a paper, which Sir E. Wilmot requested me to prepare when he was staying here, on the subject 'What is the Use of the House of Lords?' before the Chelsea Constitutional Association, Sir E. Wilmot in the chair. It appeared to give great satisfaction.

"*December 16th.*—Wrote as follows to Professor de Quatrefages, enclosing a prospectus of 'Treatise on Man:'—

"'I ought to have thanked you before for your interesting work "La Race Prussienne," which I have perused with much pleasure.'

"*19th.*—A long letter from Professor de Quatrefages in reply to mine, who says he shall be very happy to see his little volume translated into English, and thanks me very cordially for my kind thought in respect to it. He also says what he has suffered from the war, being confined in a cellar during the bombardment of Paris, which brought on rheumatism, and obliges him to resort to the mineral waters. So he fears he shall not be able to fix a day for a long time to profit by my hospitable invitation to visit me.

"21*st.*—A letter from the Anthropological Institution of New York, informing me that they have elected me a foreign member.

"31*st.*—A letter from Sir E. Wilmot, asking me 'if I would mind repeating my lecture on "The House of Lords" to the Westminster working men,' and saying he thinks they will be very pleased to have it.

1872.

"*January* 18*th.*—A letter from Mr. Russell, of Edinburgh, forwarding me his Father's 'Recollections of the Early Days of Lord Brougham,' which will be very valuable to me in completing my memoir, and for which I wrote and thanked him, and sent him the etchings of Lord Brougham's chateau and the view of Cannes from it.

"*February* 6*th.*—At the Anthropological Institute yesterday afternoon and evening. In the chair at the council meeting, and elected a member of the publication committee in the room of Professor Huxley, who is gone abroad for a time. At the evening meeting read a paper on 'Hereditary Descent,' which was very well received and discussed, and a good attendance. Captain H. Burton (the great explorer) said in his speech, 'It is a most valuable paper, but I do not agree in any single thing.'

"18*th.*—Attended council meeting and evening meeting of Anthropological Institute, and read my paper there on 'Longevity,' which produced a fair discussion.

"28*th.*—Completed a design in oils for a memorial window to E. Hume ; subject of Christ walking on the sea.

"The *Athenæum*, alluding to Earl Stanhope, says, 'All historians and students of history owe him a heavy debt

of gratitude.   Without his aid the historical manuscripts
commission might never have been started.'   So far,
however, from aiding, Lord Stanhope decidedly opposed
the manuscripts commission, as his cousin Mr. Pitt
Taylor informed me in his letter which I have with the
other correspondence on the subject.

   " *March* 29*th*.—Called yesterday morning on Collins,
and took him the four pictures to frame.   When he
first saw them, he exclaimed they were Fuselli's, which
I thought a high compliment.   Asked him if he had any
of Fuselli's works.   He said, ' No ; they would not sell
now.'   The contempt for Fuselli and the fondness for
high finish, with the contempt for intellectual excellence,
are the eccentricities of the present age, as I have
remarked in ' Theory of Arts.'

   " *April* 29*th*.—Went yesterday to Fairford, to see
the celebrated painted windows in the church there,
by some persons attributed to Albert Durer.

   " *May* 22*nd*.—Attended council and evening meeting
of Anthropological Institute.   Read my paper on ' Moral
Irresponsibility and Resulting Insanity,' taken mainly
from one of the sections in the preliminary dissertation
to ' Treatise on Man.'   It was extremely well received,
and there was a very good discussion upon it.   I said,
in reply to the different speakers, that ' this Society was
well qualified to form an opinion on this very important
subject, and that, by devoting attention to it, it might
hold and exercise an important influence.   It was not
too much to say that it was better qualified than the
Home Secretary to deal with such topics.'   I referred
to the acuteness of lunatics in many cases, and cited
one where the lunatic, getting the first word with the
manager of an asylum, persuaded him that he was the
keeper and that the keeper was the lunatic.   I also referred to Lord Thurlow's saying that when the plea of

insanity was set up he would hang them all. If they were not mad, they deserved it ; if they were, they were better out of the way.

" 24th.—Had a very urgent letter this morning to attend a council meeting of the Social Science Association on the Jury Bill introduced by the Attorney-General, and in which I am very glad to see he has inserted a clause for carrying out my proposal for having a special jury in cases of murder. I have twice brought this matter before the Social Science Association and Law Amendment Society, but they have done little or nothing to forward my views. Attended the meeting accordingly. Serjeant Pulling in the chair. I suggested that the qualifications for jurors should be lowered, so as to make them representative of the class they tried as well as of the prosecutors, which was the original principle on the establishment of juries. I proposed that all who are admitted to the franchise ought also to serve on juries, and my proposal was agreed to. Intelligence and integrity certainly do not depend on, and are not ensured by, a property qualification. I said I wished we could have an educational test on qualification for juries

" 25th.—Attended another committee meeting on the Jury Bill yesterday, and proposed and carried an important amendment : to make a certain amount of income, from whatever source, a qualification for both special and common jurors ; also one to pay them by the day, and not by the number of juries they were upon, as at present proposed.

" June 20th.—Delivered this evening, at the Society for the Encouragement of the Fine Arts, my lecture on 'Glass-painting, and its Capacities as a Branch of the Fine Arts.' The room quite full, and the lecture well listened to, and appeared to give much satisfaction. A good debate afterwards, principally on the capacity of glass-painting for epic composition and the desirability of attempting the classical instead of the mediæval style in art, particularly in reference to the decoration of St. Paul's, in which my views were strongly opposed. In reply, I said I was very glad to have the whole subject so fairly and freely discussed. I urged, however, that because some had failed in classical attempts in glass-painting it was no reason why all should do so. I allowed the efficient colouring in the old glass, as seen at Chartres, etc., but contended that expression with this was quite compatible, as seen at Fairford. With regard to what had been said about the impossibility of representing the works of Michael Angelo and Raphael on glass, I appealed to the glass paintings at Sèvres, where they had been most efficiently done, and added that if it was objected that the subject was too mechanical for this Society to take up, what I proposed was the intellectual, not the mechanical, branch of it, to which attention should be called.

"*July* 3*rd*.—Had our garden-party to-day, which was postponed from June on account of the unsettled state of the weather. The weather to-day charming, indeed perfect : sunny, but breezy ; and though warm, airy and fresh. Everything went off extremely well.

"10*th*.—Matthew Arnold walked over here on Sunday evening to see Mr. Hill, and told me that he admired the grounds very much.

"*August* 10*th*.—A letter from Mrs. Hume to E. about my window at Mearstoke, in which she says, 'My sister was at church in the evening on Sunday, and very much pleased with the window. Every one is pleased with it and by it, for we feel it is a gift of such affection and interest, and we are very grateful for it.'

"17*th*.—At Brighton. Went to the evening meeting

of the British Association yesterday, to hear the inaugural address of the new President. I got a capital
place near, and just in front of the President. The
ex-Emperor of the French, Napoleon III., sat near me,
so I put him into my notebook, and Mr. Stanley, the
colleague of Livingstone, who was also near me.

" 20th.—Read a paper before the Association on
' Renovation and Waste, and the Possibility of Pro-
longing Life by Artificial Means.' It was strongly
criticised by some of the medical men, though I
fortified myself well by quotations from high and
scientific authorities. I told them, however, that I
had made suggestions only, not assertions, and treated
the question merely as a naturalist, not as a medical
man.

" My paper on ' Instinct ' came on in the afternoon.
After I had concluded it, the chairman, Colonel Lane
Fox, called on Mr. Wallace, who said the paper was
unscientific, being mainly made up of opinions. He
had a great contempt for those who derived their
opinions from old authors. My paper was fairly
cheered ; Mr. Wallace was vociferously so. Mr.
Robertson said he had a contempt for what was
only got from old books, but that I had given an
able summary of past opinions. Dr. King said he
must compliment the author of this paper on its production, and proceeded to commend it. In reply, I
said, ' I must in the first place express my warm
thanks to Mr. Wallace for the contempt he has
expressed for me ; and in the next place I must
express my thanks to him for the contempt which
he has expressed for Aristotle, Lord Bacon, Willis,
Locke, Newton, and the other great men whose
authority I have cited, and in whose company I am
proud to be placed, even though it be to express

Mr. Wallace's contempt for us all in common. I am astonished that a paper should be condemned as unscientific which contains an epitome of the opinions of some of the greatest men who ever adorned the world of science. I have as great a contempt for the despisers of old books as others have for those who consult them exclusively.' I was well cheered when I concluded my speech, which I delivered with considerable energy.

"*September* 11th.—Addressed the following letter to Mr. Darwin, sending him with it a copy of my 'Theory of the Arts,' my papers on 'Longevity' and 'Descent of Qualities,' and the analytic prospectus of 'Treatise on Man:'—

"'Having studied with intense interest your two valuable works on "The Descent of Man" and on "The Origin of Species," I read with much gratification the announcement that you are about to produce another work on "Expression in Animals," carrying out perhaps the ideas expressed in your former works. I therefore take the liberty of asking your acceptance of the accompanying volumes, in one of which I have adverted to the same topic, and the use which artists might make as regards the exhibition of character and expression (in which the English school is peculiarly deficient) in the study of animals (*vide* vol. ii., pp. 74, 80, 116).'

"*October* 8th.— At Chester, which I left at 9.30, and stopped at Prestatyn, where I had not been for nearly sixty years—about 1813 or 1814—when I was quite a little boy, and was sent there on account of ill-health, at which place we stayed about two months, first at the 'Fox' inn and then in lodgings. Curious to ascertain what I could recollect of the place, and made a plan last night of the streets and sketch of the inn, church, and principal objects, which I found singularly correct. Could not have made such a plan of places I had seen the first time only six years ago. The quondam ' Fox ' still standing, but mainly used as a shop. A small appendage to it is called 'The Cross Foxes.' The church has been rebuilt. The churchyard securely padlocked alike against parishioners and visitors. Wished to have gone in on account of the view from it, which I recollect. Applied at the post-office, where the key is left, but was told it was away. Applied at the parsonage to be allowed to go through their garden to the churchyard, but the gardener refused. This is the true way to alienate people's affections, at any rate from the fabric of the church.

" 9*th.*—A letter from Mr. Darwin, in which he says he is much obliged for my very courteous letter and kind present of ' Theory of the Arts.' He hopes soon to read it, but the part about expression cannot aid him in his work, as his book has been printed some months, though it will not be published until Mr. Murray's season in November. He will feel it his duty and an honour to give me any zoological information in his power, whenever I may think fit to write, but must mention that he has very little spare strength, for being much out of health, he is compelled to leave home to-morrow morning for three weeks, in order to get some rest. He thanks me for my kind offer of books. Has read long ago White's ' Gradation,' and is much in doubt whether the others would be worth his reading, as his reading powers are now very limited. When his little book on ' Expression ' is published, he will do himself the pleasure of sending me a copy ; but whether the manner in which he has treated the subject will at all interest me he really does not know.

" *November* 4*th.*—A present from Mr. Darwin of his

new work, for which I wrote and thanked him as follows :—

" 'I beg to return you my best thanks for your kindness in sending me your very valuable and interesting work " On the Expression of the Emotions in Man and Animals." Artists, especially English, not excepting even Landseer, would study it with considerable advantage.

" ' I was much struck by the ancient statues of animals n the Vatican, and possess some spirited original etchings by Rembrandt, depicting animal passion.'

" 12*th*.—A letter from Dr. Rogers, informing me that I was enrolled a member of the Royal Historical Society.

" A present from Professor de Quatrefages of his new work 'On the Negro Race,' for which I wrote and thanked him.

" 17*th*.—Attended the council meeting of the Historical Society, and read a paper, illustrated by diagrams, on 'Materials for a Domestic History of England.' It was well received ; in fact, I could not have wished for a more decided expression of opinion in my favour.

1873.

" *January* 28*th*.—Plumptre says in a letter to me that his late pupil the Brahmin Gamendon Motum Tagore is a great admirer of my books.

" Mr. Wilton tells me that he has been reading 'Theory of the Arts,' and that his 'interest has been much excited in the contents,' so I sent him a copy of the book.

" *February* 7*th*.—A note from Plumptre asking me to the party at the Brahmin Tagore's yesterday evening, where I went. Theatricals from eight to eleven ; then supper ; excellent. Tagore very pleasant and friendly. We, Cox, Tagore, and myself, are to meet at Plumptre's to dinner on the 27th inst.

"*12th.*—Attended a meeting of the Committee on Sir J. Lubbock's Bill for the Preservation of Historical Monuments at the Anthropological Institute ; and, at the London Archæological Society, proposed and carried a resolution in support of his Bill.

"*27th.*—Dined at Professor C. J. Plumptre's with E., meeting the Brahmin Tagore. Had much talk with the Brahmin, who is a most intelligent man and a Christian. He thinks the Jews will ultimately be converted to Christianity, but will become infidels first and then rationalistic Christians. Agrees with me that in the end all Christians will be merged into two grand sects —Rationalists and Catholics. Thinks the main conversions in India are by the Roman Catholics.

" *March* 19th.—Attended for the first time on Monday a meeting of the Psychological Committee. Galton and Lane Fox there. Made several suggestions as to the programme of subjects settled, some of which were agreed to.

" *20th.*—Yesterday read papers on ' Renovation and Instinct ' before Anthropological Institute.

"*28th.*—Went with E. to the annual dinner of the Historical Society at St. James' Hall, the Marquis of Lorne in the chair, to whom we were introduced, as were all the Council in rotation. I was put down to reply to the toast of ' Prosperity to the Historical Society,' which was proposed by Rae, who sat next to me, and who in doing it said that the manuscript commission was entirely owing to my exertions.

"'I said Mr. Rae had been too complimentary to me as regards my being the author of the manuscript

commission, though I had used great exertions in the
cause. I was gratified that the Historical Society was
associated on the present occasion with one connected
with Scotland, as to Scotland history owes so much;
and it was remarkable that the two great histories of
England, that of David Hume and that of Lord
Macaulay, were both written by Scotchmen. Sir
Walter Scott, too, had done much for history in the
Waverley novels, which, combining instruction and
interest together, made us acquainted with many remarkable events in history which would not otherwise
have been brought home to us. Dr. Arnold had said
that he never properly understood the history of Scotland until he read Sir Walter Scott's "Tales of a
Grandfather." I was gratified also to see ladies present
at the dinner, and to meet them at the Historical
Society. If, as some supposed, they were to be our
future legislators, it was important they should study
the history of their country. That portion of it which,
however, would be most attractive to them was its
domestic history, which had yet to be written, and who
so fit to write it as those who were the ornaments of
domestic life? Much had been done for history of late
years by the ladies. Miss Strickland and Mrs. Jameson
were highly distinguished among our historians in
their respective spheres. Scotland indeed was the
land of romance. London too abounded in objects of
historic interest, and constituted quite a museum of
relics of this character. A great impetus especially to
historical research had been given by the granting
of the manuscript commission, and I begged to suggest
whether this Society and that commission could not be
made to work together, they giving us access to their
papers, and we in return showing how those effects
might be best rendered available. For instance, I

could point out how in the Hardwicke collection there was a mass of documents of great interest relating to the Scotch rebellion of 1745, of which no general report of the collection would give an account.'

"Made the acquaintance of George Cruikshank, which I was very glad to do, and asked him to pay me a visit at Iselipps, and he promised that he would.

"The analysis of my two papers at the Anthropological Institute which I drew out appears at length in the present number of *Human Nature*. That on 'Instinct' appeared also in the *Athenæum*, and they mentioned that I read a paper on 'Renovation,' etc., as well.

"*April 21st.*—Attended in the evening the meeting of the Law Amendment Society (at which Lord Westbury was to have presided, but did not come) on 'A Codification of the Law.' A very full attendance, and a very animated debate, in which I managed to get a hearing, though I did not expect it until the last moment. I said that the one great question to which all the speeches alike pointed was how the grand work of codification was to be effected. As to the desirableness of that work all were pretty well agreed. 'It appears to me that to accomplish this properly it must be the work of one single mind. It has been said that if the building of Noah's ark had been left to a joint stock company or to a royal commission, it never would have been completed before the Flood commenced.' The only plan likely to be efficacious was to entrust the work of codification to one man capable of grasping the subject, giving him power to call to his aid such coadjutors as he deemed desirable, subjecting of course the conduct of the whole proceeding to the control of parliament. Until this course was adopted there was no chance of an efficient code being framed. What I said was very well received, and the chairman and F. Hill told me afterwards that my remarks were quite true, but that parliament never would consent to give up the superintendence of the measure, and would be jealous of leaving it to one man.

" 22*nd*.—In the evening read a paper on 'Domestic Everyday Life and Manners and Customs in the Ancient World' before the Royal Historical Society. The paper appeared to give great satisfaction.

"*May* 17*th*.—Wrote to Mr. Moultrie, saying I should much like to present a window of the same character as that at Ashbury, of which I sent him a photograph, to the Trinity Church at Rugby, which might stand as a memorial to my father, mother, and grandfather, for each of whom I believe he felt a sincere regard, as I am sure that they each of them did for him and for Mrs. Moultrie.

" 19*th*.—Received yesterday a letter from Mr. Moultrie, stating his willingness to have the family memorial window as proposed, to which I replied that I was extremely gratified.

" 22*nd*.—Our garden-party, which went off most satis- factorily in every way. Weather perfect, and everybody seemed gratified.

"*August* 21*st*.—We made a short tour in France this autunn, but were driven home on account of the con- tinued bad weather.

"*October* 16*th*.—Brought with me to Rugby, where I came on Tuesday, the coloured sketch of the memorial window, which I showed to Edmund and also to Miss Moultrie, who expressed themselves much pleased with it. Mr. Moultrie, however, called on me about it in the afternoon, and said he should like to consult the archi- tect who is restoring the church.

"A copy of the *Revue Scientifique* sent to me, which

contains an outline of my paper on the ' Hereditary Transmission of Faculties.' It occupies three columns. The part relating to the explanation of the phenomena from a supposed flux and reflux in the system is placed in inverted commas.

"*December* 3*rd.*—Two more scientific suggestions occurred to me recently, one for 'increasing the area of land by undulation,' the other for 'strengthening indoor light by reflectors.'

1874.

"*January* 3*rd.*—Think of writing to Dr. Vaughan and making to him a proposal to put a painted window into the Temple Church, composed entirely of pieces from Palestine, say twenty.

" 15*th.*—Came to London on Monday.

" 16*th.*—Called on the Brahmin Tagore, who asked me about my ' Treatise on Man,' of which he had heard from Plumptre, and said he should like to see the proofs and to write some notes to the work. Invited us to go to his house on Monday, and to stay until Wednesday morning for the purpose. His knowledge of Indian philosophy and mythology may be of great use to me.

" 20*th.*—E. and I went to London on a visit to Mr. Tagore's, where we stayed until Tuesday night. Discussed with him ' Treatise on Man,' and he has promised to write notes to it if I will send him proofs of the passages to which they are to be supplied, containing an account of the Brahmin and Hindu notions as to the soul and the nature of angelic beings.

" 25*th.*—In the *John Bull* is my letter about Dr. Hayman, respecting which Mr. Mortimer Collins in last week's *John Bull* writes, ' An old Rugbeian's letter in your last is very much to the point as regards the traditions of the great middle school. When he remarks that Arnold turned out great schoolboys, he hits the exact blot. I have known one or two of Arnold's pet pupils, and they are schoolboys to this day.'

" I proposed to Matthew Bloxam that he should supply the elevation for the church at Rugby, making it of pure Norman, the style of the tower, which is the only original part remaining.

"*February* 10*th*.—At the Anthropological Society, where I read my paper ' Tests Adapted to Determine the Truth of Supernatural Phenomena.' A very spirited discussion. The paper well received on the whole.

" 13*th*.—Wrote to-day to Mr. Darwin respecting ' Treatise on Man,' sending him proofs contained in the passages referred to, and telling him that I had made several references to, and quotations from, his works. ' Any suggestions, corrections, or notes, that you may be pleased to make, will be highly prized.'

" 15*th*.—A reply from Mr. Darwin, in which he says he has read the proof-sheets, but has no criticisms worth sending. He is, however, not sure that he fully agrees with me on all points. On so obscure a subject as the distinction between actions performed through instinct, habit, and intellect, he supposes that hardly two men would fully agree, but adds his best wishes that my new work may be in every way successful.

" A note from Dr. Maudsley, saying he shall be very glad to look through the proofs and to give his opinion upon the points that come within the range of his special work.

" 21*st*.—A letter from Mr. Darwin in answer to one of mine, in which he says he begs pardon for not having returned the proofs, but he thought that they were spare copies. He really has no criticisms or remarks worth sending which he could make in a reasonable space, and

has no strength or time to spare, as he is much out of
health, and is overworked at present with the tedious and
dispiriting labour of preparing new editions of two of
his books. 'Pray forgive.'   Mr. Tagore sends me some
notes containing the Brahmin notions of the supernatural and spiritualism.

"28*th*.—A letter from Mr. Tagore, sending me his
notes on the Hindoo notions respecting the soul and
death in a future state, to be used in 'Treatise on
Man,' and which will be very serviceable for the purpose.

"*March* 1*st*.—Received a valuable contribution of
notes on the soul, according to the Hindoo notion,
from Mr. Tagore.

"24*th*.—A reply from Mr. Sopwith, thanking me for
my 'interesting volumes on art and forty-four etchings,
which he will value very much.   He adds, 'I have
already read to my daughters several of the introductory
pages of your first volume, and promise them and myself
much interest and enjoyment in the further perusal of
them.   Many of the etchings are most amusing.   Pat
would have been quite Pat in the house last night to
back up Sullivan.   Dear Darby and Joan are capital.
The Belgian pig is assuredly not the porker which was
the only object that really interested George Stephenson
in Brussels.   Your Durham is very good, and gives
the tone of one of the sweetest landscapes in Europe.
Some of your views as to what really constitute wealth
are pleasant reading to me.   Your kind remembrance
of me is most pleasing.'

"*April* 1*st*.—A letter from Mr. George Cruikshank, in
which he says, 'I have to thank you very much for
your kind present of the proofs of your etchings, some
of which I think very highly of, and from these specimens of your skill as an amateur feel confident that,

had you been brought up as an artist, you would have drawn yourself up to the top of the tree.'

" *28th.*—Attended on Tuesday evening the meeting of the Anthropological Society. The paper by Serjeant Cox on ' Hybridism.' I spoke first in the debate, being called on by the President. I said ' the subject was as old as Aristotle, some of whose works contained curious discussion and speculation upon it. But the matter was now as far from being settled as ever. The descent of qualities in the case not only of man, but of animals, afforded an illustration of the extent to which in some cases both parents, in others only one, supplied the qualities of the child. This was more clearly seen in cross-breeding among animals, dogs for instance, where in a litter different puppies were of the several breeds of their respective parents. The subject was an important and an interesting one, and had been treated not only ably, but suggestively, which was of more consequence still in a paper of this description.'

" *May 28th.*—Our garden-party came off on Wednesday, and was extremely satisfactory and successful. Matthew Bloxam remarked that it went off capitally. A good many speeches were made, and every one seemed pleased, and to enjoy the day. Exhibited my sketches and Rembrandts. Bloxam said, ' I never saw such a set of Rembrandts as you have got.'

" A letter from Mr. F. Galton, F.R.S., yesterday, saying he had referred to the passages marked in the proof-sheets, and pointing out what appears to be an inconsistency, which will afford scope for a note on the subject, embodying his letter and explaining an apparent anomaly.

" *June 18th.*—Professor and Mrs. Seager came to us on Wednesday. He brought me the proofs. Thinks I am correct in what I have said about natural deformity, but gives me no opinion as to notion of ancients about conscience.

"24th.—A long and ample reply from Professor de Quatrefages on Saturday afternoon, extending over four pages, which was much more than I expected, and did not calculate on getting more than "yeses" and "noes," or only "perhapses" in reply to my interrogations. His letter seems to afford matter for three good and valuable notes on each of the points inquired about, though at present I have not been able to decipher his epistle thoroughly.

"26th.—Wrote to Mr. Tagore for his opinion of 'Treatise on Man' as to the Hindoo notions about conscience, both in man and animals; and to Seager for his opinion whether I was 'correct in denying natural proneness to evil, as mentioned by Burgess and the Calvinistic writers' (pp. 27—31); and 'am I correct in the rendering, etc., of the Greek words cited?' (pp. 32—34); also as to whether 'the ancient classical writers, more especially Plato, Aristotle, Cicero, and Horace, have any definite and distinct notion of conscience as a separate, independent endowment of itself, or did they regard it as a mere exercise of the reason on moral subjects?'

"*October* 10th.—In Paris. A note from Professor de Quatrefages, saying he was 'enchanted to learn of my arrival at Paris,' and should be glad to see me any day between eleven and one. Called on him at the Museum on Friday. He said he could not speak English, though he could read it, so obliged to talk to him in French. I told him I believed that his English would be better than my French. Told him that I read in the Belgian papers of the meeting at Stockholm and his address there. He said Mr. J. Evans and Mr. Franks were there, and that he knew Sir J. Lubbock

and Mr. Hyde Clarke and Dr. Charnocke. Told him
of our tour in Germany and Switzerland, and showed
him my sketches, and talked of our tour in Brittany
last year, and of the Celtic remains there. I thanked
him for his assistance to me in my work, and said I
should be very glad if he would pay me a visit, but he
thought there was no chance of his coming to England.

" 13*th*.—Returned home.

" A letter from Mr. Sopwith, F.R.S., giving me his
opinion on my ' Theory of the Arts,' in accordance with
my request to him to do so. After telling me that he has
gone through the book very carefully, not merely reading
but studying it and re-reading it, he says, ' My opinion
of your work is that it is evidently the result of much
deep thought, of very careful analysis, and of a large
acquaintance with the subjects treated of. The reasoning, to my humble judgment, is correct in the main, for
I would not, unless after much closer acquaintance,
presume to offer even a complimentary or favourable
verdict in matters where a variety of opinion exists.
Yet instances have come across my reading in which I
heartily approve your opinions and admire your sentiments.' He afterwards in conclusion remarks, ' Your
two volumes are hard reading for continuous reading.
The subject is not consecutive in its bearings, but
rather detached into separate divisions, each requiring
separate study. In this I am not speaking of chapters
or greater divisions of the work, but even of short
paragraphs, some of which are pregnant with suggestions of a very extensive character.'

" A letter from Mr. Tagore, sending me his replies
to queries as to Hindoo opinions on conscience.

" *November* 14*th*.—Read my paper on ' Domestic
Life, etc., in Ancient Worlds ; Religious Rites and
Superstitions,' at the Historical Society. Room full.

"*December* 26*th.*—A note from Professor Huxley in which he says he has glanced over the extracts from my work which I have been kind enough to send him, but the questions which they raise are so large that he cannot give them the attention they deserve at present, occupied as he is with pressing work of a very different character. But as soon as leisure arrives he will look at them carefully and communicate what remarks he may have to make to me.

"I attended the Council of the Anthropological Institute, being the nomination of the Council for 1875. Sir John Lubbock proposed me as vice-president, in the room of Professor Huxley, who retires.

"31*st.*—Wrote to Dr. Vaughan, Master of the Temple, asking his opinion whether conscience was known to the ancients, and as to lay inspiration. He replies in favour of the first, but against the second, and terms it 'too speculative' to offer an opinion

1875.

"*January* 2*nd.*—With the new year I received a most complimentary letter from America, accompanied with degree of LL.D., *honores causa*, from Grenville College.

"11*th.*—Wrote to Matthew Bloxam on Friday and asked him, 'Is there likely to be anything done about the rebuilding of the parish church, and are you disposed to give a plan for it? What say you to preserving the tower and adding a Norman church to it? I should like to have the design by you, and would in that case do what I could to organise a committee in London to raise subscriptions.'

"16*th.*—Met Mr. Daldy at the Junior Athenæum, who said he had a party of friends going to dine with him, Mr. Wood among them, to whom he introduced me, and asked me to join them, which I did, and a very

pleasant party it was. A good deal of chat with Mr.
Wood.   He asked me to supply him with some matter
for a new edition of his ' Man and Beast.'

" *February* 13*th.* —In the evening read my paper at
the Historical Society on ' Domestic Life, etc., in Ancient
World,' embracing modes of sepulture and funeral
rites. It was very well received. Mr. Tagore made a
good speech respecting Brahmin and Mohammedan
modes of disposing of dead bodies. Mr. Tagore and
two friends retired to Serjeant Cox's to tea after the
meeting, where we had a *séance*, spirit-rapping, and
table-moving.

" Attended the inaugural meeting of the Psychological Society, where Cox delivered an address.
Asked to speak, but did not, as so many were to
take part in the discussion, and no particular opening.

" A letter from Mr. Tagore, sending me a note about
the Hindoo notion of the soul and its faculties. But
I doubt whether it goes sufficiently to the point to be
available.

" Wrote on Tuesday to Dr. Bloxam, telling him that
I much wanted to get a note or two from Dr. Newman
on my ' Treatise on Man,' of which I sent him a
prospectus.

" 24*th.*—A letter from Dr. Bloxam, containing an
extract of one from Dr. Newman, in which the latter
says, ' Mr. Harris flatters me considerably when he
wishes to ask my opinion, but I do wish you would beg
me off. I am sure I could not satisfy myself or have
proper confidence in myself. I am very shallow on all
those points of which he is treating, and just now I am
so far knocked up with what I have done, and have
such a rush of arrears of work and of correspondence,
as to be quite incapable of accurate thought such as he
would require. *Don't let me seem uncivil.*'

"*March 6th.*—A note from Dr. Bloxam, who says that if I can wait he should be able to persuade Dr. Newman to answer any question I may be pleased to send him. 'Besides other duties, his correspondence is immense, and I therefore do not wonder that he would wish to escape any great addition to it.'

"A letter from Serjeant Cox, sending me the resolutions at the meeting to establish a Psychological Society. He says, 'We are now constituted. You are placed upon the first Council, but you will be one of the vice-presidents. I have no doubt that in two years we shall be the most popular Society in London.'

"10th.—Wrote to Serjeant Cox, sending him two extracts from chapter ii.,—on Man,—and asking his opinion as to 'the correctness of the principle I have laid down in asserting the existence of certain faculties in the mind in which consists its power of action of different kinds.'

"13th.—At Mr. and Mrs. G. Cruikshank's levée to commemorate their silver wedding. A great crowd. Met several that I know.

"Attended the dinner of the Historical Society. Lord Houghton in the chair. The toast of 'The Historical Society' was proposed by Mr. Sopwith, and I was put down to respond to it.

"Wrote to Sir J. Lubbock, sending him extracts from 'Treatise on Man' relating to language and the communications of animals, and I asked him and Professor Huxley (to whom I wrote again, sending him the extract on this subject) 'whether you think there is any ground for supposing from the almost intuitive knowledge which certain animals appear to possess of the virtues of particular herbs, and [other substances, earths, and] also of mineral waters, that they considerably exceed us, owing probably to the greater acuteness of their sensorial organs and their acquaintance with the essences and essential properties of many substances ?'

"24*th*.—A letter yesterday from Dr. de Sainte Croix, in which he says (of 'Theory of the Arts'), 'The translation was finished some time since, and I have sent it to one of my friends in Paris to find an editor [publisher] who is willing to undertake the business.'

"A letter from Mr. Newman, of Warwick, in which he says, 'The window [in the church] was completed this morning. As far as I can venture to judge in such a matter, I have no hesitation in pronouncing it to be a most successful work and a great ornament to the church.'

"A concise reply from Sir John Lubbock, in which he says he has read the extracts, and agrees with much that I say, but that I open out too many subjects to be discussed in a letter.   Makes two short remarks which may be, and which I have, embodied in a note.

"A notice this morning announcing my election as a member of the Burlington Fine Arts Club.

"31*st*.—A note from Miss Buss, saying that her late father, Mr. R. W. Buss, 'desired me to ask your acceptance of a copy of his work on "Graphic Satire," printed for private circulation.'

"A reply from Mr. F. Galton on Thursday, which will serve for three notes, which I have also made out of Sir J. Lubbock's letter.

"Drew out the following circular note to send round to those to whom I shall submit the paragraph about animal perception of essences :—

"Will you kindly give me your opinion on the enclosed paragraph, respecting which there is a wide diversity of sentiment ? If animals do not perceive the essential properties of substances, by what means are they able to detect and avoid those substances which contain ingredients that are poisonous, and to select those whose ingredients are beneficial in particular emergencies ? '

" Received on Thursday from Serjeant Cox his book on ' Heredity and Hybridism. A Suggestion.'

" A reply yesterday from Mr. Wood, answering my queries very concisely and referring to his book. He asks me to send him some anecdotes of animals for the new edition of his work, which I have jotted down and forwarded to him.

" A letter also to E. from Mr. W., thanking her for some etchings which she sent him. He says, ' Let me thank you very sincerely for the parcel of etchings, with which I am greatly pleased, and value much, as, according to my taste and judgment, they are exceedingly clever, interesting, and amusing.'

" *April 8th.*—Wrote to Dr. Bloxam and sent through him to Dr. Newman some queries respecting extracts from ' Treatise on Man.'

" A reply on Wednesday from Dr. Richardson, who proposes to qualify my statement, to which he would then assent.

" *24th.*—A note from Sir J. Lubbock in reply to mine, in which he gives me his notions on certain points, of which I can avail myself for a note.

" Wrote again on Monday to Mr. Wood, and sent him another anecdote (on animal antipathies) for the new edition of his ' Man and Beast.'

" A reply from Mr. Alfred Smee, in which he criticises my expressions, but thinks that the idea might be thrown into a different form which would be unexceptionable, or at any rate in accordance with his system. In reply I wrote to him, ' Allow me to thank you, which I do very sincerely, for your kind note, which is the more satisfactory from its candour, and is at once explicit

27

and scientific. What you say deserves deep consideration.' Sir John Lubbock and Dr. Richardson have
written to much the same effect. Others to whom I
have applied take a different view of the matter.

"A note on Wednesday from Dr. Bloxam, enclosing
one to him from Dr. Newman, replying concisely, but
very satisfactorily, to my queries. His notes will be a
great acquisition, and add much to the value of the sum
total of them. He says, ' Mr. Harris has taken a great
subject, and I am sure he will make a good book upon it.
This I feel, though I feel also, or rather feel therefore,
that I am quite unable to criticise the passages which he
sends me. It almost requires to think out and write
down one's self the points treated of in them in order to
be able to form a judgment upon them.' He then goes
on, in a letter of four sides of notepaper, into the
different points briefly but pointedly, and concludes,
' And now please make my apologies to Mr. Harris for
saying so little. I may appear to him very ungracious
after his kindness to me when in this place. But he
must recollect I am an old man, and cannot do everything I should wish to do.'

"Serjeant Cox sent me on Thursday a very good
note to the paragraph about animals perceiving
essences.

"A card of invitation to a ball at the Mansion House,
sent to the President of the Royal Historical Society.
Declined it, however, being so inconvenient to get
there, having no London residence.

"*May 1st.*—Wrote on Monday to Mr. Darwin, enclosing the paragraph about animals perceiving essences,
in the same form that I did to Sir J. Lubbock and
others, asking his opinion, and stated there was a wide
diversity among those whom I had consulted. Wrote
in the same way to Professor de Quatrefages, sending·

him the paragraph also, and asked him in addition
whether, as regards memory, animals possess recollection as well as retention, and whether sensations
only, and not ideas, are what are retained in their
memories. Wrote to Dr. Newman on Tuesday,
sending him a copy of my 'Theory of the Arts' by
railway, of which I enclosed a prospectus in the letter.
Wrote on the title-page, 'The Rev. Dr. Newman, etc.'
With the author's respectful compliments and sincere
regards, added also the following note :—" My dear Sir
(if I may be allowed so to address you),—I cannot allow
Dr. Bloxam to thank you for your very great kindness
and condescension to me in the valuable note which
you addressed to him in reply to some queries which
I took the liberty of propounding to you in reference
to my forthcoming work without addressing to you a
line myself to express a deep sense of the favour done
me, and to say how much I value the assistance which
you have been so good as to render me.'

" *8th.*—A note from Mr. Darwin replying to my query
about animals perceiving essences, also one from
Professor de Quatrefages, replying pretty fully to it,
but which I have not yet been able to decipher. One
from Sir John Lubbock, thanking me for 'Theory of
Arts.' One from Dr. Newman, in which he says, ' It
is very kind in you to think I have said anything to
your purpose in the short remarks I made in answer to
your questions. I cannot get myself to think so, but I
accept your words with gratitude. Thank you also for
your " Theory of the Arts," which has come to me quite
right, and promises at first sight to be as full of matter
and as interesting as your former volume which you
kindly gave me.'

" A letter from Mr. Coleridge, thanking me for a
letter to him about the Moultrie memorial. He says,

'I agree with you about the memorial, and have already made a similar suggestion to Dr. Jex-Blake.'

"Wrote to Mr. Smee, asking his opinion as to the mind possessing faculties of its own, also as to memory, and asked him if he could give me a definition of genius.

"15*th*.—Wrote to Dr. Richardson, sending him extracts and queries as to the early manifestation and development of genius, the imaginative efforts of the mind, the operations of genius, and their capacities for training.

"A letter from Miss Child to E. about the Warwick window, in which she says, ' I went to Warwick, and saw the window, and thought it truly beautiful in every respect.'

"A reply on Thursday from Dr. de Ste. Croix, who sent me four ample notes, which seem very good, for Chapter IV., 'On Man,' also one from Mr. Tagore, sending me a note, as requested, for the extract from Chapter III., and one from Dr. Beddoe, sending replies to queries.

" *June* 5*th*.—A full report in the *Spiritualist* of the debate at the Psychological Society on my paper on ' Memory.'

" 13*th*.—Attended the meeting of the Psychological Society on Thursday evening. I read two short papers about facts respecting memory, which excited some discussion, and I replied. Then Cox read a paper on 'The Duality of the Mind,' on which I spoke first. Said ' no subject could be more full of interest or more suggestive, that there were difficulties in the way of the theory, but that it also removed difficulties. The fact of the mind communing with itself strongly in support of two minds, and still more the case of conscience, where deliberation between two opposing parties appeared to be going on.   Many organs of the body besides the brain dual, and the material organs in many respects reflective of the spiritual being.'   Sir J. Heron Maxwell, Mr. Tagore, and others spoke.   A very good attendance, and Cox considers the Society on the whole a great success.

" 19*th.*—A note from Mr. Smee, referring me to his second chapter for his definition of genius, but saying that to do it justice would require the writing of a dictionary.   Each writer uses the word in a different sense.

" A letter from Wake on Thursday.   Says he will write me a note on the extract respecting animal reasoning, but wishes for my definition of reasoning. ' Your work will be most representative in its character and I trust it will be successful.'

" 22*nd.*—Our garden-party on Tuesday, which wen off very well.

" 23*rd.*—At dinner given by Cox, as President of the Psychological Society, to the Council, and which was in a very handsome style.   I sat by Mr. Tagore and Mr. S. C. Hall, and had a good deal of pleasant conversation with them.   Mr. Hall said he was present as a reporter in the House of Commons when the famous encounter between Brougham and Canning took place, of which he promised to write me a description for my ' Life of Lord Brougham.'

" Dr. Richardson, who was there, told me ' he wondered how I managed to miss the bench.'   I said I might have had an Indian judgeship, but I was afraid of the climate, and having no family, had no occasion to go abroad.   He had told Mr. Norman Lockyer, F.R.S., that I was bringing out a work connected with biology, respecting which I was in communication with most of the leading authorities both in this country and on the Continent, Professor de Quatrefages among them, and that they had given me their opinions on some of the most controverted points in footnotes.

"25*th.*—Wrote to Mr. Sopwith. Sent him queries on extracts for notes as to memory. Also to Dr. Maudsley as to memory. A proof came yesterday morning of extracts from Chapter VI., which I corrected and returned.

"E. and I went to The Grove, Chalfont St. Giles, yesterday, to stay with Sir Adam and Lady Bittlestone, returning home this afternoon.

"*July* 3*rd.*—A proof of extract from Chapter VII., on 'Man.' A letter from Dr. Maudsley, containing notes to both the extracts sent to him.

"Miss Whitemore Jones wrote that 'the day of our garden-party is the one enjoyable day to her of the whole year.'

"A notice of the party in the *Spiritualist*, giving the names of the principal persons, and mentioning the toast of 'The Psychological Society.'

"A copy of 'Men of the Time,' containing concise biographies of all the men of the day of any note, arrived lately, in which the short memoir of myself, which I sent them at the editor's request, is duly inserted.

"Yesterday I wrote to Mr. Gladstone, sending him extract from Chapter V., on 'Man' (pp. 87—92 in the manuscript) on the general constitution of each of the capacities of the mind and the bad results of inattention to the rule. Told him I had extracted in a note his observations respecting mode of teaching Homer.

"10*th.*—Replies on Monday from Sir J. Lubbock and Dr. Newman both very concise, but will serve to make notes of, as they are definite, and to the points raised. Wrote also to Wake, and sent him, for a note on it, an extract from Chapter IV. (p. 100) on imitation by animals.

"17th.—A letter from Mr. Gladstone on Thursday, sending me a very nice note on the extract I sent him, and which will be valuable to me. Wrote to Mr. Delamotte, of Harrow, offering him a copy of 'Theory of Arts' as a prize for the drawing class this year, which he writes me word he should like very much to have.

"*October 9th.*—" Wrote Dr. Maudsley, sending him extract Chapter VI. (p. 147) relative to Shakespearian test of madness, and asked his opinion upon it; also to Mr. Derwent Coleridge, sending him extracts for corrections and notes. In my letter to Mr. Coleridge I said, 'The work contains several quotations from the late Mr. S. T. Coleridge, which makes me the more anxious to have a contribution from his son.'

"Made our tour this autumn on the Continent through Germany and part of France.

"Wrote to Mr. Smee, sending him extracts with the queries on them prepared; also to Serjeant Cox, with extract Chapter V. ('On Man') with query upon it; and to Dr. Richardson with extracts, and asked him his opinion as to the notion of Coleridge of scrofula producing genius. I said that Dr. Johnson's was perhaps a case in point as regards scrofula. Many imaginative poets and painters have been undoubtedly mad, but many as undoubtedly sane. But may not the fine susceptibility, and which aids imagination, be allied to or conduce to insanity?

"A letter this afternoon from Dr. Maudsley, replying fully and satisfactorily to my query respecting Shakespeare's test of insanity, which will supply a valuable note.

"19th.—A good note from Cox in reply to my query to him on memory.

" 23rd.— Revising and adding notes completed when
on the Continent on Thursday to Chapter VII.
'Mental Discipline and Cultivation'). Made an important alteration and improvement in this chapter by
splitting the last long section—§ 10 : 'Diseases of the
Mind and Mental Regimen'—into three, viz., § 10 :
'Mental Disease, its Essence, Source, and Development ;' § 11 : 'Mental Pathology, its Principles and its
End ;' § 12 : 'The Complete Discipline and Cultivation of the Mind the Correct Aim of the Study of the
Constitution of Man.'

" 30th.—A letter from Wake, sending his notes,
which appear very good. We dined at the Coleridges'
at Hanwell. C. alluded after dinner to his letter to
me, implying that it had cost him much time and labour
to write.

" 31st.—Called on Dr. Richardson, and with him
two hours while he discussed my queries and wrote out
his notes on them. Got him to give me the rough
draft of one, full of corrections, which he had copied
out again—an autographical curiosity. He told me I
differed from most men he knew in not objecting to
have my opinions questioned, but that I was quite
right. Said Sopwith had suggested putting the notes in
an appendix, but which would perhaps deprive them of
their main value, and prevent them being read.

" This morning Plumptre dictated to me his notes in
reply to my queries and extracts.

" *November 4th.*—A letter from Mr. Smee. He sends
replies to my queries to him.

" 6th.—A note from Professor Huxley, in reply to
mine. As to the first query, he refers me to his 'Lay
Sermons' and his address at the Belfast meeting of
the British Association. He adds, 'Lord Brougham's
opinions on scientific or philosophical subjects are

in my judgment valueless.' As to the second, he refers me to his Belfast address.

" Dined with Mr. Smee on Wednesday, and found him very pleasant and affable, and had an agreeable evening. He was very ready in reply to my queries, but could not get a great deal direct from him ; enough, however, to supply the notes.

" 18*th*.—Called by appointment on Dr. Richardson on Thursday, and obtained from him the remaining notes on Chapter VII., for the matter of which he referred me to one of his addresses, which I may quote from, and out of which, and his conversation with me, I must make notes. In the evening read a paper on ' Caligraphy as a Test of Character ' at the Psychological Society. About forty present, and it seemed to take well and to excite a great deal of interest, and with ladies as well as gentlemen. A very animated debate upon it. I exhibited autographs of Napoleon I., Wellington, Nelson, Brougham, Horne Tooke, Sheridan, Cobbett, Cowper, Macaulay, Walpole, Dr. Parr, Dr. Whewell, Lord Lytton, Charles Dickens, etc.

: " 20*th*.—Completed Chapter VII. this morning by adding notes of Dr. Richardson and others not yet put in, which completes the entire work, and sent it off to the printers. As I added original matter to-day to the work from notes I composed lately, I may consider to-day—Saturday, November 20th, 1875—as the real day on which this great work of my life was finished. It was commenced in February, 1833, nearly forty-three years.

" 28*th*.—Wrote the following letter on Tuesday to Mr. Norman Lockyer, to whom Dr. Richardson introduced me when I was staying with him on our meeting him at the railway station :—

" ' When my friend Dr. Richardson introduced

me to you, and told you of a work on which I am engaged, I was not aware that you were a native of Rugby (my native place) and a son of Mr. J. H. Lockyer, whom I used to know many years ago in connection with the Rugby Literary and Scientific Society, of which he was honorary secretary and the founder as well, and of which Dr. Arnold was an active member. If your father is alive, I should much like to see him again, and to talk over old times. I lost sight of your father many years ago on my quitting Rugby to reside in London and practise as a barrister, which profession I quitted on being promoted to an appointment, which I since have resigned on a retiring pension.'

" *December* 11th.—Two letters from Serjeant Cox on Wednesday and Thursday, sending me his paper on Tyndall's article on ' Materialism,' and in reply I said, ' I have read Tyndall's article twice, but I am not quite sure as to the precise point at which he is driving ; I am quite sure he does not know himself. From some passages it would seem he agrees with you, from others that he denies altogether the existence of a soul.'

" 15th.—At the meeting to-day of the Anthropological Society I was proposed by Captain Pim, M.P., a vice-president, and elected.

" 20th.—A long letter from Professor Stokes, of Cambridge, secretary to the Royal Society.

" 23rd.—Went to the meeting of the Psychological Society, and opened the debate from notes. Wrote out, as I told Cox I should do, a condensed report of it, which I gave to Harrison for the *Spiritualist*."

CHAPTER XXV.

TO THE DAYS OF DEATH.

1876—1886.

" *January* 1st.

"I BELIEVE I shall fix the date of my completion of the 'Treatise on Man' at the 15th of February next, that being, as nearly as I can calculate, the anniversary of the day on which I commenced the composition of the work in 1833.

"*7th.*—A letter from Sir Eardley Wilmot, sending me the draft of a Bill he is preparing respecting homicide, etc., and notices of motions respecting law reform. In reply I wrote to him :—

" 'Something ought to be done to render criminally punishable cases of gross culpable negligence resulting in death. Cases of fraud also should be made punishable when the object of the transaction *ab initio* was to defraud. I think that you will do great service in stirring up these questions, and that you are exactly the person to take them up.'

"*25th.*—Completed the printing of my work the 'Treatise on Man.' Awfully fagged by it, but I have really enjoyed the work, though it has been too much for me, together with the enormous correspondence involved in it about the notes, of which there are twenty-five contributors, and others I have corresponded with on the subject as well. This book, however, has been the great object of my life, of the best part of it, intellectually speaking, at any rate. I like much the concluding parts, but whether the public will do so as well remains to be seen.

"*February* 5*th.*—An official notification to me that I was elected at the annual meeting on the 25th a vice-president of the Anthropological Institute.

"12*th.*—E. and I went to London on Thursday. Attended the meeting of the Historical Society. I read a paper, the first of a series, on 'Domestic Everyday Life; Manners and Customs in this Country from the Earliest Period to the End of the Last Century. I.—The Ancient Britons.' It was illustrated with diagrams. The paper was well received, and a good discussion followed. Presented my diagrams relating to manners and customs in the olden time to the Historical Society.

"15*th.*—I dined at the Historical Society's dinner at Willis's Rooms. The room was decorated with my diagrams. I had a seat at the table, next to Mr. Cave, M.P., who was next to the chairman, Lord Aberdare. I was down to propose the toast of 'Historical and Antiquarian Societies.' I said, in reference to what had fallen from the speakers, that the late Lord Stanhope had in my hearing cast a sneer against the Historical Society, and that he had also opposed the issuing of the manuscript commission, and that he said in a letter to me that the family papers already disclosed were more than we wanted. This, I thought, much diminished the value of his attack on the Historical Society. I said that dryness was usually associated with antiquarianism, but that Sir Walter Scott had done much to show that matters of the highest interest might be drawn from antiquarian researches. Even the dullest documents have occasionally produced very interesting matter. For instance, the Anglo-Saxon wills in the British Museum threw great light on the domestic history of the times, as where a nobleman left his daughter a legacy of two thousand swine. So of deeds. In an ancient marriage settlement provision was made for the marriage of an eldest daughter with the son of a neighbouring squire. But in case the young lady proved disobedient and would not wed, the second daughter was to have the offer of the young lord and the land. Provision was also made in the settlement respecting the entertainment to celebrate the wedding. Household inventories, too, threw much light on manners and customs, showing the domestic articles then in use, as did household regulations, and even tradesmen's ledgers. Old laws, too, dry as they were, threw great light on the manners of the day, especially those about highways and robberies. The object of the Historical Society was to unite together instruction and entertainment, to make the instruction entertaining and the entertainment instructive. I was talking with a lady lately, who had lived in China, of the extraordinary food eaten in that country—dogs, snails, earthworms, and the like. But she said that their cooking was so exquisite that whatever might be in the larder, what came to the table was always palatable. So with the Historical Society. However nasty and repulsive the documents from whence we derive our information, they are so well cooked and seasoned when we present them before our audience that they are always received with a relish ; and while we impart solid instruction, we afford substantial pleasure as well ; and great as our success has been, this, I believe, is the real secret of it.

"*April 8th.*—Accomplished to-day the launching of my work the 'Treatise on Man.'

" The following theories propounded in this work I believe to be entirely original :—

1. Threefold mode of originating beings;
2. Theory of instinct, originating in sensation ;

3. Distinction between selfishness and self-love ;
4. Intellectual as well as material senses ;
5. Our medial condition ;
6. Emotion of irritation ;
7. Human essence of love ;
8. Animal attachment ;
9. A general but no universal resurrection ;
10. Animals no notion of death ;
11. Animals have souls, but no faculties to them ;
12. Vibration essential to memory ;
13. Theory of the intellectual constitution ;
14. Natural as well as artificial education, and of each capacity separately ;
15. Theory of pathology ;
16. Theory of disease ;
17. Theory of mental disease ;
18. Spiritual beings devoid of intelligence ;
19. Some souls only reunited to bodies ;
20. Mental deformity ;
21. Genius of inspiration innate ;
22. Memory reflective of understanding ;
23. Essence of property ;
24. Sensation distinct from ideas.

" Called on Bell and Sons about ' Treatise on Man,' and had the satisfaction of seeing a copy of my work, bound up in cloth, in modest dark green. But Mr. Bell thinks it will be a week before the book is ready to send out for sale.

" *22nd.* —In the evening I attended the meeting of the Psychological Society. A paper by Serjeant Cox on ' Wit and Humour.' I spoke first in the debate, and said that the difference contended for by Serjeant Cox between wit and humour had been pointed out by Coleridge, who went further and said that humour generally denoted genius in the person endowed with it, but not so wit. Punning appeared to some to be effected mainly by words, wit by words and things together, and humour by things alone. I hoped the paper would be printed, as it would be a valuable addition to the archives of the Society.

" In a letter to Dr. Richardson I added :—

" ' I suppose there are some points on which we shall not altogether agree, though I hope there are several where we coincide. I trust that the book as a whole will meet with your approval. It is perhaps, taking it altogether, more suggestive than calculated to lead to any definite results. Possibly in a work which is to a large extent necessarily speculative, this may be the right line to pursue.'

" In a letter which I wrote to Dr. Bloxam, in reply to one thanking me for sending him the book, and asking for my autograph to place in it, I said :—

" ' The two works which preceded it, " The Theory of the Arts " and " Civilisation considered as a Science," referred to in the preface, ought properly to accompany it.'

" *May 5th.*—Attended the meeting of the Psychological Society in the evening, and read a paper on ' Objections to Psychological Phenomena,' which drew forth a very animated discussion. I replied to the criticisms upon it with some spirit and effect.

" *8th.*—A letter on Monday from Professor de Quatrefages thanking me for my book. He says that ' he observes I have entered upon some very obscure and exalted problems, which he has generally avoided, not wishing to wander from the domain of science properly so called. He has not therefore formed an opinion as to the manner in which I comprehend the human soul, as being in its nature more or less material, and as to its mode of union within the body. But he takes great interest in what I have written on this subject, and congratulates me on having completed the great work which appears to have occupied many years.'

"13*th*.—A letter from Mr. H. Bloxam, who says, 'Your old tutor, when you were at Bilton, died on Thursday evening in his eighty-fifth year. I am one of the pall-bearers at his funeral, which is to take place on Tuesday next.'

"In reply I said, 'I am very much grieved by the intelligence in your letter, though it is only in the natural course of events. But I had quite hoped to be able to call on the good old man once more, expecting to be in Rugby in the course of the summer. There was no one for whom I had a greater respect in every way. The advice that he gave was always so very impressive, not least from the air of sincerity that accompanied it. This too was the case with his religion, and yet so deep and sincere. I often think now (though nearly sixty years must have passed) of advice and information which he gave me while I was with him at Bilton, when I fear I was a sad plague to him, though he was always most kind and considerate to me.'

"Letter also from Dr. Newman, saying that my book 'is full of thought, and laborious persevering thought. Treatises so large and deep appeal to the future. The work is emphatically a library book, and he feels much gratification in placing it in his library. He has read quite enough of it to be sure that it contains great truths.'

"A note on Tuesday from Mr. Gladstone, thanking me for my book, and in which he says, 'It is by forces and influences drawn from the field in which you labour that the fortunes of the human race are principally made, and I look forward with great interest to making myself acquainted as speedily as I may be able with your views.'

"*June* 24*th*.—Dined at Serjeant Cox's to meet the

Council of the Psychological Society.   Plumptre told me
he likes my book better the second time of reading it
than the first, and that he has been much struck by my
observation that 'God did not intend all mankind to be
of the same religion.'

"28*th*.—Received on Wednesday a copy of the
Dundee Advertiser, which contains a review of my
'Treatise on Man,' in which they say of it :—

"'This is a most elaborate and learned production,
and testifies, on the part of its author, his immense
research and great ingenuity.   It is, without the name,
an Encyclopædia of Man—a great collection of facts ;
most of them thoroughly sifted by himself, and many
of them subjected to the correction of acknowledged
authorities.'

"We had our garden-party on Wednesday.   The
first toast proposed was 'The Queen,' afterwards the
'Prince of Wales,' with which I coupled 'Prosperity to
India,' and the name of Mr. Tagore, who replied in a
very interesting speech, giving his opinion as to the
effect produced by the visit and the mode of it.   He
alluded to my book, which he said bore relation to
Cudworth's, and was a complete compendium of the
natural system of man.   Mr. Beavington Atkinson
proposed 'Art and Artists,' to which Mr. G. Cruikshank replied in a very humorous speech.   In proposing 'The Magistracy' I said that art did much to
soften men's minds, but with all that they required
magistrates to keep them in order, and I coupled with
the toast Mr. Flowers, magistrate at Bow Street.   I
added that it was a very disagreeable thing to be
brought before Mr. Flowers at Bow Street, but that it
was very agreeable to have Mr. Flowers brought before
us.   In proposing 'The Bar' I said that the magistrates were very useful to keep the people in order,

28

but that the Bar was required to keep the magistrates in order. In proposing 'The Medical Profession and Dr. Richardson' I said that that was naturally the last toast, as the doctors were the last persons we had to deal with. That they were people I was always glad to see : if I was ill, because I wanted them ; if I was well, that I might welcome them as friends. Mr. Tagore proposed 'The Ladies,' and coupled E.'s name with it, for which I returned thanks. Everything went off extremely well.

"Mrs. Cruikshank brought me a bust of Mr. Cruikshank, a cast from that taken by Behns, as a present.

" *July* 1st.—A very fair and temperate review of the 'Treatise on Man' in the *Anthropological Journal* for July of three pages, in which they say that—' added value is given to it by the interesting circumstance that the proof sheets of several portions were submitted to learned friends of the author, such as Sir John Lubbock, Dr. Richardson, Dr. Newman, and many others, and have been enriched by their comments.'

" 15th.—A review of nearly two columns of my 'Treatise on Man' in the *Dumfries Standard* of Wednesday last, July 12th. They say of it, ' This work may be said to be one of the most exhaustive treatises ever written on the subject of man's physical, intellectual, and spiritual being. The Third Book, on the intellectual nature of man, is one that will prove a valuable help to every student of mental philosophy. This last book we should be inclined to rank highest of all. It is a full, systematic, fresh, and vigorous dis- cussion of a most important department of knowledge, one that is by way of pre-eminence called Philosophy.'

" 29th.—In London for the day. In the *Westminster Review* of this month, among the literary notices is a review of my book. It says, ' There are, it will be seen, many blemishes in Mr. Harris' two volumes, but it is only fair to say that the work contains a painstaking and comprehensive discussion of the proper study of mankind.

"*August* 5*th.*—Preparing a plan of education according to the principles enunciated in ' Treatise on Man,' dividing it into natural and artificial, and specifying that which is properly and peculiarly adapted for each capacity, individually and exclusively.

" *September* 12*th.*—Made a tour in Devonshire this autumn.

" *October* 7*th.*—Returned home.

"21*st.*—A note from Miss Hall, whom we met last year at Schaffhausen, asking me to let her have some more of my etchings, which, she says, 'we have been looking over with great interest and amusement,' and that her 'nephew, who was with us, greatly admired them.'

" The newspapers mention the death of Archibald, whom I have not seen since he was made a judge.

" *November* 18*th.*—I read a paper on the Anglo-Saxons at the Historical Society on Thursday evening. A full attendance, and it was extremely well received, and a good discussion after.

" Brought, at Mr. Tagore's request, the books to be presented to the University Library at Calcutta, and wrote in them accordingly—' Lord Hardwicke's Life,' ' Theory of Representation,' ' Civilisation as a Science,' ' Theory of the Arts,' and ' Treatise on Man.'

1877.

" *January* 19*th.*—Attended the meeting of the Psychological Society, where Plumptre read a very good paper, which produced an excellent discussion, on ' The Psychology of the Human Voice.' The President,

Serjeant Cox, called on me first to speak, which I did, and said that ' much of what the paper had remarked respecting the effect of the modulation of the human voice was forcibly illustrated by the voice of animals, in whom it was often very monotonous, but they so varied it by modulations that they contrived to express every passion and emotion, and to convey their feelings and wants one to another. Pain, joy, and fear were vividly expressed, and their calls to one another and to their young were perfectly understood. This was particularly observable in dogs and in rooks, who had less power of articulation than many other animals. In the case of infants, too, by modulating their voices they could express many wants long before they obtained the power of articulation. Articulation itself became developed correspondingly with the acquirement of the ideas it was required and adapted to express. The language of passion and emotion, which was expressed without words, was indeed the most powerful and affecting of all languages, and this it was, when combined with it, that gave such effect to the language of articulation.'

"*April 5th.*—A letter from Dr. Burges, thanking me for the Devizes window of painted glass in St. John's Church, which I have lately erected to the memory of Mr. Charles Innes, formerly rector, and grandfather of my valued wife, ' and at the same time congratulating me upon the excellence of my work.' He adds, ' I only wish it had been up in the west window, which would have shown it off marvellously.'

"A copy of the *Devizes Advertiser* containing mention of my window, in which they say of it that it is ' A stained-glass window of very handsome design and colouring . . . the design being illustrative of the Sermon on the Mount. In the centre compartment is our Lord, seated, and in the attitude of teaching ; while in the sides are the disciples and others listening in rapt attention. All the figures are admirably drawn, and there is a lifelike form and spirit in them which contrasts pleasingly with the subjects drawn in mediæval style which one sometimes sees. . . . The window has been wholly designed and painted by the husband of the deceased's granddaughter, a gentleman who has a wonderful taste and skill in such works.'

" *20th.*—Attended meeting of the Psychological Society, and read a paper on the ' Hereditary Transmission of Endowments and Qualities.'

" *June 12th.*—A letter from the new President of the United States, thanking me for copies of my works :—

"' EXECUTIVE MANSION, WASHINGTON,

"' 20th May, 1877.

"' My DEAR SIR,—I beg you to receive my sincere thanks for your valuable works. I shall preserve and prize them, and hope to have an opportunity to enjoy and profit by them.

" ' Sincerely,

"' B. B. HAYES.'

" *19th.*—A long letter on Saturday from the Baron de Bogonshevsky, of Pshoss (Pleshewn) Russia, member of the Privy Council of that country, asking me about my papers in *Long Ago* on ' Ouissant,' and begging me to give him the etching of it, which, he says, will be valuable to him. He also states, ' Your notes on battle-fields are very valuable.' He mentions that he is a ' Fellow of the Imperial Russian Archæological, Moscow Archæological, and St. Petersburg Societies.' In reply I thanked him for his letter, and said I should be happy to forward him the engraving of Ouissant, and

some others which are of historical interest; and I
said that I should have much pleasure in proposing
him as an honorary member of the Royal Historical
Society.

"*July 9th.*—A very long letter from the Baron de
Bogonshevsky, in which he says, 'I certainly would
esteem myself very happy if a communication and
exchange of ideas could be permanently established
between myself and you.' Says he has read several
of my papers in the Transactions of the Historical
Society, of which he possesses some of the volumes
only. He mentions, in a private manner, that H. H.
the Grand Duke Cæsaravitch, President of our Historical
Society, has read my work, 'The Theory of the Arts,'
'and I have reason to say he has much admired its
contents, as has his brother Grand Duke Alexis.' He
say that he shall be glad to be a member of the
Historical Society.

"*August 3rd.*—A letter from the Baron de Bogonshevsky, saying he was afraid I had not received
his last, as no reply to it. But to-day a letter from
him acknowledging my reply, which I wrote before
leaving home,—a very long letter of four letter-paper
sides. Says that his library contains above twelve
thousand volumes, and that he has a large collection
of autographs, above fifteen thousand, and has added
my letter to them, and asks for my photograph. Asks
me to pay him a visit, and promises to show me St.
Petersburg, Moscow, etc.

"*September 5th.*—Made our annual tour on the
Continent, visiting parts of France, Belgium, and the
Rhine.

" *29th.*— Returned home to-day.

" *30th.*—A letter from the Baron de Bogonshevsky,
who says that he has been reading my 'Treatise on

Man,' and that he has been 'astonished to find so much
strength of argument, such natural and simple comprehensive explanation of things which were, and until
now, considered inscrutably hidden in darkness inso-
luble to the human mind. Indeed, your volumes will
stand together with Darwin's most sublime works, and
they will form a sufficient treasure in themselves, a
treasure of knowledge of things unknown and unsolved
before. After reading your philosophical researches
I comprehend many things which were dark to me
in Darwin's theories, and both will form the only
philosophy of the future. You ask me my sincere
opinion. You have it, but believe me it is not a
flattery.'

"*November* 1st.—A number for November of the
Intellectual Repository arrived this morning containing
a review of ' Treatise on Man,' in which they say of it,
' Dr. Harris has given us, not a book, but elements from
which many books might be formed. Disconnected as
the sibylline leaves, paragraph after paragraph, even
phrase after phrase, is full now of information, and
then of suggestive conjecture. The author has read
largely, and maintained a wide correspondence with
distinguished thinkers, and this is his commonplace
book, enriched with brief but not always consistent
meditations of his own. We recommend this work to
all earnest thinkers, and only to them. It is valuable
for much that is contributed by Dr. Harris himself, and
for the citations which he gives of authors who uphold
or controvert his views. Its very defect, the incom-
pleteness of the author's thinking, will render it a
valuable school.'

"*2nd.*—Obtained to-day a copy of *Nature* of September 6th, containing a review of ' Treatise on Man.'
Among other things, they say : ' In a word there is

scope in these volumes for the critic of all minds, all intelligences, and all sentiments. He tells us that during the progress of the work many hundreds of minds have been dissected by the author. In the mode of constructing the chapters of these volumes there is an originality in dealing with the accumulated learning of previous authors. Another feature, which is quite novel in literature, is also introduced by the author. He has laid other living authors under contribution, and whether they agree with him or differ from him. . . . We have no doubt that in a future day, when all the writers are silent, their protestations will be quoted—as extracts from letters of past men are quoted now—as evidences of thought quite unpremeditated, but still as correct references of the minds that gave them birth. . . . Those who have to think, write, and speak on the subjects submitted for study will often find the matter in Dr. Harris' volumes most useful as well as interesting, and they will be grateful to our author, who has spared neither time, nor labour, nor expense to give them the work of his life. We add, without hesitation, that Dr. Harris' work, though it be little read in this age of luxurious reading, will remain to be read as one of the solid and enduring additions to English learned literature.'

" *6th.*—A letter from the Baron de Bogonshevsky to-day, sending me his photograph, at the back of which he has written : 'To my most kind and respected patron and kind correspondent in England, Dr. George Harris, LL.D., F.S.A., etc., this humble effigy of a humble original is respectfully offered by its prototype, Nicolas Casimir, Baron de Bogonshevsky, Pshoss, Russia estate. October, 1877.' I wrote and thanked him for the photograph, and also for the kind and complimentary expressions contained in his letter.

"*December* 13*th*.—Read my paper on 'Domestic Life and the Anglo-Normans,' at the Historical Society.

"15*th*.—A letter from the Baron de Bogonshevsky, in which he says: 'I should very much like to translate your splendid book into Russian; I am not sufficiently acquainted with the depths of the German language to undertake the translation of a book of so much sense and deep signification. I intend, therefore, to translate your splendid book little by little, a page or so per diem, as a book of the sort cannot be translated roughly, but requires all the efforts of one's knowledge and comprehension. I have now finished reading your work, and am re-reading some passages which struck me particularly.'

1878.

"*January* 15*th*.—A letter this morning from the Baron de Bogonshevsky, in which he says: 'I have already commenced translating your vast and splendid work, and have indeed translated as well as I could six pages (of printed matter). I will go on translating (in Russian) whenever I have time.'

"19*th*.—Wrote to the Baron de Bogonshevsky, and told him about his paper. Said I should be glad to have my book translated into German as well as Russian, and would assign copyright in any form he wished.

"*February* 1*st*.—A long letter this morning from the Baron de Bogonshevsky, in which he says: 'We shall be very happy to translate your valuable work in Russian and German, and, as I have said, I have written already several pages of the rough Russian translation, and we will arrange all about the copyright when work is completed.'

"2*nd*.—Saw the death of George Cruikshank in the paper to-day. A leading article on him in the *Times*. Compares him to Hogarth and to Dickens Not so natural as the former, or perhaps as the latter either. Indeed he was essentially rather a caricaturist than a humorist. He had more of the intensity of the former than the strict adherence to nature of the latter. He excelled greatly in effect, and perhaps he succeeded best where he had to realise the ideas of others rather than to originate some of his own, as in his illustration of 'Oliver Twist,' for instance. His representations of nature resemble rather the reflections in running water than those in a placid pool. His intensity of feeling induced to over-doing, if not to distortion ; and this was the case as regards his conduct in respect to charities, the temperance question and other matters also.

"*June 7th.*—At dinner of Royal Historical Society, Dr. Richardson in the chair. Had deputed to me the task of proposing the health of the chairman. Referred to his labours as a physician, a man of science, and a sanatrian, especially his valuable work for the Historical Society.

"*13th.*—The archæological gathering at Charleton House took place to-day, and all went off very well.

"Made a tour on the Continent, through part of France, including the Vosges Mountains.

"*October 3rd.*—A note from Mr. Denny, in which he says he has been at Warwick, and went to St. Mary's. 'Your window is a wonderful success in colour. The robes, the drawing of figures, the animals, the woman on the right window and the male figure on the left ; everything in fact in it quite astonished me. Your works will indeed live after you. Even the faces of the figures I liked.'

"*December 17th.*—Gave Dr. Richardson my copy of 'Harvey on the Circulation of the Blood,' the original edition in the original binding ; also his work on the generation of animals, 'Frauds of Physic' (a very scarce work), and some books on the Plague. A letter from him this morning in which he says, ' I am very much indebted to you for the books. They will be of very great use to me, and I shall treasure them the more as being a gift from so old and valued a friend as yourself.'

1879.

"*February* 22nd.—A present from Archdeacon Denison of his ' Articles on Philosophy,' sent for me to Bell & Sons. On the cover is written, ' From G. W. Denison for Dr. Harris.' In reply I wrote and thanked him, and sent him a quotation from Bacon applicable to his views.

" 30th.—"At Rugby. Dined at one o'clock at Matthew Bloxam's. He asked me to meet at a two o'clock dinner on Thursday, Mr. Woods, Mr. Crossley of Manchester, Mr. Harrison Ainsworth, and himself ; but we must return home before then.

"*March* 1st.—A note from Archdeacon Denison, with hearty thanks for the very kind and interesting letters received this morning.

" 3rd.—Wrote to Archdeacon Denison to tell him of the exact reference to the passages they referred to in Bacon on the Book of Job.

" 6th.—Came to Mr. Tagore's to-day until Monday. He showed me an article in the February number of *Modern Thought* on the Resurrection, by Mr. Earle, referring to my ' Treatise on Man.'

" 14th.—Engaged this morning arranging materials for and making a compendium of contents of ' Life of Lord Brougham,' with which I now hope to progress. Mr. Tagore expressed a great wish that I should complete it.

" 16th.—Wrote to Mr. Tagore to-day : ' I have

received so many communications respecting my "Treatise on Man," and find so many points open to discussion, that I mean at some future time to publish *Addenda* to it.'

"*May 1st.*—In my original design for the window at Warwick I represented the lambs as nibbling white flowers from the shepherd's hands. This was altered by Baillie and Mayer into making the lambs drinking milk out of earthen pots. I think mine was the prettiest and most poetical idea.

"*6th.*—Wrote to Mr. Earle thanking him for his reference to 'Treatise on Man' in his article in *Modern Thought*, and said, 'I should like to be a contributor to it on one or two subjects, if there is an opening, but should not care about remuneration.'

"*7th.*—Wrote as follows to Dr. Bloxam respecting Cardinal Newman. 'When you next write to the Cardinal on his return to England, I should be very much obliged to you if you would add my respectful though not the less sincere congratulations to your own. He is a man for whom I have a very profound respect, and regard as one who is ready to make sacrifices, however great, to what he considers truth, and whom persons of all parties and creeds ought to honour. I should have written to him myself only it might seem presumptuous, besides boring him unnecessarily when he must be overdone by the multitude of epistles to the same effect.'

"*9th.*—A reply from Dr. Bloxam, saying he is 'anxiously looking out for all notices of the new Cardinal Newman, for he was afraid that his journey to Rome would prove too much for him. And it seems that he has suffered much, partly from fatigue, and partly from cold, since his arrival there. Should he return in safety, he will take an early opportunity of greeting him, either by letter or in person, and will not fail to convey to him my congratulations.'

" *June* 23rd.—At Baillie and Mayer's. Working at, correcting, and completing the heads for the window in the church at Fulham, and darkening them. They are now, I think, quite satisfactory in every respect.

" 28th.—A note on Tuesday from Mrs. Gibbons, in which she says, ' Yesterday Mr. Gibbons went to call on Sir James Cockle, whom you may remember on the old Midland Circuit. He has served his time as Chief Justice in Queensland, and has now returned, wife and eight children. He inquired after you and Mrs. Harris, and would be pleased to see you if you could make a call convenient.'

" *July* 10th.—At the meeting of the Historical Society in the evening. Read a paper on ' The Original Records relating to the Visitations of the Plague to this Country,' which was very well received, and excited an animated discussion.

" 11th.—Called on Mr. Earle about *Modern Thought.* Arranged to advance some money to carry it on to August, when an arrangement to be made for me.

" 23rd.—Drew up a prospectus for carrying out my plan of a ' Gallery of Copies,' which I mean to have printed with the ' Plan,' soliciting subscriptions, and shall make an effort to carry it out.

" *October.*—Made a tour on the Continent, returning October 6th. Composed several Scientific Suggestions and Diagrams for them when abroad.

" 29th. —A letter from Dr. Bloxam, saying he had been staying with Cardinal Newman, and had presented my congratulations to him on his being made Cardinal.

" *November* 26th.—Saw to-day in paper the sudden death of Serjeant Cox, whom I have known nearly forty years, and with whom I have been closely associated in several literary undertakings. He has been a steady and good friend to me, and assisted me in several good notes to 'Treatise on Man.'

"*December* 18th.—Read my paper on 'Domestic Life,' etc., at the Historical Society this evening. A good attendance, and it was attentively listened to and very well received.

1880.

"*January* 2nd.—Called on Dr. Richardson to hear his judgment on some scientific suggestions I had submitted to him, and which he said he had gone thoroughly over. The artificial corn-dryer he says he liked the best, and that it was very ingenious and valuable, and that I certainly ought to publish it. Self-acting irrigations he also thought good and ought to be made known. He said the ventilation for public buildings ought to be worked by a water-wheel. That the suggestion for a horse blindfolded has been already tried. That the one for an aërial observatory was not practical, owing to the impossibility of keeping it steady in a high wind.* That for an aërial carriage he said he could not recommend, but the steamboat steadier was worth publishing.

"*7th.*—A letter from Victoria Institute and from Junior Athenæum expressing much regret at my resignation, and asking me to reconsider it, but which I do not feel inclined to do.

"*23rd.*—A copy of a Dundee paper sent me by Mr. Foulger, which contains an extract of nearly a column from my paper in *Modern Thought* on the differences caused by sea.

"*February* 17th.—Lady Cockle called on us to-day at

* But this has been satisfactorily adopted at Woolwich.

the Norfolk Hotel, and we had a very warm greeting from her. She said Sir James would be very much delighted to see me, and I told her to give him my warmest regards.   He is away from England at present, but she promised they would come to Iselipps when he returned.

" 26th.—Poor little Fog [my favourite Skye terrier] has been lately very ill, and is no better to-day, and seems very weak.   So I sent to Hanwell for the veterinary surgeon to see her.   But at four o'clock the poor dear, affectionate little thing died quite easily, just as she was trying to get out of the basket.   I shall miss her much.   Cook, who came to tell me it, was quite overcome.   Fog was a very great favourite with all the house, and with everybody who came to see us.   She was buried at five o'clock on the lawn behind the study, opposite the drawing-room window.

" 27th.—This morning a little dog, very like Fog (I fancy a pup of hers which belongs to some one in the village), which has been here occasionally of late with her, came and looked for her on the ledge of the dining-room window, where she generally sat in a morning watching for me till I went out, and not finding her there went to the spot where she is buried, and sat there a long time, as if quite conscious of what had happened.   Fog used to come into the dining-room the last thing at night to wish me good-night.   She was let in at the garden-door, when she rushed into the dining-room wagging her tail and jumping upon me, and we had a nice little romp together, but directly I said 'Good-night, Fog,' off she would rush to her bed in the kitchen without any more warning.

" *March* 15th.—I have had a small round rockery, planted with flowers, placed over the spot on the lawn where poor little Fog was buried, and which serves as a very suitable monument to mark the place.

"18*th*.—Read my paper on 'Domestic Life,' etc., at the Historical Society in the evening, the concluding one of the series, and probably the last I shall ever read at this Society. It was very well received, and excited a good discussion. The chairman, Mr. Heywood, F.R.S., termed it a 'very valuable paper.' The diagrams excited a good deal of attention.

"*May* 13*th*.—A letter from Foulger, in which he says:—'Your article in *Modern Thought* on Ruskin has already created some stir. I hear opinions are divided, but the majority think your strictures very just. I have about ten reviews, and nearly all expressing approval. I have a letter this morning from Mr. Swinburne, who says he thinks Mr. Ruskin ought to take some notice of your criticisms. I wish he may.'

"14*th*.—We went this afternoon to Ealing, to dine and stay all night at Sir J. Cockle's, late Chief Justice of Queensland, and an old colleague and great friend of mine on the Midland Circuit. Had a very hearty greeting from him and Lady Cockle, and enjoyed our visit exceedingly.

"*June* 9*th*.—Plumptre has asked me to give my 'Theory of the Arts' as a prize to the Jews' College, in Finsbury Square, which I have consented to do, and sent him three copies for that and King's College.

"A notice of *Modern Thought* in the *East London Observer*, in which they allude to my article on Ruskin, and say that I have 'not been slow to point out Mr. Ruskin's faults as well as his wonderful success.' They give my summary of his character, adding, 'In our opinion, if this summing up of Mr. Ruskin is severe, it is just.'

"21*st*.—A letter from Mr. Perry, who, in reply to

one from me, says, 'I am so thoroughly disheartened by the refusal of Mr. Gladstone to consider my scheme for the establishment of a Museum of Art, that I am not inclined to make any more efforts in any other direction. But the number of wealthy people who take an interest in *real* art is very small.'

" *27th.*—A long letter from the Baron de Bogonshevsky, who says : 'Some of the papers in *Modern Thought* are very valuable and interesting indeed. I shall follow your kind and friendly inclinations, and shall do my best to contribute a paper early in 1881.' In regard to my 'Treatise on Man' he says, 'I am going on steadily with the translation, and I am but sorry that you have such a poor translator of your really monumental and magnificent ideas and expositions in my person.'

" *31st.*—A reply to-day from Mr. Flood Jones, who will come and see us in the summer, but as regards a proposal of mine for a memorial to Archbishop Ussher he writes :—

"'A year or two ago our dean had the name of Archbishop Ussher cut upon the stone beneath which he rests, so that all who pass now into St. John's Chapel will see the name of the great man who was buried by order of Cromwell in the Abbey.'

1881.

" *May 26th.*—A letter from Miss Whitemore Jones thanking me for the copy I sent her of what she terms 'your capital and most amusing farce' of the 'Lottery Marriage.' She also says, 'The farce reads capitally, and I have been laughing over it this morning. Your paper, too, in *Modern Thought* [on the 'Danger in this Country of a Famine'] I like immensely.'

" *June 1st.*—June number of *Modern Thought* came

to-day. Article by me on 'Railway Grievances,' and a scientific suggestion accompanying it.

" 10*th*.—A letter from the Duke of Westminster, in reply to one of mine asking him to become president of a society for forming a gallery of copies of the principal pictures of Europe. He says :—

"' I fear I must decline undertaking the post, though obliged to you for offering it to me. Some few years ago Mr. Perry and others brought before the then Government the advisability of establishing a national museum of casts. Lord Beaconsfield appeared himself favourable to the proposal, but nothing has been done. The difficulty in our way must be the expense attending the housing of the collection, which must also apply to a picture gallery such as you suggest. Both are schemes which would appear to be desirable and useful for the further education and development of art in this country.'

" 11*th*.—In reply to the Duke's letter, I said that I regretted that he would not become president of the society, but that I hoped he would be a member of it.

" 21*st*.—Completed and coloured the diagram for the scientific suggestions on 'Super-marine Causeways,' etc., etc.

" 22*nd*.—C. E. Innes told me that some of my suggestions were highly thought of at the Horse Guards.

" A note from Foulger, in which he says of a game I had invented, called 'The Tourist,' that ' it seems to be a capital game, and one which ought to have a very large sale, and that it will be a very valuable property.'

" 24*th*.—Wrote to the Duke of Westminster about proposed Raphael Society, hoping that he would become a member, and that he would also be on the council.

" 29*th*.—A letter from Major Scotland, the Duke's secretary, saying he is directed by the Duke of Westminster to inform me that his Grace has no objection to become a member of the Raphael Society, but he regrets he cannot undertake to act on the committee.'

"Wrote to Major Scotland, thanking him for his letter, and added, 'May I take the liberty of requesting you to ask his Grace whether he will be our vice-president? It is intended to ask H.R.H. the Duke of Albany to become the president of the society.'

"*August* 3*rd.*—A letter from Major Scotland, who says that 'the Duke of Westminster has no objection to become vice-president of the Raphael Society.'

"*7th.*—Several fresh suggestions came into my head while travelling on the Continent, and which I noted down and made a rough diagram of.

"*13th.*—A scientific suggestion for substituting a slide for wheels to railway carriages and fastening the carriages to the slide; and another for an apparatus for rescuing drowning bathers, and of which I sketched rough diagrams in pencil as they occurred.

"*17th.*—Made another scientific suggestion this morning, and sketched a diagram for it in pen and ink. It will be 'A Cloud Cooler,' and will be a sort of counterpart for obtaining heat from the interior of the earth.

"2. Designing diagram for scientific suggestion, 'A Tree Feller,' in pen and ink.

"*25th.*—On the Continent for a tour. Several scientific suggestions composed while travelling.

"*September* 24*th.*—Returned to England.

"*October* 31*st.*—Preparing an improved diagram of scientific suggestions, No. XXIX. C. E. Innes tells me that plans for carriage and water bicycles have been formed, which (as he remarked) proves the soundness of my suggestion.

"*December* 22*nd.*—Midwinter Day, according to my

calculation, making the winter commence on the 15th of November and allowing three months for each of the four seasons, which commence respectively on the 15th February, 15th May, 15th August, and 15th November.

" *24th.*—A letter from Mr. Munton, asking me to be a member of the council of the Railway Passengers' Protection Society, a society of which I suggested the formation, and to which I consented.

1882.

" *March* 11*th.*—Wrote to Bloxam, proposing eventually to establish the Raphael Society at Rugby, as a central accessible town, and offered to give four copies of pictures, worth £100, to start it, if subscriptions to that amount were raised for the society.

" *15th.*—A letter from the Baron de Bogonschevsky, consenting to join the Raphael Society, which, he says, 'will be a most useful and magnificent institution.' Says he will do all he can to assist it, and ask his friends to join it ; and hopes to present some pictures to it.

" *24th.*—A letter from Mr. Hopewell of Rugby, about the Raphael Society, in which he says, 'The inhabitants speak flatteringly of the scheme. One gentleman has offered to become honorary secretary, and he, as well as others, seems confident that money will soon be forthcoming to the amount of £500.'

" *25th.*—A letter from Manchester from Mr. Horsfall, dated the 17th December, 1881, saying the attention of the Manchester Art Museum has been called to the Raphael Society, and asking for papers respecting it, and adding they would be glad to cooperate with them, though I told him that I doubted if Turner's pictures, which they have selected to have copies of, were suitable as studies.

" A letter from Hopewell, of Rugby, which says, 'I

am quite assured that the town and neighbourhood will doubtless raise eventually the requisite £500.'

"I hope that Rugby will have them, as I should be pleased to have the opportunity of doing something for the town. Really good copies made by artists of eminence from the original pictures are rare, as copies are generally made by inferior artists from inferior pictures, or from engravings.

"*July* 14*th*.—Designed a new scientific suggestion which may be substituted for one of the others which appears doubtful, being an appendage to Scientific Suggestion, No. II., and which is for filling a tank in the first instance by another pump worked by a wheel in a stream at some distance off.

"24*th*.—Wrote to Sir Eardley Wilmot to thank him for his book on Fair Trade, which he sent to me. I thought there was one point to which sufficient attention had not been paid. The danger of our being in want from the stoppage of foreign supply of food, and of our navy not being sufficient to prevent our supplies being cut off in case of a war. Referred him to my article on this subject in *Modern Thought.*

"*August* 8*th*.—In the papers to-day is the announcement of a new mode of constructing railway carriages, which has been adopted on the London and North-Western Railway, nearly coinciding with what I have proposed in my Scientific Suggestions, No. XI.. It is very satisfactory, as confirmatory of the soundness of my views.

"22*nd*.—To-day I sent to Mr. E. Watkin, M.P., my scientific suggestion for a railway viaduct over the sea, as also that for improving the construction of railway trains; much has been (though only partially) hit upon by the London and North-Western Railway Company. So wrote to him on the subject.

"*September 8th.*—Wrote to Mr. G. Allen as follows : ' Did it ever strike you that the account of the creation of man (taking it that all sprung from Adam and Eve) supports evolution, as Adam is first described as simply created a living being, who held converse with the animals, and afterwards received and became a living soul ? '

"A letter from Mr. G. Allen, who says, ' I am struck with your remarks on the agreement between the Mosaic account of creation and evolution. This is the very view worked out by me in my article, " Evolution agreeable to Religion."' He adds, ' I am quoting again from your work' [' Treatise on Man'].

"16*th.*—The *Times* of Saturday week gives a summary of the proceedings of the British Association, in which they say, ' Connected with evolutionary theories was Dr. Harris's paper on the ebb and flow of mental endowment, in which the author attempts to give a rational explanation of the frequently noted fact that men of extraordinary talent have often sons of extraordinary stupidity.'

"*October 27th.*—A letter this morning from Dr. de Ste. Croix, saying he has completed the translation into French of my 'Theory of the Arts,' and is willing to bring it out in the *Revue Artistique.*

"In the *Times* to-day it is remarked in a leading article on the weather that ' there are physical constitutions that are peculiarly sensitive of electric changes, and that will be thrown into a continual tremor and a flutter a good hour before the first flash of lightning.' This is exactly my case.

"*November* 13*th.*—A circular letter from the honorary secretary of the Clarendon Historical Society, Edinburgh, asking me to accept a certificate of free membership of the Society, as a slight recognition of valuable services in the cause of historical research. In reply I said, 'I feel much flattered by the honour conferred upon me by the Clarendon Historical Society. For some years I have been engaged in preparing a life of your distinguished townsman, Lord Brougham.' Proposed to give them the manuscript to publish. Of course in this case the manuscript would become the absolute property of the Clarendon Historical Society, to deal with the work as they think proper.

"A letter from the Edinburgh Clarendon Society, in which they say: 'As regards the "Life of Lord Brougham," the committee, while fully appreciating your very generous offer to place the manuscript at their disposal, fear that the work will be too large for the means at present at their disposal.' But they say there are some letters, etc., in my 'Life of Lord Hardwicke' which the committee think would make a most interesting pamphlet.

"In reply I wrote as follows: 'You are quite at liberty to print and circulate any extracts from any of my works that you think proper; but I think that in this case it will be but fair to the author to state his name, and that of the books from which the passages are taken. You will find in the three first chapters of volume ii. of my "Life of Lord Hardwicke" some interesting original matter relating to the rebellion of 1745, which is not, I believe, printed elsewhere. I send you by book-post a short "Life of Lord Brougham," which I brought out soon after his death at the request of the National Association for Promoting Social Science. With regard to the "Life of Lord Brougham," I will send you the manuscript when I have completed it, and you can do what you like with it. It may perhaps be best to keep it for a few years, and either print part of it, or the whole, as opportunity offers. Here and there are parts (the account of the Queen's trial, for instance) which would do well to publish separately. My Life brings his career down to 1868, when he died. His own memoirs terminate in 1838.'

" 28*th*.—A letter from Mr. Goldsmid on behalf of the Edinburgh Clarendon Society, in which he says : ' With respect to your "Life of Lord Brougham," since you are willing to entrust it to us, I am authorised to inform you that the Society will undertake to publish it, in sections, until the book is complete, and I am instructed to convey to you the very best thanks of the committee for your very generous gift. Personally I have been reading your "Treatise on Man," and I feel convinced from my experience that, with such a subject and such advantages as you had of knowing him, your "Life of Lord Brougham" must needs be replete with information and interest.'

" *December 7th*.—A kind and courteous letter from the Baron de Bogonschevsky, who would like to be a member of the Clarendon Society.

" 27*th*.—A note from him sending me a valentine of a Russian rose, and saying he cannot let the 23rd December (their Christmas day, I suppose) pass without wishing me a merry Christmas and many happy returns. He says that ' if his letter was ever so long, it could not express adequately all his good wishes, and his sincere esteem and gratitude to me.'

" 28*th*.—Wrote to the Baron de Bogonschevsky to thank him for his letter. The flower, I told him, was much admired by Mrs. Harris and myself, and his good wishes I begged heartily to reciprocate.'

1883.

April 10*th*.—A letter from the Clarendon Institute, Edinburgh, to say that they are getting on with Lord Brougham's Life, and hope to begin printing soon.

" 20th.—A letter from the Clarendon Society about Lord Brougham's Life, in which Mr. Goldsmid says : ' The more I read of it, the better I like it. The task of cutting it down is terribly hard ; there is so much one would like to keep, but which we cannot.'

" *May 8th.*—Composed this morning the outline of a romance to be entitled 'The Romance of the Black Baron of the Black-rock Castle,' a story of the Black Forest ; sketched the outline of it. Lee used to tell me I had talent for sketching out first principles. I can hew the marble into rough outline, but I cannot finish.

" *June 10th.*—My valued and devoted wife was taken very ill last night, and lost the use of her right hand and arm. Woke me about six, and wished me to rub her hand and to send at once for Dr. Tonge, which I did. He said it was an attack of paralyis, but might go off, or might be the prelude to a severer attack or one of apoplexy.

" 11th.—Dr. Tonge, when he called, said that he did not think there was any immediate danger (in E.'s case) or cause for alarm as if she were unconscious, and that it is a case of incomplete paralysis. Says she will have to keep her bed for some days. Recommended her having a professional nurse. Not to see friends, and not to talk with them. Said it might bring on another attack. Gradually, however, she became better, though obliged to keep her bed for several weeks, and eventually got out of doors in a Bath chair. During the winter she was again confined to her room, but seemed in wonderful health and spirits, and was able to see and converse with friends, to whom also she dictated numerous letters.

"*November* 2nd.—A letter in the evening from Mr. Edouart about the Leominster window to the Harris family, to which I replied : 'The only plan will be to have the window in the town hall, representing the delivery of the Law by Moses. By placing the window in the town hall all difficulty may be obviated.'

"19th.—Wrote to Mr. Beresford Harris, and told him I have not strength or health to carry on the Leominster controversy, and that the only way will be simply to say whether my proposal to present a window, as designed by me, of Moses delivering the Law is declined or accepted.

"Another letter from Mr. Edouart about the Leominster window, asking me to meet him in London. In reply I said that 'I could not enter into any controversy about the subject. They must either accept my offer or decline it for the church or the town hall.'

"30th.—A correspondent of the *Rugby Advertiser* the other day mentioned that the Rugby people had made a great mistake in ignoring the proposal of the Raphael Society.

1884.

"*June* 6th.—Wrote to Dr. Vaughan, the Master of the Temple, and offered to present to the Temple Church, to be placed on the north side belonging to the Middle Temple, some views of Palestine, if he thought such a donation would be acceptable.

"A reply in which he said he had not forgotten our former intimacy, and offering to bring the matter (of which he expressed his approval) before the Benchers.

"*July* 12th.—A letter to me from Sir George Innes, in which he says : 'We think it delightful to see two (pardon me if I write old people) so full of simple fun and joyousness. To me it proclaims the hope, faith, and peace within.'

"*August 1st.*—A very nice letter to E. from Arthur Halcomb, in New Zealand, about Charles Marriott, who says of him :—

"'He was, I think, one of the kindest, most earnest, self-sacrificing, and unselfish of men. Like a good many other earnest religious men, who shut themselves up too much with their books and their own thoughts and alienate themselves from the every-day world, I think that his utter ignorance of everything outside his college walls deprived him of much power of good ; and I think that the knowledge that he was considered to hold extreme views made him much more reticent on religious matters with young men than he would otherwise have been.

"'His power of work was wonderful. He was never idle a moment ; and he generally had two or three letters in hand which he would take up at odd moments, sitting or standing, his desk being an old book-cover.

"'He was very fond of getting young men round him ; and he was very much loved by the undergraduates, although they used to laugh at his peculiarities, especially of dress, for he was the most careless and untidy man possible, and his rooms were one awful chaos of books, paper, and anything and everything else, with the dust of years on all. He took no care of himself whatever, and this no doubt was partly the cause of his body and mind giving way so comparatively early as they did. When I was with him he was very much interested in the Radley "school," in which I have heard he lost a considerable sum of money which he had advanced to help his friend Dr. S—— in starting the institution, and I often walked down to Radley on the summer's afternoons, and I

thoroughly enjoyed the expeditions with him. When
I was at Oxford lately I tried to find any one who knew
him well. I should so like to have heard more about
him. I saw a good deal of Dr. Pusey at his rooms in
those days. It was just about the time that the
" Tracts for the Times " created such a sensation at
Oxford, and all throughout the Church of England, and
I think Charles Marriott inspired, if he did not write,
a great lot of them.'

"The following character of Mr. C. Marriott is
given by Mr. Maurice * :—

"' Charles Marriott has been staying in the island.
Our acquaintance, I think, from Marriott,—who, I find,
is known to you,—through my fault, has become somewhat stiff, and I was particularly delighted that we
could meet again, and with freshness and openness;
and to see something more into one of the deepest and
noblest characters to be found anywhere. His generosity and self-devotion, in the most unobtrusive way,
are quite marvellous. If there are ten such, I think
England is not Sodom.'

" *September* 15*th*.—Sent to Mr. Podmore (by his
particular request) at the Psychological Research
Society the extract from my ' Lecture on Ghosts'
respecting Treen's apparition at Rugby, containing
full particulars as far as I could obtain them.

" *October* 1*st*.—Sir Thomas Chambers, Q.C., M.P.,
Recorder of London, and Mr. Anderson, Q.C., came
down here to see me about the proposed window for
the Temple Church, which I have offered to fill with
painted glass containing about twenty views of
Palestine, of which they appeared quite to approve,
and to prefer them to figures.

* " Life of Frederick Denison Maurice." Edited by his
son. Vol. ii., p. 351.

" I told them (to which they assented) that I should wish to put up a small brass plate beneath the window, stating that it was my gift. On the brass plate I proposed to state, ' This window was presented and the designs were selected and arranged by George Harris, LL.D., F.S.A., Barrister of the Middle Temple, A.D. 1885.' It strikes me also that the names of the different views should also be inscribed under each of them.

" 27*th.*—Working at the revision of my ' Principia Prima Legum.' The last effort I shall make at any work of mine, and much fagged by the portions out of order which I have set to right. Propose to lay it by, with the correspondence about it, as it may serve at some future day to aid in the composition of a complete codification of the law, about which Lord Westbury wrote to me, when he had the charge of it, to give him my ideas on the subject.

" *November* 11*th.*—I wrote to C. J. Plumptre and told him, ' I have a romance in my possession which was intended for *Modern Thought.* It is entitled " The Romance of the Black Forest," and is, I think, likely to be popular. It is rather sensational, being intended to afford an idea of the scenery in the Black Forest and on the Rhine, and of the tragic events which took place there during the Middle Ages, including the style of living in the old castles, banditti, and the use of torture, etc.'

" Determined this evening to bequeath to Sir James Cockle, by a codicil, the ' Principia Prima Legum ' and ' Scientific Suggestions,' as he will be the best person to bring them out.

" 26*th.*—A letter from Mr. Anderson, Q.C., and Sir Thomas Chambers, Q.C., M.P., about the Temple Church window, saying there is a misapprehension about the side lights, and that ' it is not probable that the Benchers could be brought to agree to my proposals.'

" I wrote in reply as follows : 'As I am now in a very precarious state of health, and appear to be gradually getting weaker, I think it would be better and more prudent that the proposal for the window should be suspended, at any rate for the present, say until Easter, when I shall probably be able to judge, if then alive, how far I am capable of proceeding in the matter, and possibly by that time some plan may suggest itself to you of getting out of the difficulty.'

1885.

" *February 3rd.*—Wrote to Dr. Richardson as follows : ' When the spring advances I hope that you and Mrs. Richardson, and any of your party that would like to accompany you, will come and spend the day here. I have several books that I should like to show you, and in which you would be interested . . . and shall be glad to give any of them to you, as I think you would value them more, and they would be more useful to you, than those who come after me here. By the time you come here I hope that the manuscript of my 'Autobiography' will be complete. Some of the correspondence and notes of conversations will, I really think, be interesting and valuable, and if you will write a preface to it, I shall be much obliged.

" *13th.*—Wrote to Edmund as follows respecting my anthropological paintings : ' I send you a painted catalogue of the pictures I have painted, designed to express the actual character of the persons represented, and which may serve to some extent to illustrate the mode in which I have attempted to carry out my purpose. In the second volume of my "Theory of the Arts," under the head of Graphopnemata (souls of pictures), you will see the theory further explained. The mode in which I have proceeded is as follows : I have first of all selected a head (very often that of a real person), which has appeared to me most to resemble the person I wish to represent, and I have then altered it so as more completely to agree with the features I intended to portray. Curiously enough (as I believe I have remarked in the catalogue), when I have attempted to design a head without having an original model before me, I have sometimes found that the face which I have depicted nearly resembled that of some real living character, who in turn nearly resembled the character I intended to represent.'

" *17th.*—A letter from Edmund, who says, 'I have been exceedingly struck with some parts of your " Civilisation considered as a Science," which I have been looking into. It seems to me to be in advance of us all. In another fifty years it will probably be really appreciated.'

" *April 15th.*—Wrote to Mr. Shaw, the sub-treasurer of the Middle Temple, and told him that I was in error in proposing Lord Somers instead of Lord Hardwicke (as I mentioned in my former note), to whom memorials should be placed in the Temple Church, in the side windows next to those in which the views of Palestine are to be placed, and the reasons for which I would explain when we met.

" *May 1st.*—Edmund wrote me word that he was greatly pleased to hear that I was preparing an autobiography, and asked me to send the manuscript of it to him, and to allow Matthew Bloxam to see it, who could make some additions to it.

" *17th.*—Went to London. Lunched at Dr. Richardson's. Took him my autobiography to read.

ADDENDUM TO 'TREATISE ON MAN.'
April—1885.

" Sight and size. There is in reality no such thing as absolute or definite size, which is in each case only proportional or relative, and depends entirely on the organ of vision by which the object is viewed. Thus, print appears large or small according to the medium through which it is viewed. So also different objects vary in size according to the distance from us. Indeed, as regards the subjects of the senses, many of them must be determined in the case of all objects to be relative rather than absolute or definite. This is the case undoubtedly as regards weight, distance, size, colour, form, and other apparently perceptible and ascertained qualities or relations. Animals, especially insects, differ entirely from man as regards the power and properties of vision. In the case of animalculæ, for instance, the human frame must appear like a world. To the Deity a world may appear no larger than an insect. To different beings different degrees and qualities of light are also essential through which to view objects.[*]

" *July* 20*th*.—Two notices of scientific discoveries in the newspapers identical with two of my 'Scientific Suggestions,' one for obtaining heat from the interior of the earth, the other for a floating bridge to conduct railway trains over rivers and creeks.

[*] Note to " Treatise on Man," vol. i., p. 232.

"*August* 12th. Had thought of making an ADDEN-
DUM to the 'Treatise on Man,' on the subject of 'Free
Will and Liberty in the Case of the Deity,' in addition
to what I have said in vol. ii., pp. 13, 14. But on the
whole, I do not think that I can add anything to that
which will make it more satisfactory. His Will has in
fact been already in several ways solemnly declared and
asserted, as also His power, and that in the most
complete and perfect manner. The only other exercise
of either would be undoing what He has already accomplished, which it would be irrational to suppose that
He would do. Our knowledge in this respect must
necessarily be imperfect.

"*October* 8th.—Matthew Bloxam refers in a note to
'Cabinet Colloquies,' which he says were very clever, and
remind him of Swift, and mentions that he is making
a catalogue of the antiquarian papers he has written.

1886.

"*January* 27th.—Saw in the paper to-day the death of
poor dear old Flowers, the police magistrate at Bow
Street, one of my best and oldest friends, and I quite
believe one of the worthiest, too. A capital, because so
true and touching, description of his character by his
colleague Vaughan. He had an exquisite vein of
humour.

"*March* 15th.—Wrote to Mr. Goldsmid, of the
Historical Society, Edinburgh, respecting my "Life
of Lord Brougham,' suggesting that his plan of
printing portions at a time be adopted, so that a thousand copies of them, together with the table of contents,
be sent out to solicit subscriptions to the proposed
work, of which I should purchase some copies. Told
him he ought to try and get the Queen and the

principal people in Scotland to join the Society, which should be a national one.

"*June* 1st.—Completed to-day the revision and correction of the " Romance of the Black Forest,' which is now all ready for printing.

" 19th.—Wrote to Messrs. Baillie and Co. that I was ready to have the painted window in the breakfast room put up any day that is convenient to them. Enclosed them a plan of the window, with the names of the different paintings.

"Wrote also to Mr. Shaw, the under-treasurer at the Middle Temple, that I was ready to have the window in the church put up at once, but that I must leave it to him and the Benchers to see that it is satisfactory. Offered to send a cheque for £100—£80 for the views and £20 for the two figures.

"A note from the under-treasurer of the Middle Temple informing me that my offer of a window in the Temple Church is not such as the Benchers would be likely to approve of, in the opinion of Master Anderson and Master Thomas Chambers, and they do not, therefore, feel justified in taking any further action in the matter.

"Wrote to Dr. Vaughan, and told him I thought it but fair and courteous, after his kindness to me in the matter, to inform him of the decision of the Benchers, owing, I believe, to a difference in opinion of the body as to the desirableness of my proposal.

"A reply from Dr. Vaughan, who says he is sorry that my kindness should be thrown away.

APPENDIX.

GOVERNMENT OF IRELAND.

"WROTE to Sir E. Wilmot, sending him a plan for Ireland, by dividing it into north and south, which is supplemented by my plan, made some time ago, of uniting Ireland and Scotland by a tunnel or bridge of boats.

"A letter from Sir E. Wilmot on Ireland. He says that my proposal promises many and great advantages, and advises me to make my proposals through the medium of the press.

"Since writing in my journal a plan of reform of Ireland, I have considered matters fully, and believe that the following scheme will be more complete and satisfactory, and also practical.

"Ireland to be established as an independent country or state, still subject to the following restrictions and conditions.

"One of the princes royal of England and his heirs to be the sovereigns of Ireland, whose deposition is not to be allowed without the assent of the British Parliament and Crown, and for whom a suitable residence in Ireland is to be provided by the English Government, but maintained by Ireland; such Sovereign to reside in Ireland at least eight months in every year

"He is to hold perpetual alliance with the English Crown, and to do homage to the Sovereign of Great Britain, with whom he is to form a perpetual treaty, offensive and defensive.

"Ireland to have its own independent Parliament, consisting of House of Lords and Commons.

"The House of Lords to consist of the present Irish peers, and with such additions to it as shall be made by the Irish Sovereign. Also of the Irish Roman Catholic Bishops.

"The House of Commons to be elected by the Irish people, but each member, and also each elector, to have a certain parliamentary qualification in land or money. This to be fixed by the Irish Parliament, and every member of either house to be a native of Ireland or a naturalised subject.

"Ireland to maintain its own expenses without any aid from England.

"The Roman Catholic Church to be the established religion, but a full toleration to all Protestants, whether Churchmen or Dissenters, who may have their own congregations there, but which they must voluntarily support.

"Processions or the display of party-coloured banners connected with political or theological questions or societies to be strictly prohibited under a penalty, and any person attending or displaying them to be subject to a penalty of £5 for first offence, to be doubled and trebled afterwards.

"Songs, pictures, or verses of a political or theological and inflammatory character to be also prohibited under penalties. Arguments in private houses, political or polemical, at which three persons only are present, are not to be prohibited.

"All denunciations, by any party or person, from the altar or pulpit, to be prohibited.

"Where disputes arise between Roman Catholics and Protestants, the jury before whom the case is tried to consist of six of each, the majority to be accepted in all cases. A verdict of 'not proven' to be substituted for 'not guilty.'

"No law to be in force which has been out of use for two hundred years prior.

"All landed estates belonging to Englishmen and others to be guaranteed to them on condition of their residing upon them at least six months in the year. They may be compelled to sell at a fair price in default of so residing.

"Every peer and landowner to be obliged to reside on his estate in Ireland, and in default of so doing, in addition to the other penalties, to be incapable of holding any office of dignity or power.

"The annual value of each holding to be fixed by a Board of Commissioners, to be appointed by the Lord Lieutenant of the county. Two-thirds of such commissioners to be landowners, the remaining third tenants.

"The rent fixed by such commissioners to be recovered by distress, and the non-paying tenant to be evicted, and not to have any other lease or holding granted to him; and the grantor of such lease not to be able to recover the amount of his rent, or any part of it, by distress or otherwise, and the tenant not to be eligible to any office or appointment, or to follow any commercial business, or recover any money on account of transactions in it.

"English laws to be in force, unless altered by the Irish Parliament."

Printed by Hazell, Watson, & Viney, Ld., London and Aylesbury.